PICTURES OF DORIANNA

CATHERINE STINE

Konjur Road Press
Forays into Fictional Magic

Pictures of Dorianna
Copyright © 2019 by Catherine Stine/Konjur Road Press
All rights reserved.
Cover art by Najla Qamber
ISBN: 978-1-7333901-0-1

"So intense! Incredible story with epic climax. Darkly enchanting" - Page Unbound

"Amazing modern remake of Dorian Gray!" - Bookworm Babblings

"Vividly written. The characters stepped out of a creepy version of "Gossip Girl." - reader review

5 stars "Devilish and enchanting" - reader review

"Pictures of Dorianna is the creepiest thing I've read in a long time. I mean that in the best way!" - reader review

5 stars "Careful! By the time you remember what real love and friendship are, you may have already lost them for all time." - reader review

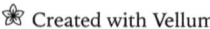 Created with Vellum

PICTURES OF DORIANNA

Catherine Stine

***

Also by Catherine Stine:

Witch of the Wild Beasts
Witch of the Cards
Fireseed One
Ruby's Fire
Heart in a Box
Refugees

1

Hell is other people.
—Jean-Paul Sartre

On the way to my new school, I catch a glimpse of my face in a shop mirror. Even though I hate mirrors, I force myself to look. No one needs to remind me I'm plain.

Leaning forward, I examine my pale skin with its tracery of blue underneath. It looks like granny spider veins. And I never smile all the way. That would expose my wonky teeth —one front tooth slightly over the other.

My hair's limp, but it's auburn with peachy highlights. I've got that going for me, at least. Lifting up a lock, I admire its warm glow in the September sun. And there's still a hint of eagerness in my eyes—they haven't knocked that out of me. It's hope, whispering, "Maybe this place will be different. Maybe they won't walk past me as if I'm floating dust."

I've been here in Brooklyn for four days, shuffled away

from family chaos to my Aunt Carol's house. She's nice so far, but I don't really know her. It's too bad we could never afford to fly east for family reunions. I do know she's a fundraiser for a public radio station, and owns one floor in a brownstone. And that she eats vegetarian, and neatly folds the nubbly throws on her earth-tone Pottery Barn couch.

And she's the sister of my screw-up father.

I'm not sorry I left Wabash. School there was a train wreck. It got so lonely, watching the reigning couples kissing their way down the halls. I wanted someone's arms around me, too, or at least another good friend after Jen. But it wasn't meant to be, after gossip spread that my father was sent to jail for committing moral turpitude. My mom took to her bed, and I took over. We were struck with loss and horror and shock all at once. Mom needed me last spring. I tried to help in any way I could, until she insisted that I needed a total break from the family. Or was it Mom who needed the break?

I'm going to suck it up. I *am*. If she needs the break, she can have it. Maybe I need one, too. I'm determined to pump myself up to face a different army of kids. Ambling down Montague Street, past the cute boutiques, I soak in the balmy September sun and survey my new stomping grounds. These Brooklyn streets are as delicious as strawberry shortcake. The narrow shops are a wonder of necklaces, handmade with glass bits and bottle tops, and leafy bracelets fashioned from green computer chips.

The caffeine-laced scents wafting from the cyber café draw me in. As I walk by, I sneak looks at the lean, fox-quick boys with scruffy hair, low-slung belts, and tees that read *Neon Pandas* and *Oubliettes of Onyx*. Bands I've never heard of, since out in Hoosier Land they mostly play country music.

I smile, picturing myself talking to a slinky boy who

makes me my very own playlist—he'd call it *Songs for a Brooklyn Beauty*. A girl can dream, right?

Turning down Court Street, a woman breezes past me in a black jumpsuit. Another dramatic beauty in thigh-high boots floats by, with two dachshunds tugging against their pink leashes. As I glance back at her, I imagine her working as a Broadway actress, dancing across a stage in those fancy boots.

Just then, one of her dogs works free of her grasp, and streaks into the street. "Hey!" I call. "Hey, pup!" I dash after it, grab the pink leather strap, and coax it back toward the curb as a bakery van careens around the corner, the driver pounding on his horn.

The booted lady runs over to me. "Thanks so much!" she says, breathless.

"Happy to help. Couldn't let your sweet dog be hit." Our eyes meet as I hand her the leash, and her smile touches me. I watch for another moment as she walks demurely on.

Everything here vibrates with possibility, if I block out my dread of school. It's my chance to figure out who I want to be, which I couldn't quite do back home. I can't wait to let my old, stale-kernel life rot on the vine, and start over.

Reading the sign on a red colonial stone building, I sway with sudden trepidation: School. I'm here, no turning back. Look, you're smart, I tell myself, you tested in and even got a scholarship here. Ivy sprints up its scholarly walls, and its walkway is marked with marble planters. Each one bursts with purple chrysanthemums, as if this is the cheeriest high school ever. Maybe private school kids are easier on new students. Unlikely, but I'll give it my best.

I grip a planter and wait out a sickening flood of school memories: like when I was in fourth grade and couldn't get a gym partner, because kids said I stank of the watermelon hippie incense my father burned in his church. At least I had

Jen then, whose mom belonged to the congregation. Jen and I bought hamsters together, and went ice-skating on Fridays. We sat together during the long, boring services, and whispered about the boys we liked at school. I liked Tommy, who was obsessed with horse-riding competitions. Jen liked Bo, a cute Chinese guy who'd moved to Wabash from San Francisco.

That all changed three years ago, when I was thirteen. Kids started telling rumors that my dad was a perv, chasing after the moms in school—even Jen's mom, Lynn—and Jen slunk away from me.

That's when my nickname changed to 'It'.

I take a breath and reason with myself. No one knows my father here. No one can ask my former classmates for the embarrassing dirt on Dorianna. No one will ever know my heinous history.

Tossing my hair back, I march past the kids hanging out on the steps. They're all dressed differently—jeans, dresses, leggings—so I guess my skirt and ruffled, floral top will fit in okay. I smile, but they're already deep into conversations.

My Indiana school was cinderblock, with low-paneled ceilings. This place has shiny halls with high arches. Different, I chant, it's different here. The place is only beginning to flow with people, so I have time to practice my padlock combo.

Inside my locker, I tape a page I tore out from *Marie Claire* magazine. It shows a leggy model, with long brown hair like mine, her head tilting against the backdrop of the Brooklyn Bridge. Photos aren't like people. They're always there if you need them. My heart leaps. No more invisibility. Somehow, soon I'll be that proud, carefree girl. I'll look at her every day and take lessons.

As I'm standing back to admire the photo, I grow acutely aware of the boy who's stepped up next to me. My eyes dart over to him. Tall and sandy-haired, he's wearing jeans and a red plaid button-down over a tight jersey. It's cool how his top shirt's wrinkled as if he doesn't care to be that perfect hipster. He's emanating heat, sweating along his upper lip as he transfers new school supplies in and out of his locker.

One away from mine.

I catch him glancing over. "Hey," he says casually.

Who's he talking to? "Me? Oh, hi."

He shrugs, as if he only said hello to be polite. "Thought you might be new, 'cause I've never seen you," he says. "I mean, until today."

"Yeah, I'm new. I'm Dorianna." My belly does cartwheels.

"Oh, okay."

That's it? He's not going to tell me his name? Guess not, because he's already turning his head toward a girl walking toward us. She stops across the hall and begins to dial her locker combo. He's studying her with keen, guarded eyes, as if he knows her well, but isn't so sure he wants to see her.

Under the pretext of twisting around to readjust my shoulder bag, I take a long look at my competition (Wishful thinking, I know).

She's a platinum blonde, sleek and muscular, as if she spends afternoons doing laps with the varsity swim team. Her red dress barely covers her butt, while her white handbag is so massive it could stun a boxer. I try not to stare, but it's hard. I've never seen someone my age so polished. The closest comparison in Wabash was a bleached-blonde sports nut, who wore fake gold chains and bragged about hooking up with the hottest guys from the football team. No comparison.

Looking closer, I see this girl's ears stick out like fingerling potatoes from her milky blonde hair. Not quite perfect after all. That's a relief.

She opens her locker and hangs her bag on it. Pulling out

a cell, she begins to text someone as her eyes flicker to me, then to the boy, and away.

I fumble some more with my bag and try to look hugely busy.

The boy says a sharp, "Hello, Lacey," to which she nods dismissively before returning to her texting.

I'm used to people pointedly ignoring *me,* but this girl's rude brush-off is blatant even by my standards. I offer the guy a sympathy wince.

He sends back an uneasy grin, which zaps me with electricity. "I'm Ander James," he explains. "You're from?"

"Indiana."

"What do you think of New York so far?"

"It's amazing. I've seen some of Brooklyn, and a tiny bit of Manhattan."

"Yeah, it takes years to discover all the outskirts. I like to explore the edgy areas."

To which Lacey looks up abruptly from her texting and stares at him, openmouthed. "What would *you* know about edgy and cool?" she snipes. The tangled energy racing between Ander and this girl is so troubled, I start to clench my own fists.

"See you around." Ander says to me. He marches away, taking the high road.

I click my combination lock shut and turn to walk to class.

"You wish," I hear behind me.

Lacey's words are a hot slap to my back.

What if I *do* wish? Who says Ander and I can't talk? Is she the chat police?

Later that morning, I share Lit class with Lacey and Ander.

It's crowded, so I can't get close to them. After class, he leaves first, with only a distant look my way. When Lacey prances out, a bunch of girls gather around her—looking like a devoted flock, worshipping the Holy Grail. Reminds me of how my dad always strived for a following for his church. Certainly, Lacey's followers are more chic than my father's fifty-something, hair-extension groupies. Can't let that scare me, though. I picture my *Marie Claire* girl with her head thrown back in total abandon.

Ava, one of Lacey's friends—I learned their names in class —has glowing ebony skin, and strands of bangs that fall jauntily over her forehead. She's model tall. The shorter girl, a redhead named Bailey, has on cat-eye glasses, ballet slippers, and striped leggings under a tunic that match her violet-sunset swaths of eyeliner. Others lurk on the fringe, but Ava and Bailey seem to complete Lacey's power trio.

Will Lacey chill out if I try to be friends with her? No one here knows I'm incredibly shy. But I can get over that, too. I'll sketch in a new self-portrait, of a bold, talkative me. "Hi," I manage. My eyes jump from one to another of the girls.

Lacey looks blankly at me. After an uncomfortable silence she mumbles, "Hi," while the others cluster around her in bodyguard formation.

"Your locker's right across from mine, remember?" I persist. "Going to lunch?"

At that question, Lacey gives me a grimace that says she'd rather pet a cobra than walk to lunch with a transfer from out-of-state. "Not right now," she replies, unsmiling. She nods at my top. "Unusual, um, shirt for New York. Just sayin'."

"What's wrong with it?" I'm shaking, half from anger and half from nerves. This outfit was part of the pricy new fall line at the Village Mall back home. I spent two months' babysitting pay on it.

Ava, the dark-skinned beauty, speaks. "I model for Ford, and they never dress models in hokey florals or baggy A-line skirts. Complete no-no." She's wearing torn black tights under torn black shorts. Her outfit's pretty weird. Maybe it's a New York thing.

Bailey, the girl with cat-eye glasses, offers me a faint smile. "Aw, cut the newbie some slack," she says before they strut away, their laughter trailing like sour perfume.

I'm grateful. It's not a lot, but I'll take it.

The next three days aren't much better, though I'm determined to launch into a real conversation and make a new friend. Every morning, I pump up my courage by staring at *Marie Claire* girl, my silent, two-dimensional life counselor.

Every morning, Ander says hello, loudest and most emphatically when Lacey's across the hall. He's obviously using me to make her jealous. And Lacey is eavesdropping. She slams her locker closed as a clear signal of disapproval.

It's not as if Ander is saying anything deep, or even inviting me to walk to class with him. On the second day, he asks if I have a spare pen. On the third day, he asks me if there are music festivals in Wabash.

I loan him a pen and answer his questions. Despite whatever game he's playing with Lacey, he seems to enjoy talking to me. Ander's lopsided grin is so darn cute, and his eyes stay on me when I talk about the Lotus music festival I went to in Bloomington, and how I especially liked the Indonesian gamelan music.

On the fourth day, at lunch, I see my chance to approach Bailey, the girl in Lacey's clique who called off her wolves that first day. Aside from my chats with Ander, Bailey's comment is still the nicest thing someone's said to me. She's come early and is still alone. I don't ask permission, just plunk down across from her and offer up a smile.

She looks up, startled. She's switched up her look to aqua glasses, a scoop-neck dress, and dangly bluebird earrings. She doesn't smile back this time. Instead, she makes a sort of I'll-make-do grimace, and returns to her salad.

"Love your earrings," I start.

"Thanks. Made 'em." Bailey swings around toward the door, as if she's eager for her friends to arrive and help her deal with this unexpected intrusion.

I picture *Marie Claire* girl, and brave up. "Where'd you find that great dress? I'm kind of fashion challenged." I giggle. Using their actual criticism of me from day one at my own expense should show her I'm strong and unshakable.

She shrugs, casting a glance at the beige pullover I substituted for that flowery shirt, worn with my same beige skirt. "Your clothes aren't bad. And you're wearing nice makeup. Don't apologize for yourself." My makeup's wobbly, but it does hide the blue veins under my papery skin. I'm happy she approves.

Before I have time to respond to the surprising no apology comment, Lacey and Ava bound over. "What are you doing here, Bailey?" Lacey spits out as if she's just chugged rotten milk.

"New girl, you didn't follow my fashion advice—no baggy A-line skirts." Ava tosses her ropy bangs. "People *pay* me for that."

Why did they have to come over and make me feel like shit? Bailey's not their property. But they've caught me off guard. I'm no match for their venomous charm. Bailey looks down at her plate. Her red hair shrouds her expression.

Lacey leans over her, her own pale hair cascading over Bailey's shoulder as if they're one smooth being in a silky cocoon. "We've got much better seats with the *guys* on the other side of the lunchroom."

Finally, Bailey looks up at me. I blink hopefully at her to see if we've shared any kind of meaningful moment. Am I only imagining a look of regret?

She toys around with a piece of broccoli for about a second before she leaps up, tray in hand. With a perky, "Got to go!" she flies off with her friends.

I feel like smeared mystery meat on the slimy floor. What was I thinking when I imagined it would be different at this school? They're clueless about my past, yet they still run. Why?

2

Illusion is the first of all pleasures.
—Oscar Wilde

fter the last bell, I hurry to my locker to grab my jacket and a new textbook. I need to get out of here. Now. Not even *Marie Claire* girl is lifting my spirits. Lacey's at her locker across the way, and the hater vibe is overwhelming. As I brace for one last possible verbal snipe, Ander strolls over.

"Where're you rushing off to?"

"Going home. You?"

"Oh, uh, I'm off to the beach." He shrugs.

"Sounds like fun," I say. "A beach around here?"

"Yeah." Ander glances at Lacey. She's narrowing her eyes at us. In a voice meant to broadcast across a rowdy hall, he adds, "Hey, want to come out there with me?"

"Oh, w—wow," I stumble.

"You said you wanted to explore the outer boroughs."

Ander tilts his head and studies me in a way he hasn't done yet. I'm alternately melting and getting chills. His pale blue eyes remind me of a Husky dog's: spooky, blue-gray, and hard to read. "I'm headed to Coney Island to walk the boardwalk. Won't stay warm forever." His mouth twists as he glances, lightning fast, over at Lacey again.

Marie Claire girl isn't holding back, so why should I? "Sure, I'd like that!"

"Got to grab a book from the library," he says. "Meet you on the front steps."

"I'll be there." My. God. Is this really happening?

Snickering, Lacey grabs her handbag and slams her locker closed. She marches off, heels clicking against the freshly polished linoleum.

I might be plain, but I'm no dim-bulb. It's obvious Ander only invited me out to irritate Lacey. Even so, to go out with a dream guy like Ander is something I'd be a fool to pass up.

I'm smoothing down my wrinkled skirt when he finally emerges. In a flat tone he says, "Let's go, then."

Noticing his slight limp, I slow down, and we make our way to the subway station right by school. We quickly hop a train but the subway is screechy, so I don't have to get conversational just yet. Whenever it stops to let in waves of people, Ander turns to me with an oddly guilty grin, and asks questions. "Do you like our Lit teacher?" "What was your old school like?" He moves on to the next question before I'm done answering. Not many people are talking. Riding seems mostly about clinging onto the cold pole for dear life, and saving your vocal chords for later.

My theory seems accurate, because once we get out of the subway, he's more talkative. "I used to play soccer. Team captain. Number-one center," he informs me.

"Really! You don't play anymore?" I ask as I gawk at the gaudy arcades we're approaching. There's one for bumper

cars, one for video games, and one for the purple neon head-
quarters of a turbaned psychic, Maria Suprema. The air's
dripping with sweet caramel and buttery popcorn, mixed
with twinges of car exhaust and hot-dog smoke. A roller-
coaster, a Ferris wheel and other carnival rides soar over the
boardwalk. Wow, a gritty urban version of the Indiana State
Fair, but set on the edge of an ocean.

"I'm a *former* soccer star," Ander says with bite. "Last
season someone mangled me." My gaze moves to his left
thigh as he gives it a brusque pat.

"That's awful. You okay?"

"Not so much. My doctor shoved a metal rod in my
femur."

"Ouch." I ache for him. "That really sucks."

"Yeah. He told me he's seen more serious soccer injuries
than football ones. Unfortunately, the association has no
mandatory protection other than shin guards."

"They ought to change the rules."

"I wanted to be the one to get the team to state. Killed me
not to." He rubs his leg again. I'm surprised and flattered
that he's revealed something so personal.

On the boardwalk, rival speakers blast a mix of old disco
and hip-hop. We stroll past guys selling Gucci and Rolex
watches. Ander clues me in that they're fakes. Who knew?
Next we pass a pair of old ladies in hot pink whose dark
roots leach into platinum. These people sure let their inner
freak out, I'm thinking, as we pass by toothless, tattooed men
on a bench, whose hooded eyes stay glued to a flock of bare-
shouldered girls.

I follow Ander down a stairway and onto the sand, which
is studded with overflowing trashcans and people of all
stripes relaxing on towels. We choose a spot near the surf.

Ander flings off his overshirt and plunks down on it. I try
not to blatantly drool over his ripped chest and arms pressing

against his tight jersey. I've never been this close to a guy this handsome, and it literally takes my breath away. Stretching my skirt under me, I sit, and then arrange my leather flats side by side.

"Sorry, bad with names. I know you told me before," Ander cups his hand over his eyes to glance at me in the glare of the sun.

Figures. I never got much attention from the meaty jocks *or* the arty guys. Ander seems kind of in the middle. He has an athlete's body, but a far-off gaze, as if he's thinking of things that happened a long time ago. Things he can't quite shake.

I did have a few dates with a classmate named Len, whose dad owned a chain of shoe stores. We went bowling, and to the movies. On the third date, over burgers at Denny's, I stared at my wilted lettuce while he laid down a final verdict.

"No offense, but I'm bored." He peered at me over his glasses.

"By the dinner?" I'd asked.

He coughed. "My burger was okay."

It wasn't as if Len was so exciting. He mostly talked about his dad's business and how Indiana was experiencing urban sprawl. How boring is that? Still, his comment stung. Will Ander find me any different?

Digging my heels into the sand, I fluff my hair and sit up straighter. "I'm Dorianna."

Ander nods. "Ah, that's right, sorry. Dorianna. . . unusual name."

Extraordinary name for an ordinary girl—that's consolation.

"So, uh, were you into sports back at your old school?" he asks me.

"Ha! Yeah, gardening." I snort. "I harvested cabbages and brussels sprouts with my trusty hunting knife."

"That's one way to exercise." His husky, sexy laughter fills my chest with quivery chills. "Don't they race motocross in the Midwest?" he asks.

"I knew one girl who did that." A classmate who raced in a skintight jumpsuit and flashed her photo on the bike every chance she had. "Hey, I got to mow the lawn with my cherry-red, sit-down, four-wheel Dixie Chopper."

"Sounds cool." Ander pokes at the sand with his toes.

Not sure how to fill in the lull, but it's my turn. I figure I can talk about school, maybe ask him about that unfriendly girl, and some of the others, too. "What's the story with Lacey?" I start. Ander throws me a blank look. "In the morning, the girl across from our lockers you said hi to on the first day?"

"I said hello?" Ander shrugs. "Don't remember that."

What do I do with that response? How could he forget? I try again. "You know, the one with the blonde hair and big handbags. What's she like?"

Ander rakes a hand through his hair. "She's a snob. Big into parties. Her posse shadows her every move like a bunch of airhead zombies. She lives in Manhattan and actually has a car. A *car*. In *Manhattan*. Her parents pay to park it in some overpriced lot."

In Wabash, lots of kids get cars at sixteen, but I guess not here, what with all the cabs. "What kind of car?"

"A yellow freaking Mustang," Ander adds wistfully.

I sense his energy locking up. Does he have a bad history with this girl, or is he bummed that his parents can't afford to buy *him* a Mustang? "Who do you like to hang out with, then?"

"Guys from our Lit class, and a dude from another school," he says vaguely.

"What about the soccer guys? You still friends with them?"

Ander pats his thigh. "A few. Like I said, steel rod in there. I'm done." He picks up a handful of sand and tosses it. A baby sand crab, ejected in the toss, skitters away. "Those jocks are full of themselves. Most other kids, too. They have superstar lawyer and TV-producer parents. You'll see."

Doubtful he has *all* the kids at school figured out. And why would he give up his popular status so easily? Something seems wrong here, as if Ander has a serious chip on his shoulder. I understand those. "So, your dad's not a big-shot TV producer?"

"Nah. He's an editor for a legal publisher. Yours?"

I flinch. Ander told me why he limps, so fair is fair. Besides, something about him inspires me to be open. "My dad's a minister." *Was* a minister, before he got thrown in the slammer.

"Is that why he named you Dorianna? Isn't that, like, a Bible character?"

"Hardly!" I erupt in a full-tilt belly laugh. Feels amazing. Familiar with all of the Bible stories, I'm positive that Dorianna is neither a biblical woman nor a saint.

Ander rises on his elbows. For the first time, he looks really interested. "What kind of church is it, anyway?"

I want to be open, yet . . . it's so hard. My father originally had his own fledgling flock—of around forty-five. "Generic New Age doctrine, with eco-twists."

"Seriously? Tree huggers?"

I laugh. "Yeah, sort of. They used to sing a song called *Look Into the Eyes of the Sun* that one of Dad's faithful wrote. They also performed the Woodland Walkabout—a weekly group hike in the woods for God."

"Weird. Like a walking meditation?"

I nod. "Looking into the sun is dangerous. Your retinas would fry. I worried that people would interpret the song literally."

"That'd be crazy, wouldn't it?"

"Sure would." I sigh. "Where are you supposed to find God? Not from staring at the sun, and not under a rock like a newt. I don't know where I stand with religion."

"I hear you." Ander flicks his hair back.

Wherever I stand, it's nowhere near that church.

"Anyway, my father wanted more attendees, but only seemed to get less." I can't talk about it anymore. It's too shameful. Before they shut him down and sent him to jail, he was left with about seventeen congregants, mostly divorcées, bunched on the front benches, singing that homespun hymn to the roof beams. He was desperate to grow his church.

But I never knew how desperate until I found that sleazy list in his desk. My eye flashed on the number ten but then scooted, super fast, back to the top. So I only read his first entry—enough to practically make me heave.

I stuck his list in a daily inspirational he gave me when I was six, along with a few family photos, and brought it here to Brooklyn. I can't bring myself to throw it out. I keep telling myself I should read the next nine entries. Yet I secretly hope that the next time I unfold the paper I won't have to learn what the other items are, because the rousing words of the devotional will have cleansed my father's list of its tainted ink.

After his arrest and my parents' separation, Mom decided it was also best for me to go east until they got their divorce straightened out. No matter how open I want to be, it's too humiliating to tell Ander. Especially about that list. Mom doesn't even know about it. She's depressed enough.

Ander looks over at me, probably wondering why I got so quiet. "So, is he still practicing? You talk about it like it was in the past."

I wedge my toes in the sand. "He's done with his church." I tell Ander about staying with my aunt, but not why. "My turn." Eager to shift the focus off me, I point to a folded spiral-bound notebook in Ander's pocket. "What's that?"

"Oh. I write about stuff." Ander taps it with the flat of his palm. I'm surprised by how big and muscular his hand is. As if he's spent the summer doing construction.

"What kind of stuff?"

He wipes sweat off his temples and then looks out at the ocean. "A novel. I'm collecting material for my future novel."

"You're sure ambitious. I've never met an author, and I love books. Have a title?"

He blushes. I'm shocked that anything I say can evoke such a reaction. "I don't usually tell people," he admits.

"Trust me." I smile. "I don't exactly know anyone yet to blab it to."

"I s'pose." Ander turns and stares at me, like, really *stares*. I soak it in, even though it makes me squirm.

He's gorgeous, all angles and sexy stubble. His arms are tanned, strong, perfectly formed, and I'm sure he's wrapped them around plenty of other girls. Yet, in his eyes I see distance—between Ander and other people. Is that why he chose me, a total non-threat, to hang out with, instead of a popular girl—like Lacey? He's endured athletic battles and he's smart, even if he's slow on his feet with that unfortunate limp. Must've had at least one or two girlfriends. Girls like flawed good guys—in movies and stuff. I do, too. Perfect guys are like Greek statues—too faultless, stony. Dare I dream that Ander could ever be my boyfriend?

"*Extortion Portraits*," he exclaims.

I bob my head, though I don't get it. "Extortion?"

"Obtaining information by threats."

"You don't seem like the threatening type."

His handsome face falls. "Well, you don't know me. Plus, it's *fiction*."

So he'd like to be more dangerous? "A thriller? I like

those," I say to bolster his ego.

"You could say that." He grins.

We gaze out at the surf, at the little kids whizzing about, jumping over the white water and screeching. Ander asks if I'd like to grab lemonade up on the boardwalk. I say sure, since it's even hotter now than in the morning. I'm busy brushing sand off my feet and slipping on my shoes when someone shouts Ander's name.

Spinning around, I see an outrageously tall guy speeding toward us. Lordy, he must be over six and a half feet tall. His tousled hair is so black, it glints blue. Two strappy equipment bags dangle from his shoulder and bump against his wiry chest as he walks closer. His shirt is silky purple, open to his chest, with Gothic flowing sleeves as if he's one of those dangerous male models you see in rock magazines who grin impishly and straddle a motorcycle. Swallowing hard, I study his belt buckle: a horned goat creature with ruby eyes.

Inexplicably, I'm tempted to tell Ander I need to leave. It has to do with the intense energy jumping off this guy. Instinct screams at me to dash all the way to the subway without looking back. But that would be ridiculous. I'm not about to pass up the opportunity to hang out with Ander, no matter how offbeat this new guy is.

Don't stay here, my protective instincts warn again. There's a bloody twinkle in that spirit's eye. Now my gut is babbling nonsense. What the heck does that even mean? I shove down my panic, but my heart keeps on racing.

"My man, you didn't tell me you were heading to Coney." The guy fist-bumps Ander, who wears a faint frown, as if he doesn't relish me seeing how edgy it can get with his friends. Does this goth weirdo go to our school? Looks like the type who would wear white zombie contacts to wig people out. I've seen those guys on TV.

"What're you doing out here, Warren? That's the real

question," Ander asks.

The guy pushes his smoky shades back onto his unruly mop. "Didn't I tell you? My uncle split to Russia until next summer and left me his apartment. So I moved out. Couldn't stand the drama at home in Park Slope with my brother, Charlie. It's all here." He waves an arm toward Surf Avenue, past the boardwalk.

"Couldn't stand Charlie, huh?" Ander looks less fazed. More intrigued.

So, Charlie's this guy's brother. Judging from Ander's reaction, I'm guessing Charlie looms large in Ander's world, too.

The tall guy strokes his knuckles as he appraises me in a slow up-down that doesn't as much make me feel he's undressing me as appreciating the art of my curves. I'm *so* not used to this. It's not as giddying as Ander's stare. More like the bracing swerves of an out-of-control carnival ride. My heart is doubly rattled. He's got tons of rings—a snarling dog's face, a rusted nail forged into a circle, and an onyx-and-amethyst orb. "Who's the lady?" he asks Ander.

Ander looks at him blankly. What gives? Has he forgotten my name yet again? I'm about to introduce myself when he says, "Dorianna. And Dorianna, this is Wilson Warren."

I suppress a laugh. Who's named *Wilson* these days? "Should I call you Wilson, or Warren?"

"Wilson. Only Ander calls me Warren. Pleased to meet you." Wilson bows as he waves his hand in concentric circles —an odd but charming gesture.

"Shooting video?" Ander inquires. So that's what those official-looking bags are.

"Yeah. Took some great footage of the cougars, and the new rides at Luna Park." Wilson chuckles low in his throat. "People reeling off that new airplane ride." He demonstrates with fake-drunk steps.

Ander smiles. He has a honey-sweet smile. He should smile more often. I wonder what kind of cougars Wilson's referring to. Old ladies who chase young guys? Or are there caged jungle cats over by the rides?

Like some fabulous praying mantis, Wilson lowers his sticklike exoskeleton next to me and tucks his limbs into his concave chest. He pulls out a sleek black camera from one of the bags. Must have serious cash for all that equipment. Way beyond the basic Olympus my mom bought me years ago, which I baby so it won't break.

I startle when Wilson sticks his camera near my face and peers at me through it. "You're okay if I take some footage," he asks, more like a statement.

Ander frowns at him. "Um, Warren . . ."

He proceeds to record before I can answer. I won't protest, even though it unnerves me, because this focus on me is as new and different from Wabash as the ocean curling and uncurling ahead of us.

"Nothing much to see," I confess as I nervously brush back my hair.

"Oh, but I beg to differ," Wilson refutes, in that oddly archaic way of his I'll come to dread. He swings in for a closer shot. "You've got an angel's face," he remarks.

I snort. "You're joking."

"Not at all." He keeps on recording.

"Warren, an angel's face?" Ander raises an eyebrow.

"See?" I say, almost apologetically. Even Ander knows I'm plain.

"I didn't mean you were ugly," Ander says defensively.

That's all right, I'm thinking, I know what I look like.

Wilson keeps on capturing me. "Your nose—is narrow with a hint of upturn."

"My nose isn't so narrow."

"The forehead has a sheen of purity," Wilson speaks

about me as if I'm an ivory figurine in an art museum. "Eyes set apart like that represent a cunning intelligence cloaked in . . ."

"In what?" I'm on pins and needles.

"Pure, untested innocence!"

Ander guffaws. They don't need to humiliate me. I'm not *completely* innocent. Len kissed me at the movies, before he determined I wasn't his thing. And I've had my share of raunchy thoughts about what I'd like to do to certain guys, including Ander.

I summon my nerve. "What do you mean by untested innocence?"

Wilson doesn't answer. Instead he blurts, "It's appalling. We must corrupt you!" He winks at me. I'm strangely pulled by it—as if I'd go anywhere with this stranger. "Ander, shall we corrupt this perfect angel?" Wilson spins the lens cap in his fingers.

"You're such a drama king." Ander snickers.

"Check it out for yourself." Wilson angles the viewfinder in our direction.

I lean over and peer in. A high-pitched, *"Eeee!"* escapes me. He's captured an otherworldly quality I didn't even know I have—silky like his shirt, almost glowing.

"That's me?" I'm in awe. Longing fires up behind my eyes, spreads heat into my chest. "How did you get me to look like that?"

"Good directing. I'll give you that." Ander looks from where Wilson pressed pause, to me, and back to the image, clearly not believing I can be made that pretty.

I don't, either. "More than good. You're a visual magician."

Wilson grins, making his pointy ears shift outward. "Need a bit more video." He puts away his large camera, extracts a tiny one, and starts recording me with it.

Getting up, I brush off sand and creak into a stiff pose.

Wilson unfolds his mantis legs and stands up, too. "Let's try some surf footage."

"But, uh, we were getting lemonade—" Ander shoves his feet in his sneakers and shambles toward me as if to take my arm.

"How about in a few minutes?" I veer off, irritated that Ander's interfering with Wilson's magnetic pull, where only moments ago I was completely in Ander's sway. A primal force moves my feet down to the breakers. Self-conscious as I'm made by the attention, I have to see how Wilson will direct me. *Have* to. I jog into the foamy water. "What should I do?"

"Pretend you're dancing." Wilson wades in beside me, not seeming to care that his trendy black pants are getting soaked. Not to mention my floating skirt.

"There's no music, and I'm a horrible dancer," I wail. My arms are stiff rudders. I didn't need to rush so far in. What was I thinking?

"Sing a song then, and try to dance," Wilson orders.

Glancing over my shoulder, I see Ander at the water's edge with a look of disdain, his arms crossed. I feel judged, until I realize he's glowering at Wilson. Who *is* Wilson and why is Ander friends with him? Hasn't Ander ever felt his mysterious pull?

Oh, who cares. . . I'm tired of analyzing and second-guessing my every flipping move. I need to loosen up. I don't want to hear another guy telling me I'm boring—to heck with my wet clothes. Lifting my arms skyward, I flail them, straining to think of a song. Lyrics flit into my head, and then flit right out. I suck at remembering them. Oh. Wait—the words to that ridiculous song from Dad's church. That I know by heart.

Look into the eyes of the sun, see the spirits burning there.

Higher, faster, on the run, purified by air.

It's absurd at first. Then, after the second line, I coil in a snakelike dance. Flipping my hair, I note the faces of some random kids through my loose curls. They're staring. My excitement surges, as more eyes focus on me. It's so freeing. . . Why was I always so afraid to make an ass out of myself?

"Good!" Wilson shouts. "Dip down, scoop up some water. Yeah, wild."

Ander's voice pierces through my splashing and Wilson's stage directions. "Warren, you don't exactly work for Dior. Hey, I'm going. Dorianna, you coming?"

I glance at Ander. His face doesn't match his frustrated voice. He isn't even looking at Wilson anymore. He's gawking at me the way a male dog stares at a female in heat —with longing, with passion. I've seen that look on guys before, but *never* directed at me. It's so unexpected that I do a double take. But whatever was in Ander's mind a second ago has already dissolved. Did I only imagine his hungry gaze? I want him to look at me like that again. I'm thirsty for it. I need it like I need water.

Embarrassed by my need, I clomp out of the water with all the grace of a walrus.

"Ander's right," I inform Wilson, feeling guilty that I ignored Ander's earlier request. "We *were* headed up for lemonade." I squeeze saltwater out of my sopping skirt.

"Let's grab the drinks and go to my place," Wilson suggests as he caps his waterproof video camera and places it gently in its pack.

Ander frowns. The boy is moody. Or are these two guys in some power play?

"Come on, Ander," Wilson growls. "Bachelor pad to the max."

"Sounds fun to me," I squeak.

Ander says okay. As we buy drinks, Wilson takes more

footage: of me confessing my love for lemonade on a hot day, and of the booth's plastic daisy lights. He tapes domino players, swirling candy wrappers, and even a broken bench slat. Video addict, I decide. That must be how famous directors get started. Hey, you have to start somewhere.

As we walk on, my gut flips over—hard. Here I am, after one week of eleventh grade in the sophisticated City of Five Boroughs, and I'm already headed to a video artist's fabulous beach pad with an ex-star athlete. If only Len and my old classmates could see me now. Lacey and her tribe, too.

Adoration, that's what popular people demand. In my case, this bit of positive attention thrills me to my core. I imagine what it'd be like to have my new classmates still talking about me—in a good way—in ten years. "That girl seemed shy at first, but she turned out to be a firecracker!" "Every guy was chasing her." "I still have the note she gave me junior year."

I'd give my left pinky to be admired.

"We'll mess around with the footage," Wilson says, sliding his long body close to me.

"What more would you do with it?" asks Ander.

"Lots," Wilson promises, giving me another mischievous wink. If he can make me that pretty, have Ander look at me like that. . .

In the hard slant of the sun, the goat's eyes on his buckle ping ruby red, and fill me with anxiety over seeing my acrobatics on replay. Ander's right: Wilson is no high-fashion professional, and I'm no model.

As before, though, I'm swept along by a ravishing undertow. Its strong grip washes me forward into a release of dazzling, yet invisible spray. A joyous trill in my gut tells me this will no longer be an ordinary afternoon, or me, an ordinary, boring girl.

3

T'is magic that hath ravished me.
—*Doctor Faustus*, by Christopher Marlowe

I'm stagestruck when Wilson opens his apartment door to a sea of white couches and leafy, floor-to-ceiling plants. Ander rushes in first.

"After you, angel." Wilson ushers me in with a firm arm to my back. I catch a whiff of his cologne—like woodsy pine.

Ander is already studying the bookshelf. Stepping toward him, I see most titles are in another language. "The Russian Cyrillic," he explains.

"I'm impressed. How do you know Cyrillic? You sure are a book guy through and through."

"I like languages." Ander uses the book to gesture around the space. "Dude! I need an uncle to unload an apartment on me. I'm jealous."

"How can you afford to buy groceries and things?" I ask

Wilson. "Do your parents give you money?" Pretty brave, living on his own when he's still in high school.

"Those misers? Ha! No cash to the black sheep." Wilson snickers. "I sell my videos and photos on Getty Images and online. Very lucrative, if you know the ropes, and the kind of footage people are looking for."

"For example?" I ask.

"Classic emo stuff," Wilson replies. "Pink sunsets and sparkly athletic kids, playing a clean game of beach volleyball, but with skimpy things on." Ander and Wilson fist-bump.

I can't help but feel sympathy for Wilson as the family's black sheep. Must stink. I'm an only child. Though my father's church was New Age and hippie, he'd been strict as a cop about honesty and upstanding behavior. If I told a small lie, or took a larger-than-normal portion of rice or chicken, I'd get it. Ironic that he taught me to play by the rules, when he didn't. Living with a hypocrite. Still, being a black sheep must've been worse.

Wilson motions for us to follow. "Made a makeshift studio in my uncle's storage room." He leads us down a shadowy hall, decidedly bleaker than the sunny front room.

Inside the double doors, he flicks on a halogen lamp and scurries around lighting candles in wall sconces. These walls, unlike the clean beach-whites, are papered with coppery fleurs-de-lis. Ander looks as surprised as I do at the contrast. I warm when I see his brows arched and his mouth open. He's so little-boyish like that.

In the flickering, I make out a large, semicircular mahogany desk. It faces out from a wall, and three state-of-the-art monitors claim its center. On either side of these, Wilson's arranged blinking digital gadgets. For rendering multimedia, I guess.

The space is growing on me. I marvel at the candlelight

casting leaping patterns on the coppery wallpaper. "Your uncle only used this for storage? Why wouldn't he use this room, too? It has so much . . . atmosphere."

"Said a guy died in here. Gave him the willies," Wilson murmurs. "My uncle's superstitious." Wilson's long face eases into a sly grin as he arches his bony fingers over the workstation. "That stuff doesn't scare me. I've been around for centuries, seen it all—beheadings, hangings. Prince of Darkness and all."

Ander and I exchange uneasy glances as Ander shakes his head in disbelief. "Warren's our favorite theatrical villain. Pay no attention."

I stutter out a giggle. "Geez, Wilson, you scared me there for a minute."

"Madame, beg pardon." Wilson bows. "But don't tell me I didn't warn you." The way his black brows cross over his deep-set eyes makes me step back.

"There *is* a heavy vibe in here." Ander taps on the wall. "No windows, huh?"

"Perfect for editing," Wilson replies.

If you like editing in a medieval dungeon. My eyes settle on a stage with a green paper background, across the room. I point to it. "What's that for?"

"A platform to record objects and models, and a green background that you can replace with anything, once it's loaded into your software. Green screen, they call it."

"Give me an example?"

Wilson guides me to a monitor. He sits, while I lean over his shoulder. Punching in keys, he fills the screen with four separate images of the same preppy guy posed in soccer gear, with a smug, almost goofy grin on his face.

"That's Charlie, Warren's brother, and my ex-friend," Ander remarks, coming over to stand by me. I'm glad he's close. This studio's intriguing but strange.

Each video background is distinct. In the first, Charlie is plopped into a throng of blubbery cartoon cherubs. In the second, he's peeking out from a glinting guillotine. In the third, he's among slithering rattlesnakes, and in the last, he's in a pile of maggoty sausage.

"We love the guy," Ander says dryly. I fake a laugh.

Wilson glances around at me. "I'm visualizing backgrounds for you, too."

A troubled silence falls between us. It would be cool to vamp onstage, luxuriate in a Wilson Warren video—say, with a tropical background, or in a wildflower-strewn forest. But studying what he's done to his very own brother, I doubt our visions would ever sync. "The green screen sure gives the videographer tons of control," I mutter. "What did Charlie do to deserve this?"

"Besides being a jerk?" Wilson nods at Ander. "He stole away Ander's Eve."

"More like Charlie ate her poison apple," Ander snipes.

"Either way, Ander is lovelorn over a malicious blonde minx who left him."

"Lovelorn, my ass." Ander jabs Wilson hard in the ribs. Poor Ander. Is Wilson referring to Lacey? She's a blonde minx. That would explain the tension sparking between them. If it's true, why did Lacey dump him?

I feel a stab of jealousy. I'd give anything to be Ander's— to feel his strong, reassuring arms around me, to massage his sore leg and read his novel-in-progress.

Wilson touches my arm. I jerk away. "Unlike Charlie, I would only do glamorous things to you," he promises. Ander pig-snorts. "Ignore the dour hog behind the curtain," Wilson adds. Are they teasing me? Playing some witty word joust? I gaze at Ander. He strokes me with an unexpected grin. No, I'm just being uptight.

I swallow my discomfort. If Wilson asks me onstage, I'll

do it. A chance to be an artist's *muse*. If Ander's friendly with Wilson, he must be okay. Wilson just likes to shock, the way I've read that some goth-style kids file their teeth to resemble vampires. Wilson clearly has talent and a generous uncle, who trusts him enough to loan him the space.

Glancing again at Wilson, in his high-backed throne chair, I see he's connected his camera's USB. He's uploading video and feverishly inputting data.

"Have a seat." He gestures to the swivel chairs on either side of him.

I sit gingerly, reluctant to douse the seat with my soppy skirt. Ander takes the seat to Wilson's left. Gulping the last of my lemonade, I shiver when a blast of air-conditioning hits me. Wilson opens an animation program and builds layers in it, pasting in footage of the plastic daisy lights on one layer, and other bits on additional layers. He has at least ten, and he's building them so fast it's hard to grasp what he's doing.

After mere minutes, he turns to me. His eyes burn with a manic intensity. "Ready for your debut, Dorianna?"

Are you kidding? I've only been waiting for it my *whole life*. I lean forward, elbows on the desk. "Ready." Ander leans forward, too. Wilson's finger, with its dash of black polish, presses play.

Onscreen, my likeness emerges with outstretched arms through a glory of sun. I'm me but not me. I'm brighter, bigger, glowing. As I shimmy, the sun settles itself into my palms. And then, in a beach-goddess bestowal of gifts, from my open palms I release a psychedelic explosion of plastic daisies, clouds, sand pails, and seagulls. They float out and up, and morph into arching sunrays. The sunrays dance around my cascading hair, and kiss my sickly white cheeks into candy-cane pink.

"I, I can't believe this!" I rasp.

"You're like an Indian deity," Ander exclaims. "You know, the ones with a zillion hands, offering up the entire earth."

"You're the Coney Island Queen," Wilson says. "Presiding proudly over toxic starfish, mermaids with piercings, and sideshow freaks."

Ander and I exchange looks of shocked pleasure. No wonder Ander's friends with this guy. He's a conjuring genius. I swing back to Wilson's screen, where his impish conjuring is still unfolding.

This time, I'm framed by playful waves and children's grinning faces, and then by sandcastles and undulating fish in jewel tones. I'm dancing my heart out to the sound of a spacey lyre. Inside, I'm leaping and dancing, too. "How'd you do it?" I gasp.

"Software called Adobe Premiere plus After Effects . . . plus enchantment. What else do you expect from an agent of the devil?"

"Lay off, Warren. You'll scare the girl. Really, though, it's incredible."

Now the cups of lemonade are soaring around. My onscreen image catches one and offers it to the viewer. As I do, the cup distorts to huge, juicy proportions.

"You like?" Wilson presses pause.

"Wait! Don't stop!" I cry. My cheeks are on fire. My chest is heaving. I want to suck in more and more. "Oh, my god," I say breathlessly, and then shiver, remembering the harsh reality. "But . . . it's not *exactly* me."

"It's a new and improved you," Ander says reasonably.

Wilson touches my arm again. This time it's not slithery. It startles me into something deep, unidentifiable. It's as if he wants me to confess something, but I don't know what. I gaze at him behind a sudden prick of tears. "If I could look like that, I'd. . ."

Abruptly, horrid memories rush in: the old nicknames, the beady, nauseating stares. When I was fourteen a friend of Len's said I was too buck-toothed to get a boyfriend, and that if I ever wanted one, I better get braces fast because my wonky front teeth cut a red line into my bottom lip.

And that final humiliation. When my dad was on trial, my classmates didn't even bother to blurt out nicknames. Instead, they passed me unblinking, the same way Lacey and her gang have done every morning and will continue to do, day after depressing day.

Nothing will be different here. Nothing can.

Through my haze of pain, Ander's saying, "Strange! You don't even look like the same girl. If Wilson puts this on YouTube or Instagram, you could be the next big thing." Ander's voice has intense heat for the first time today. "People would follow your every move."

"They used to call them 'It Girls'," Wilson informs us.

It Girl, and not simply *It?* "Oh, my God. I'd give—" Ander's hungry stare at the beach rushes into my memory. If I was that beautiful all of the time, he'd gaze at me like that every day . . . be drawn to me.

"You'd give what?" Wilson's stare is a wrestler's grip, tightening around my chest.

"I told you, lay off," Ander snaps.

"Sure, sure," Wilson drones, and then, "I have some brownies in the kitchen. They'd go well with the lemonade. Might sweeten your mood. Want some? They're on the counter."

"Trying to get rid of me?" Ander grouses, but ducks out anyway.

Wilson turns back to me with a charismatic grin. "So, what were you saying?"

I just met this guy. I shouldn't blurt out personal stuff.

He's scaring me, but I want acceptance so, so badly. It's so much easier to admit that without Ander in the room. Wilson must sense this. "If I could be really popular," I start, "I'd give my next six months of checks from my mom to charity."

"You'd *what?*" Wilson hisses. "Never mind. I thought you cared."

I gasp for air. This feels like some creep-show pledge. But I don't believe in Hell, or the devil, or any superstitious junk. I don't know what I believe, except that I'm cynical about religion, after that mess with my father's church, and finding his list. So, it doesn't matter what I say to Wilson. It's only a torrent of words. How much sway do words have in the real world, anyway?

Wilson taps impatiently on the keypad. "You want beauty and youth forever? I can give you that. Power over those mean girls, Ava and Lacey. Power over a lot of people. It's yours for a price. Just say it."

"How do you know about them? I, I never told you." Wilson doesn't answer, just keeps on grinning. His eyes are golden and black and red all at once. Like unearthly spears, piercing me. I'm dizzy. I need fresh air, now. But I want this promise more than anything. *Ever.* "What's the price?" I rasp.

Wilson's stare burns into me. "Can't say, exactly." He takes a long breath. "But there always is." His words are ice and fire. Flutters of snowflakes pattering silently under my skin, that melt into scorching sparks.

I follow an irrepressible urge to stand up, and look down on Wilson with his narrow, feral face and piercings. I need Ander to look at me with that passion, over and over. I need those hater girls put in their place. I need a friend, and for people to want to be with me all of the time, to never, ever be bored—only to love me.

It's worth any price.

A powerful force in me breaks loose, a flu bug races rampant up my spine. Like when I got hooked into rooting for the Pacers one season—the burn of wanting them to smash their opponents. I had their plastic ball hanging from my window, and concentrated on its hypnotic pendulum as I fell asleep. Team fever.

"Would you . . . give your soul?" Wilson's whisper invades my gut, my brain.

Ander's aching gaze from our time at the beach shimmers in front of me. Enticing. I can almost feel his kiss. Like water. Drink it in. I've never wanted anything as much as I want this, this . . . "I'd give anything for power, easy youth and beauty." My voice comes from all around me, spreading, gluey on my skin. "Yes, I'd even give my . . . *soul.*"

The air spirals into a funnel, draining all oxygen from the room with a hiss. *So-, so-, soul.* In an instant, new air swoops in, air suffused with rich, delicious minerals. I gulp it in, openmouthed, so very thirsty.

"To be seen and accepted," I murmur.

Wilson goes head to head with me. "Forget about just being accepted—how about having a following of millions, going viral?"

"Really?" I'm whirling. "Go viral." Wilson's promises are golden brands, annointing me, conferring an otherworldly legitimacy I've never, ever felt. How does he manage to do this?

Ander returns with the brownies. I luxuriate in the sexy new glint he's giving me. Who needs sweets when he's looking at me like that? Is this vow a real thing? Is it already working?

"Something feels different in here," he mumbles. "It's colder." He puts the plate of brownies down and smiles at me. Light flickers red, then gold on Ander's handsome face as he caresses and infuses me with his body heat.

An unfamiliar power in me swells with precarious danger and weight as I study Ander and Wilson. Abruptly, I'm flung out of my body, inexplicably looking down at them as pitiful peons who will someday worship at my feet.

As two of the very, very many.

Then I'm back inside myself, stunned by how I was seeing them.

The room seems to rush with the force of souls washing through, and I flinch when I hear them moaning. I tell myself it's only the whir, whir, whir of the hard drives.

Sitting bewildered, I can't say exactly *what* took place—only that the candlelight is flickering brighter, the fleurs-de-lis are practically dancing on the walls, and Ander is still gazing at me with an expression of astonishment and lust.

He gets out his notebook and flips it open to the first blank page. "You need a script if you're going on YouTube," he says. "It'll be more compelling if you're not just rambling."

"You're the writer," I say hopefully.

"But no lame girl whining in her room in front of a laptop," Wilson chides. "Too juvenile and amateur. We need something with spark."

I'm already churning with ideas. "I need a name—Fun Girl, or Hot Girl or . . . Sungirl!"

"Good one." Ander jots that down.

I swirl around, touching the fabric of my skirt, already dry and hot. How did that happen so fast? "I'm Sungiiirrrrl."

"Not bad, —it's catchy," Wilson remarks. "I'll build you a

platform, fan sites. We'll get a meetup party going. You'll be the grand hostess, the ultimate influencer."

"A party, how fun!" I twirl around a second time.

"We should start small," Ander says sensibly. "We don't want every douche—"

"How about just people from our class," I say. "Like Ava, Bailey. . ." That makes the most sense to me. It will be my first test, to see if this crazy vow is real.

"Lacey? Count me out," Ander snaps.

"Can't deal with the femmes fatales?" Wilson baits. "Lacey might give you another ride in her infamous little Mustang."

So there *was* a last time. I shrug it off. It doesn't matter now—only the future matters.

Ander shakes his head. "I wouldn't set foot in that prima donna's toy ever again."

"Sure you wouldn't," Wilson smirks.

No more talk about the Mustang. "I never had a real party," I admit. "I'll have streamers and cake and—"

"No little girl's event," Wilson snaps. "It has to be sophisticated. Set lofty sights. Set the parameters now."

"What, like 'high tea'?" I fire back. Who is he to order me around? It's *my* big debut. I catch myself. *Attitude, attitude,* I scold silently. I'm not the spoiled type.

"High tea. That's better." Wilson sits back and affects a languid pose, one hand in the air with pinky out as he holds an imaginary cup.

"A *tea*?" Ander sniggers. "No way anyone will show up to an old-lady event with, like, finger food and crumpets."

"But that's why it works," Wilson says. "It's outrageous. Unexpected. Artsy."

Ander cocks his head suggestively at the wall sconces. "And Victorian?"

"And you're a sucker for, what, local thrift-store flair?" Wilson glares at Ander's worn plaid shirt.

"Guys, guys, we'll make it cool," I insist, a wisp of doubt in my voice. Maybe the magic takes time to set in. It's still a little bumpy here.

"According to Andy Warhol, you only have fifteen minutes of fame," Wilson says to me. "Though if you play your cards right, you'll have much, much more."

I nod eagerly, my spark reignited. "Sungirl should have a sun theme. Don't you think? Outdoorsy, everyone in yellow clothes."

Wilson must like the idea, because he's already scrolling through sites of copyright-free images. He chooses a cupcake photo with swirls. Within seconds, he's Photoshopped the virtual icing into a lemony froth. Creating an evite design, he adds a border of yellow daisies and a still of me looking up at the sun.

I panic. "Wait! That's going out to everyone in my class?"

"Well, yeah," Wilson says through an impatient sigh.

"Can't you find a section of video where my face is hidden? If they know it's me, they'll never go to my party."

"Get some confidence," Wilson scolds. His stare takes me apart in pieces.

"She's got a point." Ander steps close. His warm breath swathes me in calm. I want him there always.

Wilson shrugs and spins back around to the computer. He chooses a second still of me where I'm half-turned toward the ocean with a section of my hair flying up from the wind, conveniently camouflaging my face.

"Much better," I sigh.

"The sun looks like it's scorching your curves. It's pretty smoking hot," Ander admits.

Wow, no one's *ever* described me that way. I could get used to that.

"Thanks, it's perfect," I tell Wilson. "By the time they realize it's me, hopefully they'll love the concept."

"That's the spirit," Wilson says as he saves the file.

Ander writes the copy, with tweaks from Wilson and me.

> *Bask in the warmth of Sungirl at her Yellow Party.*
> *High tea, 3 p.m. Saturday afternoon at*
> *Prospect Park by the Music Pagoda*
> *Yellow attire only*
> *Parlor games*
> *First seven winners get a voucher from Sungirl,*
> *good for points at her next mysterious Meetup*
> *Shhhh! It's beyond exclusive.*
> *Only peeps with this downloadable evite*
> *can show up.*

Ander creates a mailing list, concentrating on the most popular kids from our class, but inviting some of his friends, too. We throw in some of the well-liked girls from the grade below for good measure.

"It's not a matter of exclusivity," I reason, "more a way to weasel into the top-of-the-class heap. Once there, we'll open the parties to more kids—even the geeks."

"Right, we'll undermine the in-crowd—stand it on its head," Ander adds.

Wilson agrees. He, like Ander, seems to like anything that provokes, that's mischievous, that rips open the tight fist of the favored.

I can't deny that I'm worried about how kids might look at me on Monday. Will the secret of who sent the evite leak out before my classmates get excited about the event? If so, will they laugh me off the planet? I leave Wilson's apartment in a daze.

At least I have the weekend to brace myself. Walking the last few blocks to Aunt Carol's, I'm a lot less surefooted than I was at Wilson's with the guys spurring me on. Wilson's enchantment is surely a load of hooey. I pinch my arms, my cheeks. There's no real proof that I'm different, only a vague buzzing in my brain, a skipping of my pulse. I could be making the worst mistake of my life with this crazy-ambitious event.

4
———

Mirror, mirror on the wall, who's the fairest one of all?
—The Brothers Grimm

S aturday morning. It takes me a few minutes to register yesterday's events. Wilson. The video. Ander's sexy gaze. . .

I brush a hand through my tangled bed hair. It feels oddly thicker. From Coney Island's sea air, or something else?

I leap up, throw on a bathrobe, jog to the bathroom, and then hesitate in front of the door. Looking in the mirror is always a huge disappointment. In one reckless motion, I fling open the door and lean into the toothpaste-dotted mirror.

"Oh. My. God," I gasp. My hair *is* thicker, and wavy with more peach tones. But that's not the only change. My normally dull brown eyes have golden and hazel flecks. My sickly pale cheeks are noticeably rosy. Even my lips seem fuller—no, *are* fuller, and pouty. I ease my mouth into a tentative smile. My rabbit choppers barely poke out at all.

Is this even possible? Really? Leaning in closer, I grip my lower lip and stretch it out to inspect its inner flesh. "No awful tooth marks," I cry. This would've taken years of braces without magic. I smile, easier and wider this time. "Wilson! How . . . ?"

I wash my face and hurry back to my room to inspect myself in a different mirror. Same results. Wilson was joking, right? He couldn't have actually done this to me. Could he?

I grab my cell and scroll to his number. But when I find it, I snap the phone shut. "Wait," I mumble to myself, "if it really is magic, I don't want him to take it all back." I'm afraid to know details about where it comes from. That might make it fade. I refuse to find out it's not real.

I also don't dare utter aloud the other thing Wilson said—something about a price, an unpredictable consequence. Hopefully, that part was a joke. Does he enjoy scaring people when he transforms them? Suddenly cold, I wrap my bathrobe tighter. This is too freaky. "Am I going crazy?" I ask my reflection, even though I'm already in love with my improved look and trembling with excitement over what it could do for me.

I need to test it on someone else—see if they see what I do. I hurry downstairs to the kitchen and to Aunt Carol pouring coffee into her favorite blue ceramic mug. "Morning," I chirp.

She wheels around. Coffee pot still in hand, she stares at me with narrowed, baffled eyes. "Why hello," she finally sputters. "You look spectacular! Did you color your hair, or put on makeup, or tweeze?"

It's real, I think gleefully. *I'm beautiful now.* A new worry pops into my head. How will I ever explain it to my aunt, or Ander . . . to anyone but Wilson? Flicking my hair back, I smile sheepishly. "I got a facial and the spa lady showed me how to apply makeup—the right way." I sigh. "My mom never taught me that stuff."

"Oh, Dorianna, I know, I know." Aunt Carol puts down the coffeepot and gives me a timid hug. She studies my hair, clearly wondering how it's gained such gleaming highlights.

This seems an opportune time to ask her about buying a yellow party dress. My aunt knows all about my mother's "troubles" and, by association, mine. I fire away.

"Oh, Dorianna, what a fun idea to have a get-together in the park. And how brave for someone starting a new school." She chews on her cuticle. "A spa treatment must've cost you. Do you have any extra savings for the dress?"

"Only about forty dollars left. Do you think I can get something for around that?" I know a nice dress costs way more than that, but I can't afford to blow my monthly check in one day. My mom is strapped for money, too. "Do you think you could pitch in, just a little?"

Aunt Carol's brow furrows even more. "I'll try, Dorianna. I'll try my best."

A wash of satisfaction courses over my guilt. It's not altogether cleansing, though—more an immoral pleasure at getting my aunt to cough up funds. This is so not me, yet I quickly shrug away the uncomfortable feeling.

"You already look stunning," my aunt says. "I can hardly imagine how much more beautiful you'll look in a sunny dress."

"Thanks, Aunt Carol. I knew you'd understand," I reply, half in earnest, and half with a melodramatic modesty that Wilson would love.

~

We've already trekked to bargain stores like Strawberry, Forever 21, and Marshalls. These stores have a precious few yellow party dresses, it being September and not prom season. Of the two we come across, one has hideous Snow White puffed sleeves and the other a stained bodice. No wonder they haven't sold yet.

"A shopper told me that Macy's is having a sale," Aunt Carol reports. "Hopefully dresses there won't cost a fortune."

I nod. Isn't that, like, an old-lady store? I look at my aunt with her glasses and tidy ash-blond hair, graying at the roots. She's wearing crunchy granola low-heeled shoes and an A-line skirt. I think of Ava's comment and wonder if a taste for outdated A-line skirts runs in our family like bad blood. I'll make sure to pick out the yellow dress myself.

Neither my parents nor Aunt Carol are exactly swimming in cash, so none of us can really afford to be that stylish. I'm sad about that, and that there's no rapport between the families. Then, there's the added icky element of sidestepping Dad's sentence and jail time. Aunt Carol's his older sister. At some point, we'll have to speak about this forbidden topic. Feels weird not to.

At Macy's, we inspect the rows of dresses. There are lots of black ones I know are affectionately called "little black dresses," good for fancy parties. There's a swirly gray number and a pink one with a red sash, but nothing in yellow. I'm beginning to feel that the yellow theme is a mistake, when my aunt calls from a few aisles over. "Dorianna, here!"

When I arrive, she's triumphantly holding up a yellow dress—the only one in the right size. Twinges of irritation gnaw at me. I wanted to make the discovery. What's wrong with me? Normally, I'd be thrilled to have help. Especially finding an out-of-season color on a chaotic sales rack. "Thanks, Aunt Carol," I squeak, struggling for a nugget of gratitude.

Aunt Carol waits patiently as I go into the fitting room to try it on. I gather my hair and hold it in a loose updo as I study the look. It's so amazing to see my reflection, and not hate it. The dress has a bejeweled, low neckline and super-cute cap sleeves. It hugs my top while arching out at the hips to accentuate my curves. Gorgeous. I picture guys in the class clamoring around me, and Ander looking, too. I picture Lacey complimenting me and inviting me to join the cool table at lunch.

I'm pumped. This yellow miracle is my ticket. Speaking of tickets, I gulp at the tag. It's marked down twice from $450—to a low of $179.

That means that my aunt will have to cough up $139 plus tax, on meager wages. And I hardly even know her. I model the dress as I approach her.

Aunt Carol lights up. "It's spectacular."

"I love it. It fits me perfectly."

"I'm so glad." Aunt Carol's eyes surreptitiously search for the price tag. "How much?" she finally asks.

Rather than saying the price out loud, I hold out the label. "Geez, dresses in Indiana are half this much."

My aunt adjusts her glasses. "It's a bit steep, even with the sale."

"But I *have* to have it!" I burst out. Why did I say that? In my next breath, I dismiss the question. That same fever I felt at Wilson's after I watched his surf video is spiking. "We've already sent the invites, Aunt Carol. I can't back out now."

"It's okay, it's okay." Aunt Carol holds up her palm as if she's warding off a swooping bird of prey. "We'll splurge, that's all."

A second wave of satisfaction crashes through me as I put the dress on the counter and the saleslady rings it up. I consider offering to put in more of the little money I have, but I hold back. I'm entitled to some happiness, aren't I? My aunt has no kids, so she must have squirreled away funds. It's as if a fight is raging between my selfish side and my better angels. My better angels strain to reach in my purse and hold up twenty more dollars. But they strain in vain.

I thank Aunt Carol as we ride down the escalator. There's a pinch in my aunt's, "You're welcome." After that, we go to a diner. Over coffee and blueberry muffins, I ask her about her fundraising work. I need to make my better side feel okay.

"I'm in charge of overseeing pledge calls," she explains, "and figuring out what we'll gift the benevolent donors." Her shoulders droop. "In this economy, it's a struggle. Most people don't have extra money to fund even the things they love, like our new jazz series."

Is this reminder of the shaky economy my aunt's subtle way of punishing me for being materialistic and greedy? I sit there feeling horribly uncomfortable about the pricy dress, sandwiched between my legs in the shopping bag. Before I figure out how to respond, my aunt goes on, in a warmer tone.

"Have you made any special friends yet?"

Certainly not Ava or Lacey. Bailey's passing smile and comment don't really count. I know better than to mention Wilson. Coney Island is seedy between its glitz, and even though I'm almost seventeen, I suspect that my aunt wouldn't be thrilled I've been out there and intend to go again. I settle on mentioning Ander, but no details of how I feel about him.

"He wants to write a novel. Imagine. He's preoccupied, though. Guys."

"Men and their questionable behavior?" Aunt Carol blurts, before catching herself.

I never said *what* he was preoccupied with. I meant his writing, but she assumed I meant it in a negative way. She's never been married, and I wonder if she's ever thought about it, or if she's a rare breed that never pines for a long-term

love? There's another terse silence while we yet again avoid
any mention of Dad, serving a year in jail for a serious misde-
meanor involving manipulation of women that cost him his
ministry license. At least my aunt's stable enough to take me
in. But it's as if her brother doesn't fully exist for her.

As a child, I remember only two times when she flew out
to Indiana. On her first visit, we went to the zoo and saw
zebras. The next time was when I was eleven, and my dad's
church was probably at its zenith. Aunt Carol attended his
service. After lunch at the house, I overheard Aunt Carol
talking with my dad.

"Ned, where do all of your wonderful followers come
from? How have you managed to collect them so fast?"

"That's my business, Carol. You say that as if you're
suspicious," he'd snapped.

"Why, of course not, Ned," she'd coddled. "I admire your
business savvy."

As usual, Mom stayed silent and escaped to her room to
take one of her many catnaps. Though perhaps my dad's
hostile response was better left to fester, unexamined.

So, now, instead of trying to talk more, I focus on tearing
into my muffin—its spicy blast on my tongue, its sprinkle of
blueberries that bounce on the plate when I break the muffin
in half.

Aunt Carol seems focused on sugaring her coffee. I wish I
knew *how* to relate to her. She's kind to keep me for the year,
or whatever it ends up being. God knows my relationship
with my own mom is strained. I love Mom, and I tried to
help her however I could—giving her neck rubs, going on car
rides to cheer her up—but she's always on the verge of a
breakdown, and mostly too fragile to have taken care of me.

In fourth grade when I asked Mom for help dealing with a
classmate who was teasing me, she simply said, "You'll figure
it out," and slunk to her room. And last year, when I confided

in her about that horrible last date with Len, my mother
burst into a bitter litany of offenses about my father—his
flirting, his sullen disregard, his bad way with money—before
wanly floating off. I gave up telling her my problems. She had
enough of her own, and I was afraid that one more might
send her over the edge.

After coffee, Aunt Carol and I go shopping at the local
green market. The simple act of reaching for cereal and pasta
and chatting about the meals is so much easier than the land-
mine of conversation.

Back at the house, I march right up to my room with the
shopping bag and put it in my closet. Why did I act like a
rotten princess in that store? That's so not me. But another,
new, more entitled voice in me silently scolds back, *Sungirl, no
need for sappy remorse.* It's bizarre how this new hard side
seizes my mind. I shake it out.

Shutting my door, I put on the yellow confection and twirl
around and around. The skirt part flies out like sunrays. I
really do look like a sun goddess. Those snobby kids will *have*
to take notice. Picturing them fighting for a place at my lunch
table, I can hardly wait.

5

Pain is no evil unless it conquers us.
—George Eliot

On the following Monday, the lunchroom looks like Grand Central Terminal at rush hour. I hardly know where to turn. Around fifty tables are crammed in, each one bursting with students. I weave through the crowd to the food line, grab a tray, and choose a tuna salad and an iced tea.

Inching along in the line toward the cash register, I crane my neck over the rush of kids to see who's sitting where. This was always major anxiety time—where to sit. At my old school, and during my first week here, I suffered through lunches alone. Holding my tray, I decipher the cliques, which even after a week of school are clear.

There's a table of smarties, one of greenie save-the-planets, and another of school orchestra musicians. Some carry nylon instrument bags and must've come directly from band practice. There are also tables of kids who don't quite fit into any groups, apparent from their random seat choices and their heads painfully deep into chip bags, books, or laptops. I'll avoid those. I already feel out of place enough. Plus, as Wilson says, I need to set my reputation early on.

Sungirl would totally pick the right spot, wouldn't she?

I see the soccer girls holding court at two large tables that they pushed together with the guys who also play varsity. Charlie is the new soccer captain, Wilson tells me. But Charlie isn't at this table. The soccer guys are impossibly good-looking, but not my type. I like the more tortured, intellectual guys . . . like Ander. Ander isn't around, either. Besides, I don't want to seem clingy. I'm almost to the checkout lady. I need to figure this out, fast. It's depressing how, despite my increased beauty, I still feel gangly and out of place.

A few tables over from the sports kids, I spot Lacey, Ava, and Bailey sitting with a couple of cute guys. Charlie's there, sitting next to Lacey, his arm draped over her chair back. He has dark wavy hair like Wilson, but Charlie doesn't share Wilson's aura of danger. Dressed in a red Polo shirt and a mix of bright twine friendship wristbands, Charlie's definitely no mirror of his brother. Chuckling, I picture Wilson's sinister goat's-head belt buckle and his spiky rings.

I imagine Charlie between practice and home, hanging out at a diner near the field. He and his teammates would probably talk about who scored goals as they wolfed down burgers and traded playlists. I sigh. Decision time. There's an open seat at the band table. Musicians are a tad nerdy, though they're open-minded and chill. I'll take a chance on them.

This move puts me only a couple of tables from Lacey's. Kids shift to make room, and I say hello. Lisbeth, who's in one of my classes, says a cheery hello back. Then she returns to her conversation with a girl who has long black hair and a T-shirt inscribed *Beethoven U.*

"So, Cat," Lisbeth says to her friend, "did you get that Yellow Party evite?"

"Yeah, who's Sungirl? A senior or what?" Cat asks. My ears prick up.

Amazing. My party's already gossip worthy.

Lisbeth shrugs. "You can't see her face. Her hair's all blowing around."

Smart move to camouflage my face.

"She must be in our class. How else would she have gotten the list?" Cat says.

Lisbeth turns to me. "What do you think about it, Dorianna?"

"Sounds cool to me." I weigh whether or not to reveal I'm Sungirl. No, there's something luscious about hearing gossip, incognito. I'll wait until the party. Surprise them all.

Cat takes a pull of her cranberry soda. "Well, I'm going. That party blurb was, like, the coolest thing ever." Excitement surges through me. I want to jump up and down. Instead, I manage a cool nod of agreement.

"Me, too," said Lisbeth. "Got to see what it's all about. Plus, what a great location—the Music Pagoda."

"Yeah," Cat agrees. "Remember when we played there for the UNICEF benefit?"

"That was big fun," pipes up another girl with red lipstick. "Playing in Halloween costumes. Remember? I was Little Red Riding Hood." She and her friends burst out laughing. "Though who knows where I'll score a yellow dress in September?"

"Want to go shopping with us?" Cat asks Red Lipstick Girl.

"Yeah, come with us," pleads Lisbeth. "We'll go through the vintage places."

"Good times!" exclaims Lipstick Girl.

I'm jealous. Sucks being the new girl. It would be fun to shop with people my own age.

Lisbeth turns to me. "You going to that party?" Her eyes linger on my lips as if she's realizing they're much fuller than last week. Will she blurt out something about my new and improved look? No, she must be too polite.

"Yup, I'm going," I announce, and wait for Lisbeth to invite me shopping. When it's not forthcoming, I add, "I've already gotten my dress."

Cat's eyes get wide. "That's fast. We just got the invite. Where in the world did you find a yellow dress?"

"Macy's."

"Nice. If you have the money."

"Yeah, my aunt treated." I'm pleasantly surprised that they think I come from money. If they only knew.

After I deposit my dishes on the moving rack, I sashay by Lacey. Lacey gives me a critical look, followed by an obvious shock of recognition that I'm not the same girl as I was last week. Her gaze follows the revised contours of my narrower nose, thick, wavy hair, and amber-flecked eyes. I'm humming with secret delight.

Behind me, I hear Ava say, "That new girl looks much better today."

"Midnight makeover?" sniffs Lacey.

"By the way," Bailey interjects. "Did you get that Yellow Party evite?"

Lacey snorts. "High tea is silly. Who the heck is Sungirl, anyway?"

"Don't know, but it's brilliantly elegant," Bailey counters.

Though my pulse is racing, I continue to take my sweet time passing the table. Artfully, I fling off my jacket to reveal my new black pencil skirt. After Macy's, I stopped into a Brooklyn Heights boutique. With the rest of the monthly check Mom always sends me, I totally splurged on the pencil skirt. It shows off my curves and legs even more explicitly than the tight yellow dress. I have no intention of being called "out of touch" by Lacey or Ava again. At the last minute, I impulsively lean over to Charlie. "You're Charlie, right? I know your brother, Wilson."

Charlie looks up, startled, his square jaw slack. "Um, who *are* you?"

"The new girl," Lacey says, as if that explains everything. As if I was the only new girl in the whole school. "Apparently, New Girl got a face-lift over the weekend. Cut-rate deal?"

Ouch. I want to snap, That's uncalled for. But I'm Sungirl, and Sungirl would rise way above. I take a breath, willing the words away.

Charlie takes a long second look at me. I wonder if he likes what he sees, even if Lacey won't admit it's cool. "Wilson's over the edge," Charlie says, in a final dismissal.

I don't know what I expected, but by association his comment chafes. Prettier or not, I'll have to work really hard at this.

A girl rushes over and taps me on the back of an arm. "Is it *you?*"

I spin around. The girl looks young: a ninth-grader?

"You're her, you're Sun—"

"Shh!" I whisk the girl out of Lacey's hearing range, but not so far that Lacey and her crew can't crane their necks high enough in greedy suspense. "What makes you think it's me?" I whisper, with a twinge of dread.

"I saw your video on YouTube," says the dark-haired girl. "Freaking amazing!"

"My video?" I sputter. Has Wilson already uploaded it to YouTube?

Holy horrors, everyone will see it now, know it's me, and shun my Yellow Party.

"The one on the beach, with you dancing around." The girl arches her sculpted brows.

"Um . . ." I force a mysterious grin, before sneaking a peek back at Lacey. Charlie and Lacey and the whole lot of pampered sheep are giving me and this other girl sidelong glances, in a clear attempt to eavesdrop. A moment ago, I was knocked off my game, but now? Their sudden curiosity is infinitely satisfying.

"I know who Sungirl is," I whisper. "But you can't tell a soul until the party or you'll totally blow the suspense. She'd have to *blacklist you.*"

"What party?" The girl frowns.

Oh, right. I didn't invite anyone below tenth grade. "You're in ninth?" She nods. "Yes, I'm having a party. And yeah, *I'm* Sungirl, but no telling a soul."

The girl's face lights up. "I knew it! Amazing."

"Thanks. I'm Dorianna, by the way."

"Tory." The girl's auburn ponytail bounces as she speaks and she's painted her green eyes with sparkly eye shadow. She smoothes her sweater and gives me another dazzling grin.

In my side vision, I see Lacey taking more quick peeks my way. This is better than eating a chocolate double-dipped ice cream cone, even better than fantasizing what I'd like to do with Ander. Well, maybe they're tied for first place.

I warm at this opportunity to shine, starting with one younger girl. "Hey, Tory," I whisper, "My Yellow Party's this Saturday in Prospect Park. Give me your cell number, and I'll text you an evite."

"Absolutely." Tory scribbles it out on a napkin. "Can I bring a few friends?"

"Sure. Everyone has to wear yellow, though, so tell them to get creative."

"On it. I'll send more people to your video, too," Tory promises.

Panic seizes me. "Uh, wait on that. Don't blow my cover. That's an order."

"Order taken." Tory performs a fake salute.

As I watch Tory prance off, I feel a hot rush of authority. Tory's bound to bring in at least a dozen followers. After all, she's a Lacey-in-training. I can tell. Younger girls are easy marks, and soon, everyone in Tory's class will be my fan. I'll find a popular freshman girl, too, and a senior to spread the word. Before I know it, the whole school will be in the palm of my hand.

Immediately, I'm disgusted. Where did I learn to be so bitchy? I've never been a conniving person.

Nothing wrong with gaining followers, I convince myself.

On my way out, I loop back one more time past Lacey's table, pausing to eavesdrop. They've exploded into gossip, abuzz over why Tory was so gushy.

"That freshman is freakin' in love with the new girl," Ava says.

Lacey snickers. "Poor, desperate thing."

"The new girl does look good. Wonder what she did to herself?" Bailey asks.

"Head transplant," cracks Charlie.

"Big yuck. Wonder what she and that freshman were talking about?" Bailey says.

"Stuffed animals and Rainbow Brite perfume," scoffs Lacey.

It will be a miracle if I can actually lure them to the Yellow Party. "Hang on for a fast ride," I mumble to Lacey's back.

Only Bailey acknowledges me with a kittenish grin as I walk on by.

On my way home, I buy two boxes of lemon cake mix, yellow paper napkins and tablecloths, confectioner's sugar, and yellow food coloring from the grocery. I'm an expert at making cupcakes. Before those last few years, when my father's church fell apart, there was always a bake sale or a Sunday potluck.

Aunt Carol is still at work. During the week, she doesn't get home until at least 6:30, so dinners often consist of pizza or Indian takeout, which is exotic for me. Back home, my mom cooked plain homemade fare—potatoes, meatloaf, and more potatoes—day after day.

I toss the grocery bags on the kitchen table and rush up to my room, switch on my laptop, and click into my Yellow Party event site.

My spirits leap. Sure enough, Tory has already RSVPed, and so have about fifteen of Tory's friends. But the real coup is Bailey.

Bailey has not only RSVPed, she added a note: *I'll b there in full head to toe yellow!*

"Yes!" I thump the desk with my palm. Bailey's considering being my friend after all? Next, I click into YouTube and search "Sungirl."

Wilson's uncanny video pops up. It already has seventy hits. There are some comments but thankfully none are from from classmates. I shiver. At least in the photo we used for the evite, they can't see it's me. I can only keep my fingers crossed that none of my classmates goes on YouTube before the party.

I press play. Same footage, sort of, except in this version I'm juggling even more flowers—dahlias and crazy-big blossoms. On my arm is a new tattoo of a blue beetle, fanning its antennae. And my face . . .

My enhanced features are on this video, too, as if Wilson's Photoshopped me like art directors do to models in *Vogue,* where they retouch inches off waists, and turn up the saturation on makeup so it pops.

But the thing that I'm not crazy about, besides that beetle, is my scheming look.

I'm wearing a subtle but devious glint that wasn't there before—or was it? Suddenly, I'm confused. I feel myself flushing, and I'm glad I'm alone. Has Wilson doctored my face even more in his editing suite? Why didn't he ask my permission first? That wasn't part of our deal. Why would he want to paint a shoplifter's wily expression on my face?

In a sour cocktail of emotions—delight, disquiet, and anger—I recheck my Yellow Party site. There are seven more RSVPs—from the musicians I sat with at lunch.

Delight wins out.

6

Four legs good, two legs bad.
—George Orwell

I find Ander at his locker the next afternoon. His sandy hair is deliciously tousled, and he's wearing a tight green T-shirt that accentuates his ripped chest and shoulders. I swallow hard. "How's it going today?" I venture.

"Not great. I've got to write a seven-pager tonight for bio." Ander loads books into his pack without looking up.

Is the magic of Friday already a memory? I haven't talked to him all day, and I want him to look at me, to see the new beauty etched on my face. I've only looked in the mirror like forty times today, to make sure I didn't imagine the changes. I veer into Yellow Party news. "People love your writing on the evite. I already got a bunch of RSVPs."

Ander padlocks his locker. "I do have a flair for it." Hoisting his pack on his shoulder, he finally looks over at me, and his glance turns into an openmouthed stare. "Hey! Wow, you look great. Are you wearing hazel contacts? Did you do something to your hair, or face, or—?"

"Something like that," I say mysteriously. "I look decent, huh?"

"More than decent . . . you look really pretty." Ander's face blooms red.

This hunk of a guy is blushing over *me*? Doesn't get better than this. Enchantment is back with a flourish. "Wilson uploaded the video," I tell Ander. "I didn't know he would post it so fast."

"That's an okay thing, right?"

He's forgotten how horrible I said it would be if the kids here knew I was giving the party before the fact. He'll never understand what it's like to be a pariah, and I don't want to spell it out. I was on the verge of telling Ander about the freaky video changes, but I decide not to. Don't want him thinking I'm paranoid. "It's all good. I had ninety hits by this morning, and great comments."

Ander leans against his locker. He looks huggable today in his ripped jeans with the tight top. I love the rugged, urban, mountain-guy look. He smells yummy, too, like spicy soap. "Wow. What kind of comments?"

"Like, 'Flower child reborn' and 'I'd take a juggling lesson from Sungirl any day.' Stuff like that."

Ander laughs and touches me lightly on my shoulder. "Hey, I could use some rays and another of those lemonades before I tackle that paper. Want to go back to Coney?"

I nod, even though I'm not ready to see Wilson yet. Although, I *should* call him on the video changes. Lacey approaches. By the way she slows down, it's obvious that she's heard the part where Ander said he wants to hang out with me again.

While Ander grabs his jacket and goes down the hall for a minute to talk to a guy from Lit class, Lacey turns to me, scowling. "Just because you got some skeezy makeover and push-up bra, if you think you're going to wrap Ander around your little finger, new girl, you're deluded. He likes naturally beautiful girls, like me. You'll just be sloppy seconds."

Bitch, where do you get off?

I want to yell, 'You have no reason to be mean to someone you don't even know, even if she's hanging out with your ex!' But I catch myself. It's not my normal way to curse at people. Rather than return Lacey's catty putdown, I have the oddest impulse. I want to offer her a beatific smile, and bestow the expansive sun rays a true Sungirl would naturally offer a princess spoiled rotten by being so effortlessly popular.

I hold the smile, and use every ounce of energy to increase its warmth and intensity.

Clearly, Lacey isn't expecting this reaction. She breaks the gaze, stumbles over her heels, and hurries down the hall, leaving a trail of floral perfume. I check to see if Ander has witnessed any of this nasty back and forth.

He's put on his jacket and finished the conversation with his friend. Now he's staring at Lacey. When he sees me look at him, he tears his eyes away and his hand goes to crunching his writing notebook into his back pocket.

Clearly, Ander's bitter. It figures. His ex-buddy Charlie is dating Lacey now. When he comes over, I can't help saying, "It's obvious she cares," in order to gauge where Ander stands in his feelings for her.

"Well, *I* don't care," he protests. But the spark of hope in his face hurts me.

By the time we're on the Coney Island subway, he and I are laughing at how I bewildered Lacey with my glowing smile.

"What did she say to you, anyway?" he asks as he gets out

his notebook. Is he going to write down what I say? That would be strange.

"Nothing I can't handle." No way I'm admitting she said I'd never win him over.

"Oh, come on, tell me."

"Show, don't tell, that's my policy," I say cryptically. I'm not even sure what I mean. Lately, my responses are so unlike me. We hop off the train. My senses fill with sea air and hot-dog smoke. In fact, I'm acting less like myself by the day.

After Wilson lets us in, he starts to pace. The formerly neat living room is piled up with his dark array of clothing and video equipment. "I'm hyper," he says between paces. "Don't take it personally."

"What's the matter?" Ander shoves a heap of Wilson's clothing farther down the white couch and takes a seat.

Wilson stops pacing and rakes a hand through his hair. "Got into it with Charlie."

"Over what?" Ander leans forward.

Wilson throws me a brooding look, as if I know why he's upset. I almost suspect he's wearing dark kohl around his eyes, they're so exaggerated. "My brother's a narrow-minded dolt," he spits. "I put him in his place."

I hope it has nothing to do with my comment to Charlie at lunch that I'm getting friendly with Wilson. Why would Charlie care about that?

It's bad timing to ask Wilson about his video if he's in a funk. Plus, I'm totally chicken. I try to reframe how I feel about it—instead of wondering why he tampered with the footage, I try to concentrate on how alive it is, and how each pixel is continually reinventing itself. I read about nanotech in science, where the "smart atoms" in a tiny, implantable device can literally change the organic matter they're implanted into. I have no clue as to how the real science works. But that's what Wilson's video seems capable of.

But my positive reframing isn't working. Why did he make more changes, and why did he upload it to YouTube before the party? What if people see it's me and decide not to come?

"Something on your mind?" Wilson steps up in such an aggressive way that I'm intimidated. He presses in on my personal space, employing his height to dwarf me. Heat rises off his body.

Abruptly, I sit down next to Ander. "No, not really."

"Not really?" Wilson's eyebrows shoot up.

Crap, is he psychic, too? Can he hear my thoughts or what? "I didn't know you were posting the video on YouTube so soon," I fumble. "It's gotten tons of hits already, but . . . seems like you changed it. That strange beetle tattoo, and, um, I look different?"

"You look different in person, too." He winks. "Do you like how I changed you?"

Ander erupts in derisive laughter. "Warren, you're going to tell me you magically altered her face? She just made changes to her hair and makeup, or whatever. Don't embarrass her."

Wilson raises his hands in a glib, you-got-it gesture. "I told you I had powers."

I throw Wilson a stern look. We don't dare talk about my bodily transformation in front of Ander. I'll have to wait until I'm alone with Wilson for that. "I . . . I'm pleased, but I was referring to the *video.*"

Wilson sighs. "No one thinks they look like they really do on video," he says quizzically. "Or acts the way they really do. Right, my man?" He turns to Ander.

Ander shrugs. "Like your brother not knowing he's an asshat?"

"Touché. Let's head over to the boardwalk before it rains. I'll show you around."

I'll gladly do anything that distracts from the conversation. Wilson grabs a pearl-tipped cane from his uncle's umbrella stand on the way out. Why does he need a cane? If anyone does, it's Ander, with his limp.

"Dressed for a Dickens novel?" Ander cracks.

"Never know when you might wander into one." Wilson twirls the cane.

During the elevator ride down, I study him, trying to figure out his look of the day. Wilson's black velvet top hat is turn-of-the-century. Yet, he's also fashion current in a clingy shirt and skinny black jeans that hug his lean legs. A tri-circled necklace hangs low on his chest. And of course, his video bag dangles from a shoulder. He's sexy in an agitating, almost threatening way.

We order relish-covered hotdogs and Pepsi from Nathan's, and eat them on a boardwalk bench, facing the ocean. Discussing plans for the Yellow Party, I explain how I got Cat and Lisbeth to play music by claiming that I'm helping Sungirl organize things.

"Great," says Ander. "I'll borrow my dad's car to help pick up the cupcakes on Saturday."

"Really?" That is so gallant—chauffeuring me like I'm the belle of the ball.

Wilson says, "I'll maintain the design of your Facebook fan page. Update links to your website, Instagram, YouTube. Make more party trailers."

Will he keep making changes without consulting me, I wonder? But I only say, "I'm thrilled. You're way ahead of me. Isn't that asking too much?"

"No. You need to build your brand, your platform," he insists.

"I'll bat around new party meetup themes," Ander offers.

I giggle. "Feels like I'm some grand school project."

Wilson gets out his camera and takes footage of us wolfing down the last of our hot dogs, and of Ander doing a gimpy dance. He takes a close-up of me, basking in the afternoon sun, which is starting to slip in and out of the clouds.

After we eat, we stroll down the boardwalk, past some skater kids and two ladies eating soft pretzels. We come to a garish mural painted on the side of a building. It has old-style circus characters on it, even though it seems newly painted.

I read its headline aloud. "Sideshow by the Sea?" I glance over at Wilson.

"A bunch of young performers got together some years back," he explains, "and started a new kind of sideshow. They have sword swallowers, human pincushions, strong men— you name it. Let's go in. See for yourself."

Inside the building is a bar, tended by a twenty-something dude sporting a waxed curlicue moustache and red suspenders. The walls are a crazy quilt of deer antlers, clown portraits, beer ads, neo-pinup girls, and dusty images of the Cyclone roller coaster.

We wander around. In one corner, a Coney Island Sideshow museum is set up, displaying Victorian-era photos of the boardwalk and the rides. I love the ladies' long bloomers and the guys' hokey black jumpsuit shorts. The boardwalk back then was alive with ladies dressed in flowing skirts holding parasols, and men carting people around in wicker rickshaws. The museum is selling posters of the new sideshow, T-shirts, and mugs.

In the café section, urban types a little older than us are sitting at tables and talking quietly. I see where the sideshow entrance beckons, but the performers are apparently on hiatus. They advertise a fat lady, a human pincushion, and an armless artist who paints with his feet. Another poster features a lineup of high-step ladies.

"That's it!" I shout as I study the poster.

"What?" Ander cranes his neck to discover what I'm staring at.

"My next party theme! We'll invite the voucher winners to perform burlesque. We could even do it out here."

Wilson comes over to look. "Genius idea, Dor." He arranges me in front of the circus ladies poster. I vamp for his video, sticking one hip out and then the other, feeling way more comfortable than during that first awkward performance in the surf.

Ander's eyes linger on my poses, which thrills me. "We'll give them catchy stage names," he suggests.

"Absolutely," Wilson says. "Limited vouchers will drive people to the Yellow Party, in hopes of being first to grab one. It'll also drive traffic to your fan page. Exclusivity does that."

"Yeah, but the ultimate goal's to get everyone there, not just the popular kids," I remind them.

Wilson taps his cane on the floor. "Let's open the next party to my high school, too," he says. "Hell, to all of the Brooklyn high schools."

Ander cringes. "We don't want a mob. She needs to build it up organically."

"A mob is good, my man. They'll all worship at the altar of Miss Dorianna."

I flush with heat. A delicious tickle goes up my spine.

"Dude, see how the Yellow Party goes before we pull out the stops," Ander says.

"I love the idea of a huge party," I admit, "but Ander's idea of building up my fanbase in an organic way makes sense." How else will I ever pull it off?

"Organic, schmanic," Wilson scoffs. "Forget about ever

adding my school, then. It'll be too late if we wait. No more access to the school database. I'm dropping out."

"Why?" I blurt. We need his list to add warm bodies. But as soon as I think that, I'm put off by how calculating it is. The bottom line is, Wilson should stay in school. Anyone should.

People at the next table over cast us curious side-glances.

"I'll get my GED," Wilson says. "You don't need a diploma to be a video artist."

"No!" I insist. "We'll add your class next. . . just stay in school."

"Ever humbled by your passion," Wilson tips his hat. "M'lady, you have me mesmerized to study the dreaded advanced calculus."

Ander and I tell him how silly he is, and Wilson captures it on video. "One day, you'll see Wilson Warren's art videos in the Met," Ander promises.

"Mr. Ander James's signature will grace his novels in every bookstore," Wilson predicts.

"And everyone who is anyone will be following my fabulous events," I say, twirling as Wilson focuses his lens on me.

"That reminds me," Wilson says. "One more thing to capture on video. Follow the leader," he adds in his typically curious fashion.

As we walk away from the crowded part of the boardwalk, I notice a massive gray building ahead, soaring over the others. "What's that place, a school?"

Wilson snickers. "A school of juvies."

"Juvies?" Looking closer, I make out bars on the windows.

"A detention center for druggies and kids with public intoxication raps," Ander explains.

"Sucks to have it right here in your neighborhood," I say to Wilson.

He pulls his cloak tighter. "If they're stupid enough to get caught, they deserve it."

"You'd never catch me in one of those places," I promise.

"Me neither. They don't allow laptops—or pens." Ander jabs his chest and sticks out his tongue as if he's doing himself in with a pen.

I shift my gaze to the other side of the boardwalk, where the waves roll in free of obstruction.

Nearing the rides area, we pass a large wooden cage with a sign that says, "See Poncho, the World's Biggest Rat." It's padlocked. Empty.

Wilson taps on the sign with his cane. "I know where they store that thing."

"Is it really an overgrown rat?" I ask, shivering.

"Judge for yourself."

Wilson leads the way around the booth and down the boardwalk, tapping his cane on the weather-beaten wood. Farther from the vendor booths and the Cyclone roller-coaster, we approach a set of shuttered shops.

A bald muscle man sits on a stool by one of these unmarked buildings. Smoking a cigarette, he nods to Wilson as if they've had more than a few nefarious encounters. I don't know why, but I imagine them exchanging cash for black-market goods, or even for drugs. Wilson hands the guy a ten-dollar bill, after which the guy gets up and fiddles with the door padlock.

The guy cocks his head toward the opened door, and Wilson guides us into the dimly lit space. The first room has a gutted look—papers strewn about, a trashcan overturned—as if a business has packed up quickly.

"In here." Wilson opens another door, into an interior space. The place reeks of hay and stale urine. Flicking on a light, Wilson starts to video the space as he leads us to an oversized wooden crate. Short, startled grunts come from inside it, as if the creature senses what might follow. Wilson lifts the crate lid. "Hello, Mr. Rat," he says. He records our reactions.

With a combination of fascination and repulsion, I examine its red, bristly hair and deep-set eyes. "That's no rat."

"Right, what then?" Wilson studies me.

"A capybara," Ander declares. "Also called a water hog. From South America."

"Smart boy." Wilson claps Ander on the back and then keeps on shooting footage.

"It lives here all year until summer?" I ask, incredulous.

"Apparently," says Wilson.

Ander and I watch Wilson use his cane to stroke the beast in the side of its thick neck.

The four-foot-long capybara whips its head up and bares its teeth, after which it launches into seemingly involuntary jaw snaps. *"Clat, clat, clat!"*

"Maybe it's hungry," Ander says.

"There's something incredibly sad about its teeth," I note. "They're covered in tartar."

"You think it likes gum?" Wilson asks.

"God, no! Maybe bread." Ander holds out a piece of hot dog roll. "I saved it to feed to the gulls, but this thing needs it more, the way its ribs stick out. Aren't these animals usually fatter?"

Wilson pulls back Ander's outstretched hand using the pearl hook part of his cane. "Not so fast. Make Poncho do a trick."

"Hey, I don't know about that," Ander gripes.

He looks as if he's thinking about how everyone has to beg for scraps, how no one's free, except the seagulls that can trail off. Or maybe that's just my projection onto my new writer friend. One thing's for sure, Wilson's treatment of

Ander and the water hog is pissing me off. Why would
Wilson want to tease it? Does he really get a rise from that? I
haven't seen this cruel side of him before—or have I? I flash
on his green-screen video stills of Charlie. It's one thing to
mess with a video image, another to provoke a live animal.

"Going soft on me, brainiac?" Wilson goads Ander.

Ander laughs it off. Again, it prompts me to imagine
Ander's feelings. It's strange, almost as if I can read his
mind. He's probably thinking about how he wants to punch
Wilson out, but how it's not worth the drama. Or he's
thinking how this mean animal treatment is weighty material
for his future novel about extortion. He could write about the
surly man outside, smoking that stinky cigarette, and how
the guy extorts cash, or how a different extortionist might
provoke the boar and set it loose on an enemy.

What gallows humor I'm capable of. I snicker to myself.

"Care to share, Dor?" Wilson asks.

"No. It's nothing." I step away from him.

Wilson snatches the hot dog roll from Ander and holds it
up over the animal pen. The capybara grunts loudly as it
strains to reach it.

I squeak, "I'm pretty sure that capybaras can't jump." Or
even rise up on their hind legs, so at this rate the poor beast
will never eat.

"Cut it out, Warren," Ander snaps.

"In a minute." Wilson's face animates with that impish
grin.

Of its own strange accord, my simmering anger builds to
a volcanic rush of energy that propels me forward. In a split
second, I'm nose to nose with Wilson. "Don't mess with my
friend—or that animal," I growl. *"You feel me?"*

A molten charge seems to fly through the both of us as if
we've short-circuited one another. A mutual awareness of my
growing prowess? That's farfetched. But how else can I

explain it? It frightens me, what I just did. Has Wilson changed more than just my looks? His gaze bores under my skin—tense, questioning. Do I have a physical effect on him, too? Like magnets attracting and then repelling? Ander's looking at me now, with wide-eyed curiosity. So, he saw it— me rushing over. As fast as this unexplainable energy has welled up, it leaves me, with sudden fatigue.

Wilson spins away, too. He offers Ander his hot dog roll back. "Okay, softie… here. Toss it to Poncho. We've got bigger business to take care of."

The second Ander tosses the roll, the capybara snatches it in its shovel jaw and swallows it in one famished gulp.

I linger there by the animal, as Wilson and Ander start toward the door. How did I move that fast? It's as if I blanked out, and a moment later I was eyeball-to-eyeball with Wilson, yelling at him. I'm glad I did it, because he was abusing that thing. But for me to get all in Wilson's face is such crazy-odd behavior for me. The capybara stares at me mournfully. I sneak in a quick pat, to which the creature snaps at my arm. Thankful for my new, quicker reflexes, I hurry outside.

The three of us walk silently. The silence makes the clicking of Wilson's cane all the more crisp.

Ander eyeballs it. "Why do you need that pretentious cane? You're not a vaudeville-style performer or anything."

Wilson taps the cane with more vigor. "You can always borrow it, if you like." Pointedly, he studies Ander's limp.

"Or we could stick that thing right through your eyeball," I say, only half in jest.

Clearly, there's a side of Wilson that likes to goad. What, is he jealous of me protecting Ander and the capybara? That's hard to believe. As much as I'm flattered by Wilson's atten- tion, I don't want him hurting Ander.

Before we say good-bye, when Ander's in the bathroom, Wilson comes up to me really close, as before. Again, heat and intensity rise off him like steam. "Don't forget, I inspired your powers," he says under his breath. "You're one of me now."

"Jerk, what's that supposed to mean?"

"I told you who I am. You see what I did."

"Whatever, whoever you are, so-called Prince of Darkness. You don't own me. Why did you post that trailer before the party? I told you I didn't want people to know who I am. And how about removing my sneaky expression and that beetle tattoo off the surf video? That wasn't part of our so-called deal. Why would you add that?"

He looks offended. "I did nothing of the sort. I told you there'd be unpredictable consequences. It must be showing you from the inside out."

I look back at him, incredulous—stare at his black, gleaming animal eyes that put a wordless fear in me, of living under a sunless, heatless orb. And fill me with recognition of my own untamed stirrings.

Wilson's unexpected guffaw sounds like someone gargling sawdust. "You're so serious, Dor. Don't be so serious."

His laughter worries me more than his radar gaze. "Keep our so-called deal to yourself," I warn.

He winks. "Our own little secret."

On the way back to Park Slope on the train, there's an easy silence between Ander and me. As if we're both way relieved to be away from Wilson and in each other's company —alone together. When we're almost to Ander's stop, he strokes my leg, only for a moment.

And I like it. A lot.

"Thanks," he says simply. Then he gets up and disappears behind the closing train doors.

7

More and more, it feels like I'm doing a bad impersonation of myself.
—Chuck Palahniuk

S aturday morning, I leap out of bed and check the
Yellow Party page. A shocking eighty-seven kids have
RSVPed yes. Nervous excitement wells up as I step
carefully into the fancy dress. Studying myself in the dresser
mirror, I gasp. In the last few days, my face has blossomed
even more. My nose seems even narrower, my complexion
more dewy. Or is it a matter of my growing confidence? Who
knows, but I'll take it.

I fasten an amber necklace around my neck that my
mother gave me. It's missing one stone I lost on a bus back
in Indiana. I shift that part to the side, so it's not as obvious.
Next, I slip on a wooden bracelet that I tinted yellow with
fabric dye. Last, I strap on my new yellow heels, a real coup
from the Payless sale bin. I attempt a couple of updos, each
deconstructing in a mess of loose strands.

Aunt Carol calls up the stairs for me, and I yell back, "Give me a minute. My hair's acting crazy." I love my thicker hair, but not its rebellious nature.

As I'm taking out the clips from my third failed attempt, Aunt Carol peeks into my partially opened door. "Need help?" she asks shyly.

"Sure, I don't know how to make it look decent." I hand her the clips.

Aunt Carol brushes my hair upwards with one hand, while gathering it in her other. "Your hair is so full and shiny," she exclaims. "Did you use a special conditioner?"

"Um, yeah, some trendy new product. Can't remember the brand," I ad lib. Easing back into the vanity seat, I glance at her in the mirror. Her hair's pulled tight in a no-nonsense style that doesn't offer much hope for her ability to whip me up a current look. But I'm grateful for a reprieve after our awkward shopping excursion.

"So, your friend's picking you up to help with the cupcakes?" she asks me.

"Yup, everything's under control." I'm not as sure as I sound.

"What drinks are you serving?" Aunt Carol expertly rolls a clutch of hair into a loose coil, and then places the clips in strategic areas.

I bolt upright. "Gah. I was so busy with the cupcakes I forgot about that." Earlier in the week, we discussed the possibility of me using her porcelain cups for tea and hot chocolate. But we decided that if most of the people showed, we wouldn't have enough. After that, it slipped my mind.

"Starbucks sells big cardboard flasks with paper cups included," Aunt Carol suggests. "We use them at office parties." She puts in one last clip and stands back to look at her handiwork. "I suppose I could contribute."

I flash on that scene in Macy's, when I pushed her to pay

for most of the dress. The impulse is bubbling up again. I stuff it down. It would be too greedy, though I've spent so much of my monthly allowance on the pencil skirt and shoes that I'm already tapped. "Nice of you to offer, but I'll cover it."

In the mirror, she relaxes into a smile. Clearly, she's relieved by my response. She makes a final fluff to my loose chignon. "What do you think?" She's no fashionista, yet she's created a very cute look.

"Thanks, Aunt Carol. It's totally great."

As I'm wrapping the last cupcake pan in foil, the bell rings. Heart aflutter, I run to get it. Is this what prom will be like next year? Is it an impossible dream to imagine I might go with Ander?

He stands there in a baggy yellow pinstriped suit. The effect is rather clownish. I wonder what he thinks of my dress, my look? His thirsty eyes drink me in, but he's not offering a compliment. Holding back on purpose?

"Nice suit," I say.

"Thrift-shop score."

When he turns to help put the trays of cupcakes into his dad's Ford Focus, I spot his folded notebook jammed into his pants pocket. His coattails are caught up in it. Obsessed with writing, I note with glee.

We load the folding chairs, card table, and bags of supplies. I tell him about the drink dilemma and he takes a side route to Starbucks. Once we've ordered, I realize I'm short about five dollars. He offers to cover it. Ander is not only cute, he's generous.

He parks as close as he can to the gazebo, a five-minute hike over a green field from the lot. It takes us fifteen minutes of back-and-forth, hauling everything over the rambling field. It's really windy, but once we're there, the sturdy granite gazebo offers good protection. Still, it's a challenge to tether the yellow balloons to the nearby benches.

As we survey our hard work, I say, "I wonder what people's reactions will be when they see me? What do you think they'll say—you know, Ava and stuff?"

Ander frowns. "No offense, but, uh, I doubt the super-cool kids will come."

"Bailey RSVPed."

"Really?" He looks at me in disbelief. "Okay, she's the friendliest. She doesn't take herself seriously. Only seems to do the snob trip to maintain her standing."

"Is it possible that Bailey's coming because she might actually *like* me?"

He shrugs. "She doesn't know you. She's probably coming to report back to the clique."

"Do you think she dislikes me as much as Lacey does?"

"No one seems to need a reason to hate on people these days," he muses.

My face tightens. I worry if my "makeover" will be any boon to my popularity after all. We're mounting yellow streamers from the overhanging roof when the orchestra girls approach, hauling their instruments in padded fabric bags.

"Hi, Dorianna, is Sungirl here?" Lisbeth puffs from the weight of her cello.

"When's she coming?" Cat asks as she brushes back her shiny, black hair.

I grin nervously. "Didn't want to blow my cover at school, but . . ." I give Cat and Lisbeth a crafty look.

"What?" Lisbeth screeches. "You're . . ."

"Why didn't you say so at lunch?" Cat grimaces. "That's off the wall."

"Kind of," I admit. Then I think of all the times on my

birthday that I never had a party, only a cake in the kitchen with my parents. And the times kids sneered at me for my screwed-up family. They'll never get why I clung to secrecy. "I wanted to surprise people."

"You got that right!" Cat exclaims, still giving me the stink eye.

"Sure shocked me," Lisbeth admits. "The pagoda looks pretty."

Cat, seemingly recovered from being weirded out, tunes her violin, and they set up in the pagoda. Both girls are dressed in yellow shirts and long black skirts—a regulation band outfit? Thrilled that they didn't bail, I let the black skirts slide.

Little by little, people filter in. From the vantage of the pagoda, I watch their yellow dresses drift over the green of the park and cycle into the party like so many yellow finches coming to roost. Guys, too, with funky yellow jackets, elegant piss-yellow ties, cheesy faux-gold sunglasses and hats. Lots of guys have on joke clothes. One is even wrapped in yellow crime-scene tape. Another guy is squeezed into a child's rain-coat. Still another dude is jumping around in a felt banana costume, and I drink it all in. It's exhilarating. I'm filled with a heady sense of pride in my creation, and terrifically grateful that no one seemed to have watched that video on YouTube —yet.

The band strikes up the chamber music. I greet the guests while Ander pours them drinks.

Tory dances over. Clearly, her parents spent major bucks on her outfit. It's an above-the-knee formal dress with a frothy, lemon meringue-y top. Over it is a chiffon shrug. "Dorianna, you look beautiful," Tory gushes. "And the park looks like it's bursting with yellow daffodils."

"In September. Imagine," I say.

"Did you shock anyone yet with your true identity?"

"Completely."

Tory's laughter is high and infectious, and I laugh with her. "Meet my friends." Tory reels off way too many names of the freshmen girls gathered around for me to remember. They're all Energizer Bunnies like Tory, and all fawning over me, asking how I came up with such an unlikely fall theme. The attention takes away some of my fear.

"Does it have to do with the sun?" asks the boy wrapped in crime-scene tape.

"Well, duh, she's Sungirl," Tory answers for me. As if everyone should know that and love me for loving the sun and being Sungirl, the same as everyone loves a Hollywood 'flavor of the month' starlet for being glam, not for being a great actress or anything.

A guy from class frowns when he sees me. "It's *you,* from math? I thought it'd be some popular girl," he says bluntly. "Sungirl, huh? What's so special about liking the sun? Everyone likes the sun. What makes you so different?"

"Yeah, that's lame," chimes in the guy's friend.

No doubt the questions will get harder. My back steels against the onslaught. "I'm special because . . ." Filling my diaphragm with fresh park air, I stare at him as I fish for the right words. Over his shoulder, I see more people in yellow approaching. And then, in a rush, the words come. "I'm special because *you're* special, and I'm a reflection of you, and I've brought you all here and . . . *Hey!*" This last exclamation is more of a shout, to wake the kid up, though he's already awake and looking quite perplexed.

"You sound like you're in a cult," he scoffs.

I wince, horrified to be compared to a cult, the exact thing I compare my dad's church to. I wipe my clammy palms on my dress. I'm *Sungirl,* and Sungirl would rise above this idiot's slight. I muster up an intentional, focused beam of energy like that smile I gave Lacey in the hall. It's the kind

that's been powering through me more and more frequently
since that first time at Wilson's. A vitamin sort of rush,
mixed with an endorphin high as if I've just run ten miles.
The only downside is that the sensation comes and goes. Like
that time I whooshed over to Wilson to chew him out, and
then afterward I was drained and weakened. If that's part of
my new power, I wish it would be steadier.

I send another burst of high octane out to the doubter
guy.

His mouth is half open, as if to lob another cynical
putdown, but his face smoothes as he stares at me with
glassy eyes. "Wh—when's your welcome speech?"

"In a few." It *worked*. So far, so good. I breeze off to greet
more guests as I notice the earlier trickle is fast becoming a
steady flow.

Where's Lacey? I glance at my watch. The party started
forty minutes ago. Darn, she's a no-show. A part of me is
relieved, but mostly it's a letdown.

From the pagoda, I survey the meadow and swallow
another swell of panic. Ander comes over and puts a hand on
my arm. My skin warms to his touch. "How're you doing?"

"It's strange: one moment I'm fine, and the next, jittery."
In response he gives my shoulders a quick massage that radiates pleasure all the way through me.

"Time for cupcakes?" Tory, already my most loyal subject,
bounces upstairs with her adorable flock of minions—like a
spray of golden wildflowers.

"Yes, serve them half of the trays."

"On it," said Tory. "Girls? Bring the dessert down to the
folding tables. It's windy, so make sure the tablecloths are
secured with clips." Clearly, Tory loves taking orders from her
queen, but loves even more dishing them out to her maids in
waiting.

I float over to the railing and pronounce loudly, "Yellow

cupcakes, now being served at my Yellow Party." In a mad
dash for the colorful pastries, they go quickly. We uncover
more and Tory's girls serve a second round. People seem to
be enjoying themselves. They're eating, and talking in little
huddles. A few look bored. Maybe I should pick up the pace,
get people involved. But I have no idea how. I've never
thrown a party.

Glancing over at the meadow, I spot a girl approach with
blazing red hair flowing from a wide-brimmed hat. *Bailey.*
She's with a shaggy-haired guy, and they're waltzing forward
with an air that suggests their presence will grace my whole
enterprise. It's been painful so far, dealing with the rude
comments from the guy in my math class. Bailey's endorse-
ment will mean so much. I struggle for the right greeting as
they climb the stairs, and her eyes widen at seeing me hold
court. "Welcome, Bailey," I say.

"Hi." She looks past me, at the band girls and at Ander
fussing with the hot chocolate. "Where's Sungirl?"

"That would be me!" Again, my shaky confidence wavers.
I'm overly aware of my dress, my posture, and how Bailey's
gaze is alternating between amused shock and hesitation.
Also the way her date is looking at me sideways. It seems
Wilson's apparent magic has not stopped my knees from
knocking, or me feeling utterly gawky and out of place at my
own party.

"*You?*" said Bailey.

A moment of suspended animation follows, punctuated
by Bailey's sudden shriek of laughter. My cheeks burn.

Then Bailey leans forward and loudly air-kisses me.
"*Mwah, mwah.*"

I'm in shock. I can't believe that I'm pulling this off. "I'm
so glad you came. Your dress is so creative. You made it?" I
gush. Bailey nods.

The true artiste of Lacey's clique, Bailey is in a fifties-style knockoff with a tossed pattern of lemons and oranges, and a hat straight off the set of a vintage film. Its straw brim is decked with shiny plastic lemons and kiwis.

Bailey fingers my dress. "Let me guess. Bloomie's?"

"Close. Macy's." I don't reveal it was on clearance.

"Macy's is so underappreciated. Dorianna, this is Cole. He's an artist."

"Hi, Cole." I notice Tory's friends checking him out. He *is* awfully cute in his preppy khakis and yellow jersey, but also sporting a whacked-out yellow polka-dot bow tie and Bogart-style smoking jacket.

Ander offers them drinks. "Hey, guys, good to see you here," he says with a rare smile. "Dorianna's worked hard on this." He swings an arm around me. I'm paralyzed in stunned elation. His arm—around me—warm, intentionally protective. It lasts for two seconds before he shifts away and I'm famished for more.

"Let's get this party started," Bailey crows as if she's the designated co-host. She walks to the balustrade ledge and shouts, "Everyone! Up and dance."

Dance. Of course. That's how to get people involved.

The band begins a plucky Renaissance jig. In a brave move, I take Ander by the hand. Surprisingly, he's game. We sway tentatively to the music.

"Classical sucks!" some guy calls up to the musicians. "Play rock."

"Yeah, really. Like, what *is* this?" his girlfriend complains.

Ander turns toward the band. "Know anything more upbeat?"

In response, the musicians launch into a plucky adaption of the grunge classic, Nirvana's "Smells Like Teen Spirit." One guy uses a stool for a drum. Down on the lawn, guys ham it up, especially Tory's friend, mummified in the crime tape. His binding unwinds as he shimmies. He looks like a wigged-out punk mummy.

Ander leads me down to the lawn. The faster, louder music loosens him up. His moves are a bit jerky, but I find that sweet and sexy. I take shy glances at his spectacular, translucent eyes. The simmering vulnerability of his soft upper lip and hint of blond shaven beard just above it melts me. My fingers trace his strong shoulders shifting under his big jacket. Muscles, of an ex-athlete. I turn wistful, aware that he's already experienced injury.

As we move together, I sense him connecting more with me. His gaze follows my mouth, my hair sliding down, loose. His hand takes mine with a sort of hunger of its own. When we twirl, I notice his tails are still caught in his notebook. Will Ander read his story to me? I want him to. I'm eager to know what he thinks, how he sees the world. Is this what falling for someone feels like?

A hip-hop-inspired song follows, and more couples bounce and swoop around us. "It's going great," Ander whispers in my ear, sending sparkly sensations through me.

"Yeah, high-energy," I whisper back.

Tory and a tall boy in mustard-colored pants perform an expert street dance with popping and locking. Bailey and Cole do coordinated kicks. Some guys dance free-form. Still others lurk on the sidelines, watching. That would've been me last year.

Ander says something.

"What?" It's hard to hear over the music.

He mumbles it, again too quickly. Then abruptly, he breaks away from me, to stare at something in the distance. The glint of alarm in his stare startles me. What's going on? Wheeling around, I crane my neck to see over the dancers.

Lacey. The blonde queen has finally arrived, on Charlie's arm. By the way her cold stare is fixed on me, she's already witnessed us dancing, and Ander whispering in my ear. My pulse speeds up exponentially. The big kahuna, skewered on my own enchanted fishhook. Well, not yet, but biting.

My surge of dark joy is cut short when I see that Ander's already heeled it back to the pagoda. Our dance is over almost before it began. That stings. In the past, I would've run after him. Now, this alien part of me is almost more interested in luring Lacey closer. While I'm thinking about how weird that is, I'm already weaving furiously through the crowd toward her. In clear disregard of the rules, she's sporting a black hoodie. Charlie, too, has on a navy hoodie, with the red varsity soccer-ball logo. They're both wearing navy jeans.

Unwieldy anger gushes up as I study their renegade colors. I swallow it down. "Glad you could make it, but, um . . . my evite specifically said *Yellow* Party."

"*Your* evite? Now I've heard it all," Lacey sniffs. "You're not Sungirl. Where is she?"

"Surprise, surprise, I am Sungirl!" I giggle nervously. "Welcome to my Yellow Party." I genuinely hope they'll relax and be friendly. Drop their snotty posture. My heart is open, beating hard, so eager to forgive.

Lacey and Charlie exchange exaggeratedly stunned looks, as if they might suddenly bust a gut laughing. "Now I've heard it all," she spits out.

That strange power surges up me, as it did when Wilson was goading Ander. It creates an invisible shield. If Lacey wants to continue being shitty, I guess I'm ready for battle. *"You haven't heard it all,"* I counter. *"Not at all."*

"Whatever. Be grateful for me showing up," Lacey snaps.

I really am grateful, my old side whispers silently, though I raise my brows noncommittally. Two can play the game of I Don't Give a Rat's Butt. "Bailey's here," I mention, "in an amazing yellow dress." I point to where Cole and Bailey are doing their coordinated kickbox moves. When Lacey's eyes narrow at Bailey's betrayal, that mischievous, pleasurable tide surges harder through me. A crashing breaker of molasses on fire mixed with lighter fluid.

"Pretty nervy, inviting the whole class here. Or was this Ander's idea?" Charlie explodes. "We don't even know you."

"No, you don't. I have many sides you know nothing about. Isn't that the point? To all get to know each other?" I challenge. Charlie stares at me with a condescending leer that makes me want to punch his lights out. No wonder Wilson hates his little brother. No wonder Ander doesn't hang with Charlie anymore.

Where *is* Ander? He was so on the case before, right by my side. I can't blame him for wanting to get far from Charlie and Lacey, though. Or is it that he didn't want Lacey to see us dancing together? I hope he hasn't gone home. I hope he's biding his time until my essential business is done—working the party. Massaging friends *and* enemies until they morph into my followers. Wilson calls this skill 'spinning your social spider web'.

"Have a drink," I offer. "Tory's girls are serving. See you. Time for me to address my lovely partygoers."

With that, I sashay away, fluffing the skirt part of my dress as I go. I've practiced this in my mirror at home about thirty times. Do I even need Lacey's blessings, now that I've extended my hand and she's bitten it a second time? Now that I've seen her up close and even uglier, perhaps Lacey better ask for *my* blessing before I scorch a hole right through the girl's rotten heart.

Time to talk to your audience a new, authoritative voice within me insists. I gather up my uncanny energy, advance to the front of the pagoda, and raise my arms like a princess overseeing her royal subjects. In a Shakespearian voice I start, "Classmates, friends, and solar beings . . ."

It's intimidating, these kids staring at me, waiting, and especially Lacey and Charlie, scowling up at me. Where's Ander? I need him. My heady power stutters. I only recall bits and pieces of the script he's written, but I dive in anyway.

"Some of you wonder what caused me, Sungirl, to throw this Yellow Party in September. What better time, when the beaches are clearing out, and we're hitting the books? What better time to bask in the glory of the sun's radiance? You are *all* radiant, hot and awesome." Everyone is looking around and murmuring. Encouraged, I improvise in an even more poetic vein.

"I am Sungirl, and Sungirl craves all things yellow and magical—gold jewelry, lemonade, and yellow-lined notepads. Meet me where sun sparkles on the blond sand. Where we all can dance to the beat of the breakers."

"Crappy poetry," shouts the guy who confronted me earlier.

"Yeah, you suck," chimes in his doubter friend.

Tory and her minions began an enthusiastic counter-chant: "Sungirl! Sungirl!" Gah, I've never been so grateful for supporters in my life.

I'll have to ask Wilson what exactly these supposed powers can do, and how to get them back when they suddenly dissolve and leave my knees quaking. "Time for people to come onstage, one at a time, please—and shout out your own odes to the sun," I add in a quivery voice.

"You're full of yourself," Charlie calls from the front of the audience.

"Where do you get off?" Lacey jeers.

"C'mon, let her speak," Bailey reasons, turning to Lacey with a frown.

"You peons don't deserve to bask in Sungirl's glow," bellows a deep, familiar voice. "So, fly. Fly on out of here."

I gasp. Towering over the rest of my classmates, a guy in a lemon velvet jacket strides confidently to the center of the crowd. His mop of blue-black hair is stark against his sunny costume, and his shoulder is studded with camera bags. "Get lost, ye non-believers," he commands in faux biblical lingo. With a tiny handheld camera, he begins taking footage of me.

"Wilson, kiss my gluteus maximus," Charlie shouts.

"You wish you could speak in golden verse, like Sungirl. In reality, you can hardly read," Wilson shoots back at his brother.

I'm not sure if I should let Wilson go on or tell him to chill out. It's strange to see him out of his Coney Island Batcave. Kids pivot around to see who's talking.

"Reveal more, Sungirl, about the prize vouchers you're giving out for your next party," Wilson exclaims loudly. He pushes through the yellow throng toward the pagoda.

"Yeah, Sungirl!" Tory and her friends shout from their post by the stairway.

"This is only the first of many parties, each with its special theme," I promise. "Let's hear your pledges to the power of the sun. The first to earn vouchers will be special participants in my next party performance. Who will be the lucky first?" I pick up the jar of vouchers.

Despite Charlie's put-downs, some people scramble to the pagoda. Crime-scene tape guy is the first to grab a voucher and spout an ode.

"I love the sun, because I dig surfing," he starts. "I surf over at Rockaway, or in Miami when my folks fly us down. The sun, on my back, yeah, it's magic." He shrugs, as if unsure how decent his blurb is. I cheer him on.

Next up is Bailey.

"Bailey, don't fall for it," Charlie warns.

"Put a sock in it," she counters. "I'm pumped that Sungirl threw this bash. We need more creativity and less negativity in the world." With this, she glares at Lacey and Charlie. "Without the sun we'd all freeze and the earth would be one huge ice crust."

Lacey yells, "Bailey, you've sold out, you—"

"So, Sungirl, meet me in the lunchroom on Monday," Bailey interrupts, totally ignoring Lacey. "I'll treat you to a lemon sorbet and a place at my table." She reaches for a voucher.

Not to be outdone, Lacey abruptly marches to the stage. I'm too shocked to stop her. You can't deny the girl's beauty. Even in jeans and a loose hoodie, she glows as if she dwells in some higher goddess realm than even Olympus. Looking down, I finally see Ander in the crowd. The way he gapes at Lacey makes me hurt all over.

"This girl is not in yellow," Wilson protests. "She can't be part of this gathering." In bounding steps, he makes his way to the stage as if to cast Lacey out with his bare hands. A clamor of worried speculation rises up.

"You've got no authority, either," Lacey spits. "You don't even go to our school."

She glances at me with a curious mix of anxiety and arrogance. I'm not sure what to do.

Wilson does it for me. He towers over Lacey. "You, Color Offender, buzz off!" Everyone except the kids in her inner circle bursts into uproarious laughter. No doubt the less-cool kids are thrilled to see Queen Lacey get her comeuppance.

"Hold on," I squeak. "Let her speak." This is something that absolutely needs to be played out—whatever the outcome.

Wilson glowers at Lacey, but regains his charismatic authority. "Sungirl has spoken. The offender may speak." An oversized bat, he swoops to the back of the pagoda, behind the band, where leaves from overhanging trees cast jagged shadows.

Lacey gazes out into the crowd, as if these are her own followers, and this party was all her idea. I'm seething with sudden jealousy. What was I thinking when I said she could speak? I don't understand myself. Parts of my personality are absolutely at war with each other.

"I may not be dressed in yellow," Lacey begins, "but I drove here, in the sickest yellow Mustang you'll ever want to see. So, you're wrong about the yellow thing, Mr. Wilson effing Warren." She beams, revealing flawless teeth.

Charlie hoots loudly, as do a bunch of guys.

"What's more, the first five people who want a ride out of this dump in my li'l yellow Mustang, come get *my* vouchers." Lacey holds up some cards. Business cards, really? She's in the business of shooting people down for sure. "Each card stands for a personal invitation to shop with me some after-noon." She grins at me in self-congratulatory satisfaction.

I return the smile to prove I'm unfazed. Then I concen-trate my energy on stopping the flow of takers, like I did stopping that rude guy's putdowns. I beam mesmerizing energy toward the crowd.

But it's not working. Lacey's 'groupies' rush the stage. I'm no match for her, even with any supposed powers I've been granted. She's too good with crowds, and making people feel special. Even Tory grabs a card. She gives me an apologetic glance as she dashes for a sweet spot in Lacey's car. Charlie stands at the foot of the pagoda stairs, head cocked at a rakish angle, clearly savoring the uproar.

I look over at Ander for sympathy, but he's unmoving, only casting Lacey sharp glances. I'm repelled by his sour passivity—and by my own inability to bring this disaster back under control. People are spilling out. The party is over. Even the musicians are packing. This is so not how I planned to end things. I've been trumped.

A swift, hot wind blows on my back, and Wilson's at my

side. His searing eyes fix on mine, reminding me of his glinting ruby-eyed goat buckle. "You going to let that no-account Jezebel do that to you?" he asks. "Use your powers, woman."

"What powers? Your magic is bogus." All I have is a bitterness I can taste.

"It's in you," he insists. "You need to believe in it." He gives me one more maniacal stare with his scalding eyes. Then he lopes away.

My gut knows he's right, though I can't prove it. It has something to do with the fact that now I can spout forth and the person in front of me, however judgmental, can't ignore me. I've never felt such overpowering impulses. As if its sway is so great that to resist would be like gripping a light pole in a storm, using every muscle to keep from being carried off into the thundering clouds. But the power is unsteady. It surges and ebbs. Is that the price Wilson warned of, or will the cost be worse?

Tears prick my eyes as I watch Bailey and Cole head toward Lacey's Mustang. The Mustang is already packed with kids, shrieking and laughing. My bones turn icy as I watch Bailey speak to Lacey. Are they discussing me?

Then, Bailey and Cole swerve away from Lacey's car and walk toward the subway. I let out a gust of relief. Lacey burns rubber as she zooms past them.

"Mean bitch," I hiss as I swipe away the mist in my eyes.

Wilson is up in my face again, so abruptly it's as if he's literally flown over—soundlessly, effortlessly. Goosebumps spike up over my arms. "What now, Wilson?" Before he can say a word, I add, "I'm out of here. Need a ride to the train?"

"Not today." His voice is flat, disappointed in his protégé.

In the car, Ander's in quiet mode. He's helped me a lot today, but I need to ask him a hard question. "What happened, Ander?"

"What are you talking about?" He's focused on the road.

"You did a disappearing act."

When Ander glances my way, his eyes are kind. "I knew you could handle it. You're Sungirl, right?"

"I am," I say uncertainly.

"I wanted to give you full tilt. Wilson was wrong to upstage you. Lacey, too."

I hadn't thought of it that way. Was Ander simply trying to give me the space to fly? Was that all it was? Some of my earlier strength flows back in, this time with gentle fluidity. The end of the party was disastrous, but at least I garnered a crowd. Even Lacey showed. That was more than I imagined possible.

I just can't stop thinking about how Ander pulled away from me the second Lacey arrived. Why does this pain, this constant hole, always reveal itself?

Ander parks by my house and unloads the supplies by the stoop. He asks if I need help getting stuff inside. I smile gratefully. "You've done enough, thanks."

He returns the smile. Then he kisses me gently on my forehead. His kiss is sweeter than all of those yummy yellow cupcakes put together.

8

It is a fact that cannot be denied: the wickedness of others becomes our own wickedness because it kindles something evil in our own hearts.
—Carl Jung

"Dorianna, over here," Bailey calls from the lunch table in the center of the room, where she's sitting with Ava, Lacey, Cole, and Charlie.

I wave nonchalantly as if I get invited to sit with the cool kids every day. Ander's at a table in the corner with a few of his friends from Lit class. I'm torn, but I need to do this, and I know Ander's aware of that. Sitting with Lacey and Charlie and Ava will be rough, but the new part of me relishes the challenge.

As I walk over, I can't help wondering why Bailey hasn't totally renounced her clique. It seemed that's what she was doing back at the Yellow Party, when Charlie and Lacey started dumping on me. I'm sure it isn't easy to reject old friends, though, especially if they're the most popular kids.

Besides, in a minute I'll be sitting here, too, basking in Lacey's shiny but malicious glow. At least Bailey is honoring her word, and being surprisingly welcoming. Her warmth wasn't just a fluke.

I'm wearing my pencil skirt again. No more cash for clothes until my mom's next check. At least I've switched it up with my clingiest magenta top. It draws out the auburn highlights in my hair that grow uncannily brighter each day.

Ava reluctantly shifts to make room as I set down my tray. She was the only one who I didn't lure to the Yellow Party. *Work on this diva,* says a silent, unbidden voice in me. My neck heats up even though no one's heard it but me.

"Everyone's blabbing about your Yellow Party," Bailey reports.

I sense all eyes on me, judging my reactions, and subsequent words. This news is supremely satisfying. I'm itching to find out *what* people are saying, but it's most important to put on a chill front. "Really! Did you have fun?" I ask her.

"Big fun, especially the medieval jig. Right, hon?" Bailey nudges Cole.

"I go more for the rock, madame."

"Well, I'm a sucker for English high tea," Bailey admits.

"I'm not," Lacey grumbles. "That theme was lame."

"You didn't have to go," Bailey reasons. Lacey ignores her.

"I agree with Lacey," Ava snaps. "No way I was going."

"Your choice," I breeze, trying not to show the quiver inside. I'm still not feeling the power. Does it only show up every other day, or what?

Charlie studies me with cold eyes. "Is Wilson your spokesman now? You're aware that he's living in a fantasy world. He thinks he's got *woo-woo* powers."

Ava chuckles. "Powers? Do tell."

"Powers, yeah." Charlie rolls his eyes. "He used to sit in that depressing cave of his, burning his candles that stunk up the house, while he edited his morbid videos. He even had black sheets like some Satanist." Everyone laughs, except Cole and Bailey.

"What's so messed up about black sheets, bro?" Cole asks Charlie. "They're good for, uh . . . romance." Bailey giggles.

"I'm glad he moved out." Charlie opens his chip bag with a loud pop.

"Glad your own brother moved out?" Bailey scolds. "That's just sad."

"You had to be there." Charlie shrugs. "Not that it's any of your business."

I'm tempted to tell Charlie that Wilson said his music reeks and that Charlie cheats on his girlfriends. But I can't slam the clique on my first day at their table. *Save that for another choice moment,* snaps my mean voice in silent rage. It's awake now, churning.

"That party was grade-school stuff," said Charlie. "Yellow cupcakes?"

"I'd like to see you put together such a creative venture," Bailey challenges.

"Yellow's a power color," I say.

"Yeah, dude, what about the whole Sungirl thing?" Cole adds. "Isn't that what lured you to the party? Me? I kind of dug it."

I toy with my salad. It's weird hearing people discuss me like I'm not there. I'm unsure of how much to say, what to say. I've never, ever been privy to an inner circle's conversation.

"It's just a girl juggling, dude," Charlie insists. "A sneaky girl at that. Did you see her expression on the YouTube video? Like she's stealing something."

"Yeah, breaking and entering into our circle," Ava snorts.

I flinch. So, Charlie saw the *video?* Oh, no. The devious

expression on it *is* obvious! *Shit.* "Look, Bailey invited me to sit here," I squeak out.

"I can't believe you, Charlie and Ava. You're flipping green with jealousy." Bailey has a playful way of saying things that would sound blunt from anyone else. It increases my respect for her. I wonder again, what a free spirit like Bailey is doing with these spiteful twits? Sighing, I realize she's doing the same thing *I'm* doing: trying to keep it real, while still treading water for a place in Lacey's exclusive pool club.

Using my inner turmoil as fuel, I focus on Lacey and send her one of those cold then hot laser-beam smiles. "You took a voucher for my next meetup. If my party was so lame, want to fork it over?"

Her face goes slack, but she quickly finds her words. "I'll think about it, but don't hold your breath." She flashes her own ultra-smooth smile. "If your next party theme is slightly more interesting, I may go, to see people make fools of themselves."

"You have a *performance* voucher," I state.

"I'm aware of that."

"Lacey, what kind of performance?" Ava leans forward. Her bejeweled dreadlocks shift over her well-defined cheekbones.

"Not open to discussion," I warn.

"You don't have the control," Ava growls. "Who *are* you, anyway?"

Only a budding Princess of Darkness who you don't want to mess with, a voice in me affirms. Sounds alluring. I almost believe it.

"Why is everyone acting like such a butt-face?" Cole jumps up. "Bailey, catch you after school. I'm off to Bio." They kiss and he darts off.

Ava wags a finger at me. "*You're* the butt-face, for butting into our thing."

My strength comes back in a hot rush. I send another one of those incredibly intentional vibes Ava's way—my pain mixed with an unspoken demand to treat me better. It scorches my own chest on its way out.

"Ouch!" Ava yelps. She rubs around her collarbone as she scowls at me.

I *couldn't* have hurt her. It was only a thought. I was only granted power, easy youth and beauty, not the ability to literally *burn* people. Right? Bailey sends me a questioning look.

"What happened?" Lacey's soft forehead creases in concern. "You okay, Ava?"

Still rubbing the spot, Ava nods warily.

Lacey narrows her eyes at me. "Look, I don't know what you're trying to prove by having these parties and weaseling over to our table and being so in our faces, new girl—or should I say, Sungirl." She snickers. "But it's backfiring. And let me tell you something about your boy toy, Ander. Supposedly, he's been writing that stupid novel for years. Have you looked in his notebook? There's nothing there besides a few scribblings. Yeah, uh-huh, that's right."

I'm speechless. Ander is writing a novel about extortion. Or is the notebook just a bunch of loony ramblings, like that writer guy in *The Shining?*

"Enough!" Bailey leaps up. "Lacey, you have no right. Have you ever tried to write a novel? And what do you have against Dorianna? You don't even know her. No one forced you to come to her party. You *are* jealous."

"Of *that* pushy psycho?" Lacey's laugh is way high-pitched.

Bailey smiles over at me. "Walk you to your next class?"

"Sure."

"Yeah, Bailey, hang out with Dorianna," warns Lacey. "Go for it. See how far that gets you. But don't come running back to me."

Part of me is flattered that Bailey's told Lacey off at her own expense. Another part of me knows I should've done it myself. And then, something else nags at me.

As I follow Bailey out, I have a flickering image of Lacey as a spoiled young girl, in a house full of state-of-the-art monitors and skinny laptops and a walk-in closet brimming with expensive garb from Bloomie's and Versace and Juicy Couture. I picture one of those ratlike, ribboned lap dogs at her feet. I see Lacey getting her way but not getting any real attention—pathetic, if true. Seeing that, I don't hate Lacey. I understand that kind of loneliness.

It dawns on me I'm not out to reject Lacey as Bailey just did. I want Lacey for myself, but not as-is. I want to change the dynamics.

Get to know her, whispers my untamed side, *win her over and shape her, even if it takes you all year. In the end, Lacey will be wrapped around your pinky.*

Wildness surges through me, like a pack of feral wolves, howling, tussling. It feels so good, so freeing. Ava's dead wrong about me not having the control. Okay, so I'm not in control yet, but I've already begun to work the plan. I will not deviate from my purpose until every person in this godforsaken high school is my groupie. And if Charlie thinks his brother is dabbling in the dark arts, well, I'll use Wilson, too, to reach my goal.

I'm almost out of the lunchroom when the burst of wildness ebbs in a dizzying shudder. I spin around to see if Ander's still there. He is. He waves at me, and I wave back. I don't mind hurting Charlie, or Ava, or even Wilson if need be.

But sweet, sweet Ander, I plead… I hope I never, ever hurt you on my way to the top.

9

I either want less corruption, or more chance to participate in it.
—Ashleigh Brilliant

ocking myself in my room, I check my fan page for
the third time today. This morning, I had 126
followers. At 4:00 p.m., I had 178. Now, at 7:30
p.m., it's up to 337. *Incredible...* and all of it, even with that
dreadful end to the Yellow Party.

Next, I click over to the YouTube Sungirl video and press
play. On it, I'm still juggling the same stuff, but the sun is
glinting at a sharper angle. My face still wears that slimy
expression as if I'm about to spill incriminating secrets I
promised to keep, but there's something new as well. I rub
my eyes and focus harder, hoping for different results. I press
replay, fingers crossed.

No luck. My chin's upturned at a severe angle and my
stare scours the viewer with . . . scorn. I clench up. My
altered expression can only be described as contemptuous

arrogance. I've been a lot of things—overeager, a wallflower —but never arrogant. What will my budding fans think? My hateful disdain will turn them off. "This can't be happening," I hiss.

My YouTube video certainly has a ton of hits—1,989, to be exact. I'm amazed. But this shitty sneer on my face is bound to poison my image going forward. "Wilson, you lied. You definitely messed with this," I shout at my laptop. "And this wasn't part of our deal!" I snap the lid closed and throw myself on my bed.

When I'm calmer, I'll come up with a plan to find out once and for all if he's altering the footage of me.

"Wilson, what did you do to my YouTube video?" I'm standing at his Coney Island apartment door. I'm going to dig my talons in him, no more nicey-nice. Just hope he doesn't take away the good part of that spell.

Wordlessly, he leads me back to his studio and offers me a seat. He leans back in his swivel chair, raises his arms, relaxes his head in his hands, and studies me. Today he has on a heavy silver chain under his black Edwardian shirt with flared sleeves, and his cologne smells of that same musky incense that might billow from a Gothic castle bedroom. Despite my anger, a flush of unwelcome desire rustles through me. "You're referring to, specifically?"

"The look on my face," I sputter. "I told you before, but now it's . . . it's worse."

Wilson rights himself, and gets out a camera. He starts clicking still photos of me. "This look? He asks, clicking a shot and showing to me. "Or this?"

"Stop that." I pivot in the opposite direction so he can't get another shot.

"But you're exquisite when you're mad. You've no idea," he breathes heat on my back.

I wait until it cools and then spin warily around. "Enough. I won't be swayed by compliments."

"Yes, Sungirl, yes. I bow down to my Yellow Queen." Inserting his camera in its bag, he places it among the others on his console. "What were you saying?" As he leans toward me, a moonstone on his silver chain dangles and gleams.

His eyes, framed by his black constellation of hair, draw me toward him like two forceful magnets. Unbidden, my belly does a taut flip. "I look condescending, I'm leering, okay? You changed my face on that darn editing program. I know you did."

His laughter is brusque. "The camera reveals what's under the surface. It's always a shock."

"It's more than that. Are you denying what you did?"

"I did nothing. It's your doing—the change comes from inside you. I told you that before."

I snort as I fold my hands across my chest. Though I do wonder. "When you make your next compilation, I want a copy *before* I go home."

"I should be hurt." He affects a pout. "If you don't trust me, then why do you want me to make more videos?" He cocks his head at me in a challenge.

I sense that he's not hurt at all. That he likes baiting me, even thrives on it. I glower and shake my head to make it clear I'm repelled. In truth, though, it turns me on against my own will—this joust—at least this new "me" I hardly recognize.

This new person who is plotting to hook Lacey, enjoyed baiting Charlie, and is gleefully sparring with Wilson this very second. The old Dorianna is literally shrinking in horror under my skin—it's a physical sensation, a pulling and ripping. She's drying out. Crinkling up. Pieces are disintegrating. Is this the consequence that Wilson warned me of? Will the sweet, shy Dorianna waft away like dust? My blood runs cold at the thought.

In my room earlier this afternoon, as I worried about the day's activities, I tried to rub my arms and legs and face back to a pink, innocent glow. Other times, like in the lunchroom with Lacey, I welcome the freedom to be someone else—even someone rude, incorrigible, and devious. Is *that* why the promo trailer changed?

No, I reason silently, that's impossible. The video changes are all Wilson's fault. As for me, I need to hold onto a fistful of conscience, even if some of it withers. I don't care how good it feels, I don't want to turn into a cold, conniving witch. I'm a good person.

Wilson flicks on his monitor and clicks into his editing program. "You're so alluring that I couldn't wait to make my next video. It's already done."

"What?" My breath catches in my throat. I roll my chair close to Wilson's. My jaw drops as I watch.

It begins with a close-up of the capybara, but this beast has on Wilson's own black top hat. Wilson's pearl-tipped cane is in the capybara's cloven hoof and it's gesturing to the audience with the pointed end. "Come one, come all, to the big top. See the painted ladies of the Coney Island Burlesque. We've got Busted Betsy, Pheromone Patty, and Ms. Candy Tattersal. We've got 'em all." With that, the beast releases a lusty, monstrous *oink*. "See them kick their heels at the moon," it brays. "The moon is full tonight, gentlemen. And the pinup girls are full of sass and sassafras. The glorious dame leading the pinup pack is the insatiable, larger-than-life Sungirl, Lady of Cosmic Rays. Watch her high-step on her giant burning suns. Come one, come all!"

The capybara ringmaster clacks his teeth and tips his hat. With that, Wilson's mystical camera pans from the beast to me, using footage of when I vamped in front of the old girlie poster in the Coney Island Museum. My close-up morphs to the stuff Wilson shot on the boardwalk—a headshot of me gobbling down my hot dog. Then I become truly insatiable, gobbling down lemonades and signs and even people. I'm about to eat the sun, when I balance it on the tip of my tongue instead.

As the sun wobbles on my tongue, it expands to the size of a car. I blow it, with one ladylike *poof*, onto the floor. When it stops rolling, I leap on it, and do a cancan. Impressive.

As I watch, what really throws me is that Wilson has magically changed me out of my school clothes—the pencil skirt and simple top—and into a yellow fringe bikini, barely covering my thighs.

An immediate protest boils up. How dare he virtually strip me. But as I stare longer at the image, I realize how stunning he's made me. This is no porn slut image. This is the masterful, painstaking work of a cutting-edge filmmaker, amplifying tenfold the glory of his muse.

"You like?" Wilson asks, clicking stop.

Muse—I roll the word silently in my mind, taste its honeyed essence. All the concerns that crowded my mind minutes ago drift off. Things like morality and conscience seem like dirty rain clouds bumping by. Life is good, I am awesome, and Wilson's video kicks serious butt.

Placing my hand on his long, curiously delicate fingers, I whisper, "Am I your muse?" I remove my hand only when it starts to heat up, and before he gets the wrong idea that I want more.

Or do I?

He shifts slightly in his chair, in order to line his eyes up with mine. "You could say that you're my muse," he admits. In his gaze, I know I could have him right now, in this room, as easily as he's captured me on video. I could rip off his shirt and run my hands through his forest of hair. Plant a firm kiss on his lips and force them open. His tongue would taste of smoke, of musk, of infinite need. For that second, I see past his charming façade into the hunger, lodged in his soul. A lonely, desperate soul that seems to have lived for centuries, yet not quite at all—stuck in some netherworld where a virus might exist.

It takes real effort to pull away. But I have to. This is dangerous, this audacious forgetting. I don't want Wilson. I want Ander. I hold out the thumb drive I brought. "Copy the burlesque demo on this, then I'll take it and keep an eye on it. That way, I'll know the difference between what was on in the original and what you edit on YouTube. End of story."

He shrugs, and takes the drive. The hypnotic moment is broken. "There," he says, after it's done. "You'll see for yourself I had no hand in any digital personality changes." He toys with his moonstone. "Don't come whining when it's not what you expected."

My chest tightens in panic. "What's that supposed to mean?"

He places his arms firmly on my shoulders, and gives me a threatening glare. "Dor, you made the bargain, not me. It's a spectacular but perilous slope." His voice dips, into a perverse dankness that feels like slippery, hidden stairways and banished souls.

I want to demand that he tell me what the specific parameters . . . and consequences of the magic are. He must know if he's the grantor, but now? Now I'm too afraid to ask.

As he continues to stare at me without taking his hands from my shoulders, I sense his anger shift to lust and I realize he might kiss me. Do I want that? My will is like smoke in fierce wind, blowing here, swooping there. Was that how Ander felt when he was with me at the Yellow Party and Lacey barged in? For another crazy moment, I sense Wilson is a genius, with his video art, even more so than Ander who hides his writing as if he's ashamed of it. Is it the dark magic that's yanking me back and forth as if I'm in the throat of a hurricane?

I have to see Ander's notebook. *Have to.* Especially after Lacey hinted about Ander pretending to write. Very serious charges. Abruptly, my senses fill with Ander's kind and wounded spirit. Like being surrounded by warm, clear, healing water.

I pull away from Wilson. The magnetic bond is broken again.

"I have a great idea," I say, as much to fill the negative charge I've created as to reveal my clever new brainstorm.

"Do tell." Wilson turns his back to me, disappointment evident in his slouch. He fiddles with his computer, a sign that I've disturbed him and this is the only way he knows to regain control.

In a move more characteristic of Wilson than of me, I step around to his front, where he can't avoid me. "Lend me your smallest camera. I'll take photos of the backs of people who picked the performance vouchers. We'll post them on the Burlesque Party page with their carnival names. It'll be a game for my fans, to figure out who's who." I hope Wilson likes my suggestion. Despite my misgivings, I want to please him.

"Nice idea, Sungirl." He wheels around, grinning. Wilson is back. He paws through his equipment and holds up a marshmallow-sized device with a clip. "Fits inside your shirt-sleeve." He demonstrates by sticking the thing inside his Edwardian cuff and shooting one of me.

"Perfect!" I giggle. "You don't mind if I borrow it?"

"Why would I? The sneakier, the better." We exchange sly grins.

Sneaky. This was the first negative change I noticed in my

own video. Guilt seeps in, followed by a surging exhilaration. *What's so wrong with some devious behavior? It isn't against the law, for shit's sake. Nor is a bit of arrogance,* I decide as I think about the second quality that emerged on my face.

I need to be more arrogant. I've been way too humble and compliant. Like on that first day when I let Lacey and her thugs criticize me without fighting back. Other times, too. I give Wilson a conspiratorial peck on the cheek. "Ander will write the new meetup copy, and we'll get this party started."

"Ooh, I do love a good burlesque." Wilson does a lascivious bump and grind as he walks me out.

10

I want your leather-studded kiss in the sand.
—Lady Gaga

On the subway back from Coney, my cell pings. It's Ander.

hey, where r u? wanna hang out?

coming back from coney... where r u?

@ havanas wanna meet me here?

b there in 15

All of this attention in one day is intoxicating—Ander texting me? More, please.

When I get to Havana's Cafe I see through the window that he's hunched over his notebook. The urge to sneak up behind him and skim a page is naughty but too perfect an opportunity to pass up. I wait until someone has the door open to leave and then slip in, noiselessly.

Tiptoe up, crane my neck, and read.

Every time he was finally over it, Angie would send him a coded

look with those luminous eyes of hers. It made him nuts not to know
what she was thinking when she did that. Did a part of her still want
him? That familiar ache welled up in Padro—the tiny, dirty nugget of
his heart that still loved—

"Miss, did you want to order?" asks the café waiter,
padding up behind me.

I jump out of my skin. Ander slams his journal closed and
wheels around. "What are you doing?" he snaps.

This is all wrong. I need a quick comeback. "I . . . I
wanted to give you a surprise hug. I didn't see a thing.
Really."

"I'm just doing a free write about some dude named
Padro."

I nod. His blurb has me neurotic that Angie is actually
Lacey, and that a part of Ander still loves her. But who am I
to protest, after flirting with Wilson? Or whatever that was.

"Have a seat," Ander offers in a friendlier voice. "Sorry to
bark at you. My notebook's private, that's all. God forbid I
should leave it here or at school and let some asshat pick it
up and get a rise out of it. I'm kind of paranoid about it."

"Makes sense." Not really. He must have something to
hide in there.

"Want something? A drink?" His inviting smile melts
away most of my discomfort. The waiter comes over and I
order a fruit smoothie.

Settling in, I glance around. Havana's tacky plastic
coconuts on the wall and tablecloths with garish tropical
flowers comfort me. It smells of baked garlic chicken and café
con leche here. Always, there's the hum of the fan, struggling
to clear the air of grease and smoke, and the warm buzz of
conversation.

"What were you doing at Warren's?" Ander asks over his
café con leche.

"I wanted to brainstorm ideas."

"Why cut Lit, though?" he presses.

"I wanted to go out early. Coney Island creeps me out after dark."

Next to Ander is the novel we're reading for Lit class, *Notes from Underground*. What a wimp Dostoevsky created in the Underground Man. He lived in his cellar in Saint Petersburg, accumulating book piles, and massive grudges. The guy couldn't relate to women, or anyone. He'd risk getting hurt. Does Ander identify with the Underground Man? Hard to believe.

"I had this neat idea." I raise my arm, click on the minicam, and describe the picture-matching game I devised to build another round of winners for the party, after party number two. Breathlessly, I add, "Wilson already made the Burlesque video. With the capybara as a ringmaster."

Ander's handsome face hardens into a grimace. "I thought we were all in on this." Now he's peevish, too? After his disappearing act at my party, he doesn't have the right. And yet, I'm pleased with his jealousy. It's such a novelty, I can't help but like it.

I pull the memory stick out of my bag. "Do you have your laptop? Let's watch it here. You can write the evite copy now."

Ander's gray eyes flash with glints of curiosity and competitive spirit. That's better. We watch the event teaser. "Got to admit," he says, "it's hilarious, using the water hog as ringmaster."

Hilarious, even if Wilson's treatment of the beast was harsh. I figure you can't exactly hurt a capybara by playing around with it in the editing room.

Over a piece of shared pie, we cobble out the Burlesque Party copy and match winners to stage names. Earlier, I had to give out some vouchers for free, since Lacey crashed the giveaway event before they were all claimed.

Sungirl, Lady of Cosmic Rays, leader of the Coney Island Dancers,
invites you to another fabulous party!
BURLESQUE
On the boardwalk at Coney Island, behind Nathan's Famous
Hot Dogs
Sunset, October 6th
Winners of Yellow Party vouchers form the lineup of Stars.
Stay tuned for details.
For a winning ticket to Sungirl's third exclusive meetup, guess the
identity of these burlesque lovelies. First ten right answers win secret
perks!

We match the names to the dancers, leaving spaces for the photos. Candy Tattersal is Bailey, Pheromone Patty is Tory, Lil Laurentine is Lisbeth, the musician, Ms. Givem Heck will be Lacey, if she deigns to show up. Your Fyne Selfe is Cole, Bailey's hottie boyfriend, and Busted Betsy is Jake Steinberg, the guy who wore the crime-scene tape at my Yellow Party.

"The perfect two guys to dress in drag," I giggle. "Funny photos, here we come." I unclip the mini-cam from inside my cuff and show Ander the shot I took of him when I first sat down.

"I look awful," he protests. "Where'd you get that camera? From Warren?"

I muss up his hair. "You're not jealous of The Prince of Darkness, are you?"

"No way." Ander's face flames up, further evidence that he cares more than he admits.

"How'd you guys meet anyway?" I purr.

"I met Warren last year, at one of his brother Charlie's

debauched parties," Ander says with bite. "Truth be told, I still don't know him *all* that well." He pauses. "I stayed up late, drinking and talking with him about the corrupt state of the world, and, as Warren puts it, how you have to 'bigfoot your digital profile' if you're going to get traction. It was fun talking with him, but . . . such a weird coincidence the next day."

"What coincidence?"

"Charlie booted me hard during that soccer game. He was struggling to steal the ball from Poly Prep's wingman."

"And?"

"And bam! I was belly-up in unbearable pain. I happened to glance into the bleachers. Warren was staring down, amused." Ander snorts. "Okay, maybe with intense curiosity? Whatever it was, it spooked me."

"That would bother me, too." The misgivings I feel for Wilson ooze up like black tar.

"I can't decide about Warren, though, because he also has a heart." Ander slugs down the last of his coffee. "A few days later, I hobbled into Havana's on crutches and Warren was there. He said what a drag it must be to have a steel pin in my hip, and how his dumb brother ruined my chance at varsity."

I sit there, wishing Ander would say something definitive about Wilson, to help me make my own decision about him.

"Warren has other good points, too. He always shows up when I need cash for a burrito at Havana's, or an informed opinion on how to be a writer these days. Warren has a more creative head than Charlie, hands down."

"He is full of ideas," I agree.

"But, I don't trust Wilson freaking Warren. He's a little off."

"Specifically?" My stomach clenches.

"Why would he even show up at that game when he hates sports, hates his brother, and doesn't even attend our school?

"Good point." Wilson bothers me, too. How he acted to that capybara, his hostile side. I wonder what Ander would think of me if I told him I made a screwy vow with Wilson. Uneasiness rumbles through me. Ander must see it, because he strokes my wrist, and stares intensely into my eyes as if he's worried.

"Dorianna, it's startling how pretty you are—prettier than the day before, and the day before that." He reaches out for my hand. His touch is electric. "How is it possible?"

I inhale sharply. I so wasn't expecting that comment, or his touch. Ander's going through a checklist, I sense it: my walk is confident now, my gaze stays on him, my posture's proud. He's asking himself how someone could transform that fast, even with a healthy dose of attention. To distract him from his silent questions, I brush my wavy auburn hair over one ear, showing off my new dangly earrings and silver ring.

His gray-blue eyes glaze over. His animal need wafts over in a hot rush that takes my breath away. "Do you know how much I thought about you today?" he whispers.

"No." I'm trembling. "How much?"

"I thought about you when I was in Lit, and wondered where you could possibly be. I thought about you when I waited for you by our lockers after school. I thought about how I split on you at the Yellow Party, and how that wasn't cool. How I took you out to Coney on a whim, but you charmed me. You're the first person who's been able to make me forget about . . . other girls. I'm into people seeing us more together, you know?" He strokes my cheek. Each fingertip sends a delighted chill of desire through me.

Charmed him? Is that part of Wilson's magic? My rational side scoffs at the idea. No matter what, or how this happened, Ander knows what to say to open me up in a way I've never dared before. His grin says, Take a chance, and you won't regret it.

He eases his hand gently around the nape of my neck. Runs it through my hair. Gently pulls me in closer, an inch, and then three. I thrill to the warmth of his skin, the loose strands of his bangs tickling my face. He smells of cream and coffee. The sudden press of his mouth is rapturous. His lips part mine and his tongue explores, shooting tiny violet and blue flames all over me.

Over our steamy coffees, we envelop each other in a greedy, steamy embrace, and we kiss for a good long time.

11

Everyone carries around his own monster.
—Richard Pryor

I'm in an upbeat mood after hanging out with Ander, and I get this idea to share it with my aunt. I liked it when she fixed my hair, but since then we've been so busy, we've hardly spoken except for mumbled words over the nighttime news before heading off to our rooms.

She's a vegetarian, so I decide to buy a veggie pizza to surprise her. At 7:00 p.m. she calls to say she's sorry, but she has to attend a last-minute business meeting. Slumping in my chair, I wolf down two slices. If there isn't a live person around to share my good mood with, there are always my followers. Upstairs, I switch on my laptop.

My fanbase is *way* up. The Surf Dance video, despite my weird facial expressions, has over two thousand hits on YouTube. And lots of kids from other schools have visited the Sungirl fan page. There are tons of comments.

when's your next meetup? purple party this time? —sparklgrl
sungirl, I'll hop in yr tanning bed - yr boy from bayridge
I go to Parkside in Manhattan. forwarded your rockn video to my friends -Luv ya, perrie
do u glo in the dark? - noodleboi
No fair!!!!!! open your meetups to kids from Poly Prep!!!! -Jessie
you are a stone cold diva -Alex G
sneeekey gurl come steal me -ray ray

I scowl at the screen. I hate that some people think I look sneaky and cold. Also, some comments are too raunchy for my taste. Still, I inhale all of the love aimed my way. It fills up a place that so often feels caved in. Wilson hasn't sent the official Burlesque evite to our school, or posted the video yet. So, I compose a teaser for my fans, offering tantalizing clues about the event and game prizes.

Dearest fans,
I shine my warmest rays on you, a little summer in chilly fall.
Party #2 is about to drop. Hint: bring back the days of showgirls and sequins!
The first fans to win the next guessing game will get secret prizes for meetup #3.
Keep checking back here. You may be the lucky winner!
Shine on, Sungirl

I'm hoping that the kids at Wilson's school will become entranced. They'll certainly be less biased than the people Lacey's tried to poison against me.

I shake off my heels, and run a fragrant bubble bath. Sinking under the steamy bubbles, I picture admirers, crowding around me, offering presents and invitations to places. I think of Ander's delectable kisses and how I want more. I wonder how jealous Lacey will be when she sees us together—really together. That makes me worry about what will happen if either Lacey bails on Burlesque, or goes, and causes a hot mess of a scene.

Why am I always obsessing over Lacey?

Lathering up my legs and feet, I try to switch to positive thoughts: of Ander's arms around me, and of Tory being so very friendly and helpful at the Yellow Party.

Tory's a committed worker bee. I'll get her to work even harder for me—embed links and compliments about Sungirl and Burlesque on every possible social media site. Then I remember Ander's comment, about how we should only open events out in "organic" stages: first our school, then Wilson's. I slap at the bathwater. *"That's way too slow. I need the stakes raised now."*

As I towel off, I think of how Ava is a stubborn, narcissistic holdout, and how my sudden irritation at lunch seemed to burn her. "Impossible," I spit, "I didn't do that." Or is literally scorching people part of my new power? No matter how afraid I am of the answer, I need to find the nerve to ask Wilson. From the shadowy corners of my room, I swear I hear whispers, first a few, then louder . . . a full chorus, yammering.

"Stop that girl, it would be so easy," Wilson taunts.

"My brother thinks he's *woo-woo*," Charlie hisses. "Black sheets like some—"

"Look," Lacey snaps. "I don't know what you're trying to prove, but—"

"You're breaking and entering . . . Ouch!" The indelible image of Ava rubbing her chest invades my vision. And Ava's challenge: "Who *are* you?"

"Shut up, all of you. Shut up!" I yell back at the nebulous voices in the shadows. Without bothering with pajamas, I dive under my covers and yank them over my head. This is bullshit," I say, into the sheet. "I'm exhausted, that's all."

A sob pushes its way up my throat, but I swallow it. Like a tiny pea of a girl, I'm terrified of the cobweb monsters under my bed. Where's Aunt Carol? I need her to be home. A vision of the house in Wabash, after my father was carted away, darkens my mind. Gray and creaky with a glaze of chill. My mother was always sleeping. Sleeping off her sad little life. Even before my father left, he was never there. He was over at his church, or scouting around for a flock, or off in his den, writing odious, hippie-come-lately sermons. One time I badly needed him to help with trigonometry problems. I'd called and called him at the church. He never answered, and I cried myself to sleep, math homework left undone. It wasn't just the math, either.

That vacant spot in me that I filled with adoring comments from my fan page minutes earlier is already empty —famished, in fact. That video, of me inhaling Cokes and flowers and hot dogs and even trying to gobble the sun, thunders into my consciousness. I roll over in bed, moaning. By the time my aunt comes in downstairs, cold sweat is trickling down my back.

The next morning, I'm in better spirits. The sun does that— offers the promise of a new day.

"I'm Sungirl, and Sungirl is always beaming," I whisper to *Marie Claire* girl in my locker, and keep on chanting silently as I amble through the hall. It seems to be working some simple magic. People greet me warmly by my avatar.

"How's it shining, Sungirl?" a friend of Tory's asks.

"Wassup, Sunny Delight?" Cole gives me a fist bump as he passes.

"Sun's up," I chirp.

Just before lunch, Ander meets me at the locker with a kiss. "Eat together?" he asks. I nod and we walk to the cafeteria.

"Can you stand sitting at Bailey's table? I need to work the crowd a little."

He makes a face. "Will Charlie and you know who be there?"

"No clue." Of course they will. As much as I long to spend every second with Ander, Wilson's words ring out: "Work fast, because your fifteen minutes will fly." The pressure of time weighs heavily on me. Lacey needs to be lured back in, and Ava. "What if we sit next to their table?" *So they can see us kissing.* "I'll talk to Bailey before that."

"Sounds like a plan." Ander swings an arm around me, and it vibrates warmth. After his disappearing act at my party, his touch is still a pleasant shock.

We arrive early. Ander goes off to talk to a friend while I start to snap the candid photos I need. My models catch me, and protest until I coax them into a side room for privacy. It isn't hard to talk Tory into it, though. She's an eager model until I tell her to pose with her back to the camera.

She wrinkles her nose. "Not my best angle."

"So not true. You have a great posterior, Ms. Pheromone Patty."

"What's a pheromone exactly?"

"A sexual chemical you release, alerting the male species that you're fabulous and available."

"In that case . . ." Tory gives a flirty back kick that shows off her silver heels. I snap away.

It's a cinch to rope in Tory's friend Jake, the crime-scene-tape kid. Jake's a fruitcake and loves the idea he'll get to perform as Busted Betsy. "I'm so busted," he quips, "but yeah, drag's cool with me." He strikes a hammy she-model pose with his index finger on his pouty lips and one narrow hip cranked out.

By the time Ander and I reconvene, the room is teeming with people. I subtly point out Lacey's table and, after we make our way through the food line, we hurry to claim the neighboring one.

I make a show of waving cheerily to Bailey, who waves back. Not only that, she calls, "Can I sit with you guys?"

My heart leaps. Bailey is publicly choosing me over Lacey and Ava.

As she makes her way over, I catch Lacey frowning at her, and then sneaking a peek my way. Ander's sitting closer to me than a simple classmate would, with his back to Lacey. This gives me extreme satisfaction.

Bailey looks awesome today, as always. Her pink corduroy vest over her black suede skirt over purple leggings is wacky, but perfect. To top it off, she's tamed her cascading red hair with a wide purple headband.

"What's up, Bailey?" I ask her.

"Not much, what's up with you guys?" Bailey unwraps her burrito and takes a bite. "Planning your next fête?"

"Matter of fact, yeah." I squeeze Ander's arm. "He writes smokin' copy." I pretend I'm cooling off a hot pen by blowing on it. Whispering the party details to Bailey, I add, "Your stage name will be Candy Tattersall."

She lets out a delighted shriek.

"Lower the volume!" Charlie bellows from the next table. "You're not in third grade." That only sets us off, even louder.

"I *adore* my stage name," Bailey says after we calm down. "A sweet yet hard candy of a girl, all in tatters." She gives me a melodramatic hug. "You already know me so well, darling. I live for art and fashion and I already have a cool idea for the costume." In a conspiratorial murmur, she explains, "I'll get floral upholstery fabric for the bikini and make a short cape to fling off for the sensational reveal."

I nod eagerly. "Good, good, good."

"I have a state-of-the-art industrial sewing machine, so I make most of my outfits." Bailey points to her skirt and vest. "It's so fun to mix between modern and classic. Lady Tattersal will absolutely fit into that head space."

"You girls have big ideas," is all Ander says as he eats. Poor Ander. Guys have no patience for clothes.

If I could look down on this lunchroom scene, I would swear this couldn't be me. It's so uncanny to have made a fun new friend and found a boyfriend all in a few weeks. My old life is a faded print on peeling wallpaper in a dusty Indiana farmhouse, hundreds of miles away. Is this totally the work of Wilson's magic, or did I have any natural hand in it?

I shoot Lacey a sudden, wicked grin. She snaps her attention back to her own table, pretending she hasn't been staring with obvious longing. I wonder why this moment of triumph over Lacey is the most delicious. A moment that gives someone pain. My old self would have been fretting over this—but today? It's already seeping from my mind.

By this time, Cole has made his way to our table with a ham panini and coffee. If he's surprised that Bailey has suddenly changed her seating plan, it doesn't show. The only hint is the nod and the "shit happens" grin he offers Charlie, Lacey, and Ava over at the next table. Ander says a friendly hey to Cole, as if he's already accepted this new lunch quartet.

"What's up, dude?" Cole says gamely. "How's the writing?"

"Coming along." Ander pats his notebook, as if to check it's still there.

I explain about the posterior-shot guessing game to win a voucher, and he agrees to pose after lunch. The guys munch on chips and check their text messages, while Bailey and I blab. I tell her where the next party will take place.

Her face pales. "Will people go all the way out there?"

"Why wouldn't they?"

"I have an idea," Bailey says. "My mother's a painter and, um . . ."

"A good one, too," Cole chimes. "She does these surreal backgrounds with weird half-human, half-animal creatures—like Bosch. You know Bosch?"

"Bosch painted hellscapes," Ander says.

"Cool, but what does your mom's art have to do with my party?" I ask.

"We live in a huge loft space in Chelsea."

"With a view of the Hudson River to die for," Cole adds as he texts someone.

"So, listen," Bailey says, "if you need a party space, my loft could be perfect—private. Free." She makes a face. "You don't want the performers being ogled by Bosch-like cretins out in Coney Island, do you?"

"She's got a point," Ander says.

Coney Island for a party featuring girls in bikinis does give me pause. I remember how I felt when I first went out there. The subway spooked me, as well as the seedy folks loitering on the boardwalk and around the arcades. Those creepsters sure would get an eyeful. Plus, some kids' parents might protest. Not the senior parents, but the ones who have kids in Tory's grade.

But if it's at Bailey's loft, I worry that it'll become more her party than mine. And it won't be in the sun—but then again, we could create a sunscape indoors. "Generous offer, Bailey. You sure you want to host *my* party?"

"Sure I'm sure. Why not stop by?" Bailey urges. "Check out the space."

"Today?"

"Yeah. Be fun to have you over. Show you my mom's artwork, my messy room."

I glance at Ander. "What are you up to this afternoon?"

"Oh, I have plenty of things to do." He puts his cell in his pocket.

"Like what?" I ask playfully. "Go see Wilson, without me?" I push out my lips in an exaggerated sulk.

"I seem to remember the shoe on the other foot." He runs a finger lightly down my nose and then rests his hand on my knee. "Go for it, Sungirl. Just let me know what you girls decide."

"About what?" Ander's rugged good looks and sexy touch are slowing my thought process.

"If it's going to be at Bailey's loft, we'll need to change the copy before posting."

"Oh! Right."

Ander kisses me. Each kiss is sweeter than the last. But I must admit, what's *most* yummy is the envious look in Lacey's eyes. That vulture still has a thing for my man. It's glaringly clear in her hateful stare. I kiss Ander back, with renewed passion.

After lunch, Bailey and I sneak up behind Lacey and I take a shot of her.

She wheels around. "You girls stalking me now? Want my autograph, too?"

We laugh with abandon. It's great to have an ally, to not be worried about being uncool. This is the closest I've ever been to Lacey. Her flawless skin, leaf-green eyes that glint with self-assurance, and hourglass figure under her expensive sweater catch me off guard. I've seen her draw people in with her dazzling gaze and whispered words that she saves for her chosen few. The ones that make people feel like a star.

"You're still considering performing in my next party, right?" I ask her.

"Maybe." Lacey studies the tiny camera I've unclipped from my sleeve. "What's up with that?" I describe the guessing contest for event number two. "Not happening!" she shrills. "Any photo of me has to be pre-approved." She lunges for it.

I back off. "No, no, no," I scold.

Bailey narrows her eyes at Lacey. "You want in on this, or not? 'Cause if you don't want to perform, plenty of other girls would gladly take your place."

Lacey frowns at Bailey as if to say, Mellow out, frenemy. Don't be a drama queen. Then she throws up her hands. "You want the derrière shot, what do I care? Here, get another one while you're at it." She purposely sticks her rear out in a raunchy pose, but she doesn't know I've already gotten the perfect shot.

Bailey starts to talk about all of the things she'll show me when I come over—in a loud voice that Lacey can't help over-hearing. I'm torn. I want to hurt Lacey for all of the pain she's put me through, yet I don't want Bailey to totally alienate her.

So, when Lacey walks away, I say, "Don't worry, you look good from the back." She doesn't turn, or acknowledge the compliment, but with my newly heightened senses, I sense her energy spring to a happier place. In fact, with this new power surging in me, it's almost as if I can read minds. I'll have to ask Wilson about that.

"Why throw her a bone?" Bailey challenges, when we leave the school. "Lacey's treated you horribly from day one. Plus, I stuck my neck out for you."

"True."

"Bringing you in was risky." Bailey gives me a playful poke. "I might've been stuck with a dork for all I knew."

"What you did was huge, so thanks." But that doesn't mean I'm going to deviate from the path I've set.

I just wonder what Bailey would think of me, if I ever get Lacey on my side—as my very best friend.

12

If anything, we have to make it darker and meaner
than the boys.
—Angelina Jolie

On the way to Bailey's Chelsea loft on the west side of Manhattan, we walk past blocks of trendy galleries. She explains that these used to be meat-processing plants and biscuit factories. I ogle the flashy abstract art and installations inside. Nothing like this in Wabash.

Pausing in front of a renovated warehouse near the Hudson River, Bailey announces, "We're here." We zoom up ten floors in the elevator and walk down a wide hall. Bailey unlocks a wide metal door and ushers me in.

"Your place is amazing!" I gush.

She points to a line of mural-sized canvases that soar over the spare, cube-shaped sofas. "Here are some of my mom's paintings."

I study them—washes of rich brown and golden ochre under what looks to be a nasty hobbit village. Trolls, ogres, and faeries with fangs buzz about. I immediately relate to these creatures. They're cute yet full of malicious mischief, which I suppose they can't always control any better than I can. "Trippy! How does she come up with these?"

"She got hooked on fantasy when she was our age. She loved the dark stories—like Edgar Allen Poe, Mary Shelley's *Frankenstein*."

"Wow, my aunt's place is so plain compared to this."

"I'm sure it's as nice."

"It's comfortable." I shrug. "Your mom's work is so, like, nervy! She's not afraid to make a bold, outrageous statement and stand by it."

Bailey arches a brow. "I guess I got that from her, too. How I let Lacey have it."

I feel a wave of guilt. "Look, I hope I can pay you back for that someday."

"No need to pay me back. Other than don't get all simpatico with her."

I won't be making any more oaths.

Bailey's smile tightens to a line. "Look, I'm not trying to tell you what to do, and it's fine if Lacey's in the burlesque show. It's not like I'm all exclusive and territorial. But I'd look like an idiot if you got all buddy-buddy with her. Make sense?"

"Perfect sense." I can say that much without being a liar. "Where's your room?" I chirp, eager to change the subject.

"In here." Bailey leads me through double doors. This area contains the bedrooms, each with arched windows that stream in sunlight and panoramic views past the building tops, to the glorious Hudson. I see sailboats, and a barge being pushed by a cute red tugboat.

Bailey shows me her room. Her windows are draped in

velvety blue fabric, tied back with golden, braided ropes. Against one wall, she's set up what looks like wooden drying racks that hold fabric swaths—prints, stripes, and crisp geometrics.

"I call that my Inspiration Station," she explains, going over to it and shaking out a swath. "I hang up my favorites to inspire me. I've even helped make costumes for Mom's client who's a designer for Broadway shows."

"Oh. My. God. You're incredible!" I'm totally intimidated—Bailey's out of my league. These days I'm only talented at conniving. And I'm not into manipulating people I really like.

Bailey flounces down in a beanbag chair and pats the one next to her. "Thanks for the compliments. Here, come sit."

With her friendly invitation, my nerves settle down. "Want to advise me on the burlesque costumes?"

"Let's do it!" Bailey gathers drawing pads, fabric swatches, and a coffee can brimming with colored pencils. We google *burlesque* on her laptop. A bunch of fun costumes load onto the site—ones with feathers, jewels, and even bananas on them. "Let's use these to jump off of, make some sketches," she suggests.

I draw myself balancing on a giant 3D sun and color in my version of the yellow fringe bikini that Wilson created digitally. After my first shock at the skimpy costume, the provocative look has grown on me.

Bailey peeks over my shoulder. "Cool! Do you own that outfit?"

I laugh. "No, Aunt Carol would shit a brick if she saw me in that. Plus, an outfit like that would cost serious cash."

"Save your money. I have tons of fabrics. I can make it for you." She points to her industrial machine, up on a platform in a corner by the windows.

"Man, that would be a lot to ask."

"It'd be fun. Pay me back by helping me sketch costumes."

"Good trade." My first reaction is pure joy, followed by secret anticipation for Lacey's reaction when she finds out Bailey's level of involvement in my next party. What's my problem? I would never have thought about that kind of thing before. I'm becoming as wicked as the mean girls. I shrug off that feeling as I sketch.

Bailey's cell rings. She hoists herself out of the beanbag chair, fishes her cell out of her messenger bag, and flips it open. "Oh, hi, Ava, what's up?"

My nerves jangle. Ava's even icier than Lacey.

Bailey gives me a conspiratorial wink as she launches into a conversation. "Yeah, I invited the new girl over. . . . So what? I don't care. . . . Yeah, I'm going to perform at her burlesque party. . . . No, I'm not insane. What's Lacey's issue? . . . You don't have to agree with everything she says. Want in on it? . . . It'll be a riot, yeah. Not dumb. . . . Decide soon. . . . Girl, don't be hard-core stubborn. . . . Yeah, what?" Bailey shifts her head away from me and lowers her voice. "Later on that. Don't assume stuff," she whispers. "No! Suck it up." Bailey spins back toward me, and grins. "Okay, bye Avey-Baby. *Mwaah!*" She makes a lip-smack sound and clicks her cell shut.

I'm dying to pepper Bailey with a million questions about what Ava said about me, about Lacey, but I don't want to appear nosy. Instead, I strain to read Bailey's mind. My budding powers seemed temporarily blocked, probably because I don't relish manipulating Bailey. Still, the urge for info is irrepressible. "So, um, is Ava upset?"

Bailey plunks back down on her beanbag chair and shrugs off her buttery leather ballet slippers. "Here's the dirt. Ava says that Lacey still likes Ander. No, revise that thought. She doesn't like Ander, in the sense that she wants him back. She just hates the idea of anyone else having him—like *you*."

"Aha. That explains why Lacey was so evil to me from day one."

"What do you mean?" Bailey wiggles her toes in her purple tights.

"She saw me every morning, talking to Ander. My locker's right next to his, I mean, what do you expect? We would naturally say hi."

"So, what'd she do?"

"She gave me the stink eye. Told me, 'You wish!'"

Bailey laughs. "Sungirl, you are hokey. 'Stink eye' is such a hokey phrase."

I cringe. Wabash is rearing its clunky self again. "He's not quite my boyfriend." *Yet.*

"That's even worse," Bailey exclaims. "Lacey hates that you guys are friends. That he talks to you and you talk to him, and hang out and just, you know, enjoy each other's company."

"For real? That's too bizarre."

"No doubt in my mind. In a way, all of that talky-talk stuff is more intimate than getting it on." Bailey's eyes gleam as she delivers the next bit of juicy news. "Lacey told me that she and Ander used to go to her place and lie on her bed and they'd talk for hours with, like, just their shirts off. I'd bet that's what she misses the most. I can't picture Charlie doing that. He's no intellectual." Bailey erupts into gleeful cackles.

Jealousy stabs me. I hate hearing that Ander shared that heady part of himself with anyone but me. But it does help me understand why Lacey's feeling so distraught. I'm newly resolved to have Ander all to myself, to insure that he'll never talk up in Lacey's room with her ever again—clothes or no clothes. "How long were they together?"

"A long time. Two years. They broke up in December of sophomore year."

Another sharp pang hits me. I resent the years they shared. "That's quite a while. So, why did Lacey break up with him?"

Bailey curls a strand of hair around her finger as if she's having a hard time thinking of an accurate answer. "No one really knows."

"She never talked to you about it? I'm shocked. You guys were such good friends."

"I know…it's strange. Lacey *was* turned off by Ander limping on crutches."

"Only because of his soccer injury? That's a horrible reason."

"No, there was more—"

"Like what?" I sink back into the beanbag, not wanting to look overeager.

"She seemed scared. Scared and disgusted, and sad."

"Scared of what? Or who?"

"I don't know exactly. But that was when Ander and Charlie were having a problem. Fighting. Charlie felt really bad about causing Ander's injury. And Ander was starting to spend time around Charlie's older brother."

My nerves prick to alertness. Bailey's referring to *Wilson*. "Was Wilson involved in Lacey's breakup? That's farfetched."

Bailey shakes her head. "No clue. Lacey never said that. What she *did* say was that the scene at Ander's was uncomfortable. One time she went there with Charlie when Wilson was hanging out with Ander. She said Wilson gave her bad vibes. Charlie told me that, too. But I chalked it up to Charlie not liking his brother horning in on his friendships. I mean, Charlie and Ander have been friends since grade school."

It's my turn to shrug. "Ander and Wilson have lots in

common. They both like to talk about the state of the world, the future of publishing and social media and—"

Bailey gives me a hard stare, as if she's studying something in my face that wasn't evident before. "So, you hang out a lot with Wilson? I heard he doesn't live at home anymore. That he moved out even though he's still a senior."

"True." Not sure how much I want to tell Bailey. I trust her, but instinct warns me to hold back, especially with this new information about Wilson. Even with my powers, it makes me nervous that I'm not in control of how people see me. How Bailey sees me.

"Where does he live now? Have you been to his place?" She's studying me even harder.

"Once or twice. Wilson lives out in Coney Island."

"What's he doing out there? Doesn't he go to a school near us, in Fort Greene? That's a long commute. He and Charlie must've had a serious issue."

"It'd be interesting to find out more." Good excuse to question Wilson. Bring Ander along, too, so Wilson can't get up in my face with his mesmerizing charm. Maybe, back at my place, Ander and I could talk about the universe, the way he and Lacey did—without *any* clothes on.

After snacking on gourmet cheese, crackers and sparkling lemonade, Bailey and I design more costumes. She rummages around in various drawers, pulls out one spectacular fabric after another, and finds threads to match them.

Lady Tattersal, Bailey's character, will have a floral cape over a naughty Victorian-inspired bathing suit. She'll clutch a maroon parasol and wear high-button boots—items that Bailey actually has in her closet from one of her antiquing forays.

We sketch Cole and Jake's drag outfits—banana skirts with bikini halters that can be filled with coconuts. I'm starting another costume drawing, when I check my watch and let out a screech. "*Gah!* I've got to go, my aunt's cooking for me tonight."

On the way out, I weasel in a touchy question. "Do you still like Lacey, a little?"

Bailey bites her lip. "She can be nice. Lately, she's been acting like a jerk."

"Still, we should design her costume. Not a peace offering, but just in case she decides to perform. We want to make sure her outfit fits in with the style of the burlesque—so she doesn't mess us up." Bailey nods. "I'll talk to her," I say in a rush before Bailey can volunteer.

Her mouth twists in a cynical grimace. "You think she'll talk to you, huh?"

"I'll work my magic."

On the train home, I'm buzzing with renewed purpose and determination. I used to shy away from challenges. But I'm gaining a taste for them—especially when uncanny powers lend me an advantage.

I choose my approach the next day following bio, a class I share with Lacey but none of her groupies. Ander isn't in this section, either, so he won't cause an inadvertent roadblock. Following Lacey out the door, I tap her lightly on the shoulder and dance around to the front of her. "Did you decide if you're performing?"

Lacey screws up her face in an obvious attempt to look fierce. "You should be so lucky. That last party of yours was a bust. I told you I'd let you know."

"Yellow Party was amateur hour, compared to what Burlesque will be. Here's the thing, I need to know now, Ms. Givem Heck—that's your stage name. You would so rock as Givem."

"Anyone tell you that the hard sell is a turnoff?" Lacey tries to scoot around me. "You'll have to wait."

"I won't, though." I blast her with my scorching Sungirl smile—the kind that almost burns, but not as hot as on Ava that day. I know Lacey feels the heat by the way her hand races to her chest. "There's a pretty senior girl clamoring for your spot," I warn in a low sizzle. "Plus, everyone who's anyone will be there." I pause for dramatic effect. "Even your bestie, Ava."

"You don't know what you're talking about. She'd never go to your stupid party. She told you that last week." Lacey sounds sure, though she's stopped trying to wind around me.

"I have the inside scoop," I promise. "I was at Bailey's. Ava called. Said she was thinking of joining the lineup. Bailey's already designed Ava a costume." This part isn't true —yet. But Ava will be all the more intrigued once she knows that Lacey is considering performing—and vice versa. "You don't want to be the only one not there, do you? This party will go down in history."

Lacey throws back her head and howls, causing her milky hair to pour down her back. "Now I know you're nuts."

I'm filled with that old longing for thick, silky hair like Lacey's, until I remember that my own hair *is* thicker and wavier than ever. "You'll be the nut," I snap, "when you're a no-show and Burlesque gets rave reviews on a zillion podcasts and instagram sites. When my meetup parties go viral, don't you want to say you were an early participant? It could make you a star, too."

The glint in Lacey's eyes is unmistakable.

She's in the trap, a voice in me purrs, *now snap it closed.* "Bailey and I designed you the most incredible costume." I focus all of my brute strength on emitting those mystical rays of energy at my disposal. It's as if I'm turning my white-hot thoughts into one taut, athletic muscle that, at a second's notice, I can flex for a knockout punch. This is fiendish fun.

"What's the costume?" Lacey's voice oozes curiosity. "Not that I'm going."

"A bikini, beaded with rhinestones." I don't mention that the jewels are cheap costume baubles. "You'll have a matching headpiece. You could be the highlight of the line-up," I add reverently, "and the most gorgeous girl there."

"Is your dad a salesman?" Lacey snorts. "'Cause you're using every cheap trick in the book, trying to clinch this deal."

"Salesman, you could say that." A sick feeling flickers through me as I think of my father's list. Hard sell—not even the half of it. But I'm not breaking any laws like he did. "You have until tomorrow morning to decide," I snarl, unable to keep up my slick facade with the shameful memory of my father's deeds.

"We're done here," Lacey says. "So let me on by."

"Twenty-four hours before that pretty senior nabs your part," I caution, as smoothly as belladonna disguised in spicy wine slides down a throat.

I wait all day for a note from Lacey, a text, even an obnoxious snipe as we pass each other in the hall. Nothing. And then, as I hop off the bus on my way home, my cell pings. I snap it open.

I'm in but just biz no hanging out. Lacey

"Score!" I pump my fist in victory, not caring if people on the street think I'm mental.

13

---

*Charm is a way of getting the answer yes without having asked any
clear question.*
—Albert Camus

T
he next few days are filled with taking the
performers' measurements, rushing to Bailey's
after school to work on the costumes, and
indulging in major shopping sprees. Sungirl, a.k.a. yours
truly, will need mad outfits to uphold her new level of visibil-
ity. I toss out my boring skirts, baggy cotton blouses and my
corny Little-House-on-the-Prairie cotton print dresses.

In the space of two days, I plow through the entire four-
hundred-dollar October check my mother sends early.
Thankfully, Aunt Carol helped co-signed a teen checking
account for me when I got here, or I'd be begging her in vain
for permission to withdraw funds. I splurge on tight, clingy
tops that show cleavage, a chic pair of hip-hugging black
pants, glitzy costume jewelry, two pairs of insanely high

heels, and a bitchin' yellow trench coat that reminds me of Yellow Party—the part before Lacey got there—when I first felt my strength. It advertises, in no uncertain terms: SUNGIRL.

I'm not done yet. My closet's only half full. Shamelessly, I beg my mother for more cash in one of our first conversations since moving.

"You don't know how expensive it is here, Mother. I have to dress up for school. To even get a burger, I spend a good twenty dollars with tip."

"I thought Aunt Carol was cooking for you. You know how to cook, too. I taught you how to make meatloaf and tuna casserole."

I heave a great, impatient sigh. "Sure, I cook some meals. But I need a social life. You want me to make friends?" I aim the next sharpened arrow that's bound to sting and fling it through the phone. "You don't want me to be a wallflower like I was back in Wabash. Or get desperate like Dad."

I know that as much resentment as Mom feels about her marital breakup, and as much hatred as she expresses toward Dad, she still has sympathy for the guy—and by default, me.

"You sound different," Mom notes.

"How?"

"Remote."

"I am. By six hundred miles or so. I didn't ask to be sent away."

"I was going through a hard time. I, uh . . ."

"I know, Mom. I felt so bad for you." The old, dreadful pain shoots through me, remembering how I'd give her head rubs when she cried, or cook dinner for us when she was too wiped out. Then, I feel my new, dark heart harden—clay in a fiery kiln—into heavy stoneware. *Your parents were never there for you*, it seethes, *they were too busy being screwed up.*

"Of course I don't want you feeling like a wallflower. I

want you to have friends," she insists. "Have you made friends? Do you have some good friends?"

I'm fighting hard to lure people in. Even with enhanced beauty and wit, it's a pitched battle. Out of my emptiness, I feel another twinge of pity—for my father, surprisingly. Did he ever feel as frantic? It's a real struggle to build up a loyal flock. I haven't talked to him since he was thrown in jail. I might never speak to him again.

I think about Wilson Warren and his complicated gift to me. I'll keep confronting him, too. Force him to define the harmful limits of my power. I don't want to hurt Bailey, my mom, or Ander. Perhaps my events could raise money for a charity, or for my mom to get a better house, or to help propel Ander into print. Publish his novel . . . if he's writing one.

Ander. I think of the heat of our kisses and his private notebook. *I can't wait to violate it.* Violate it? Why, I ask silently, why if my powers might also be used for good do I always end up thinking of the worst actions? It's like I can't sustain the good parts. A shudder of fear passes through me.

"Dorianna? Are you still there?" my mother asks.

"Um, yeah. I've met some interesting kids." It seems as if I was lost in a netherworld of chaos, but according to my watch, it was only a few seconds. "Very sophisticated kids." I let that sink in before I go on. "So, you can imagine why I might need. . ."

"Okay, okay, I see your point," Mom says in a guilty rush. "I did get paid the other day. I only need half of that for the mortgage and—"

"Only what you can afford," I say in a reasoned, yet deadened voice.

When we hang up, I'm filled with a unsavory stew of remorse and perverse satisfaction. As much as I've been frustrated by Mom's problems, I've never manipulated her the way I just did. It's easy, wielding this power that's forever welling up in me now. It's become as organic to me as my blood. Yet, it's alien. Or am I my own flu, using my body to multiply bad aspects of myself?

I picture a bunch of kaleidoscope bugs, all with my leering image and multiplied, all with amoral cores, whirring furiously inside me. Too much past the tipping point to get rid of them now, and besides, I'd have no idea how. I pray for a few more innocent moments. Moments where my old, kind self can still peek through before I'm engulfed in night.

Right after the second installment of money comes, I dash off to Bloomie's with Bailey. We have a blast trying on outfit after outfit and doing catwalks for each other. After that, I treat her to lunch at a fancy midtown café.

I sneak the bulging bags of clothing upstairs while Aunt Carol is cooking dinner. All week, I revel in wearing new outfits to school. After all, Lacey and Ava always have a new look. As Sungirl, it's my duty to upstage them. It's expected of me now that I'm cultivating stardom. I'm delighted that Tory and her crowd fawn over me, amazed by my new fashion sense. Cat, who normally wears boyish T-shirts with slogans, starts to echo my low-cut shirts and tight black-flared pants look. Even Lacey, who I supply with a constant stream of compliments, is slowly coming around.

"Nice necklace," she admits coolly in passing. "Where'd you get it?"

"On Fifth Avenue. Designer stuff, you know."

"How's my pinup outfit coming along?" Lacey ventures.

"Amazing! I was over at Bailey's yesterday," I say, emphasizing Bailey's name, "and she was hand-stitching the jewels on your costume—very elegant look. You must come over for a fitting this weekend," I add casually, as if I'm almost living there now. The shock and jealousy in Lacey's eyes is pure nirvana.

Bailey would be pissed to discover I'm getting so chummy with Lacey. I'll find a way to finesse that, too—to insist to Bailey that each friendly exchange is necessary for the benefit of the upcoming performance.

My aunt makes frequent couched references to the cost and cleavage of my new threads. "Funny, I haven't seen you in that before. Is it new? Looks expensive. Make sure to stretch out your mom's checks." And, "That's a very *different* style for you. I don't remember that shirt. Did you bring that to New York with you?"

I provide vague answers. "It was lying around," I say, or "This shirt was looser, but it shrunk in the wash."

All of this bitchiness and conniving is exhausting, but I can't seem to edit it—it flies from my mouth before I know what I'm saying. By Thursday, I feel as if I want to give back to Aunt Carol. She's been patient and nice to me, and my better side is poking through. I want to do a good deed, in part to prove to myself I still can. "I'd like to cook you a special dinner," I announce when she gets home from work. "A vegetarian dish? I know you like that."

"That would be lovely." Her tired eyes brighten.

"Any favorite veggies?"

"I'm not picky. Anything's fine."

"You work so hard. C'mon, you name it."

"I like cauliflower," she giggles. "Au gratin and with carrots, too?"

"Over brown rice?"

"Sounds delightful."

I grab the reusable shopping totes and head out. It's fun picking out menu items at the grocery: fresh cauliflower, carrots, onion and garlic, along with organic brown rice, and milk for the sauce. My aunt likes granola, so I toss that in, plus yogurt and cookies for me.

After I unpack all of the grocery bags, I put on a mix that Wilson gave me, of Gothic trance. It's good for slicing the veggies with the sharp kitchen knife, but by the time I get to making the sauce and setting the table, I want more upbeat fare, so I change the playlist to rock mixed with a few sentimental but satisfying pop tunes from home.

My aunt pokes her head in the kitchen. "*Mmm,* smells wonderful."

"Hope so. It's almost ready. Have a seat in the dining room."

Funny, I'm much more excited about seeing my aunt's reactions to the meal than I thought I'd be. I feel literally lighter. Could it be that all of my overwhelming surges of dark energy and shady impulses have melted away with this act of kindness? My earlier impulse to ask for more money to help fund the next party fades. Why burden my aunt again? It would ruin the closeness of the moment. I could even get a part-time job after school, at the grocery or at Havana's, to help cover my new clothes and the parties. Wheeling around to hang up my apron on the pantry door, I see Aunt Carol's pocketbook hanging there. Don't even think about it, I admonish myself. Don't spoil things. You can be good.

Proudly, I present the dishes—first the steamy casserole, then rolls I heated in the oven with fresh butter. I pour natural sodas made from mixing cranberry juice with seltzer. I light two candles I bought as a last-minute table decoration, and we shake out our napkins.

"*Mmm,* this is the best vegetarian dish I've ever had," my aunt exclaims after the first couple of bites. It's great to hear such appreciation in her voice.

"I'm happy to do something for you, Aunt Carol. You've been generous, putting me up and all. Must be a lot after living alone . . ." I stop, hoping I haven't broached a painful subject, about never getting married or having kids of her own, and how lonely that might be.

My aunt only raises her glass in a toast. "To my lovely niece and her wonderful cooking." After that, the sounds are of us wolfing down the food. Finally, Aunt Carol wipes her mouth with her napkin. "Did I hear you talking about another party?"

"Yes, Bailey and I are figuring out a dance-performance party."

"What fun." My aunt winks. "Do you have a special guy you want to dance with?"

"Aunt Carol!"

She laughs. "I live solo, but I'm no stranger to love. I've had two great boyfriends."

I'm shocked. What happened to them, if they were so nice? "There's one guy I like to talk to."

"Wonderful! What's he like?"

"He has a notebook he writes in. He wants to tackle a novel, get it published."

"Ah, a writer—very ambitious. Has he read any of it to you?"

"Not yet." If Ander doesn't make that move soon, I'll get it done. My mind fills with ways I could tease it from his pocket—in class if he sits in front of me, on the subway, *if I slide a sneaky arm down his back.*

How thieving can I get? The nefarious impulses that I thought I'd so successfully conquered by the happiness of doing something for someone else spring up like warty three-headed dragons, ready to blast fire. This upsets me so much I grab the dinner plates and run into the kitchen, away from any chance I'll blurt out something rude. "I'll clean up the kitchen, Aunt Carol. Take the night off."

"Really? Oh, thanks." Her grateful, weary voice filters

from the dining room to the kitchen, where I'm hunching over the sink.

I'm sweating and my heart starts racing as if I've taken a really toxic drug. *Take it,* growls a demanding voice in my head, *take it now.*

With dishes left in the sink, soap bubbles on my trembling hands, and in a frantic daze I hardly recall, I steal ninety dollars from my aunt's purse on the pantry door.

Sweating, I press the start button on the dishwasher. I'm itching to run upstairs and hide. Sick with disgust, I long to put the money back. But if my aunt walks in, and sees me stuffing cash back into her wallet . . . I couldn't handle that.

There's time to put it back, argues my better side. You can still risk it. But that overpowering muscle, trying to strangle my very being, won't allow me to take the action. I'm weary of fighting these negative bursts—so weak and weary. This must be one of the consequences Wilson warned me about.

I'll spend the money on something to entertain people, I rationalize. Entertaining, that's a good cause. Walking fast toward the stairs, I pass by my aunt, alone on the couch.

"Do you want to sit for a while, and listen to music?" she asks. Makes sense. We had a perfect time together before I went and ruined it. No wonder she looks befuddled.

"I'd love to but, um, I have to write an essay for school. It's due tomorrow." Truth be told, I do have more Dostoyevsky pages to read for Lit.

"I'd be happy to line edit for you, anytime," she replies, probably to cover up the awkwardness of the lost moment. "After all, I'm a wordsmith at my job."

I call from the head of the stairway, "Generous offer. Take you up on it soon." I lock my door, the door my aunt has never, ever barged into. With clammy hands, I remove the stolen cash from my pocket. Choosing a book from my bookshelf, I open it midway and stick in the four twenties and the ten.

Staring at the money, I'm torn—part of me wants to pad into my aunt's room and plunk it on a chair, where she'll assume she misplaced it. Another part of me weighs the ethics of taking from my mother, struggling with the mortgage, to taking from my aunt, who has a rent-stabilized apartment, no kids, and a good job. I know this is a wrongheaded argument, but it brings me to my third thought.

Bottom line, I need money for my next event. And I have cash in hand. *You're already bad, so what's the difference? It's too late to be a goody-goody,* my inner voice shouts. The dragon part of me, sticking its scaly neck out and breathing fire, has won.

So be it. I slam the book shut and stick it firmly back on the shelf.

That's when I remember the thumb drive that I forced Wilson to copy the Burlesque video on. *That* could settle the argument raging in me: Am I still a tiny bit good, or am I incorrigibly, fatally corrupted?

I retrieve the drive from my pack, and slide it into my laptop.

Chuckling, I watch the ringmaster capybara, in top hat and tails, announce the show and gesture to the viewer with Wilson's pearl-tipped cane. This part is funny, but by the time I'm about to appear on camera, my hands are trembling. I clench my arms around my chest and lean forward to study my every onscreen movement.

There I am, balancing on the enormous, happy-faced orb. Smiling, having fun. I uncross my arms, breath a huge sigh of relief, and press the pause button.

This is clear proof that my karma is repaid, that my gift of dinner to my aunt has canceled out my other bad behavior. Wilson was wrong.

I fling myself onto my bed and laugh with relief until tears roll down my cheeks and into my ears. "I can still have powers and be a little bit good," I murmur.

Abruptly, I stop rolling around when a soundless voice whispers, *Ah, but there's more.* Who are you and how do you know? I ask myself. But I know. It's that new, malicious being in me. Panic upends every hair on my scalp. *Watch the rest of the trailer,* it demands. I press Play.

After a moment of black, I reappear, glowering out at myself. "Yeah, you, thieving con," shrills my onscreen self. "A home-cooked dinner won't erase your core darkness." My likeness erupts in a punishing cackle.

I play it again, to the end—same dreadful diatribe. "Screw this!" I yell to my laptop. How could this video thing know what I just did? It's not alive. Did this garbage go viral? My followers. Gah! What will they think now?

I log onto YouTube and type in "Sungirl at the Beach," and when the video comes up I play it. So far so good. I'm frolicking in the water, singing the Sun Song, and juggling. I see only that devious look, and the arrogance—nothing newer, nothing more disturbing.

"Please, oh, please," I mutter. "Let it only be on that thumb drive, not on all of the videos." My heart leaps . . . a beat too early. Onscreen, my likeness pauses from her juggling and snickers at the viewer—me—in a crazed manner. "Yes, my pretty," she growls. "It's true. I'm changing—*and so are you.*"

This isn't happening. I hunch over and clutch my ribs as I play the thing again. At least the YouTube verbal shit-storm isn't as bad as the one on this copy, I rationalize. What can I do? Each video is changing in its own way, at its own pace.

It's horrid not being able to control this. It's as if some insidious spam keeps infiltrating no matter what.

Scrolling down to see the latest YouTube comments, I gasp.

the lady doth protest too much—cackle, cackle, cackle

u might b hella changin but u still shine big

Sungirl's turning into a sun witch. Bring it on, evil girl

hangin' out @ sungirl.com to watch u turn b-b-bad to the bone

There's a huge amount of hits—over five thousand. Where do these flipping trolls come from? I can't take my evil outburst, even if my viewers can.

I make a beeline over to my bookshelf to get my aunt's money. "I'll return it," I pledge, but my hand freezes in midstream. Finally, I understand the phrase "frozen in place"—more than I ever wanted to.

Wilson might've lied about not altering the YouTube beach scene, but this copy? He had nothing to do with this. He was right after all. These consequences are unacceptable. I'll have to work harder to thwart them. That revolting trailer on the drive cannot stay on my desk. No one can ever, ever see it. I hide it in my bookshelf, behind a row of novels.

Where does Wilson—the so-called Prince of Darkness—get his powers? How exactly has he transferred them to me? And who's behind the whole operation? That question is almost the scariest part.

14

Love is an exploding cigar we willingly smoke.
—Lynda Barry

I'm the budding queen of the lunchroom now. All heads turn as I float in. I sense Lacey advance toward me, and hesitate, perplexed as to where to sit since Bailey and Cole have moved to my table. So have the peripheral people who once orbited Lacey, the now-deposed queen.

Tough-girl Ava is the one holdout. I'm determined to turn her around. I grab my chance when Cole and Ander are off getting food, and Ava is deftly weaving my way.

She pauses at my table. "What possessed you to tell Lacey that I was considering performing in your pinup line? Don't speak for me. That wasn't cool in the least."

"But . . ." I keep my radiant smile on simmer so it doesn't scorch Ava again. "You must want in on the burlesque. What's your favorite color?"

"I never said I wanted in."

I look her over appraisingly. "You'd look great in green. What do you wear, a size two?"

"S-size four," Ava stutters.

I raise my brows. "Wow! You're so slim, I could swear you're only a two." I let that observation sink in, and then add, "Rehearsals start soon."

Ava flicks her bangs to the sides of her elegant, carved face. "Rehearsals?"

"I'm thinking two. The first will be at Bailey's, on Saturday? The next one will be in the gym the following Friday, during lunch. We'll do the line dance and then people will practice their solos." Ava's eyes glitter at the word *solo*. "Relay that to Lacey." I increase the decibel on my smile. *"You lovelies won't want to miss it."*

"Won't want to miss it," Ava echoes uncertainly. Scanning the room to find Lacey, she shuffles away like a drugged patient.

I must've mesmerized her. Wow, I'm getting better at that. I watch Ava sit with Lacey and begin to gab. Both slip occasional side-glances my way. My panic over the awful changes in my videos is overshadowed by this heady new thrill.

I seem to be developing an uncanny sense of hearing, too. Even though I can't hear every word or sound, it's as if the gist of any conversation I focus on seeps into my head via an enchanted router. Only if I close my eyes and really concentrate . . .

Dorianna has a nerve. That's Ava.

Ava actually called me by name instead of saying, "that *new* girl". I strain harder to intuit their words.

A solo, though, Lacey says, *—could use it for your modeling portfolio.*

—any other director would video me.

Not for free.

Singular thrills skip up my spine. Domination is such a high.

Someone's heels click toward me and then they put down a tray. "Are you meditating?"

"Uh, no." I snap my eyes open and brush back my hair.

It's Tory, radiant in a white dress with black detailing.

"Taking a moment." I rub my eyes. "I was up late posting on my fan sites. Instagram and stuff."

"Poor Sungirl. Internet divas are so overbooked," Tory coos. She fishes a digital phone with a pink cover from her pocketbook and proceeds to cluck over me like a medieval chambermaid as she inputs data. "Do you have rehearsals figured out? I'll text the performers. What about the fittings? Will you need help with the refreshments, or is Bailey getting a caterer?"

I give up on "listening" to Ava and Lacey to answer Tory's rapid-fire questions. "I need more posts that link to my Website, my Instagram and stuff," I tell her. "More posts from my, you know, *fans*." I smile warmly at Tory in remembrance that she was my very first one.

Part of Tory's job now is to visit sites and proclaim, using various pseudonyms, how amazing Sungirl is, and how her upcoming parties are going to go down in history. Tory is also instructed to enlist friends to post, tweet, pin and help champion the cause.

Artfully, she thwacks her satiny ponytail over a shoulder. "Oh, Sungirl, listen to this: A bunch of amaaa-zing influencers want to interview you for their podcasts and You Tubes. They're the crème de la crème of social media queens, with a jillion followers. There's one site called PartiOn and one called Rumpusflowr. And, yeah, one called KupkakeDreemz. Oh. My. God—the KupkakeDreemz one has such cute graphics. Like, dancing pink cupcakes and floaty angels with purple sparkles and clouds floating around them? Anyway, when can they, like, FaceTime you and stuff?"

I'm pumped. To be featured on the hottest media sites is exactly what I need to blow it out of the park and go viral. "Wow, great work, Tory. Um . . . maybe tomorrow after school, at Bailey's. Can you stack up Sungirl interviews and promos for me? We can knock them out one after the other. Boom, boom, boom. Totally spread the word about Burlesque."

"Perfect. Right—on it." Tory's thumbs text at warp speed.

Ander lopes over, balancing a burger, a cookie, and a carton of chocolate milk. He deposits them on the table and offers up a warm smile. "How's my Sungirl?"

"Sungirl is very busy," Tory clucks between texts.

"How's your writing?" I peek around to Ander's back pocket to see if his notebook is tucked in its normal spot. Of course it is.

"Writing's slow," Ander manages through a mouthful of burger.

"Bro, don't talk fulla chew." Cole joins us with a tortilla. "Where's Bailey?" he asks me.

"Not sure."

"How can that be? You and Bailey are the Velcro Twins," he says.

I give him an innocent shrug. Bailey might need some appeasing. Earlier, we had an uncomfortable exchange.

"You're getting a little too tight with Ava and Lacey," she'd said. "I heard you were complimenting Lacey on her new handbag. What's up with that?"

Who blabbed this? It sucks how fast word spreads, even between enemies—like a flame in a paper-goods store. "I told you, don't worry, Bailey. It's for the performance. I'm buttering them up."

She frowned, but tried to make a joke out of it. "Don't

butter them up too much. It's fattening." I chuckled, even though she was insinuating that I was so insatiable for followers that I was literally eating people, like in Wilson's capybara video.

Now, trying to forget about the snafu with Bailey, I sidle up to Ander and purr, "Want to come over? You can write while I noodle around online."

"Yeah?" Ander leans back in his chair and surveys the lunchroom tables. He still has the annoying habit of taking quick inventory of who's sitting nearby before he gets too affectionate with me. It gives me flashes of my old insecurity.

I have to remind myself who I'm becoming: beautiful, powerful, not someone to mess with. I reach out and gently brush back a lock of Ander's hair that's fallen low on his forehead. His eyes stay on me—smoky gray and gleaming with desire—as he leans in and whispers, "Let's go."

"We'll talk about the state of the world," I giggle.

He gives me a puzzled look.

Luck's with us. My aunt's note on the kitchen table says she needs to work late, and that there's leftover casserole in the fridge. Good, no interruptions.

After I lifted the cash from my aunt's purse, it took her a few days to ask me about it. I'd acted blameless as a child, and suggested that the cleaning lady had taken it. Aunt Carol had rubbed her temples, muttering that Frannie had worked for her for years without incident.

That forced me to improvise in a way that I didn't relish. "I've seen her snooping and opening drawers."

Although Aunt Carol fired Frannie, I now notice that my aunt no longer leaves her bag on the pantry door. I shrug off the guilt.

Ander's here. Time for celebration! And maybe more.

I warm him a slice of leftover casserole in the microwave —guys are always hungry, aren't they? I take cookies to my room and put on a rock mix, while Ander revises the evite copy using Bailey's address in place of the boardwalk.

"Let's watch that capybara video again," he suggests. "You still have the copy on memory stick Warren gave you?"

"Can't find it," I lie. A shudder goes through me.

"Too bad." Ander checks out my books. "You like *The Hunger Games,* too."

"Oh, yeah, great plot." Hurrying over, I weasel between him and the bookshelf. Plucking the novel from his hands, I slide it back in place. Please don't pull out any more books or you'll find that incriminating drive copy, I plead silently. But I say casually, "Relax, take off your shoes."

"Good idea." He kicks off his sneaks, tosses his jacket and notebook on my desk chair, and then asks me where the bathroom is.

As I wait for him, I eye his notebook. It'd be so easy to open it, read his latest entry and find out if he's actually writing anything substantial. Padding over to the chair, I'm hyperaware of every swishing sound my skirt makes. My fingertips tingle as I reach for the notebook. It's in my hands. *Finally.* Holding my breath, I flick it open.

The bathroom door clunks and suddenly Ander is at my side. "Hey, don't! You weren't looking at that, were you?" He swipes the notebook out of my hands.

"I . . . I was just going to ask you to read me a passage, that's all." I glance up at him with a primitive fear. Will he reject me now, knowing that I'll steal what I'm not given? It's so, so hard, not using my powers to sway him. They're boiling up, hissing silently, *Do it, mesmerize him...you did it to Ava, so it's easy for you now.*

"It's not the right time," Ander says. "I'm—"

"Let me guess." I'll save him from himself. "You hate reading out loud. I hate reading out loud, too. In fact, I forgot all of my lines one time in class, when I had to recite Shakespeare." I suppress a fitful giggle, as I watch him shove the notebook in his pants pocket. "Are you mad at me?" I squeak.

"Guess not. I understand why you're curious."

I'm grateful. He's defending my suspicious move as if he's talking himself into believing I'm innocent. My shadow self crawls back into its invisible cave.

Can I?" Ander points to my bed.

I'm glad I made the bed this morning with my pretty quilt. "Be my guest, mister."

He plunks down, rolls onto his back, and lodges his hands behind his head. "Ah, that's better." He waves me over. "Come, talk to me, Sungirl."

His shoulders, arched up, are commanding in their bold curves. His shirt hem is raised just enough to reveal tight abs underneath. I swallow hard. I can't believe Ander is sprawled out on my bed, on my covers, my pillow. This is too amazing, too sexy.

I lie down and arrange myself so I'm facing him. That peculiar translucency in Ander's eyes makes me feel as if I can see right through them into his mind. Yet he's harder to read than Lacey or Ava. Not sure why. My heart booms so loudly he must hear it.

"You have beautiful hair," he murmurs as he brushes his fingers through it—a move that alternately relaxes and makes every nerve in me sing.

"You're kind of handsome yourself." I kiss his forehead, then his cheek. We snuggle together. God, he's warm, and his hard chest pressed into my soft one is a revelation. I feel wanted, a real first. We stay tucked together like this, him stroking my hair, me snuggling into his neck.

After a while, I'm aware that my jaded side is flying over

the scene like a surreal bird of prey, studying us. It feels infinitely satisfying that I've gotten Ander on my bed, as Bailey said he and Lacey have done, many, many times. Somehow, this aspect is almost as important as Ander's actually lying next to me, breath to breath, foot to foot, and chest to chest.

I try to ignore a question perched on my lips, but it's impossible. "Did you love Lacey?"

Startled, he raises his head in one hand, in order to look over at me. "Why would you ask me that?"

"Someone said you two used to lie on her bed"—bare chest to chest, I think—"and talk."

"Bailey is such a gossip. She needs a lecture." Ander's voice is hard. Scary.

"It's just that, I want you to like me as much as—"

"Shhh. Don't. Don't compare yourself to Lacey. It's different, you're different."

"In a good way?"

"In a good way." His tone warms, eases.

"Did you like me when you first met me?"

He hesitates. "It took a little time. I wasn't looking."

I swear I hear his mind saying that he wasn't into me, that he thought I was plain, bucktoothed. "You'd just gotten over a bad breakup," I say on his behalf.

"I told you, let's not discuss that."

"Can I ask one thing, and then drop it?"

He sighs wearily. "If you must."

"Why did she break up with you?"

His voice is clipped. "Who said she broke up with me?"

"Bailey."

"Screw Bailey. Why do you like her? Is that what you spend your time talking about?"

"No." My insides pinch. I'm taking a risk by pressing this, especially so early on in the relationship. I need to stop, and yet I need to set it to rest. "I have to feel comfortable," I explain.

His shoulder muscles ease under my arm, and he relaxes back onto the pillow. "Lacey didn't like that I was injured. She had this fantasy of being with the awesome, invincible soccer captain, the alpha dog, and when I was injured, well . . ."

Ander's no fool. There must be something to Lacey. Ander wouldn't give a totally superficial brat the time of day. I remember Lacey clucking over Ava like a worried mom, and her soft hair flowing over Bailey's shoulder when she lured her from my table. She makes people feel loved, feel special. They flock to her in order to bask in her attention. That's what I want, for people to bask in my sunlight. Is fake sunlight poison? Is hers more real than mine?

"Her dumping you for an injury is a stupid reason," I say. "There has to be more." I remember what Bailey said about Lacey being over at Charlie's when Wilson was there.

Ander shifts away from me. He rolls onto his back and looks up at the ceiling. "She didn't like me hanging out with Warren."

I spring to attention. Is Ander reading *my* mind? Not sure why this stirs me so much, except it bugs me that Lacey knows Wilson, too. "Why would Lacey care about Wilson or who he hung out with? I didn't know she even knew him."

Ander chews on his thumbnail. "She was getting close to Charlie," he says with bitterness. "Could be that she didn't want Warren gossiping to me about what she was doing with Charlie."

"Except Wilson's not that kind of gossip," I reason. "Is there something specific that Lacey doesn't like about Wilson?"

Ander stops talking. He rubs his eyes with his fists. Then he cracks his knuckles. In my heightened state of awareness,

I sense him going over tiny details about Lacey and Wilson, as he strains to remember old conversations and events.

"Look, I don't know," he finally answers. "All I know is that I got friendly with Warren at Charlie's party, the day before Charlie kicked the shit out of me in that horrendous game. I *know* that Lacey and Charlie were messing around before that. Maybe Warren creeped her out, maybe he even came onto her. We all know Warren doesn't hold back when it comes to the fairer sex." Ander grins, clearly satisfied with his use of Wilson's favorite turn of phrase.

I'm reminded of that last time I was over at Wilson's and I almost kissed him. I'm thinking about his lethal charm. *And mine.*

"I always figured Lacey just wanted Charlie, and I was in the way," Ander continues. "But it *was* weird how Warren moved out right after Charlie and Lacey became a couple."

Lacey is beautiful, Lacey is powerful, and Wilson loves white swans, spreading their wings. It follows that he may have tried to come on to Lacey. Or more than that—inject his toxic charm in her the way he did with me. My chest goes cold.

Ander must sense it. He pulls the quilt over me. "You okay? Enough questions?"

"I guess so." I catch Ander's gaze and hold it. "I'm getting a little friendly with Lacey."

"What? I thought you hated her, the way she treated you on that first day of school."

"She's coming over for a costume fitting soon. And she'll be at the rehearsal. I could slip her a question about Wilson."

"Absolutely not!" Ander shakes his head emphatically. "Stay away from that bitch. She'll mess you up. Besides, it's my business, my problem, and I've moved on."

Ander's objections seem way more complicated than simply protecting her. I don't like that. Apparently, it shows.

"Oh, now you're in a bad mood?" he accuses. "So not fair. That's why I didn't want to talk about this. I warned you."

I don't want the time with Ander to sour like this, either. I invited him here to talk, to cuddle, and to feel close. His irritation at me is my fault. I need to switch this up, lure him back into my corner. And I want to keep this natural, so I know it's real.

Should I tell him about what's happening to me? Part of me wants to, in the name of honesty. I want to confess that it isn't just his imagination that my hair's grown thicker, my lips are fuller, my skin creamier. I want to tell him how giddy it makes me. I wish he knew how I'm testing my powers, experimenting with ways to charm people, like Tory, into doing my bidding. I'm itching to tell him that Wilson turned me on to these powers. But I can't. I absolutely can't.

I'm tempted to confess the bad stuff, too: How terror-stricken I was when I realized I'd literally burned Ava with my hatred. How that copy on the thumb drive and the YouTube video changed. If I show him the corrupted Burlesque teaser, what would he think? He would flip out and dump me. I have to keep carrying this weight on my own. It must remain my secret with Wilson. I'm not ready to break up before Ander is officially my boyfriend. I like him way too much.

That's why I vow to never use my glamour on Ander—that's what it was called in medieval times. After I watched that drive copy, I'd looked the word up on Dictionary.com and shuddered as I read: *Glamour: an enchantment, illusory romantic powers, occult charm.* This is the exact description of what I'm doing. I certainly could've used glamour in middle school—on Len, on the kids who ignored me, on my father to stop his embarrassing behavior. I could use it on Ander.

No. I need to keep the relationship with Ander pure, sacred. Love doesn't jive with lust for power. I need to know that he's attracted to my *real* personality, not my conjured one. It's so tempting to push it, though. It's working so well with Tory. It's even working on Wilson. That last time out at his place, his attraction to me was a palpable force, and I'd shaped it for my own benefit. Gotten that digital copy, even if the results were damning.

I played the player.

Now, cuddled up so close to Ander that my uncanny ears can hear his pulse bumping fast inside his neck, I shake off a powerful urge to use magic. Instead, I reach out to hug him. "I'm okay. I'm not upset. I want us to be real with each other, Ander. That's all. I want us to be free of immature, jealous games."

He eases out of his frown. Bestows me with one of his rare smiles. "Sounds good to me. Did I tell you that I love your mind? Did I tell you I love that you're so into books?"

I kiss his neck, where the pulse beats. "By the way, I understand why you don't like reading out loud. But maybe I can borrow your, um, notebook, and read a few pages in the privacy of my room. I'm sure it's incredible."

Ander's anxiety spikes up and pierces my solar plexus. Darn, I said the wrong thing again. He's panicked. Then, nothing. My extraordinary sensibilities aren't always correct.

"I'm not ready," he mumbles into my hair. "It turns me on that you want to read it, though. Soon, sexy lady."

Soon, my unbidden voice answers silently, *soon enough I'll find a way.*

I push the voice away in disgust. Not now, I beg.

Ander begins to kiss me. Moving his hand slowly down my back, he rests it in the small part, where it curves. When his palm strokes me in circles, energy radiates inward, to my belly, the heat between my legs. I explore his mouth with the tip of my tongue. Run my hands down his rounded yet taut shoulder muscles. They curve gracefully into his arms, and then elbows and then solid wrists, each corded with strength.

"You're beautiful," he murmurs as he smoothes his hand over the flare of my hip and then around to my front. Eases it up, under my shirt, cupping my breast on top of my bra. Electric waves of pleasure spread all through me. My heart beats crazy fast.

Thankfully, I thought to wear nice things under my clothes. I have on my new crimson lingerie, edged in blood-red lace. In gentlemanly fashion, he stops himself from pushing his hand under it, or lifting my shirt over my head. I hear his ragged breathing, and his inner voice, lecturing him to wait, not to rush so much.

"You're amazing," I whisper in his ear and then lick it. My own hand explores his chest, then inches down to the tight ridges of his belly, and the soft hair that covers it. I linger there, wanting to savor each part.

We're settling into another round of slow kissing, when an inner alarm in me goes off, followed by the muffled clap of the front door closing. "My aunt's here!" I break free of Ander's arms, and leap up.

"Holy crap!" He stumbles to his feet, leaning on his better leg to get his balance.

"Dorianna?" Aunt Carol calls from the bottom of the stairs. "I'm home early, since they cancelled the meeting." Another pause. "You up there? I saw your coat. Dorianna?"

There's a sound of footsteps climbing the stairs, a quick knock and then the door swings open. My aunt's mouth goes slack as she stares at Ander, scrambling into his sneakers, and at me, hurriedly combing my hair. "Well, hello?" she blurts.

"You didn't knock." I turn. Not meaning to, I send a white-hot blast of anger her way.

Aunt Carol's arm shoots up and clasps her chest. "Ouch!" she cries. "My heart."

I scramble to her side. "Are you okay? What happened?" I know darn well what happened. In my fury at being interrupted, I lost control of the magic festering in me. I'm like an unstable volcano, erupting. I've spewed hurtful lava at my Aunt Carol.

Ander gathers his jacket and pack. "I was just heading out. Are you okay?"

Aunt Carol gawks at him as she rubs her upper chest just under her collarbone. "It was like I was burned with a hot poker. I thought I was having a heart attack. It's gone now, thank God." Her brow wrinkles as she gingerly probes the area. "Burning's not a symptom of a heart attack. Is it?"

Ander shakes his head. "Never heard of that symptom, but—"

"Shall we take you to the emergency room?" I cut in.

"No, child, no." Aunt Carol heaves a relieved sigh. "Honestly, it was probably the shock of seeing you two up here."

It wasn't just that, but I can't reveal the real reason.

"Sorry we scared you." Ander holds out a hand and she gives it a wobbly shake. "I'm Ander, a friend of Dorianna's."

"I see that," Aunt Carol says, her tone a bit snappy.

I've got to be careful not to inflict more injury. This part of my magic frightens me. Seriously, though, I'll be seventeen in a matter of weeks, and what I do with my new boyfriend shouldn't concern Aunt Carol. She's not my mother. "We weren't doing anything," I insist, working hard to hold back my impatience.

"I see that, Dorianna, I, uh . . ." Aunt Carol seems to be juggling words for the appropriate thing to say to a niece that she still doesn't really know.

Is it my job to make it easier for her? I'll try. "Shall we go downstairs? We were just headed down there, when . . ." I almost blurt out, *when you barged in,* but I bite my tongue. "I'll fix some coffee."

"Sounds good." My aunt smoothes down her clothes.

As I brew coffee, I remind my aunt who Ander is. The writer.

She perks up. "Oh, that's great. I love a good novel. I don't know how much my niece told you, but I work in public TV, and I often get to meet writers. Met Jonathan Franzen when he did an interview with a colleague of mine." Smiling warmly, she fills in the silences. "I often go to the library to pick up a good read. Books are so pricy these days."

Ander relaxes in his chair. "I love that branch. Sometimes I write over there after school."

"Really?" Aunt Carol adjusts her glasses. "If you see me, feel free to say hello."

A moment of awkward silence follows, as if we all feel that the conversation's jumped to a too-intimate place, and needs to be notched back.

"What are you writing?" Aunt Carol asks him as I pour coffee.

"Short stories, um . . . experimenting, really."

I study him. This is not the sardonic, sure-of-himself guy I first spoke to on the beach. And short stories? He claims he's working on a novel.

"Many writers are superstitious about discussing their works in progress," says Aunt Carol. "I've read about that."

My heart goes out to my aunt. Here she is, trying to put Ander at ease, and all of this after her shock of seeing me practically in bed with him and being literally scorched. Too close a call. I can't let my moods flame out on people around me.

Ander has to get home after the coffee. I walk him to the door, and we kiss again, beyond the prying sight of my aunt.

"Despite the, uh, mishap . . . I had a nice time." He draws me close.

"Me, too." I snuggle into his neck.

"See you in school." He kisses me again. "Let's take another jaunt out to Coney soon."

"Sure." With this mention, I'm flooded with the strange things people say about Wilson. Morbid, charismatic, unpredictable.

As I watch Ander go, I decide that I do need to go out to Coney Island soon—without him. I need more answers, and the questions I need to ask Wilson are not the kind that Ander should hear. After I put on my nightgown, I take the Burlesque copy out of its hiding place and slip the drive into my laptop for another look.

The capybara is the same, but my likeness, high-stepping on the yellow orb, leers out at the viewer and cackles. She spits out new accusations, as if ramping up for a fight with the viewer. "Dirty thief!" she roars. "Yes, you! Think you can hide from yourself? Think again."

A high shriek escapes me. I play it over. Same thing. I yank the thumb drive out of my laptop, throw it on the floor and stomp on it. One piece cracks off and lodges in my foot.

"Ow!" I yelp, as I hop over to my bed. I inch the shard out, throw it in my trashcan, and grab a tissue to wipe away the gush of blood. "I needed to show that goddamn copy to Wilson!" I hiss as I press on the wound. But there's a spreading realization that it wouldn't do any good. A sour taste seeps up in my throat. He had nothing to do with these changes. Wilson helped unearth an elemental force, but there's no denying that the good and the bad of it are all mine now.

Each of my actions is changing the videos. How will I ever explain it to my fans?

"Dorianna?" Aunt Carol calls from the upstairs hall. "Are

you all right? I heard you scream. Dorianna?" My aunt jiggles the handle on the locked door.

I never gave her a pass to barge in, I rage silently. Urges to burn, to maim, to literally annihilate the apartment, my aunt, and myself explode through me like grenades. I bare my teeth at the door like a feral animal. My backpack, hanging from a hook on the door, jolts off and smacks to the floor.

It takes all of my strength and concentration to keep from screaming, to calm my breathing and remember that my aunt is actually looking out for me. "It's okay, Aunt Carol," I gasp. "I . . . I was having a nightmare."

"You're scaring me. Open up," she pleads. "I need to see that you're okay."

"Not now. My hair's messed up. I'm in my pj's. I'm fine. Stop worrying."

"It's early for going to bed."

"I'm tired, though."

"Okay." Her voice is resigned. "Holler if you need me." Finally, she pads down the hallway to her own room.

I let out a great, shuddering sigh, and think about how grateful I am for the lock. Without it, I hate to imagine what might've happened. I feel it especially strongly when I hang my pack on the door hook, and see that an uneven section of paint is singed. I gape at it in horror.

I burned that paint clear off without a single match. Grabbing a brown marker from my desk, I color over the mark—a woefully inadequate touch-up job. I toss the marker on my desk and crawl under the covers.

"Am I being tested? If so, for what?" I ask the darkness.

Of course, the darkness has no answer. My heart bangs up in my throat as my mind cranks out desperate bargains. "I cooked for my aunt to balance out my bad karma, but I still stole my aunt's money," I mumble. "What if I tell Bailey what's happening to me?" Will that honesty scrub me clean?

. . . No, I've strayed too far from innocence. I'll have to keep hiding things—hide everything, I realize. At least Ander didn't see that horrid Burlesque trailer. He'll never see that.

As I drift into grogginess, my more rational brain shuts down and I sink into darker reasoning. *"I have a gift,"* I murmur into my quilt. How could any gift be wrong? Let me use it for what it wants. Let me revel in it, just for a while. I wriggle my toes and stretch.

Wilson said he was the Prince of Darkness. Isn't that supposedly an agent of the devil? Well, I don't believe in the devil. He's a buffoonish horror-show character that some evil priest made up to terrorize people into keeping to the straight and narrow. Horns and a tail, how comic book can it get? I raise my arms, and invite a dark spirit to seize me.

"Go ahead, you degenerate!"

No devil swoops down to punish me for poking fun at him. He doesn't set me on fire with his wrath.

"It's a crock of shit!" I shout as I slam my arms down on my quilt.

Glancing out at the night sky through my window, I think of my dad, and his church. He didn't believe in the devil, either. His church was too modern and enlightened for that kind of literal, old-school morality play.

Yet, another part of my mind reminds me that he got punished. Punished for his sins. I shiver, though I'm actually sweaty under the heavy quilt. My father's problem is entirely different from mine. His crime involved physical coercion. I dredge up my memory of the first item on his sleazy "How I Got My Church Members" list.

Marilyn: Cornered her in KG bar. Listened to her tale of woe about divorce. Pity sex in hotel. Marilyn joined my church the next day. First member was in the bag.

My stomach churns violently. It's bad enough to do it, but to have written it down as well? Dad is a hypocritical con. Is his affliction contagious? Perhaps it's not my vow with Wilson that's messing with me after all. Dad's list is still in my devotional. I could destroy it without ever reading the rest. But touching it might defile me.

"I'll *never* glamour Ander," I promise out loud. "I'll only have sex for love. I will never, ever charm Ander in any magical way, except for the part I can't help—my appearance and my extraordinary senses. Dad, your sexual manipulation was trash," I spit. "Unlike you, I will have rules and morals even when I choose dark actions."

I bury my head in the pillow. "This is different," I say into it. "*I* am different. Dad, you did it by choice. I'm struggling against powers beyond my control."

This is the best I can do. State my difference. Make weak claims. The truly chilling thing about the power is that when it's raging in me, it's an alien thing, not to be denied. Weak, weak to my bones, I hold out a glimmer of hope that my powers can still be used for good.

15

The last time I checked, a ménage à trois was not a pit stop on the road to redemption.
—Tom Kapinos

The bells on the door of the café jingle as I walk into Havana's. It's a day later, after school, and I'm meeting Ander over steamy café con leche. I've replaced last night's horror with my delight over a new outfit —a sheer bomber jacket with tons of showy chains. To top it off, I have on a roaring twenties aviator's hat, festooned with a splashy fabric daisy. "Sorry I'm late, hon, I—"

He's gawking at me in the way I crave: his eyes, hazy with lust. But Wilson's with him, and I don't like that one bit.

I set down my bags, brimming with sequined costumes, paper goods, and candy in big sacks and throw my arms around Ander, with a proprietary grin toward Wilson that says, I belong to Ander, so you can't have me.

In Ander's smirk it's clear that he's amused by my pegging Warren's narcissism down a notch. "Yeah, Warren snuck up behind me," Ander explains. "At the exact moment I realized I didn't have enough cash to pay for my burrito."

Wilson shrugs. "I like to help out a friend." He reaches for my hand and kisses it. I draw it back, all the while bestowing on him a regal smile. "It's so lovely to see the Princess of Darkness!" he gushes. "What I wouldn't do to besmirch you."

Ander shakes his head. "Warren, one minute you're a smooth operator, and the next, a degenerate. Which is it?"

"A degenerately smooth operator."

"You look dramatic today," I tell Wilson.

"You like?" He whips a corner of his cloak over his face. "Bought it last year in a thrift shop. Total Voldemort, the Gothic gentleman's answer to the woman's black cocktail dress."

At least he's not sporting that silly pearl-tipped cane. I order a lime smoothie, a specialty of the house. "So, what were you guys talking about?"

"Our mutual fixation on the girl of cosmic rays," Wilson says. "Ander was saying that he has deepening fascination with you *as a character*."

My pulse spikes as I notice Ander's notebook under his elbow.

"Warren, for shit's sake." Ander is not amused.

"Ander here, has morals, which I lack," Wilson muses. "He has mixed feelings about pirating someone's life."

"I'm not pirating anyone's life, jerk." Ander turns to me. "We were having a philosophical discussion about Chekhov. How Chekhov used his wife Olga as a trope for Nina in *The Seagull*."

"A purely philosophical discussion." Wilson winks at me.

"I'm not writing about Dorianna," Ander insists.

I level a stern look at Ander. "If you are, though, it's only fair that I read it." I'm not sure how I feel about Ander writing about me, if he is. It's kind of flattering, depending on what he's saying about me.

"I'm writing about Padro and his fictitious girl. Look, I freaking write fiction." Ander's frustration tells me to leave it alone.

Wilson turns to me. "Dorianna, I hear you're doing rehearsals."

"We start tomorrow, at my friend's loft."

"Can we go ogle you?" Wilson asks, which merits a snort from Ander.

"Not the first rehearsal. Might make the girls tense."

"They better get over that," Wilson scoffs. "They're going to be shaking their buttocks on stage."

"Guys, too," Ander reminds him. "We have two guys doing a campy neo-burlesque."

"With assless chaps and bejeweled handcuffs?" Wilson quips.

"Assless chaps, now that's a thought." Ander wags his brows at me.

I throw my head back and laugh, partly because it's a funny image, but partly from relief that Ander and Wilson aren't going for the jugular anymore. In fact, Wilson has taken out his camera and is recording Ander's empty coffee cup, a close-up of Ander's ink-stained hand, the dusty horse piñata sagging on twine in a corner, and the gaudy-bright pastries in the glass case. Apparently satisfied, he clicks the lens cap closed.

"That reminds me, Wilson," I say as I swoop my hair over one shoulder. "Did you get the photos I e-mailed of the performers' backs? For the voucher contest?"

"Done! You've already got some educated guessers."

"Awesome!"

Ander looks peeved that Warren is so into the events—and me—that he's already posted that lineup on my fan page. Let Ander stew. He'd best be careful about what he's writing. It annoys me that he won't let me read it.

The café bells jangle again, this time delivering a group of eight sophomores. When they see me, they surge around, all buzzing at once.

"I know who Lady Tattersal is! She's Bailey. Red hair's a giveaway."

"I'd know that Cole dude from any angle. Looks like a girl. He's hot, but he needs a haircut in the worst way."

I raise my arms. "Whoa! Don't tell me now. Vote on the fan page." I distribute my freshly printed business cards that show a still from that first Coney Island surf scene, where rays of sun beam out from behind me.

Wilson chuckles. "Keep up this pace, Dorianna, and you'll crash your media sites from all the fans following you at once. Did you make these business cards?"

"Ander did."

While Wilson studies one with narrowed, greedy eyes, the sophomores crowd in closer, vying for my attention like eager puppies.

"Hey, I already voted!" one of the girls shouts as she grabs a card. "I was, like, number four. Does that mean I get a special voucher for meetup number three? Huh?"

Another kid holds out his hand. "Autograph?" I write my name on his wrist so he can literally wear me.

"Take extras. Pass them to everyone you know." I give each kid a thick chunk of cards. Finally, my groupies retreat to the counter to order burritos, giving me awed, sidelong glances as they wait in line.

Wilson turns to me. "I'll invite some people from my old school."

"Good." I do a double take. "Wait, your *old* school?"

"He dropped out," Ander says.

"I told you not to do that." I shoot Wilson a hard stare.

"I know, I know, Sungirl, but you're not my mommy."

"I'm your friend."

Warren puckers into a look of sheepish appreciation. "The sentiment is warm and squishy, but I cannot tolerate the cretins who never do homework and then expect an A, who can't even read and then wonder why the Chinese are over-taking us. They're wasting their precious time, and mine. I want to create art, *devour the world*. I'll learn more on my own."

"Learn about what?" I ask.

"How sharks and eels mate, the celestial tissue of the planets, the sixth sense, the seventh and eighth senses, the midnight trajectory of the subway rats. Do they dash over to Nathan's for hot-dog crumbs and then to Toonz for a dose of live music? Or do they prefer drinking the fermented seepage between the tracks while they enjoy the scream of bad brakes? Do they get their paws read by the fortune-tellers on Surf Ave.?" He pretends to examine the lines on his palm. "I see, Mr. Rat. You'll find your future girlfriend gnawing on a paper cup. Three months hence, she'll birth your healthy litter of twenty."

Ander and I exchange bemused glances.

"I'll have more time to create supernatural divas and daring video art. By the way . . ." He rakes a hand through his coif. "How's that copy of the trailer you wanted, hmm? Was it a *good* one?"

"What copy? The one you lost?" Ander gives me a puzzled look.

"Lost, found, whatever." I glower at Wilson. "Stuff happens."

Ander looks over at Warren, and then back at me to glean clues in our faces. I sense that he's wondering if Wilson and I have been hanging out a lot behind his back, and sharing secrets he isn't privy to. I sense him also realizing his own limits to goading Wilson. That he better not pry, because Wilson could flame out in some outrageous and unpredictable way.

"Ah, burlesque." Wilson sighs. "Imagine the boardwalk spectacle, as the polluted sun sets in an acidic haze."

"I thought you were in the loop," Ander says with obvious glee. "Dorianna's friend Bailey offered to host it at her loft."

Wilson smoothes over his sudden frown. "You ought to go back to our original plan to meet at Coney. It's more decadent, juicy!"

"Juicy, right." Ander snickers. "With those dirty geezers slouching on the benches, drooling through their dentures at the virginal high-school beauties."

Wilson erupts in a hostile chuckle. "When you say it like that .. . ."

"Hey, babe, let's jump. You ready?" Ander swings an arm around me.

"Sure." I glance at Wilson with a twinge of guilt at leaving him behind.

"I'll carry your bags," Ander says with a dash of thrilling chivalry. He glances over at Wilson. "Thanks for the twenty. Pay you back next time."

Wilson's expression flits from jealousy to studied nonchalance. "Yeah, mosey out to Coney whenever. I'll be conducting interviews with the fortune-tellers and the mermaids." He winks at me. "You come out. *Anytime.*"

I will. Soon. I still have unfinished business with the so-called Prince of Darkness.

Ander whisks me out of there fast. I sense that my thrill at being fought over disturbs him, as does the honeyed come-on in Wilson's voice. Can't blame him. Ander's already lost one girl to a supposed friend. He's not about to let a second guy horn in. Especially not Charlie's older brother.

16

The golden apple, devoured, has seeds. It is endless.
—Bette Davis

The first rehearsal is going pretty well, if you don't count the fact that I could cut the tension between Bailey and Lacey with a hunting knife. Bailey's mom was nice enough to hire a theater friend's assistant choreographer, Marla, to show us a few basic burlesque steps. Marla, an athletic woman with ebony skin, takes us through a scarf dance and a slow, seductive hip-shimmy.

Lacey struts in a good thirty minutes late. "My costume?" she asks me, making everyone pause in mid-step.

"Later. We have a choreographer," I explain in a flat tone.

Lacey gawks at the teacher, who she's just noticed. Clearly, Lacey was not expecting this level of professionalism. She steps it up, and manages to keep her mouth shut for most of the rehearsal. It's fun to do the line dance, and we manage not to step on each other's toes.

After we're done, and chugging cold water, I turn on the charm, recalling a saying I used to hear in Indiana: You catch more bees with honey. "Great start, Lacey. Looks as if you've taken dance lessons before."

"Like pole dancing?" Bailey weasels in.

Lacey shrugs Bailey off. "I've taken ballet, ballroom, you name it." She stares pointedly at Bailey's ballet slippers. "Unlike those who wear dance stuff for show."

"Don't bother rehearsing with us if you're going to have a crap attitude." Bailey stares Lacey down.

"Dorianna invited me here."

"Well, it's my loft. I can uninvite you," Bailey replies.

"Hey, hey, hey. We're big kids, let's be civil," I say with a kittenish grin.

I sense Lacey's claws retracting. It was Bailey's choice to reject Lacey, so it's not my problem. Or is it?

Next week at school, I have a talk with Bailey over chocolate shakes, to reassure her I'm not getting cuddly with Lacey. "I hardly know the girl, okay? We just need her in the lineup."

"Why?"

"She has good legs. Blonde hair. She'll draw in more followers. Besides," I purr, "I have plans for Ms. Givem Heck, for exposing her inner slut."

Bailey cracks an impish grin. "How will you do that?"

"Haven't figured it out yet, but I'll let you know." I spoon in a hunk of chocolate and let it slide luxuriously down my throat. Lately, I'm so famished. For food, for clothes, for fans. Nothing ever seems to fill me up.

"Can't wait to hear." Bailey licks whipped cream off her spoon. "How many RSVPs do we have now?" she asks. The evite went out a week ago.

"This morning we had three hundred sixty-two yeses."

"Holy Moly!" Bailey's jaw drops. I study the oozy choco-late blobs floating on her tongue. "How will we cram all those people in my loft?"

"It's a good problem, right?"

"Uh, yeah, if we had a stadium. Seriously, Mom will freak, and she's normally very chill. Where are they all coming from?"

"Mostly from a friend who goes to a school in Fort Greene." More like *went* there.

"Dorianna, we need to shut this thing down—take it offline."

"We can't do that." Five thousand fan page followers and three hundred sixty-two attendees is not enough. No way. I can't wait until the third event, where I'm going to bust it wide open. "No worries, not everyone will show," I soothe.

Bailey's warm eyes turn cold. "But if even half of those people show up . . ."

"Calm down." As an experiment, I gently press a hand on Bailey's wrist and silently chant, *Calm, calm, calm,* and then, *Excitement, excitement, excitement.*

Bailey's expression changes from worry to wide-eyed eagerness, as if a master sculptor is kneading her face. "It's in a week, can you believe it?" she shrills.

"No, I can't." I feel a shiver of guilt at the discovery that I can now reliably mesmerize. Mostly, it elates me. *It's not as if you're hurting Bailey,* my dark side reasons.

"I hope my costume holds together. The top's not quite done." Bailey cups her boobs. "Wouldn't want these girls popping out."

"I bet the guys wouldn't mind."

"Cole would." Bailey takes another spoonful of her melting sundae. "Is someone documenting the event?"

I flinch. Will my charged energy change other trailers? "Um, a friend."

"Whoever it is, should totally get us on YouTube."

Spikes of anxiety puncture my easy mood. At least Bailey hasn't mentioned any changes on that beach video. She must not have replayed it. I force a grin. "He could probably do that."

"Cool! Do I know your friend?"

I can only hesitate so long. "Charlie's older brother, Wilson."

"*Him?*" She drops her spoon on the saucer with a clatter.

"What's the problem?"

"That dude is shady. Lacey told me that Wilson said some bizarre stuff to her one time she was over at Charlie's."

My ears prick like a fox on the hunt. "Like what? Tell me."

"I can't remember exactly. It was two years ago."

I lean over and poke Bailey. "Tell me. You've got to tell me!"

"Wow, back off!" Bailey's voice has that sharpness that cut me so deeply in the early days of school. My eyes must have looked too hungry, too desperate.

Abruptly, I'm filled with that time of not belonging, when everyone in the school was either ignoring me or laughing at me—especially Lacey and Ava. I'd almost forgotten what that felt like. I want to forget it again—forever. "Sorry," I mumble. "It's just that Wilson shot my Sungirl video, and did the Web stuff."

"He's talented, but uh . . ." Bailey knits her rosy brows.

"But what?"

"Lacey claims that Wilson liked her for a while, after she started dating Charlie—in secret, of course. 'Cause, you know, she was still with Ander then."

Inside, I'm hurting, but I maintain a chill exterior. "And?"

"And, well, Wilson would show up at the strangest times,

like out of nowhere."

I clench up. Just like last week, when Wilson popped into Havana's at the exact moment Ander said he needed cash. "Give me an example."

Bailey winds a piece of flame-red hair around her pinky and sucks on it—her trademark thinker's pose. Then she takes her finger out and flings the lock off it. "Okay. One afternoon, Lacey was outside of school. She'd hailed a cab to go to Charlie's, when she realized that she'd forgotten her wallet and had no money or credit cards."

I'm thinking about what Ander said again. It's like Wilson has a built-in GPS tracker on Ander, on me—on Lacey, too? "And?"

"So, Wilson was suddenly up in her face, asking her if she needed money, and he said he'd be happy to share the cab and pay, since he was going home." Bailey looks over at me and we exchange uneasy glances.

"She must've seen him walking toward her."

"No. She said he appeared out of nowhere."

I bite the inside of my mouth, and tear a piece of skin off. The iron flavor of blood fills my sinuses. "He's quiet on his feet. Um . . . I can see how that would startle her."

Bailey scrunches up her face in distaste. "She also said he went around in a cape. Like a Jekyll-and-Hyde character."

"True. He's into Gothic or Victorian or . . . Let's just say, he has a flair for the melodramatic. But how's that so different from a lot of artists?" Bailey will relate to that. Honestly, I'm not sure why I'm so defensive of Wilson. He wigs me out, too. One thing he's not guilty of, though, is tampering with that Burlesque copy. What would Bailey think of that? She can never, ever know.

"Lots of artists have flair," Bailey reasons. "But not all artists stalk people."

There, Bailey's come out and said what is obviously on

her mind. "Stalk people!" I cry. "That's a harsh judgment call. Is that what Lacey said he was doing?" I'm poised to sting like a crazed wasp. Wilson is nuts, but he's a friend. I tamp down my fury, afraid it will hurt Bailey.

Bailey's expression is challenging, questioning. "Lacey didn't *say* that . . ."

"What, then?"

"Oh, why are we always talking about Lacey?" Bailey's eyes glint. "Sometimes I feel like *you're* stalking her!"

I'm stung. My hurt flares up so furiously that my lip curls in a primitive growl. I clap a hand over my mouth to suppress it.

Bailey leaps up. "You just snarled at me! What *was* that? Your mouth. . ."

I quickly pick up a napkin, wipe my mouth with it and hold out the blood drops. "I bit my tongue. It really hurt." I'm not totally lying.

With a sigh, Bailey sits back down and lays a hand on my arm. "Oh, lord. Sorry about my stalking remark. That was bitchy. Don't know why I said that," she admits. "I'm weirdly jealous of your, um . . . interest in everything Lacey."

I wipe away more blood drops.

"You inspire obsessed followers, too," Bailey says in a backhanded compliment.

"I do?" My anger slinks back like a wild beast given warm milk.

"Sure you do. You had me at Sungirl-dot-com on, like, the third day of school. I thought you were so much more creative than the other girls."

"Ah, my arty friend, don't feel jealous. Not for a minute." I give Bailey an affectionate hug. It's the wrong time to ask more probing questions about what Lacey said about Wilson.

If I'm such a magnetic soul, I should be able to pull that out of Lacey all on my own.

17

Little Wing is like one of these beautiful girls that come around sometimes . . . a very sweet girl that came around that gave me her whole life and more if I wanted it.
—Jimi Hendrix

"Okay, Wilson, so you didn't change the new ringmaster video," I challenge. "But you must know *how* it changed."

He's pacing. The place is a fright. His clothes, usually arranged in his closet in neat groupings of blacks and charcoals, are in wrinkled, multicolored heaps on his uncle's sofa. Chinese takeout containers clutter the counter, and his camera bags, usually lined up along his console, are scattered on various side tables.

"Just a minute," he growls. "I'm hungry." He opens his fridge and I see a bowl of soba noodles and even a big, fat steak waiting to be cooked. Instead, he grabs a stale roll and gobbles it down, while pacing. Pacing and mumbling must be how he keeps a semblance of internal order.

"What's wrong with you?" I ask. Ironic, since I came over to ask him questions about *me*.

"I can't think straight. You're agitating me. Let's go for a walk."

"But it's drizzling."

"A little rain never hurt anyone." He grabs his medieval cloak and a pair of leather gloves. Hands me an umbrella.

I'll press him as soon as he walks out his tension.

We walk past nightclubs, pizza shops, and a lot littered with beer cans and rolled-up disposable diapers. Mist mixes with drizzle. Wilson hikes his hood over his dark whorl of curls.

He's right. Out here in the rain, I don't feel cornered, with his pressurized vibe charging the room with unstable electricity. With him crowding out my space, and no escape. On this gritty street, I'm stronger, and I can put the pressure back on him. I'll breathe through my fear that he'll tell me something I can't handle. "So? I was asking?"

We stop at a light, wait for the traffic to ease. "What exactly changed on it?" he asks.

I glower at him. "I heard myself *talk* on it. My image was yelling at me, saying I'm a thief, and I'm wrong if I think I can hide—hide from *what*, Wilson? That's nutty talk. How is it even possible that a digital teaser can suddenly have a new speaker on the audio, an already recorded person saying entirely new things? 'Cause, you know, I'm not insane."

His face is murky under his hood, yet his tone is unsurprised. "What are you hiding?"

I'm hiding from my corruption, from my manipulations, from . . .

Shut up, snarls the feral part of me, *Shut your traitorous mouth.*

You shut up, I warn back, silently. "Wilson, how can you be so calm about me ranting on the video copy?" I ask him. "Doesn't that upset you? It's going to mess up my following and scare people. If you're the Prince of Darkness, you have powers. Tell me how to get rid of it. Help me edit it out!"

"I told you, I have no control over that part," Wilson answers without slowing his pace, without looking at me. "If I edit it out, it will only reappear."

"How do you know? Can't you try?" I tug on his sleeve so he'll look at me.

"It's pointless, Dor."

Through the rain, heavier now, I stare at his face as it swims in watery patterns. Desperation eats at me. "I've changed in *all* of the videos. I'm *frightening*. I wasn't like this before I met you."

Wilson emits a sound between a dry laugh and a sigh. "I told you things would happen—good things . . . *and* bad things."

"Why do bad things need to happen? Can't there be only good things?"

"Impossible. I explained this to you. There are prices for everything."

"I thought you were joking."

"That's *your* problem, Dor. I warned you."

I bat at the rain. What I really want to do is to batter him. "Then at least tell me what the good parameters of my magic are."

His knotty eyes emit flickers of heat from beneath the black folds of his hood. "You've grown magnificent, you've become the diva of the school. You've become Sungirl. You'll stay beautiful and young like that . . ." His sentence trails off.

I want to hear more about staying young, what that means. But first I need to know the exact boundaries of my powers. "I mean, the nuts and bolts," I fret, "of exactly what my skills are."

"You tell me. You must've noticed things."

I think about this as we start walking again. "I can sort of read minds. I just found out I can mesmerize people into doing things."

"Good, good. Your powers will increase. You'll develop an uncanny sense of smell, be able to move very fast, conjure things—holographs, spirits . . ."

I think about those voices that seemed to be all around me when I shivered in bed that night. "Sounds interesting. But, uh, what about being able to burn people? What about that?" I ask, with trepidation. My question lingers in the sodden air as rain clatters against the parked cars. "Wilson, I'm able to literally burn holes in things. *Burn* people with my rage. I made my backpack fall off a hook. I singed the goddamn paint off my door when I was mad at my aunt. I'm afraid of what I can do. I'm not my old self."

"Thankfully," Wilson murmurs.

"What's wrong with you? Not thankfully!" I shout in extreme frustration. "I used to be nice. Now I'm afraid of what I might do next. I can't control the bad part anymore."

We've reached a corner. The neon signs strobe violet, then yellow, then red on Wilson's slick cloak. "You wanted it all before," he reminds me. "Too late now."

"If you know where the powers come from, you can stop them!"

"I can't, though. I can't stop them."

Hysteria ratchets my voice up higher, through the blare of traffic. "Who the fucking hell do you work for? Tell him I want out of this pact if it's going to make me a scary lunatic." I've gotten Ander's attention in the bargain. Isn't that enough? Wilson studies me, but says nothing.

If I burn him, will he talk then? Glaring at Wilson, I

concentrate on shooting molten light at his chest, a sharp laser beam, scorching through his clothes. He groans.

"Feel it now? Huh? Tell me how to undo the pact I made. Tell me, or I'll torch a hole right through you!" I scream this part so loudly that pedestrians turn to gawk.

Wilson inches back his hood. "You're causing a scene, Dor." Rubbing his chest where I've burned him, his tone is that of an impatient father who believes his wayward daughter is purposely disappointing him.

Infuriated, I blast him again, fully intending to do bodily harm.

This time, his head jolts forward, onto his chest. He raises a cloaked arm to fend off my fire. "Stop. This is no fickle game. What did you pledge at my place that first day?"

I narrow my eyes, picturing as Wilson edited, and then played, the beach video for the very first time. I'd imagined myself as popular. Wilson had been egging me on, saying how many fans I could have if he posted it online. I remember him getting up in my face, demanding answers.

That same manic chokehold I felt in Wilson's studio that first day is wrapping me tight, right here, right now, in a thick cord of solid dread. It makes no difference whether I'm out here or in Wilson's apartment—he's still getting to me. I start to cough and gasp. "Don't make me say it again," I plead.

The wind whips up. It blows the umbrella out of my hand. I can't see it ahead of me—only soupy fog and rain. Yet my overwrought emotions are lifting me, propelling me upwards like that almost-weightless umbrella. Flashes of metallic color ping off the edges of my vision.

"Watch out!" someone yells. Not Wilson, but a woman. A firm, forceful arm is yanking me—where?

"You almost got hit!" a lady screeches. Her face is so close to mine, I see her nostrils flare in panic. See the streams of rain gush down her rounded cheeks.

I blink hard. Back on the sidewalk, I realize I was so lost in a bleary funnel of dreams that I'd wandered into three lanes of fast-moving traffic.

"Sungirl, over here!" Wilson hollers from down the block.

Did I run away from him? It's as if I lost a chunk of time. Was I literally flying? Wilson said I'd be able to move super fast. But how could I have gotten so very far ahead of him?

"Are you drunk? Shall I call an ambulance?" The woman is still clutching my arm to steady me.

"I'm better now. I'll be fine. Thanks."

Wilson catches up with us, and slips an arm around me. I wish it were Ander's arm instead. Ander's would feel safe, warm. Ander's would feel like he did it for love, or at least for friendship. Not this . . . this magnetic charge, as if I'm simply the other half of Wilson's charismatic force, being drawn toward him against my will.

What *is* my will? Wilson didn't drag me here. I wanted to come out here.

I shake him off. "I said I wanted to be popular and pretty. You kept yelling at me to say more. I felt incredibly pressured. Why do you keep pressuring me?"

"Pressured? I was making you into a phenomenon. And you are, so why you keep getting on my case is beyond me." His face is that of an idyllic choirboy's.

"You know why! Why are you wanting me say it again? I said I'd give my soul." I swallow a scream. "Where did it go? Who took it?"

Wilson emits an animal sound from deep his throat—a mixed sensual grunt of pleasure and pain. "I love to hear you say it, Dor. Say it again and again."

When I turn to him, his innocence is replaced by a red glinting stare, a perfect reflection of the goat buckle with its bleeding eyes. And I know without a doubt what he is. But that's another impossibility, right?

"So, you're a *real* Prince of Darkness?" I whisper.

"Yes. I serve my master in the hierarchy. I'm whoever you want me to be," he breathes.

My insides freeze up. "What did you do to Lacey—Charlie's girlfriend? The one he got with, right before you moved out of your parents' house."

"I don't know who you're talking about."

"You're lying. My friend Bailey said you did something to Lacey."

"I did nothing to that silly girl."

"Ah! So, you do know who I'm talking about. I knew you were lying."

"Lacey's not even worth a conversation. She's a lightweight. A twit."

That's proof beyond a doubt that Lacey is no lightweight. That whoever Lacey is, she is surely a threat to Wilson. Otherwise, why would he bother lying about knowing her? It makes me all the more curious about Lacey, determined to get to know her better. Pinpoint her appeal in order to co-opt it. Forge a bond. Two powerful women could wreak more havoc than one.

My two sides argue: Leave her alone. *She's after your boyfriend.* She'll hurt me. *Hurt her more.*

"You in there?" Wilson nudges me.

Awakened by his prod, I burst out, "Tell your boss to sell me back my goddamn soul, then. It's not his. I don't even *believe* in that bullshit." I laugh gruffly. "So, if you're a demon, you don't exist."

"I guess I don't exist," Wilson growls. "A soul can't be returned in some store exchange, even if you do have proof of purchase. If so, I'd have gotten mine back long ago." Hearing this, new horror crashes through me. He *is* serious. He's tried and failed to claim his own soul back. "What do you know, Sungirl?" He asks mournfully. "You don't know the pain of my existence, or its beauty. Every day I'm alone, empty and ravenous. Being with you, it's—"

"If you're lonely, you didn't have to move out here by yourself."

"I was always alone, in my parents' house, a misunderstood freak. And now, I pace at night, unable to sleep, thinking of how many years I'll feel like this, watching the sunset, and you, Dorianna. Thinking of—"

"Trying to butter me up? What's your point, Wilson?" I shudder from the rain's icy chill on my bare head.

We've stopped walking again. We're standing by a streetlight as the rain streaks down. Through the deluge, the light turns, and edges Wilson in a rippled emerald sea as the traffic roars across the intersection on its way to the Belt Parkway.

"You have so much potential," he says without venom, in a deeply weary voice.

Inexplicably, I'm less enraged. I almost feel sorry for him now that he's admitted his ache, his loneliness. He hands me a knit hat from his pocket and I put it on, grateful. Studying his face, I notice the bags under his eyes, and the sallow tint of his skin.

"You could do so much with what you've been given," he says.

"But can I do good?" I mutter.

Good—how lame is that? roars my inner beast.

Wilson tucks a lock of my hair inside the cap. "Goodness is overrated. It's better to be fascinating than good. You must see the sense in that. You were the most interesting person at the Yellow Meetup. You'll be the commanding presence at Burlesque."

I lower my head to hide my grin. *Yesss,* says my beast. I'm drawn to Wilson anew. There's dreadful relief in knowing the gory details.

He goes on. "There are already many who give to charity, or work for non-profits." Wilson snorts. "All well and good. But, it's more important to wake people up, tantalize them." He bends down so he's level with my gaze. "Logically, if you don't believe in the dark magic of the vow, then why would you need to break it? You can't escape something that you're not stuck in. On the other hand, if you're willing to consider its force, and experiment . . ."

"How?" My shrillness reveals my curiosity.

"Use its magic to amplify things. Amplify your own creativity. *Shock* people. Mine takes me to the right place at the right time to catch a video opportunity, and grants me the perfect florid vision for the edit." He moves even closer and the folds of his cloak brush against my front. His scent of incense sends turgid waves all the way through me. His black eyes gleam down at me adoringly. "It connects me to the right people, too."

I allow him near, only to let him know that I don't exactly hate him, that maybe he's still my friend. "I like that I can use my talents for shocking art." I think of Bailey's mom, the allure of her wicked painted creatures. It fills me with a wave of renewed energy. "Let's walk."

We walk and walk, at a great speed, cutting through the rain. Two figures, each high on magic, still wary of each other but with new respect and freshly bonded.

We take an alternate route back, past bars and row houses with unkempt plastic ivy in window boxes, and then past a restaurant supply warehouse. Looming ahead, I see the great gray building with bars on its windows that fills the entire square block. The detention center we saw before. Flinging my head back, I open my mouth to drink the rain. I *will* continue to experiment with the dark arts, but no detention center for me. I'll never be stupid enough to be caught.

Wilson must be reading my thoughts because he says, "You're developing an attitude. Good. Arrogance is good." He drapes his cloak around me. "Shall we sit on the beach for a while before you go?"

I think of Ander, how he wouldn't like this. But I do like it, this connection I have with Wilson. "Sure, let's go."

We walk down the wooden stairs and pick a spot on a dune. He spreads out his cloak. There's room enough for both of us on it. I'm only lightly touching one of his long legs.

"So, how did you get into . . . this magic stuff?" I take care to look straight ahead at the clearing night sky. "Did you go into it, knowing?"

"This last time, no. I was fourteen. I shot my first video, featuring my black cat, Oilslick. I caught him ripping apart a mouse, and recorded the bloody feast." Wilson pushes at a wet mound of sand with his boot. "Charlie, at thirteen, won his second team trophy, this time for helping lead his junior soccer league team to state victory. All I got was a lecture from my parents about my video's morbid subject. Oh, and strong encouragement to put down the camera and join a sports team, like perfect little Charlie. Meanwhile, Charlie got a trip to Disney World."

"That's awful, Wilson."

"That wasn't the worst of it. After Charlie got back, I was experimenting with chemicals in the basement. Chemistry was my other obsession. I mixed combustibles, and blew a hole clear through the ceiling and into the family TV room."

I can't help but giggle at the thought.

"My parents shrieked and carried on. They grounded me. Charlie gloated and asked why I was such a weird trouble-maker. Influenced by tales of genies and malicious gremlins from Grimm's, I stared in my mirror that day and made a vow."

My skin crawls with dread at what will come next.

"I said to the mirror, if I could be more admired than my annoying brother, and more feared than the goblins in Grimm's, I'd sell my soul." Wilson leans against me for a moment, as if he's gleaning strength from me. "How could I possibly know, as a pissed-off fourteen-year-old chemistry nerd, how much my melodramatic vow would change my world?"

"And how could I?" I whisper. "So, how long have you been . . . around?"

"A long, long time, but not continuously. I get reborn into a new body, and it starts all over again."

"Will that happen to me?"

He ponders this. "Yours is different. Part of your vow was for eternal youth."

"I can't fathom it. Young forever. A plus or a curse?"

He laughs gruffly. "Depends."

Fear crashes through me. It's too vast a concept. I choose to focus on his pattern of being reborn. "Do you remember your last life, all of the lives?"

"Not at first. Each time, it starts out innocently. Then gradually, there's this deep, hollow longing, some desperate need that inspires the making of the next vow. Only then comes a dim, dawning memory of other times, other places." He pauses, rakes his boot in the sand. "It seems designed that way to avoid terrifying the tender speck of goodness that inevitably prevails."

I should be furious with Wilson for infecting me with my own version. But he's bared so much of his soul that I'm keen to know more. "What's your goal each time? Do you have some kind of theme? I mean, why pick me?"

Wilson gazes at me with affection. "I help girls find their power. You're number twelve."

"Really, Wilson." I roll my eyes at him. "Just when I start believing you, you become a theatrical joke."

"Suit yourself," he mumbles with little trace of humor. "The first, in 1437, was a raven-haired minstrel girl near Canterbury. Her vow helped her overthrow her abusive master and take control of the show. A female minstrel was unheard of back then. She flourished, causing quite a stir and enhancing her musical performances with perfect pitch and mesmerizing jigs. So much so, that she lined the floorboards of her carriage with gold noble coins." Wilson stops there.

I don't know whether to erupt in disbelieving laughter or take this seriously. My instincts tell me to go with the latter, as wild as this concept is. "Was there a consequence?"

"She became so famous that her jealous old master snuck up on her and performed his own lethal magic with a rusty dagger."

"That's awful. I guess her power didn't last. What about the others?"

Wilson absently toys with his necklace. "In 1642, I helped a woman in Springfield, Massachusetts, become a renowned healer."

It's getting less funny and more alarming. Who could make this all up? "The price?"

"When the town blacksmith took her sumac and pox weevil potion and suffered from an extreme allergic reaction, she was promptly drowned as a witch."

"Another powerless client."

"I suppose I should be happy that you don't trust me." Wilson stares at his rings with a frown. "I should be happy that you insisted I make you that thumb drive copy. Proves that you're devious about getting answers." His turbulent emotions spill onto me. Why exactly is he upset?

"Did you ever fall in love with a client?"

The sudden fire of his agitated heart radiates into mine.

"Twice," he mutters. "Both times it presented problems. I was involved with a circus conjurer, who set king cobras on me when I snuck into her caravan for kisses. And there was a blond painter from Rasputin's court. With her miraculous strength, she heaved me into the frozen Moscow River after I criticized her portrait of another lover."

I erupt in peals of nervous laughter. The image of Wilson's cloak billowing out as he flails in an icy river is much too fun.

"Dorianna, you . . . you're more alluring than any of those divas."

This surprises me, but I don't let on how much. "Compared to historical beauties? I'm just an American schoolgirl."

Wilson's voice is laced with bitterness. "I shouldn't care whether you like me or not, trust me or not. I shouldn't care that you're getting attached to that . . . mortal."

"Ander?" I'm about to chuckle again, when something horrid occurs to me. "You didn't have anything to do with that accident, did—"

"No! I have *some* morals, Dor."

Yet I have access to some passing channels of his unconscious. My own powers give me that. He's saying silently that they're all his rivals—Charlie, Ander, especially the athletes. I sense him wondering what else he can give me besides power.

"Do you hear them, Dorianna?" Wilson points up at the clutter of stars.

"Who?" But I do hear them: the fluttering of nomadic souls, lingering on the horizon.

"They're only one screen of gauze from the material world," he murmurs. "If you wanted, Dor, you could pull them in and steal them, simply by your powers of concentration. Some wait for a lost lover. Some are there for revenge. Others died so soon after birth that they fancy themselves still alive."

The inky sky pulses with activity. I feel them tugging on me, to help them back over. My heart's giddy with my wobbly new supremacy. I also feel the strands of my early morals tugging at me to leave my folly behind.

As if Wilson can hear my thoughts—of course he can—he says, "Your resistance to the magic will weaken." *Do you know I want you?* he wonders. *You must, because you're gaining powers of clairvoyance with the rest of your abilities. Don't fall for Ander,* he begs silently.

I startle into consciousness. Ander, I need him, I need his goodness, and light. "I've got to go," I rasp. The rain's stopped. It's chilly now. I rise, brush myself off, and glance down at Wilson.

Don't pity me, he's thinking. He smells of empty rooms and moldy suitcases.

I turn and lurch toward the stairs, longing for Ander to sweep me into his gentle embrace. As I hurry toward Surf Avenue I hear Wilson, and see him just behind my eyes.

"How dare you!" he bellows. Filling his chest with the mist of seaweed and foam, he lets forth a roar that startles the bottom-feeding fish to deeper waters.

As he does, a dangerous well of strength rises up in me, too. Its sweet venom fills my chest with wet night—a night of detonating fireworks and fornicating vermin, of tattooed sideshow ladies and prancing, biting boars. *Power is even more intoxicating than love,* both sides of me declare in unison. *Catch the rain—catch the moment. You only live once . . .*

Or forever.

Understanding does not cure evil, but it's a definite help, inasmuch as
one can cope with a comprehensible darkness.
—Carl Jung

I'm distracted from the history teacher's lecture on the War of 1812. Ander isn't here, and Bailey's sitting all the way across the room. I start to doodle random burlesque costumes in my binder when I see Lacey get up, her face mottled with deep pink. Unlike her normal, regal cool, she's bent forward, stumbling over her feet to get out of class. So fast, in fact, that the teacher—preoccupied with writing on the board—doesn't notice anything until the door closes.

A minute later, I raise my hand.

"Yes?" the teacher barks, impatient.

"I need a bathroom break. It's an emergency," I add when he doesn't respond.

The class breaks out in titters. It's all good. Now that my

star has risen, I'm confident that people are laughing at the teacher's expense, not at me.

I have a nagging intuition there's business I need to attend to that won't wait. Remembering what Wilson said about the magic guiding him on when and where to go, I know my quest is in the ladies' room.

With my growing sensory ability, even before I open the door, I hear someone crying. It's coming from behind the stalls, in the left corner by the banging steam pipes where one can have a smidgen of privacy.

Whoever's crying pauses for a moment when I step in, but then continues, unabated. It's the gasping type that means someone is either extremely overwhelmed, or in physical pain.

I rush over. Lacey is slumped over, her wheat-hued hair disheveled, her head in her hands, sobbing. After first testing the pipe with a hand to make sure it isn't scalding, I sit down next to her. Luckily, the pipe is merely warm. Even though it's still mid-October, the school has turned on the heat because of a cold snap.

I reach out a tentative arm and rest it on Lacey's back. "You okay?"

She doesn't respond with words, only a fresh round of sobs wracking her body. She must recognize my voice, yet she's not pulling away. This gives me the courage to give Lacey a few shy pats on the back.

Lacey crumbles more into herself. I'm truly worried now. This is no light crying, like over a bad test score. This is big, as if a family member has been maimed in an accident. I keep on stroking Lacey's back, hoping we'll have a few moments to talk before the barrage of snooping kids comes in to gossip as they apply fresh coats of makeup.

"What happened?" I ask, as soon as Lacey's shoulder

blades stop shaking. I hand her some paper towels from a nearby loose stack.

Without looking up, she unfolds one and loudly blows her nose. "I bet you get a kick out of seeing me like this," she mutters into the moist towel.

"Not so much. You worried me. I wanted to make sure you were all right."

Lacey laughs bitterly. "Well, I'm not."

"What happened?" I'm surprised that there's no trace of irony in my voice. My beast, as I've now nicknamed my dark energy, must still be sleeping.

"If I tell you," Lacey mumbles, "you'll tell your posse, and gloat over it." She looks up.

I'm shocked at her puffy, red eyes, cried clean of makeup and devoid of that glint. The one that used to be superiority, but lately is closer to envy. Lacey's eyes are soft, vulnerable. It would be so easy to hurt her right now. But I'm not feeling it. The beast really is sleeping. Something in me genuinely wants to connect with Lacey—at least right now, in this singular moment.

I remove my hand from her back. "I won't blab it around. Promise. I just thought it might help to talk to someone."

"Ha! To my worst enemy?" Lacey snaps. "I don't believe you."

Neither of us has ever declared it out in the open—*worst enemy*. But we are, or have been, or . . . I should be angry at this rejection of my rare kindness. Is it a rejection? Or simply a testing, in the same way I placed a hand on that heat pipe, to make sure it wouldn't burn me, before I sat down?

There's a shrug in my voice. "Archenemy, friend, what's the difference?" I pause. "We've loved the same people, hated the same people . . ."

At this, Lacey's vibe seems to shift. She glances up at me,

studies me intently. I wonder what she sees. "Who, Ander?" she asks. "Because you don't even know Charlie."

I want to press her, ask if it's Charlie she's crying about, but I don't want her to suspect I'm rooting around for her vulnerable spot in order to jab it. And that animal part of me knows anyway. So, I wait, leaving a safe space for Lacey to pour out more words, if she chooses to.

Lacey looks down at her lap, takes the paper towel, already drenched with her tears and wipes new ones away. "Yeah, it's Charlie. You would've found out anyway." She stops talking and looks over at me as if she's waiting for me to jump in and ask what happened. So, I keep on being a silent, patient soundboard. Lacey balls up the towel. "Charlie's a cheater. Yeah, that's right. I'm sure Ander or your weird friend Wilson told you that. I know Wilson thinks his brother's a cheater. He warned me once."

Lacey's talking about Wilson? *Jackpot.*

With this, my beast snaps awake and yawns, showing off its sharp teeth. I bite the inside of my mouth so I won't burst out with questions about her encounters with him. "Don't tell me if you don't want," I say with genuine kindness, mixed with a dab of manipulative savvy that this will irresistibly egg Lacey on.

"You'll find out. From Bailey, or Ava," she grumbles. "Ava, that bitch, she's come on to Charlie from day one."

I lean forward to catch every word.

"I can't blame Ava," Lacey admits. "Charlie's a cheating dog. Yeah, that's what Wilson told me about Charlie, but I didn't want to believe it." New tears stream down her cheeks. They wet her pink pullover, but she doesn't bother to wipe them off.

I could point out that karma's a bitch, that Lacey cheated on Ander first, with Charlie. But why bother?

Lacey continues. "It happened when I was at your

rehearsal. Yeah, that's right . . . Charlie was doing it with my friend, Ava." She shrills this last line.

Suddenly, a horde of girls bursts into the room, filling it with lively chatter.

"Can I borrow your mascara?"

"Let me try your lip brush. Ooh, I love that mauve color."

"So, what did Sawyer say about the date?"

"Shit, I knew this was a bad place to hide," Lacey mutters. "I should've gone home."

"Come over," I invite. "I'll fix you tea. No one's there—my aunt works."

Lacey stares at me with great suspicion. "Don't think that we're going to be friends," she says loudly enough so that the girls who are reapplying makeup rush behind the stalls to see who's hanging out in the back corner.

"Sungirl!" one of the girls screeches. "I can't wait for your next party."

"I didn't get an invite," wails another. "Text me one? Please?" She scrawls her cell number on a piece of tissue and hands it to me.

"I got one," brags a third girl. "Already made my own burlesque outfit! It's hella cool—Marilyn Monroe meets Rhianna."

"What are you wearing for it, Sungirl?" asks the fourth girl. "It'd be cool if you, like, wore an outfit with blinking lights."

The girls erupt in a round of raucous laughter before they even notice Lacey.

"What's wrong?" the prettiest girl finally asks her.

Normally I'd be thrilled at the clamor, but now? "We were just leaving," I announce as I slide a protective arm around Lacey, and lead her out. Amazingly, Lacey doesn't protest.

"Give us some space," is all she grumbles.

Down on the street, I hail a cab.

"Look, I can only stay for, like, fifteen minutes." Lacey is obviously rethinking this in the light of day.

"Fine," I chirp. *That's all I'll need to nab you as my groupie*, my beast promises as the cab speeds away.

At the house, I hang jackets in the closet, and hurriedly arrange the blankets my aunt and I use to warm us when we watch TV. "It's a bit of a mess," I admit.

"S'okay," Lacey mumbles.

I think of inviting Lacey to hang out in my room, but decide against it. I don't want her to feel cornered, plus my room is rather plain. Instead, I lead Lacey into the kitchen, a cozy room with hanging plants. I put the kettle on and offer Lacey her choice of teas. Lacey chooses mint, I choose black mango.

We sit across from each other. Lacey's stopped crying but her eyes are still red-rimmed and puffy. Even so, she radiates beauty. Her hair, normally combed perfectly, is tousled corn silk. Her low-cut pink jersey, still splotched with tears, lends her a soft princess look, and matches the pearly pink lipstick she reapplied in the cab.

Lacey's beauty is real, not the product of magic, I recognize, with an unwelcome surge of my old inferiority. Straightening in my chair, I practically have to will myself back to a sense of control. Quieted now, Lacey's sitting with her hands folded across her chest. I struggle for a good opening remark that will put her at ease, and engage her.

"So, I hope you're okay, I mean, I hope Charlie didn't hurt you or anything."

"No, none of that. I confronted him, this morning," Lacey explains as she stirs honey into her tea. "He didn't even try to deny it. He told me to lighten up. *Me*. After I took him into *my* crowd, and helped him with his image and social standing." This last is said as a person used to getting her way, used to floating on top.

I can't help but be appalled by Lacey's mention of social rank as the foremost thing she's helped Charlie with. I'm obsessed with it, too, though. Lots of kids are, if they're being honest. I grin inside. The grin must be spreading to my face.

"You think that's superficial?" Lacey's tone is barbed. She frowns at me. "What do you think you're about? Trying to be queen bee. Doing your fabulous parties. Trying to steal all of my friends." She snorts. "As if you ever could."

I can, and I'll continue to. Bailey and Cole and Lacey's whole crowd sits at my lunch table now. Charlie's escaped Lacey's clutches. Lacey sits alone with Ava, her last ally. With this news of Charlie dumping Lacey for Ava, Ava—the last jester in Lacey's royal court—might be sitting pretty with me and my crew by this time tomorrow. I reveal nothing, because I'm feeling unexpectedly close to my 'enemy'.

I'm considering what to say next when Lacey barrels on. Clearly, she needs to open up to someone, even a rival. "I should've taken Wilson up on his offer to date me," Lacey confides. "Would've given Charlie the lesson of his life."

At this, I cough up drops of tea that have trickled down my windpipe.

"Shocked? That's right, your friend Wilson was after me right around the same time Charlie put the moves on. Yup, every time I went over to Charlie's, Wilson was there, lurking in the background, playing his oppressive heavy metal. He sprayed himself to the hilt with musky cologne he thought would lure me to his room, as if I was some idiot puppy dog in heat." With this, she bursts into hysterical laughter. I can't help laughing, too. I have to admit, the girl has a refreshingly raucous side to her.

"I know that cologne. I've smelled it on him," I say.

"Yeah, right? Like cheap aromatic sexcapade candles," Lacey quips. We crumple into another round of giggling. It's a delight to see Lacey sputtering out globules of tea mixed with drool in very unladylike fashion.

When I'm able to get a breath in, I switch the subject from Charlie to the bloody gut of what my inner beast longs to feed on. "What did Wilson say when he came on to you?"

Lacey circles her cup on its saucer as she thinks about this. "Wilson's really charming, isn't he? Charlie knows it. Charlie's a cute jock, but Wilson's like an exotic star in a horror film. That's why Charlie hates his brother—oil and water, those two. I saw how Wilson lured you, too, during your first party. Wound you up on his finger."

Lacey hasn't said word-one about my relationship with Ander, and is almost talking as if Wilson and I are lovers. Why?

She leans across the table, catching my gaze. "Wilson has some strange power. You know it, don't you?"

I'm loath to admit his power because then I might have to discuss my own strange power. "Did you resist it?" is all I ask.

"I did. It was hard to. One afternoon, when I was waiting for Charlie to finish his shower after a soccer game, Wilson invited me into his room to listen to music. I told him I didn't like heavy metal. He said this was different, lighter, that he'd bought it with me in mind. I asked him why he would do that. He knew I was with Charlie, so Wilson's comment wigged me out. He just looked at me in that way— you know what I'm talking about—he looks at you with such intensity that you want to stay in it forever."

"You forget what you were doing, and why you came there, and—"

"So you know."

I nod. I want to say that no matter how charming Wilson is, I've chosen Ander. I know that this would shut Lacey down, though, that Lacey is still attached to Ander in some tenuous way. So I hold it in. It's so hard to. But there are other pressing things to ask. "Did Wilson ask if you wanted anything, like, really badly?"

"How did you know?" Lacey's eyes glint with a knowledge that seems to pass between us. "I went in and Wilson closed the door. In that moment, I completely forgot about Charlie. All I wanted was for Wilson to throw me down on his bed and ravish me like in those old Gothic horror romances. Everything else was jumbled up in confusion."

"Yes! It's like you're being thrown around inside a blinding, intoxicating cloud," I echo.

"Wilson stood close enough to kiss me, but he didn't, and I was dying for him to kiss me. My lips were burning up. And he asked me, 'What do you want? If you could sell your soul for something, what would you want?' I was so, so spooked."

"What was your answer?" I wait, breathless, for Lacey's next words.

"It took every shred of strength to get the words out. Somehow I managed. I told Wilson that I wasn't about to sell my soul, and that I wanted Charlie. The look in Wilson's eyes frightened me—they were empty and desperate—but that broke the spell."

"A spell?"

Lacey releases a panting sound, as if she's reacting anew to Wilson's presence. "It sure felt like a spell. I ran out of there like lightning." Lacey looks over at me. "But I wonder now, did I do the right thing? I've never felt that kind of intensity before. And Wilson was right about his brother. Charlie's a mad cheater. Sometimes I imagine what it would be like with Wilson."

"You don't want to know."

Lacey stare is penetrating. "You've been with him?"

I don't want to say. I haven't really even kissed him. Some things are private. "No, I only meant you did the right thing. And I didn't."

"What do you mean?"

When we exchange looks, a myriad of unsaid messages passes between us. By the way Lacey's face pales and her eyebrows dart up, she must know that I caved to Wilson's pressure, that I made a twisted vow, and I'm trapped in that vow.

Lacey leans across the table and grips my hands. Her sea-green eyes are fervent with concern. "Fight it," she whispers. "Fight it with all your might."

Love, I'm sorry, I have to have another look!
—From *Bridget Jones's Diary,* by Helen Fielding

I t's the big Burlesque night, *finally,* and I'm leaning on the counter, half watching Bailey's mom make pizza and half surveying the event layout. My costume is on under my fancy draped robe, but I still need makeup. From here, there's a view of the dining room and the makeshift stage that Ander and Cole built, at the end of Bailey's spacious living room. It's so easy to breathe in this airy loft.

"It's good your mom installed double doors for her paintings," Ander puffs at Bailey, as he shoves the unwieldy props closer to the stage.

I agree. "No way my sun props would've fit through a normal door."

"I'm thrilled we can provide the perfect venue." Bailey's mom artfully arranges basil on her homemade pizzas. She hands me a piece of mozzarella. I thank her and pop it in my mouth.

Tory's in the TV area coaching Cole and Jake on their comedy routine. "Larger than life, guys," she insists. "Shake it like you mean it!" She's been in lots of school plays, so she knows her stuff. Jake shakes his butt with such enthusiasm that his banana skirt unhinges.

"Bailey!" Tory screeches, "Need yellow thread over here, fast. Bananas are falling out, know what I mean?"

Bailey dashes over, a spool of industrial thread in hand. Tory entrusts the stitch-up to Bailey's expert hands, while she clucks over the refreshment table, arranging drinks and snacks. "Need an ice bucket," she calls to a helper, who scurries to the kitchen. Bailey's mom is already loading one up. When Tory's done arranging the drinks, I hand her a box of posters and suggest she get her team to put them up.

"On it." Tory unrolls one and gasps. "Amazing! They're like the real thing."

"I know, right?" I commissioned art majors to make Victorian-style posters of tonight's performers. Payment: vouchers to my next two parties. I had more takers than I needed.

While Tory's pretty minions flutter around with posters and an arsenal of pushpins, Ander and I do last-minute lineup corrections.

Wilson's not here yet. He likes to arrive late and make a melodramatic entrance. Part of me looks forward to seeing him. Another part is in no hurry. His intensity guarantees unpredictable shifts in the group dynamics—my dynamics, too. When he's way out in Coney, his magnetic pull fades, but I'm always drawn to him when he's near. I fear that he'll inspire my beast to the worst of its magic. And I want to enjoy this innocent, busy activity while it lasts. The burlesque group is family—one that I've chosen—not one that's dysfunctional or in jail.

Is this what happiness feels like? Creating things and having your own tribe around you, all turned on by building something together? In brief moments like this, I pray that my dark magic is a rabid weasel, who will soon choke on its poison froth.

Bailey runs over and gives me a friendly hug. "Do my makeup?"

I study her face. "What makeup does a rooster wear, anyway? I'm stumped."

Bailey's earlier idea of playing a Victorian coquette morphed after she discovered, to her delight, that burlesque had a fascinating history having nothing to do with *ooh-la-la* pasties. About two weeks ago, while I was stitching a hem, Bailey had gone online to fact-check a detail. Suddenly, she screamed, "It's performance art!"

"What is?" I'd lifted my foot off the sewing machine pedal.

"*Old* burlesque," she'd sung. "It was more like rooster costumes and parodies of Little Bo Peep and nutty, fruitcake stuff having zero to do with Vegas-style G-strings. It was 'performed at venues on the boardwalks, like in Coney Island,'" she read.

"Nice. Is there more?" I ask.

Bailey read on. "'In the 1800's, burlesque was a theater of the absurd to stand the upper crust on their heads. They did skits mocking social conventions. It was the art of the maudlin, such as having men in drag, or in satyr costumes, acting out parodies of Shakespeare.'"

"Who would've known? I thought burlesque was all about getting raunchy."

"We can make it *art*." Bailey always wants to make things into art. I love that about her.

Standing in front of me now, she looks clucking hilarious in her rooster costume with its profusion of red tail feathers fanning out from her hindquarters. On top of the red skullcap that snaps neatly under her chin is a crest of the same bright feathers, spouting up like a reverse waterfall. Her shoes are her mom's heels, which Bailey has bejeweled within an inch of their lives.

"You need red lipstick," I venture, "to match your wattle and your ruby-red slippers." I snap my feet together three times.

"Now I'm a rooster named Dorothy from Kansas?" We collapse onto Bailey's beanbags.

"Get up!" Tory shrieks, "Or you'll ruin your feathers." She grabs Bailey's hand and hauls her to her feet.

Bailey's mom comes over and riffles through Bailey's pails of eyeliners and shadows. Being a painter, her mom's adept at matching and blending. She picks a smoky brown and smudges a wave of crimson over it. Next, she works on me, painting sunny swirls on my face, and applying golden lashes that I discovered in a cheesy 42nd Street wig store.

"Ooh, I forgot lashes, I want cool lashes, too," Bailey wails.

Her mom checks her watch. "Too late, the party starts in ten minutes."

"So soon?" My chest tightens. I hope Burlesque goes better than the Yellow Party. I debate inside for the tenth time, whether I should let my conjuring go wild, or keep it tamed. I decide on setting it at medium sizzle to lure, but no fire burns.

As if you could control it, chuckles my beast.

Cole has just put on a circus-themed playlist, when the bell rings. I cinch my yellow cloak to keep my costume secret until I perform, and then, with an anxious intake of breath, I dash to the door. I need to rule this event, greet my old and new followers. Shape this going forward.

People crowd in, all trying to greet me at once, and warm me with admiring gazes. This is all so new, so intoxicating, it's as if I'm the one being mesmerized. They want to know about my costume, the burlesque performers, and they ask if they've won a voucher for a privileged spot in my next party. "All revealed soon." I wink. "Enjoy some refreshments." I ferry them to the drinks table and float back to greet the next eager wave.

Ander comes over and helps me greet partygoers. It's sweet how he stays by my side, but it's almost embarrassing how people barely greet him before making a beeline for my attention. A mere month ago, Ander was the dazzling leading man, and I a cinder girl with a virtual broom and tattered apron. Now, I feel my powers whir in my gut, as if I'm less a cinder girl, and more a futuristic machine absorbing humans into its magnetic vortex.

Never let it stop, purrs my beast.

Juniors and sophomores from school pour in next. They embrace me as if we're old friends. A flock of seniors bursts in, too, fist-bumping and acting friendlier than ever.

Strangers trickle in next—from Wilson's school? "How'd you get so pretty? You're even more beautiful in person," gushes a starstruck guy.

"She is," Ander agrees, as the guy pushes right past him to hug me.

"Is Wilson here? Are you and him, like, you know?" he asks me.

"No," Ander snaps. "She's with me."

"It's Sungirl!" crows an excited girl in a red mini who dashes over to get a selfie.

People line up to pose with me. A sea of raised arms springs up, all aiming their cells at the real-time Sungirl. Girls dressed in their own version of burlesque—minis, ripped fishnets, feather boas, and skanky heels—seek my opinion of their costumes. Shy kids hug the sidelines, mouths agape. I make sure to approach everyone with a compliment and an outstretched hand while Ander runs off to check a performance issue. He's probably overwhelmed by the attention I'm getting, but I'm too into it to stop the flow.

Wilson's coaching lines play in my mind: "An Internet diva must put her followers at ease. A smile and embrace will keep them in your corner, posting on your fan sites, your Instagram and tweeting your events. They want to feel they know you, and have rubbed elbows with the queen."

He's right. After I've worked the crowd, I notice even more people keeping a watchful eye on my whereabouts, flitting after me like nervous moths fearing to veer far from the tantalizing glow of the light.

The next influx brings in Lacey. We lock eyes and I excuse myself from the latest batch of admirers to greet her. Our relationship is a baffling knot of sometimes friendly, other times hostile, encounters. I won't untangle it now. The thing, now, is to keep my poised charm flowing.

Twice, I've helped her rehearse, despite Bailey's hair-trigger snipes. Rehearsing at Bailey's was a mistake after all. Bailey was too jealous and watchful that I keep my word. So, the second time, we rehearsed in the gym during study hall, when Bailey was busy in class. Lacey and I didn't mention Wilson again. Instead, we stuck to the mechanics of rehearsal.

"You came by yourself?" I can't help asking her now.

She shrugs. "Didn't want the complications of a new date." That means she and Charlie still haven't worked it out.

It's been a couple of weeks, so it also means that they probably won't.

Will Charlie show? If so, will Ava be on his arm, or yet another flavor of arm candy? No doubt the tension would crackle between Lacey and Charlie. My inner demon stirs and licks its chops for greasy, tainted gristle. "Ava coming?" I slip in. "We saved her a costume."

Lacey's face stiffens. "I kicked her out of my posse, but no matter how desperate she gets, she'll never be loyal to you." Lacey's catlike eyes, which a moment ago had held a hint of friendship, now study me as if I'm an unsavory science project. "I know how much that annoys you, but you can't manipulate them all."

I work hard to only scorch a little. "Look around. I have plenty of followers. Could you fill a room this big?"

"Absolutely. Done it many times. I've had smokin' parties, right here, at *Bailey's*." Lacey draws out this last word, making it painfully clear that I'm again getting her sloppy seconds: first with Ander, now with Bailey. Even with Wilson. Lacey purses her regal face into a stingy sneer. "You wouldn't know about my parties at Bailey's, 'cause you were never invited."

"The most popular people are the most generous," I retort. "That's why I extended an invite to you. I don't need to be all territorial." As soon as I utter this, I'm deeply tired of our nasty back and forth. Unexpected warmth for Lacey, even a feeling of being grateful for her brutal honesty, rushes in to replace my fury. It goes beyond whether we're friends or enemies.

What matters is our strange sense of mutual understanding, beast to bitch.

"Hey!" I nudge Lacey, to which she startles. "Are you in costume?"

She opens her coat just enough for me to see her bikini. Leather? She might hate me, I realize with a wash of satisfaction, but she admires me enough to be in my show. I check my cell, put on my game face. "Performance is in ten minutes. You up for some sociable competition, Ms. Givem Heck? I'll pin you on the mat so fast, you won't have time to blink."

"Bring it on. I've changed up my act. May the best diva win."

We exchange what feels like conspiratorial laughter, and then Lacey prances into the crowd. Changed up her act? How? Does it have to do with the leather bikini? I'm off to find Ander. The fact that Lacey's here now increases my need to stay close to him, to make sure he's not distracted by his newly available ex. He's by the punch bowl, chatting with a guy from Lit.

"Hey, beautiful." Ander swings an arm around me. "Ready for the performance?"

"Yup." I snuggle into his chest.

Across the room, the door opens to a blizzard of loud activity. Charlie is making his way inside, with Ava, in a minidress.

Ander snorts. "That lame jock piles through women so fast."

I ply Ander with kisses. I intend to show him lots of affection tonight. "Awkward couple," I sniff. "Ava towers over Charlie."

Ava's hair, in a sculptural whorl of braids and torn ribbons, adds another three inches easy to her four-inch heels. A garment bag is slung over her arm. Has she come ready to perform? *Yesssss.* This will add to the edgy chaos already brewing. "Just wait until Wilson arrives and sees his player of a brother with yet another girl," I whisper in Ander's ear. "Bottle rockets will be sparking off the walls."

Ander laughs and gives me a squeeze. "You rotten little conniver, you."

I extricate myself. "This little conniver has to greet more newbies. Excuse me."

"Go, Sungirl, do your thing. But line 'em up in about five minutes." He gives me an affectionate pat on my rump.

Charlie's soccer jersey and khakis look positively goony beside Ava's Park Avenue, thirty-room-penthouse beauty. I predict they'll last a month, tops. Breezing over, I offer them a Sungirl's-on-it grin, as if they're already my devoted fans, in order to jolt them out of their superior posturing. "Welcome to Burlesque!" I air-kiss Ava with dramatic flair.

She takes a few steps back and tucks in a stray lock of hair-sculpture. "We're party-hopping. Only here for a minute." Charlie doesn't even bother to say hi, but surveys the room—looking to see if his ex is around?

"Here for a minute, huh?" I nod to Ava's garment bag. "Brought a costume? If not, and you want to perform, Bailey's mom has extra costumes. She's the—"

"I *know* what her mom looks like," Ava spits. "I've known her since first grade."

Charlie snickers, safely behind Ava's garment-bag shield.

Coward, I think, but I only smile fetchingly as I amp up the force of my vibes. "Help yourselves to pomegranate bubbly or whatever you like. Show's about to start, so *buh-bye* for now." I glide away, like those ladies on Montague Street did when I first moved to Brooklyn, but with added swag. The admiring heat of Ava's eyes warms my back. My beast yowls silently with hyena delight.

Tory, breathless in her corseted costume, bursts through the crowd. "I've gathered the troupe," she reports. "Ander's run through the set list. Lacey's trashing her rehearsed act and performing something new. Did you give her the okay?" Tory raises her artfully tweezed brow in a panicked arch.

"Ander was ready to boot her, but she's laying on the charm and he's caving."

"Oh, let her. Who cares?"

"Really?" She looks skeptical. "If you say so. C'mon, you're introducing the show."

Flattery's a must, so I toss my most loyal follower a meaty bone. "Did I tell you that you rock as assistant producer?" On the way, we're distracted by a commotion at the door. Burly guys are arguing with people still in the hall. "What's happening?" I ask Tory.

"Too many people want in! Bailey's mom said no more party crashers. Jake and Cole organized bouncers from the football team to man the door. It's out of control."

Out of control, my beast whinnies, *I love when it's out of control.*

I feel it longing to feed off Wilson's energy. He must be close because I feel his pull. "Make sure Wilson gets in," I demand. Tory nods and scurries off.

Behind the curtains, Ander's there to help me onto the golden sun props that he and Taylor secured with wide swaths of Velcro. He squeezes me tight. "Knock 'em dead, Sungirl."

I shiver, hoping it won't literally come to that. "Wave, so I can see you out there?" He promises to, and then he scrambles to the sidelines to draw open the curtains.

Up here, with the stage lights beaming down, I'm unexpectedly intimidated. I've become a master of my fan-page posts and of my imperial lunchroom comings and goings. But addressing a rowdy audience is still hard. My powers can still falter. Sweat dampens my costume. As the slide show that Bailey and I put together flashes behind me, my heart rattles. I wheel around to triple-check it. Thankfully, my dark magic hasn't adhered a leering version of myself to the images.

Over the crowd, the door opens to more commotion.

Spotlight glare prevents me from making out a face, but I *sense* him, reaching out to me with molten eyes and scarred heart. When I adjust to the stage lights, I see the bouncers coax out another mob and let in one lone figure.

Wilson. His coal-gray shirt gleams, and his hair is untamed, abstract art. Marching forward, he shoots video of me. The crowd parts to allow him space.

Electricity streaks through me. Drawing in Wilson's energy, my rehearsed lines flow in nefarious channels up to my brain. *Ah, food*, sighs my beast. "Welcome, all, to Burlesque," I announce. "I, Sungirl, shine my warmest rays on you."

"Why burlesque?" calls out a girl who I don't recognize.

"Good question," I improvise. "As vampires have a thirst for nighttime and blood, Sungirl has a thirst for the sun, the beach, and the boardwalk. And beachgoers on boardwalks everywhere, from the 1800s on, have enjoyed sexy, fantastic burlesque."

"Take it off!" shouts a horny guy.

"Thong show, thong show!" shouts another.

I hold out my palms, emit focused beams to captivate. "Patience, lovelies, it's not just about stripping. It's the art of the tease. You'll see talented ladies, guys, too. And I, Lady of Cosmic Rays, will perform the big send-off." In response, the group roars. I revel in the thrill of the crowd, even as I tremble precariously on the papier-mâché sun props.

Steadying myself, I go on. "I'll be your guide into this spectacular world." Another chorus of catcalls buoys me. "But first, the winners of my fan-page guessing game: Senior Lucy Lane guessed that Candy Tattersal is none other than . . . Bailey Storrow." I wait for the ruckus to simmer down before reeling off the rest. "All winners have special perks at my next exclusive event, which I'll announce on my Sungirl site tomorrow night."

"Give us a hint!" shouts a girl from Wilson's school.

"Shocking truths will be revealed. Only the bravest dare sign on." The crowd begins to buzz with theories. I love how with a sample line I can create thunderous speculation.

"Take it off!" the horny guy yells in a repetitive refrain.

I raise my arms to silence people. "Drum roll, please." Lisbeth's friend, the percussionist, obliges. "First up, I present Candy Tattersal, the incredible, talented artist *chick*."

I hurry offstage, as fast as I can in teetering heels, and down into the roped-off VIP area to the left front section. Ander's waiting for me, and we exchange excited kisses, his tasting of root beer and passion. My legs tremble all over again. Wilson has snaked his way up, too. He presses me in a sensual hug that isn't lost on Ander.

Onstage, Bailey waddles out in her hilarious red hen outfit with its wild plumes. She struts along, singing a ditty into the wireless mic.

They call me Candy Tattersal, I cluck around the farm and paint for y'all,

A picture here, a picture there, ooh-la-la, a picture of your underwear!

With this, she tears off her bulky costume to reveal a slinky red bodysuit, from which more tail-feathers sprout. To a rock version of her farm song, she bumps and grinds around an easel. Picking up an outsized brush, she paints in a guy's polka-dot boxers.

Ander and I pump fists in an enthusiastic cheer, but the loudest hoots come from Bailey's love, Cole, waiting behind stage for his own act. After Bailey, Cole as Your Fyne Selfe and Jake as Busted Betsy burst onstage sporting garish wigs. Their coconut boobs are popping out of their bras and their miniskirts are studded with plastic bananas. When they shimmy, the bananas switch and click against each other. They play airhead "girls" trying to pick up two guys.

"Sample my bananas?" Cole asks a guy in a clownish man's suit.

"I never eat between meals," the guy quips.

They do more funny banana jokes and then latch arms in a clumsy, shuffling line dance.

Before the laughter dies down, Tory minces onstage. Her Pheromone Patty is a sexed-up nurse, taking care of a hot-to-trot patient. Lisbeth follows, as Lil Laurentine, a Victorian schoolgirl in a racy pinafore. She plays the cello with open legs, revealing her ruffled pantaloon, while Victorian maids in matching pinafores cavort around her and play penny whistles. Lisbeth receives the most applause from Cat and her orchestra friends.

I'm elated by how well things are going—much better than at Yellow Party. Still, I feel a rush of jealousy that I'm not a constant object of delight. The next act will be Lacey's. Glancing over at Ander's eager face, I have second thoughts about giving the green light on her new act. My preternatural senses smell a fetid rot of danger. Inside, my beast growls, *Let the girl mess with you. See how far she gets.*

Bailey's apparently gotten word. She pulls me to a corner near the stairs. "Why are you letting Lacey do something unrehearsed? It's bad enough she's in our show at all."

"Not sure what I was thinking, but we'll deal with it."

Bailey shakes her head in frustration, making her feathered headpiece quiver. She reluctantly advances to the mic. "Next, we have Ms. Givem Heck to—"

"I'm Ms. Lux Slayve Driver now," Lacey cuts in as she waltzes onstage. "I'll take it from here." Frowning, Bailey forks over the mic.

The crowd cheers as Lacey teases off her cover-up to reveal a dominatrix Cleopatra: a blunt-cut black wig, leather bikini, tie sandals and a low-slung belt with bulging compartments.

Performing a slinky dance, she forms exaggerated right angles with her arms like the profiled ladies on hieroglyphs. "Out in the desert, building pyramids, I run the workers hard," she says. "But if you're one of my three extra-*hard* workers with an oiled six-pack, I may cut you slack." She holds up paper strips she pulls from her belt. "If I call your name, report to my onstage construction site."

All the guys begin whooping. From the wings, Bailey, Tory, and I exchange horrified glances. "She's copying your voucher idea again," Tory snaps.

I let out a tinny laugh in an effort to sound effortless. "What's that saying? Oh, yeah, 'Imitation's the sincerest form of flattery.'"

"True, she'll never top the Sun Queen of Cosmic Rays," Tory scoffs.

I wave at Ander in VIP, but prickle when I can't distract him from staring up at Lacey. Then I glance over at Wilson. He's recording video of her. Infuriating. *I'm* Wilson's muse.

When Lacey draws the first paper, the crowd murmurs in anticipatory suspense. "Ed Barnes, report to the construction site," she says crisply. Ed Barnes, fist pumping, jogs onstage. Lacey calls her second volunteer. A senior in jeans bops onstage.

With the last draw, the room gets hushed. My gut rumbles as Lacey unfolds the paper.

"Read it! Read it!" chants the entire room.

She flicks her hair back and bellows, "Ander James, report onstage."

"Slut!" I hiss. I'm raring to scorch holes in her sleazy Egyptian getup. But I've already made that pledge to dazzle, not injure. If I enhance the creative magic, the scary magic should weaken. If I can only breathe through this . . .

Put on a show that will outshine anything Lacey could ever hope to do, my beast snorts at me in utter disgust.

I make my way back to VIP, but Ander's already split. There he is, one foot on the stage stairs, deciding whether or not to comply. The crowd's suspended reaction seems proof that calling him onstage is wrongheaded, because it's now common knowledge Lacey dumped him.

In a flash, their delayed reaction is over and audience opinion changes. I shudder at how fast popular reaction can flip—faster than the flipping speed of light. "An-der! An-der!" they shout. "Ander, get up there." People literally shove him up the stairs. I see him stop fighting it.

He marches over to Lacey, and stands there, arms crossed. God, he's handsome with his blond hair tousled from working on the sets, his muscles ripped, stretching his shirt tight across the shoulders. No matter his limp, Ander still has it—the golden god to Wilson's dark demon.

I feel an aching swell of love.

Onstage, Lacey sends Ander a triumphant smile. She nods to the band to cue music and the oldie "Walk Like an Egyptian" rings out. Leading the way to a sphinx prop and fake bricks she must've sneaked in, she opens a belt compartment and unrolls a leather whip. The audience gasps. Striking the thing at the guys' feet, she barks orders. "Build that sphinx. Faster! Faster."

When she reaches Ander, he says something sharp to her. Even my animal ears can't hear over the blast of music, but judging by Lacey's stricken expression, it's cutting. Ander snatches her whip and hurls it to the ground. Then he limps offstage.

The crowd goes ape-shit. Some guy yells, "Tell it straight, dude!"

I gloat. Didn't even need to use magic. Lacey caused this train wreck all by herself. I reach out to reassure Ander as he passes, but he brushes by me, unseeing. In the chaos, Ava pushes her way onstage and unclasps a green-feathered cloak.

She twirls it around before tossing it, unveiling the kelly-green bikini that Bailey spent days sewing by hand. The crowd breaks out in cheers of "Avey, baby!" She swivels to a smoky jazz number that she's obviously set up with the DJ. That's all I notice before running off to find Ander. How many times does Lacey need to rub his nose in the dirt?

Wilson spins around to record it all: Ava's wings, Bailey's mom's gremlin paintings, my downturned mouth. I clutch at his arm. "Where's Ander?"

"Watch the camera, Sungirl. Sorry, I don't keep tabs on the man."

Weaving my way back to the shadowy space opposite the stage, I see a madhouse of kids inhaling chips, making out on Bailey's sofas, and flailing to the crashing beat. My super-senses can't locate Ander. Too much chaotic energy pinging around.

Tory bursts through the mob. "Here you are! Why'd you run off? You're up after Ava. I've been trying to find you for, like, ten minutes. C'mon." I have no choice. If I don't get up there, my fans will protest. Tory leads me to the stairs. Reluctantly, I tell the DJ to cue music.

With the benefit of height, I finally spot Ander. He's in the kitchen, leaning against the fridge and talking to someone.

A girl. My heart drops.

Lacey's leaning close to him, and they're deep in conversation. Her pale hair fluffs over her cheek. When she turns, I see her face is mottled the way it was in the girl's bathroom. *Shit.* Lacey must be tearfully manipulating Ander into caring again. Any drop of empathy I've developed for her evaporates. In a consuming flame of anger, I charge down the stairs and through the crowd to the kitchen.

Behind me, people clamor loudly for Sungirl. They'll have to wait.

"Interrupting something?" I shrill. Ander's brows shoot up. He pauses mid-sentence.

"I was just apologizing to Ander," Lacey mutters.

"Oh, I bet you were," I say coldly. "Over Charlie so fast?"

"It's not what—" Ander's eyes beg for me to calm down, as if there is a logical reason for his behavior, if I'd only be patient and let him explain later.

I glower accusingly at Lacey. "You're a sadist."

"Whoa!" Ander raises his arms in protest. "The girl's upset."

"Who *are* you?" I yell at Ander, at both of them.

"Calm down. You and I are cool," Ander promises, leaning over to give me a quick kiss. "We'll talk later. Promise." He cocks his head toward the stage. "They need you up there."

Indeed, the crowd is bellowing, "Sungirl, Sungirl, Sungirl!"

An entitled gleam in Lacey's eyes replaces her tears.

"Better be a good explanation, Ander," I shout over my shoulder, as I push toward the stage. My fans give me encouraging cheers as I pass.

You don't need that weak, selfish boy, my beast belches from inside my throat, *you have your followers*. Yes, my followers.

As if seconding that, Wilson's musky energy enfolds me. *Lacey's nothing. Create a bigger spectacle than any performer here.*

Watch us, Wilson, watch us, my beast and I respond in unison.

"Our final burlesque of the evening," Bailey has taken charge of the mic, "is Sungirl, goddess of Cosmic Rays!" She gestures frantically for me to hurry.

Clambering onto my props, I'm wondering why Ander didn't tell Lacey to buzz off.

Behind me, the techie flashes the Sungirl lightshow. Rays

of hot color sizzle through the room, the way butter jumps and pops in a frying pan under high heat. From the VIP section, Wilson keeps on recording me. Mob support rises in a crescendo.

"The show must go on," I sing to myself. "My show!" The band bursts into a version of *Here Comes the Sun.* Gyrating to the beat, I toss off my bejeweled cape to reveal the fringe bikini. Fireworks of sparkling yellow light project across my curves.

"Yeah, go!"

"Wow!"

"Take it all off, hottie!" come the shouts, faster, faster.

Wilson glides closer, his digital lens exploring my every shift in movement, each of my dreamy moods. Up front, even Charlie's eyes widen. I luxuriate in the adoration of the crowd, a silken comforter wrapping my friendless childhood self in protective folds of downy worship.

Screw that playboy mortal, my beast growls from within.

But I *do* care about Ander—I can't help it. From the corner of my vision I see, with relief, that he and Lacey are done talking. She's fixing herself a drink. He's made his way to the VIP area.

He waves. His eyes are on me, yet my uncanny senses read his thoughts, spiderlike and reaching out to different parts of the room—to me, to Charlie, and then resting again on Lacey. That hurts. With his energy so disloyal, the need to prove my worth overwhelms.

Solar images flash behind me. My wavy hair is backlit by the sanctified halo of yellow pixels. From behind the curtains, Cole tosses me a golden ball. I keep it aloft by tapping it.

Amplify. Wilson's voice stokes me. He flits closer, a gypsy moth, drawn to my light. Then, I spot Lacey—double-crossing nymphomaniac—making a beeline for Ander.

"Amplify. Dazzle. Create!" I chant in a stern reminder. Shutting my eyes, I thrust back my head and stretch out my arms in an arc. Concentrating on forming energetic coils, I picture them pulsing at the speed of light from one hand to another. *Push, heat, burn,* howls the beast. I, too, release an animalistic moan as I coax my magic to a higher level. The crowd gasps. *Why?*

Opening my eyes, I see to my astonishment that I've conjured—yes, conjured out of thin air—an orb of light that wobbles above my palms. Sparks erupt from it as if a baby planet is being born, levitating and orbiting just above my arms.

"Ohhhhhh!" The crowd holds a long note of astonishment.

Audience comments fly inside me, like a wildfire online chat. Is it a hologram? No. It's burning. I smell it. It's a freaking ball of fire and it's getting bigger.

Hotter, the beast clamors.

I concentrate harder, squeeze my lids shut and groan. It's like lifting a dead weight that I shouldn't be lifting because it's way beyond my capacity, but I have an irrepressible urge to do it anyway. My arms vibrate so violently from the effort that I worry I'll drop the weighty mess on my feet and destroy my fragile foot bones. So out of a growing excited anxiety, I keep on holding this thing that's screwing up my arm muscles, my spine—my entire balance.

The cheering changes into a mass scream. My eyes startle open again. I gasp at the sight in my hands—and everything around me.

Floaty holograph daisies—half solid, half air—pour upwards from the orb in my hands, only to flutter back down, petals bending gracefully. When they hit the stage, they vaporize in sparkly whooshes. They're incredibly beautiful. *Transcendent.*

The crowd surges forward as if they'll only ever understand this trick if they can touch it. But they can't. The transparent daisies melt just above their outstretched palms. Exhausted as I am—for this effort is more than I've ever endured—I soar, exulting in wave after wave of adulation and wonder.

"Are you a witch?" someone asks. "How'd you make see-through flowers?"

"Shut up, mortals, and watch," Wilson orders.

"*You* shut up, jerk," the guy yells back. That guy trips and falls by Wilson's feet.

Good one, my beast giggles. My beast and I are frolicking. I'm not finished, not at all. In fact, I'm just getting started. Looking out, I glory in the fact that I have Ander's full attention, but wait . . . he's letting Lacey stand behind him, so close, almost touching. Protecting her.

I want to shoot fireballs to singe her hair, melt her skin, hurt her as she's hurt me. But, no. I'll gain ultimate command through more bouquets that melt like snowflakes.

More gorgeous impossibilities.

Stupid girl, scolds my beast. *Spectacle's not enough. She needs her teeth knocked out.*

Shut up, I reply wordlessly, I'll do it my way. I twirl. My bikini fringe flies out at a ninety-degree angle. Twirling faster, I focus on becoming a battery, overcharging and exploding molten acid.

"Move back! Watch out!" people shriek. I hear the thuds of feet, of falling bodies.

This time, when my eyes blink open, the room is aglow. Solar fire has erupted right in Bailey's loft. From *me*. Torrid flames lick at my feet. Hopping, I try to shuck them off. I catch myself as I start to fall backward. Someone screams. People shout and point to something beneath me. To my horror, I see it. The props underneath me have flared into dangerous fireballs.

My feet sear with pain. Flares shoot up my legs. My hands, too, are stinging and smell of singed flesh. No way to contain it. No way . . . I'm on an uneven funhouse floor, careening violently left, and then right. Outer edges of my vision darken. Before I fall, I glance into the blur of bodies, and desperately try to focus. My squinting eyes home in on the tallest figure—polecat with a black mane. Manic. My head smacks down, hard.

Lift up. Not working. Clenched hands extending. Feeling the molten, oozing skin on my leg. Where . . . is Ander? No. Where?

Wilson. Here. Scrambling over on grasshopper legs.

20

Have you ever thought that even if I am an adulterous bitch and
Satan, that I still might be the love of your life?
—- Grey's Anatomy

I hear them around me—their alarmed chatter. The *ssss*
of a fire extinguisher followed by cold, wet foam,
cooling yet stinging my scorched hands. I try to get up.
Can't even raise a shoulder. Through my glazed eyes I see
Wilson bolt onstage, fighting his way in. Bailey, too. She
slaps a throw rug over the flickering sun props. I open my
mouth to shout, Sorry, but nothing comes out.

Wilson again, dropping cross-legged by me, cupping a
steady hand under my head and settling it onto his lap. My
hair cascades over his knees like an autumn storm. "Dor, talk
to me," he murmurs.

I try harder. My mouth moves in a lazy, repetitive way, as
if I'm chewing on taffy, but I make no sound. I'm okay. But I
must not look it. Do I look comatose, or what?

"Say something, Dor," he pleads again. His black eyes burn down at me.

"You're not supposed to move an injured person." It's Tory's angry voice.

"Is she burned?" Bailey's mom says, right near me. "How did that thing she was standing on catch fire?"

"She's passed out!" Cat shrills. "Someone call 911."

"No," Wilson snarls. "She's coming around." He dribbles someone's leftover cup of water on my neck. I move my shoulders, feeling Wilson's bony knees under them. Wilson whispers hot breath into my ear. "You'll be okay. You're not hurt. This happened to me when I first did magic on Oilslick. I fell on the floor. The conjuring sapped too much electrical juice. A charge will surge back in soon. Don't panic."

"Let Bailey's mom take care of her," Tory insists in a scornful tone.

"I'll help her." Ander squeezes past the huddle. "Let me through."

His scent of guilt at having come up late to check on me spreads in the air like spoiled turnips. To the attuned, guilt is an offensive odor. Lacey's behind Ander, rubbernecking me, horrified yet tickled to see her nemesis flayed out on the floor. Ander and Lacey deserve each other, really. Sometimes it seems like the supposed innocents are more evil than the demons.

Wilson shifts over. He lets Bailey wedge in between him and her mom. At least Bailey's care has no hitches. "Girl, you okay?" She gingerly lifts my arm. "Oh! Your hands are burned."

"Burned," I finally croak out.

"She's coming to!" The crowd says en masse.

"Yes. I'm . . . here." I move my head experimentally from side to side.

Bailey's mom gapes when she peels off my singed heels.

"Only minor burns. I thought your feet would be worse. Bailey, get me get the Neosporin and gauze." Must be the magic. Already, magic must be reordering my singed cells to their former positions. By the time the salve is applied, my hands and feet will be practically healed. Better gather my strength and escape before that happens, and people start asking hard questions.

Wilson's voice sounds inside me: *Right, you can't chance it.*

"She lost her balance on the prop?" Ander squeezes all the way in.

In my supernatural sight I see he wasn't even looking at the stage when I fell. He might as well have been in another building, he'd been so removed, so preoccupied with Lacey. His mind is adrift on lovesick vibes, yet he's trying his best to rise to the situation. I also feel his worry for me. He grasps my hand and examines each burned fingertip. "Warren, I'll take her—"

"Got it covered. You were too busy flirting with your ex," Wilson accuses.

"Bull!" Ander shoots back. "It's not your business."

"This accident is none of *your* business," Wilson scolds.

"Don't . . . fight." I run the back of my hand across my neck to brush off droplets.

Bailey's returned with ointment, tape, and gauze. She and her mother bind my feet and hands. I note their astonished faces, as my skin gets pinker even before their gauze is in place.

Sitting up, woozy, I lean on Ander. "Ander? It's the magi—"

"No," Wilson says sharply. He sends me a coded grimace that says it's not safe to talk about magic, here with these fools.

"I'll take you to the hospital," Ander says. "I'll get your coat."

With what feels like a Herculean effort, I hoist myself up, pressing on Wilson's shoulder for leverage. "No hospital," I yelp. "I'm fine. It's just . . . my feet are all pins and needles."

"Understatement of the century," Cole says, a spent fire extinguisher still at his side. "You must've dropped a match on those sun props with your pyrotechnic act. They flamed up. Huge. That wasn't part of the script."

"Dropped a *match* in them?" Bailey's mother glowers at me in horrified disbelief. "Why would you do that in our loft? Don't you know that could cause—"

"A fire?" quips Wilson.

"I didn't, I . . ." I don't want Bailey's mom to hate me.

"What happened, then?" Mrs. Storrow snaps. "How could you think of using a flammable prop?"

"Mom, she didn't do it on purpose!" Bailey shrills. My supporters bellow in agreement.

"How do you know?" Lacey blares from the outer circle.

I glance around the stage, surveying the chaos I wrought: blackened sun props and pools of charred water mixed with the whipped white gook from the fire extinguisher. "I did that? No, I couldn't have."

"But no one else was onstage," Bailey's mom accuses. A small sector of the crowd murmurs their agreement.

"I'm so sorry, Mrs. Storrow," I cry. "I'll pay for the damage."

Bailey's mom glances over at her unharmed paintings. "At least the whole place didn't catch fire." Her true voice talks soundlessly in me: *This girl is dangerously impulsive. Playing with matches? Something's seriously wrong with her.* Mrs. Storrow brushes herself off. "It's midnight. Everyone, please clear out."

People filter out as Bailey helps me to a kitchen chair, first covering it with a trash bag, since my outfit is doused with sludgy water. Ander wraps a towel around my shoulders.

Wilson stands by, hands awkwardly at his sides. He must not be used to people helping each other.

Tears leak from my eyes as I face Bailey's mom. "I'm so very sorry about the mess. I need to go home, to my aunt's." Not as forgiving as Bailey, she only nods.

Ander offers me a hand as I stumble to my feet.

"I'll hail a cab," Wilson decides. "And help with Dor. She could use *two* strong guys."

Ander sucks in an irritated breath. "No need for both of us to do it."

"I'm coming." Wilson's firm tone allows for no objection.

Bailey bags my street clothes, and adds a hefty piece of cake in foil. "For later," she explains, and gives me a gentle hug. "Feel better, Sungirl. You really rocked it. Don't feel too awful about the, um . . . fire." Bailey waits for her mother to walk off. "Hopefully, Mom will get over it. Text me. Tell me what your secret magic was."

"Yeah, we need to know how you made those flower things," Cole chimes in. "And how you levitated that glowing ball."

"That sure wasn't on the set list!" Ander agrees. I catch Wilson rolling his eyes.

In the cab, I rest on Ander's shoulder, while he strokes my arm. Wilson growls silently in my head: *He's not worthy of you.* It's crazy, but I swear I hear Wilson thinking, *I'll infiltrate her light fixtures, her bookshelves . . .* What does he mean?

We decide together in the cab that there's no need for me to tell my aunt I fell and got burned. No need to scare her. But my costume tells another story. It reeks of wet smoke, and its edges are blackened.

So, I change into my shirt and pants right in the cab. Wilson sneaks peeks of my crimson bra and panties, so I hurry to pull my shirt down and pants up.

When we arrive at my aunt's place, Wilson pulls out all

the stops. "Delighted to meet you!" he gushes to her. "Anyone who's related to Dorianna must be thoroughly enchanting." Aunt Carol blushes. An audible snort erupts from Ander.

Aunt Carol scrunches her nose. "Something burning?" She follows the odor downwards. "Your hands, Dorianna! What happened? Did you cut yourself?"

"Looks worse than it is," I claim. "Bailey had candles and incense buds all around. I got too close and bumped into one. When I picked it up . . ."

"We should call a doctor, set up an appointment for tomorrow."

As we step into the foyer Wilson says, "It looks bad with all the bandages, but Bailey's mom really laid the gauze on thicker than she needed to. Dorianna will be fine in a day or two."

"Warren, it wouldn't hurt for a dermatologist to check it out," Ander counters.

"I agree." My aunt turns to me. "How'd it go . . . otherwise?"

"Amazing, but I'm tired. Aunt Carol, can my friends come up for a few minutes?"

Wilson sends her a sympathetic smile. Judging by her bathrobe and frizzled hair, it looks as if she was propped up by late-night TV, waiting for my return.

Ander flicks his head toward the stairs. "Dorianna's exhausted. Can we . . . just for a few?"

"Okay." Aunt Carol sighs. "I'm just going to have a cup of tea down here. You can stay until I head up for the night. Fair enough?"

"Quite fair," Wilson says. "I videoed the event. I'd be happy to print you out stills of Dorianna's performance."

"Oh, would you? Thanks." Aunt Carol heads into the kitchen.

Upstairs, I lower myself gingerly onto the bed.

Ander sits beside me and props a pillow under my legs. "Wilson, you really laid the charm thick on Dorianna's aunt. It was over the top."

"Nothing's O-T-T," Wilson enunciates each letter, "except your obsession for your ex."

"Shut up, Warren. Lacey was the one who called me onstage. I would never have gone if those jerks hadn't shoved me up there."

Wilson snickers. "I'm not talking about that."

"What *are* you talking about?" I ask, though I think I know. Sometimes it sucks having access into the supernatural.

"He's not talking about anything," Ander cuts in. "Wilson, I know it takes a while to get out to Coney and it's late, so feel free to take off." He nods toward the door.

"I'm not on curfew. But you?" Wilson grins. "You have a commitment."

I frown at Wilson. "How would you know?"

I sense him building up a forceful mischief and guiding its havoc into the atmosphere, into Lacey's room, branching out into her fingers. What does it all mean? No idea, but it makes me squirm.

Another focused blast from Wilson plants a strange inner sense in me of a cell phone dropping silently and a pressing urge to piss.

"Back in a minute. Got to use your bathroom." Ander stumbles up abruptly and bangs his weak side on my bookshelf. Cursing, he rubs his hip where it smacks against the shelf corner. Upon impact, I hear a dull thud, and then Wilson taps something with his boot. The ping of an incoming text message is unmistakable. "What was that?"

Wilson shrugs. "Your cell?"

I fish it out of my bag, and click it open. "No, not mine."

Wilson makes his approach. Sitting on my bed, his gaze drinks in my every detail. "You were fabulous," he gushes. "Your magic was remarkable. So creative . . . The crowd went crazy trying to figure out how you did it."

I shift higher on the pillows. "One minute I had my eyes closed and my hands out, and the next?" I hold up my bandaged palms. "The flowers that came out of my hand, just like in your video, except this time they were ghostly, not done in an editing studio. How did I—?"

"You conjured it."

"I conjured it," I echo. "And it wasn't *bad*. Until the fire . . ." My voice fades. "I don't need to do bad things." Wilson tries to hide the skepticism etched on his face. But I have a handle on the preternatural now. I sense what people wall away. I smell their lies. He can't totally fool me. "You're thinking I'll do more bad things, aren't you?" My voice rises in panic, and the two of us lock in an electric transmission of dread for the future.

Ander pads back in. "Warren, get off her flipping bed."

"You have to go," Wilson states calmly as he stands. "Your mother told you to get back by 1:30 a.m. because she's been sick with the flu, and your father's on a business trip."

Ander reflexively feels for the notebook in his back pocket —his security blanket. "Huh? How do you know that?"

Wilson only says, "Her fever's spiking. She needs you now."

"You're a freak, you know that?" Ander narrows his eyes at Wilson. Then he comes over and kisses me—one with real feeling, on the lips. "I *should* go, but you better, too, Warren."

Wilson obliges. "Get some sleep, Dor. I'll hear you if you need me," he adds under his breath as he puts on his jacket.

"Really?" I laugh. "Hear me all the way from Coney Island?"

"Warren, come on," Ander urges from the doorway.

Wilson follows way too easily. He's up to something. I glance out my window and watch them walk away, unlikely friends under the orbit of the chilly moon.

Padding back to bed on bandaged feet, I spot something silvery under my bookshelf. I fish for it. A cell phone. Clicking it open, a ragged gasp escapes me, and then a cry of pain.

21

I would rather have been shot straight up in cold blood, but to be set up? By people I trusted? That's bad.
—Tupac Shakur

W hat's that scratching on my window? I bolt upright in bed, sending a blizzard of damp, discarded tissue to the floor. I can't see anything through my closed curtains, but whatever it is, it's not just a broken tree branch. Whatever it is, is reaching out to me with sticky, hungry tendrils, wrapping me in its thrall. My heart is racing.

There it is again, the *tap-tapping*. I spring out of bed, my feet smarting from the burns, as I swipe tears off my face with my gauzed palm. Parting the curtains, I gasp. "Wilson!" and open the window to a burst of chilly night air. He's crouched unsteadily on a branch, his long limbs tangled like a tortured grasshopper. "What are you doing?" I ask him.

He opens the window the rest of the way. "Climbing in,

isn't that obvious?" Easing his knobby legs in the frame and arching his back, he starts to slide in. His leather jacket snags on a loose splinter. Cursing, he freezes in midair to pry it loose.

"Do you make a habit of breaking and entering girls' rooms?" I'm disturbed by his presumptuous action, but a little relieved, too. Those texts between Ander and Lacey were unspeakably upsetting. I need someone to talk to, even Wilson.

He shuts the window and hauls the desk chair over to my bed.

"Lock the door," I advise him. "No matter how charmed she is by you, my aunt will scalp you if she catches you in here."

While he attends to the door, I slip Ander's cell under my pillow. Then I rake my fingers through my tangled hair and brush off more tears.

"You've been crying," he notes as he wheels around. "Someone's hurt you."

Through my pain, I feel a rush of irritation. Wilson always knows too much—everything. What gives him the right? He's on target, though. In Ander's texts to Lacey, Ander has broken me. Should I tell Wilson? A ripple of sadness tells me he knows already.

"It's Ander, isn't it?" he says under his breath. He shifts from the chair to sit on the side of my bed, but stays far enough away that we're not touching.

New, hot tears pour down onto my wrinkled shirt. I rip the last tissue from its box and throw the thing on the floor. "Dammit, Wilson, he played me. I'm tired of being hurt. I've been hurt my entire life. I thought for once, I had something of my own." I pause. "You know about Ander and Lacey's texts, don't you?" I glance up at him, waiting. His normally intense gaze is softened with understanding and empathy.

"Yes," he answers in a whisper.

"Did you make it happen?" I catch myself shouting, but quickly lower the volume. The last thing I want is for my aunt to overhear us. "What did you do, Wilson?"

"The texts were already there. I only made his cell fall on your floor."

"Why?" I moan. It hurts so much—in my bones, my heart, my psyche. "Why'd you have to do that? I didn't want to see." But I know why he did it. Wilson was trying to help me in his own warped way. Trying to open my eyes.

"Dorianna, I feel bad for you. I . . ." His voice cracks.

Its rawness opens something in me—a fresh shattering breaker of grief, but also a rift in my chest that was firmly closed, moments earlier. A chink lets in what little Wilson still possesses of human, tender love, beyond any demonic love. It's lovely, yet tainted. It's incredibly tender. I let his deep understanding of my loneliness filter in, too.

The chink in my chest is also streaming stuff out. *Need*, especially. It pleads for Wilson's help. I'm aching for him to reach out his arms and allow me to smash into the burnished recesses of his leather jacket, just above his heart.

Take precarious comfort there.

Wilson does reach for me. I lean heavily on him, crying and melting and fading. His long arms pressing on my back coax me to safety. Temporary safety is better than none. "Ander's confused," I mumble. "Lacey texted him. Says she wants him back. That's not fair. She's messing with his head."

"Nothing's fair. He wants his head messed with, Dor. He always wanted Lacey, if she'd have him back. What exactly did he say in his text?" So, Wilson can't translate through the ether.

"That he wanted to try again," I admit reluctantly. "Why

would he say that? He always told me she was a bitch," I add with a groan.

"She is."

I lift my head up enough to be able to gaze into Wilson's face, see if he's telling the truth. I'm so sick of lies—Ander's lies, my own. Lacey's, too—sloppy seconds, huh? The way Lacey put it, you'd think Ander was a rotten burrito in the trash. "Why would Ander want to go back with a bitch?"

Wilson takes the liberty of brushing strands of hair from my face. "She's his kryptonite, his Achilles' heel. He loves her," he says gently, matter-of-factly.

With the touch of Wilson's fingers and his hushed, fast breath on my cheek, I know something else: that Wilson loves *me*. That he's describing himself. How I've come into his life and stolen his attention. How he loves me underneath my capacity for evil, or his capacity for evil, in a place beyond any moral judgment placed on the world by rational, mortal beings.

I wonder for a moment who's glamouring whom? It's so hard to resist Wilson—the lure of his clever wit, the desperate, sensual heat of his body. His strange devotion to me that is both exhilarating and dangerous. I still can't believe he's a hideous devil beneath his handsome, serious face. If I give in to his passion, will my own crimes meld into his evil, so that we, together might become one huge monstrosity? If I pry off his exterior, will I see a leering, red fiend underneath? Does it matter? Impulsively, I put a bandaged hand on Wilson's neck, and tug at his skin. He doesn't flinch.

"Yes, I'm flesh and blood," he whispers, as if he knows I'm making sure I can't simply tear off the mortal layer. As if he knows that my affections teeter chaotically between him and Ander.

No, I yell silently, I'm only in Wilson's arms for comfort. This strong pull of "love" I feel is only Wilson's glamour, oozing over me like dirty, sticky grease. I shift away cautiously. He reaches past me and eases Ander's phone out from under my pillow. "Hey!" I grab it back.

"Why do you assume that I'm trying to steal from you," he says wearily. "Why, Dor?"

"Why did you grab Ander's cell, then? I hid it for a reason."

"I'm helping you lose your obsession, avoiding more humiliation. Helping you, one friend to another."

Friend. It's the golden word. My clenched muscles relax. "Okay, friend, listen to this." I click into the texts. "Lacey wrote, 'I made a huge mistake breaking up with you.' And Ander wrote back,' I never stopped loving you.' Then, Lacey:

i want u back.
  that's what I want 2.
  u need to brk up with d
  give me time.
  u still love her?
  maybe
  its me or her shes a freak.
  give me time to ease her down slow
  not long I need u in my bed

"What do you make of that, *friend*? Shit!" I hurl Ander's cell down and break into angry, helpless sobs.

"Crying is unproductive," Wilson insists. "Don't be a victim. Take action. Use your given powers."

"To get him back?"

"To punish both of them."

I sniffle. "What if I still want him?"

"He's wrong for you. He'll bring you to your knees and leave you. He hurt you once, he'll hurt you again."

"I wonder when he planned to tell me what was going on?"

"Never. He's untrustworthy. Send him a strong message. Be creatively vicious."

I tremble with uncertainty, then a fledgling eagerness. "Creative? I could turn my next meetup into a mega party from hell. Lure them both over and then . . ." I run my bandaged hand across my neck.

"That's the spirit."

"I'll annihilate that blonde witch. And to think I was half-trying to making her a friend."

With his long, sensual fingers Wilson smoothes the wrinkles from my quilt. In the lamplight, his snarling dog ring gleams at me, pulls me in. "We can hold the party at my uncle's warehouse," he says. "The old Nivomonsky place has dozens of rooms. It's a spooky labyrinth, especially at night."

"Cool. We'll invite *everyone* from New York. Not that one-or-two-schools junk that Ander's always spouting. This event will make the papers. Get into the *Post* gossip column."

"That's my Sungirl." Wilson's deep-set eyes take on a sexy glow.

I grab a pen and paper from my desk and scribble notes, astonished that my burned hand hardly hurts at all. "We'll have confessional booths. Call it Confessional. Or blindfold people and have them go on blind dates. Or both. How about this title: 'Blind Date Confessional'." I giggle. "'Confess your worst, most humiliating transgressions to your blindfolded date.'"

"Love the name. We can wire the rooms, plant hidden cameras. Those preppy sheep will announce all of their secret perversions on camera."

"Ha! Totally incriminating acts." My mind brims with satisfying revenge fantasies, like Lacey getting stuck in a room with her ex, Charlie, or Ava making out with a pimply nerd and then my posting the incriminating video online. Or Charlie and Ander locked in a tiny, claustrophobic room, ripping off their blindfolds only to tear at each other's throats.

I'm gleeful at the idea of catching people who've done me dirty with their proverbial pants down. "See how they like their monstrous real selves broadcast to the world," I burst out.

Now you're talking, mumbles my inner beast.

We laugh hard. This laughing with Wilson makes me high. *He* makes me high, as if I've swallowed a horse-sized dose of a toxic hallucinogen that makes the world such a wondrous, floaty place that I never want to come down, and don't even care anymore what damage it's doing to my liver, or my heart.

Wilson and I scrawl feverish notes into the wee hours of the night. Just before the dawn, he finally makes his descent down the tree. I can't sleep, I'm so buzzed. Instead, I try to rest in bed for the next few hours. At least I have Sunday to recover. The next step is to take the train to Coney Island and scope out his uncle's warehouse.

My razor-edged spark is back, and I don't care that it's spiking out of control. I have nothing much to lose anymore. This time, I want a burn that will short-circuit the freaking pain of living out of me for good.

22

The dreamers of the day are dangerous men, for they may act their
dreams with eyes, to make it possible.
—T. E. Lawrence

Over toast and coffee at breakfast, my aunt bristles with commentary, mostly about Wilson. "I haven't seen that tall friend of yours before. He's very charming, but his clothes are something out of an old silent movie. Is he a theater major?"

"He has a flair for, um, Victorian fashion, that's all."

She takes a slow draw of coffee. A puzzled look shadows her face. "I thought you preferred the other boy, Ander. Do you like this Wilson better?"

I shrug. Spreading raspberry preserves on my toast gives me something else to concentrate on, but I'll have to look up eventually. When I do, my aunt is staring pointedly at my gauzed hands.

"We need to set up a doctor's appointment."

"It's nothing." I unwind the gauze and hold out my hands. There are only some faint reddish areas. Otherwise, the flesh is soft and pink. It surprises even me.

Aunt Carol looks stricken. She leans forward to inspect more closely, clearly not believing what she's seeing. "How could it heal so—?"

"I told you, it's not a big deal. Wilson was telling the truth."

Aunt Carol blinks at me. "Wilson seemed charming . . . too charming."

I narrow my eyes at her. "What's that supposed to mean?"

"Working too hard to win me over." She chuckles dryly. "Not that it's a crime."

I know exactly what she's referring to—Wilson's manipulations, his *mesmerizing*. But I'm not about to tell her. She won't believe me anyway. Her intuition freaks me out, it's so spot-on. "Charm's a valuable skill. Would you rather he be rude?"

"Of course not. It's just that you and Ander . . ." Aunt Carol seems to be choosing her words carefully. "You're adorable together, not that it's any of my busi—"

"Look, Ander and I broke up. And, yeah, it's private. I prefer not to talk about it."

"Oh, Dorianna, that's too bad. I'm sorry," my aunt soothes, as though I'm a wallflower like I've always been, and always will be. As if my short love affair with Ander was a complete fluke, never meant to last.

With a sharp clatter, a dish on the edge of the sink crashes to the floor. Shards skate across the linoleum.

Did I do that? Really?

"How—? No one even touched that," Aunt Carol mumbles.

"I'll get it. Stay put." I leap up, get a broom and begin

sweeping, all the while fuming. My aunt hardly knew me all of these years, and now she's my judgmental mom? With an icy tinkle, I shake the shards into the trash. "Wilson has positive qualities that Ander doesn't have," I reply in a measured voice. I need to be able to go to Coney a lot in the next few weeks, and I don't want her giving me bull about it.

"Sure, I get it." She stands up and gathers the dishes. "But if you ever want to talk about your relationships or concerns, I'm here." She gives me a look, as if she sees through my newly hardened shell and is sad that I choose not to confide in her.

I hurry toward the stairs. "I'll be out in Coney Island," I call lightly, as if our tense exchange never happened.

"Will I see you for dinner?"

"Not sure. I'll leave a message."

It's best in this new phase to keep my focus straight ahead and my heart encased in steel.

The warehouse is better than I expected—and a good distraction from those painful texts. The building is set on an entire square block, tucked on the far side of the Cyclone Roller Coaster, just off the boardwalk. The crash of the breakers and the brisk sea air add to my excitement.

Wilson fits in with the "Abandoned Warehouse from the Last Century" ambiance. He's wearing a mustard-hued vest with a dangling pocket watch, and two-tone boots resembling spats. Only his skeleton-doll necklace with mournful, staring glass eyes is modern.

I scurry around, peeking into the mostly empty offices on the first floor. Three of them are padlocked. "What's in those?" I ask.

"My uncle's fireworks, cartons of everything under the sun, and boxes of old towels."

"Old towels?" I pucker my nose at a curious sweetness mixing with the sawdust of dry wooden beams. "What was this building used for before your uncle owned it?" .

"A Victorian-era bathhouse."

Ah, that's what that sweet scent is—faded suntan oil. "Explains the towels."

"Right. You can almost smell the old body sweat." Wilson takes a deep whiff.

"Gross!" I poke him in the ribs.

"I like gross." He wags his brows. "Want to see the changing rooms?" I nod, and he tours me around the second and third-floor hallways. To either side are tiny rooms, each with a white enamel door plaque bearing a number. Inside are only benches and wall hooks. Most still have warped renderings of starlets in bathing outfits. One even has a crusty towel, still on its hook.

I imagine hoop-skirted ladies changing into shorter, cap-sleeved pinafores with bloomers and guys with handlebar mustaches stepping into black stretch jumpsuits. They would troop onto the beach, the ladies shaded under their frilly parasols.

"I would've loved to be a fly on the wall when this place was up and running," Wilson admits. "I bet all kinds of crazy sex happened in here."

"Which was, no doubt, strictly forbidden in the late 1800s."

"The more forbidden, the sweeter," he coos. My flesh erupts in goosebumps.

I perch on a bench. "These would rock as confessional booths, wouldn't they?"

Wilson sinks to his knees as if I'm a priestess listening to people declare their sins. "Oh, Sungirl, I confess that last week I enticed a young maiden's virginity from her under the Boardwalk."

"You didn't!" I gasp in jest.

"I was so, so bad. How will you punish me, Sungirl? Oh, *do* punish me."

"You must donate a hundred dollars to the Ladies' Auxiliary Beach Club and wear this male chastity belt, oh, Nympho Man!" I pretend to hand him an unwieldy contraption.

"I'll wear it with glee." He mimes putting it on. I pretend to lock it and toss the key. "There's something else you should see." He leads me down the hall.

A tremendous thunder shakes the floor and rattles the windows as we walk. Wilson explains it's only the old roller-coaster that shuts down in late fall.

"Good ambiance for the party," I reply shakily.

"Yes," Wilson agrees. "Ander told me once about the oracles . . . "

At the mention of Ander we fall silent. The space between us fills with the loss of the third leg of our trio. My grief at Ander's betrayal surges up, but it's still too deep to get rid of, like a painful splinter lodged where tweezers can't go.

"Anyway," Wilson continues, "the oracles were mostly a con game. The priestesses would drug the seekers and snake them through caves to confuse them. Stationing themselves at intervals, her cronies would call out supposed prophecies to unnerve them."

"Ha! Let's take a page from that playbook. We'll have a creepy light show, sound effects and a smoke machine. The whole bit."

"Perfect." He continues to the end of the hall and stops in front of a freight elevator. Presses the buzzer. Clanking and sputtering, it rises like an exhausted, overworked beast of burden. He hauls open its wire door and we step in. "This could be the ultimate confessional booth. Seal them in, and start the thing up."

"*Hmm*. I'd love to give Lacey the ride of her life."

"That can be arranged. I can adjust the speed to go faster or slower, turn off the lights, run a horror video in there with some metal music."

We laugh wickedly as we ride down to the first floor, a cavernous space with an elevated staging area. "Perfect for my grand entrance," I crow. "Everyone who's anyone will see me."

Wilson takes out his camera and starts to record short takes of me onstage.

I stiffen. "Wait. No. Video changes me into a monstrosity. I can't afford more of that. How about still photos instead? Make me pretty," I demand.

"Whatever you like, Sungirl. You're always pretty. You drive me wild." Wilson clicks from video to photo, aims, and clicks. "You're much too good for Ander. He never deserved you."

Wilson gazes at me as he says this. He rarely reveals his inner emotions, so I'm caught off guard. His smoldering gaze arcs with hardcore electricity. The sensual scent of his musk cologne mixed with the spicy, coconut suntan lotion invades me. All the while, Wilson's spooky doll necklace stares dolefully at me.

Slowly, surely, he moves closer and tries to press his lips to mine. When I shift ever so slightly so his kiss will land on my cheek instead, a sudden, dead emptiness where Ander has torn out my heart threatens to engulf me. I need to fill it. Now.

I lean forward and lightly kiss Wilson back, slightly left of his mouth. The touch of his stubbly skin to my lips is giddying. Immoral. Delicious. Almost enough to quell the sickening ache in my heart. He kisses me back, on the lips this time, but only for a beat. He tastes of Halloween and taffy, of rollercoaster plunges and snakebites. The pressure of his lips stings like a potent injection.

Any longer of a kiss, and I will consider it cheating. But then, Ander isn't quite mine anymore . . . *or is he?* Should I lure him back? I step away, beyond Wilson's force field. If he's insulted, he doesn't show it, only brushes off his ochre vest as if brushing off my dismissal.

After that, we walk on the boardwalk, reveling in the raw November sun. Most booths are shuttered. The beach is empty, except for the occasional hiker or person skimming the sand with a metal detector for abandoned jewelry. A lone babushka in a headscarf feeds the gulls popcorn.

"What does your uncle do now with that warehouse?" I ask Wilson.

"Once in a while, he rents out offices." Wilson kicks a child's empty waffle cone to one side as he advances. A piece of cone sticks to his boot, but he doesn't notice. "Mostly he imports things. Black-market items."

I picture his uncle's padlocked doors. I also flash on the lonely capybara in its cage, and wonder how the creature's faring, whether it's still famished. "What kinds of black-market things?" I ask with trepidation.

"Vodka, cigarettes, and, well . . ." He looks at me sneakily.

I'm tempted to egg him on further, but I need to use that old warehouse. I can't afford to be put off by it. Abruptly, I feel claustrophobic, as if it's us stuck in that warehouse elevator. "Bye, Wilson," I say as I make an abrupt turn down the ramp to the subway.

"No quick dinner at Nathan's?" He sounds injured.

Not as injured as I feel. The quick fix of Wilson's touch has worn off. Where illicit passion flowed, a mental hangover has formed. More than anything, I long to get home and under my quilt—block out the world until Monday.

On the train, I check for new texts. Ander won't be sending any my way because his cell is in my room. But wait . . . my heart soars. I can't help it.

U feeling better? -Ander

He must've sent this from someone else's phone. I'll test him. See how long it takes for him to confess, to be honest with me. For all of these weeks, I've made a concerted effort to be magic-free with him, and look where it's gotten me.

Let the games begin. I type back:

Wonderful, you?

_____

23

I've been getting some bad publicity, but you've got to expect that.
—Elvis Presley

I t's lunchtime, and I'm surreptitiously looking for Ander. He's nowhere around. Neither is Lacey. Ava's sitting with a new set of friends, including the freckled Fiona O'Riley and the striking math whiz Lucy Lane, two winners of my latest party vouchers. Strange. Why would Ava be weaseling in on my voucher-winning crowd? I shut my eyes and concentrate, trying to glean significant bits of conversation. No conversation, but an unsettled nausea ripples out a warning that my queendom is at risk for mutiny. I don't like it one bit.

Tory approaches my table with an uncharacteristically pinched expression. "Have you seen your videos lately?"

Truth is, for a week now, I haven't had the nerve to look. "Um, why?" I inquire as casually as possible.

"Because you're yelling out super-weird stuff on the beach

video. You're cackling like a witch. And on the burlesque one, you're telling the viewer that if they're not careful, you'll burn them with your sun orb. Considering what happened at your party with the fire, saying that is in really bad taste," she declares crisply.

"I was wondering about that, too," Lisbeth ventures. She's sitting at the far end of the lunch table, as if I have a contagious flu.

Crap. *It's happening.* What I've been dreading from the minute I saw that first flash of arrogance in my beach video. I struggle for a quick comeback. "I'm, uh, getting people in the spirit for the next meetup." I shrug. "Maybe the burning-orb remark went too far."

"You think?" Tory frowns, magnifying her somber, stone-washed look. "That's a horrible way to go about it. You'll scare people off. Besides, how does that relate to a blind date confessional? That party is about spicy secrets and hot dates, not about witches and warlocks. Why would you want a creep vibe on your media sites?"

Lisbeth agrees. "I showed it to my mom. I told her I played music at your event. Didn't know you'd changed the video since then. Now she's worried I'm hanging with a druggie."

"What? I don't even smoke pot," I protest.

"Is that weirdo Wilson messing with the videos?" Tory asks. "I really got into it with him when you were passed out at Bailey's. I warned him not to move you, that he should've let Bailey's mom handle it." Tory's gaze fixes on my hands. "Your hands, they're all better. How's that possible? I saw how messed up they were."

"They've healed impossibly fast," Lisbeth adds, gaping.

"My immune system's super strong." I give them each my best mesmerizing smile. "Tory, what were you saying before?

About the performance?" Anything is better than veering into this clear evidence of magic.

Tory blinks, obviously struggling to locate her thoughts from a few minutes ago. I gloat. My magic has erased her misgivings. But when she goes on, I realize that her upset is strong enough to throw off the magic and get back on track. "I was saying, um, that you better fix the videos. I can't publicize something that's going to freak people out, you know?"

"People like to be freaked," I claim.

"Not like that." Tory flicks her ponytail over her shoulder. Her continual hair flipping has become a complete irritation. It's like people who crack their knuckles all the time. Makes me want to pull their fingers out of the sockets.

I clench my fists, trying to suppress a growing rage that my beast is clamoring for. "The videos were hacked," I improvise. "Spammers."

"Delete them and post new ones, then. My reputation's at stake." Tory adds coldly, "I'm working on other people's promo sites, too."

"Yeah, from the business I brought your way." Shut up, I tell myself. I need Tory to manage the myriad of Sungirl posts. I've lost track of how many sites Tory's posted the Sungirl branding on, but there are many. And I can't exactly blabber on about how great *I* am on them. Besides, I don't have the time. So, I need Tory more than ever, especially for this latest party. News of Blind Date Confessional needs to blast citywide—even nationally. "Look, you don't have to carve me another a—"

"Down, Sungirl. I'm not your enemy. Just fix those video snafus." Tory gives her ponytail a final officious flick before clicking her cell closed and inching her notebook into her overstuffed handbag. "Got to go. Math."

"But we haven't finished the publicity blurb for Confessional. And you're the *best.*" Adding a nugget of sugar will hopefully sweeten the mood.

Tory shrugs. "Maybe tonight, after my homework." She hurries out before I can send any stronger powers of persuasion.

Cat approaches our table, and Lisbeth leaps up. "Got to run—orchestra practice." She hoists her instrument bag on her shoulder. "Speaking of that, I'm deep in rehearsals for the fall concert and, well, Blind Date Confessional needs electronica and heavy-metal tracks. Can't help you with that."

"Ask your guy friends," I call after them, but they're already to the exit door.

Abruptly, the deep frost of being alone wraps around me, as it did that first horrible week here. My easy assurance freezes as I look around. Where are Bailey and Cole when I need them? I scan the room for friendly faces. Ah, Jake's table. He's with some sophomores and freshmen that fawn over my every move. If some of the seniors and juniors are getting leery, there's always the younger crowd to impress.

They welcome me. Three guys want arm autographs, and one of their friends, a spirited girl named Rorie, asks me rapid-fire questions about my upcoming party. "Are the confessions anonymous? Are you inviting kids from ninth grade, too? Will you really set us up with a dream date?" she asks, breathless.

I answer her questions and end with, "We're devising a totally anonymous site where you make up a pen name when you log in. For the blind dates, we'll match compatible-sounding names—say, Redmayne and Foxy."

"That's so cool!" Rorie gushes. "Can't wait."

"Sungirl always thinks outside the box," Jake brags, as if he's my manager.

"Did you really make a ball catch fire during Burlesque?" Rorie asks.

"I was there," Jake says reverently. "I saw it with my own eyes."

"I heard it burned your hands." Rorie glances at mine. "But yours look fine."

"I used this amazing salve." With zest, I rub them together. It's still amazing, how within a day the magic has erased almost all of the blistery skin. I only hope these kids don't check out my videos. Magic has its downside.

"Will you do more cool magic at Confessional?" Rorie asks.

"No doubt!" I beam at my new follower, and then cast an invisible magnetic net around all the kids. *You'll go, you'll go,* I chant silently. They look at me gooney-eyed and slack-jawed. If I stay here another second I'll start laughing, because they look like robots in need of a charge. I get up to dump my trash. "Sungirl needs to go shine on Lit class."

They jerk to life in one group motion, and Jake forms a sun shape with his fingers. "Shine on, Sungirl." Everyone mirrors his move. It's a relief, but also weirdly too much.

Climbing the stairs to my next class, my sizzling smile changes to a pained frown. Ander's in this class, but so is Lacey.

Sure enough, he's waiting in the hall a good eight minutes before the class, as if he's prepared to run interference between Lacey and me. He looks hot in a pair of faded jeans and a green corduroy shirt over a tight blue tee that show-cases his ripped chest. I swallow hard, remembering our brief but luscious time in my bed. I want more, but I'm so hurt, I also want justice.

"Hey, you." He glances around the hall before giving me a distracted hug. "Feeling better?"

His touch feels so good. "Yeah, yesterday I slept lots and drank buckets of water."

"Did I, uh, leave my cell at your place?" His uneasy emotions transform into thought-forms: Dorianna doesn't know about Lacey and me, does she? Hope not. I'm not ready to break up . . . yet. I hear his thumping heart and smell his fermented, turnipy guilt. It makes me infinitely sad. "So, um, did you see my cell?" he repeats nervously.

Staring at him, I push my energy through the wet jelly of his pale irises, into his guarded mind, his lying heart. Then, out of the blue, I hand him his phone.

"Oh!" When our eyes meet, he looks so very guilty. "Did I leave it *on?*" I don't answer, and he doesn't dare repeat the question. He doesn't even notice that my hands are better, that's how preoccupied he is with getting his phone back.

Ava filters past us in thigh-high boots, along with Fiona, Ava's apparent new bestie. Smart of Ava, to eke out her own territory after Lacey's fall. I see that now.

She gives me a begrudging nod. "Slick parlor trick last Saturday."

Ha—I've won her over. Ava's no pushover. This victory was hard-fought. "Thanks," I say. "Your burlesque dance was cool, too."

"How'd you make that ball levitate, anyway?" another classmate asks me.

"Supernatural energy fields," I answer, knowing the guy won't believe me. I look over at Ander. "Waiting for some-one?" Will he flinch? Yes.

"You," he whispers. Inside, he's thinking, *Liar. I'm such a liar.*

Lacey approaches and lightly touches his arm. Her floral perfume plumes up. She looks at me, then uncertainly at Ander—*u still love her?*—her text question literally hanging over our heads. Ander's renewed passion for Lacey and his confused, heartbreaking love for me is palpable. It aches, it stabs, almost pins me to the wall.

I could still force Ander's hand with my powers. "We should go into class," I say.

He checks his watch. "Uh, oh we're late."

I go in first, followed by Ander, who makes a point of sitting next to me. Lacey sits on his other side. Why doesn't he take a freaking stand? He's playing a maddeningly passive game of Whichever Girl Wants Me More I'll Take.

Rake him across the face, urges my beast, baring his virtual fangs.

I'll do it my own way, I think in response.

Hardly listening to the teacher droning on about the long-suffering character in the novel we're reading, I draw a heart and pass it to Ander. When Lacey glances down at her book, he blows me an air-kiss. She looks up suddenly, sees me looking all dewy at Ander, and sends me thick waves of hate. Shakily, I boomerang it back, but it's like trying to stab someone with a knife when your wrist is broken.

Buck up. Injure her. Use your skills, my beast scolds.

I will, I promise.

Strange how my hissing beast seems male.

After class, I slip an arm around Ander. "Hey, handsome, I'm headed out to Coney to plan the next event. Want to come? We need your excellent writing chops for the next promo blurb." I say this loudly, because Lacey's clearly waiting for me to split.

His neck flushes. "So soon? You're hardly recovered from the last party."

"No time to waste. I'm on a roll."

"On a roll to a meltdown," Lacey cuts in.

"I don't recall talking to you," I snap.

"Ladies, ladies, come on!" Ander eases my arm off of him, and flings his backpack over his shoulders.

Better say yes, I silently fume. I won't look the fool in front of Lacey. My shame and rage surge up like hot vomit. They transform into super-charges that shoot out at Lacey. As they do, my pain twists into ecstatic spasms, and a low moan escapes me. God, it feels good to turn this torture into twisted pleasure. As the charges hit her, Lacey takes comical back-leaps. With a look of astonished fear, she teeters on her feet like an unbalanced seesaw.

In flashes of passionate rage, I turn to Ander and draw him to me. He swoops me into his arms and kisses me, open-mouthed, while Lacey gapes. God, he tastes sweet, even with this stolen, glamoured kiss. His tongue explores my back teeth, my tongue. It whips up a wicked fire in me.

With a deep shudder, he releases me and takes two robotic steps back. So crazy: I am puppet master for real. Which way should I tug the strings? I tug again on Ander's.

He shrugs. "S—sure, I'll go to Coney with you." As if the shrug has also shaken off my spell, he glances longingly at Lacey, who is now softly crying. "Give me a minute," he tells me, and takes her by the arm. He guides her down the hall about thirty paces. Let him bring her down softly. Whatever. I have the upper hand now.

I sense him promising her things. It only takes a minute, but when he turns toward me, behind his back Lacey gives me a superior gloat, and then the finger, as she minces off.

"What was all that?" I ask, the quake in my voice barely controlled.

"Look, babe, she's human. She just got dumped by Charlie, okay?"

"Since when did how Lacey feels ever bother you? I recall you telling me she was a supreme bitch and snake. After *she* dumped *you.*"

Ander sighs. "I get it. She can be awful. But she was crying at Bailey's, really falling apart, and that kiss just now .

. .″ he trails off. "She said she was sorry for picking my name out of that jar and embarrassing me."

"She should be! Where's your pride? You were the one crying over her last year."

"I told you, what happened between Lacey and me is my business. You're not my judge."

"What am I, then? I thought we had something."

His tone softens as he slips an arm around me. "We do, baby. You're my Sungirl."

I so want to believe him. But his confusion bruises me through his fingertips. His emotions for me flicker off, on, off. Curse my uncanny senses. . . it would so be less painful if I were a normal, clueless girl. Still, I could make him kiss me over and over, and—

On the train to Coney I text Wilson.

Ander is coming too. need him to write next blurb

Almost immediately my cell pings.

after his bad behavior? u dont need him . . . we can write it

I text a reply—half truth and half manipulation:

Need 2 finesse him. I want A and L at the next meetup, 2 c me go viral!

Another incoming ping:

don't go to my apt! meet me on boardwalk by lemonade stand

When Ander looks over to read the texts, I click my cell shut. "Ah, ah. . . Not until you show me your notebook."

He leans back against the train seat. "You got me."

Wilson's already up on the boardwalk, pacing and tapping the wood with his pearl-tipped cane. He's obviously brought it along to annoy Ander. The cane doesn't jive with Wilson's trendy maxi-coat, shades, and snakeskin boots. He comes off as a fashion-obsessed spy.

I wave a ten dollar bill and ask if Ander will get us drinks.
As soon as he ducks over to the lemonade stand, I button my
yellow trench coat against the stiff breeze and launch into
business. "Wilson, we need a different visual for my party
teaser. No more videos. I can't chance another video trailer
morphing into a monstrosity. The ones online are freaking
out my school friends."

He groans. "You'd think they had never seen anything but
Disney movies."

"So not funny, Wilson. My assistant's on the verge of
quitting."

"That twit, Tory? You can do better."

"My music friends are grossed out, too. One of them
showed the video to her mom. She assumed I was a psycho
druggie. It's bad."

"You don't need their hokey live music. Use a
soundtrack."

"You don't get it. The magic is out of control. It's killing
my following, and—"

"What?" Ander's back, his brow creased in worry. He
wedges in close. "What's killing your following?"

"Dorianna hates my videos," Wilson whines.

"Wilson, shut the hell up!" I fire him a withering look.

Ander hands me a drink. "What's the problem? Warren's
capybara video rocked. It got you triple the followers."

"Man's got a point." Wilson taps his cane on the bench
for emphasis. "But, Dor, if you hate my work . . ." He affects
a pout.

"Ohhh! It's not that." Groaning in frustration, I rip the
paper off my straw, ball it up and fling it into a trashcan.
"Forget it. Let's work on the text now that Ander's here." I
send Wilson a shut-up-or-else look.

"Punish me, Sungirl," Wilson sings in a private refrain to
our warehouse episode. "Punish me so good." Ignoring

Wilson, Ander gets out his journal. We tweak the copy until it's perfect.

Blind Date Confessional Meetup
Only the brave dare confess their private fantasy to their blind date!
Click into <u>BLIND DATE CONFESSIONAL</u> *to RSVP.*
Create your secret avatar name and be matched with a date to die for.
Mutual confessions!
Relax. The site is totally anonymous, so no need to hold back.
November 30th, 9 p.m., at the old Nivomonsky Bathhouse,
210 Surf Avenue, Coney Island, NY
Wear sexy party gear and bring a festive blindfold

"To die for sounds good," Wilson says, to which I roll my eyes.

"Where's that warehouse?" Ander zips his jacket. "It's freezing up here."

When we give Ander a tour, I can almost imagine things are still light and free, that there are no injuries or stolen impassioned kisses trespassing into cheating-heart territory.

But when Wilson blurts out that he wants to perform more confessional charades like we played out the other day, Ander's jaw hardens.

"You guys were messing around here the other day?"

"Scouting the location is all," I automatically defend, though the realization that *Ander* messed around without any urge to confess burns me up.

"That was some scouting, Dor," Wilson brags.

Riding back on the train, Ander's stony. He has no right to be jealous.

But I can fix that. Shutting my eyes, I invoke my energy, and envelop him within it. He leans over, mechanically, and plants a kiss on my lips, pulls them open with his teeth. I'm hungry for his mouth, the weight of his arms around me, his chest rising and falling. Too soon, he jerks away, eyes hazy from enchanted love. Does he even know what he just did?

I study the cheesy wall ads for liposuction and facial implants from a plastic surgeon. Some people have it so hard becoming beautiful. Magic has made that easy for me.

So, why is my life still messed up? An unwelcome answer percolates up. Magic won't fix everything. Forcing that second kiss from Ander feels like I've gobbled down frothy, neon-pink cotton candy. Good to take the edge off my appetite, but followed by a black-hole sugar jitter. I hate this negativity, and I force it away.

My thoughts wander to Wilson bragging to Ander about his closeness with me. It's hard to stay mad at Wilson—he almost can't help himself. Plus, he helped me that night when I was all jacked up. Glancing over at Ander, I see he's texting. *Hmm.* Not hard to guess who the recipient is.

This time, I send a blast out of the train, and direct it with every ounce of strength. *If you people thought that my levitating, burning ball was big stuff, suck on this,* snaps my beast.

Across the ether I sense a sharp cry of pain, a pop, and a bright, acidic explosion.

No more texting for cheaters.

Rings of pleasure convulse my chest all the way into my heart's blackened center.

Afterward, I sink into the seat and arrange my silky hair over my shoulders. As I relax, I have a brainstorm about finding an altogether different widget to sell Blind Date Confessional. I click open my cell, and fly my fingers over its keypad. *Ping.* Yes—Bailey says I can pop over for an hour, before her mom returns from a gallery appointment. I'm no longer welcome since the fire damage. Satisfied, I click my cell shut.

Ander clicks and clicks his own cell, in a futile attempt to send a text. He should be glad I only broke his. I *exploded* Lacy's. "Something you need to tell me?" he asks.

"No. . . something you need to tell me?"

His pale blue eyes are impenetrable, closed to interpretation.

Stalemate.

24

There are chords in the hearts of the most reckless, which cannot be touched without emotion.
—Edgar Allen Poe

It's awesome to be back in Bailey's room, melting into a beanbag chair, amongst her fashion sketches artfully strewn across the floor and the elegant swatches hanging from her Inspiration Station. I've missed coming here, spending time with Bailey. Strange, how even though my followers have soared into the millions, I still feel so alone—but not here. I shake off my newest gold-colored heels.

"Sorry I wasn't at lunch." Bailey giggles. "Cole and I made out in the park."

I smile, glad she has a fun reason for her no-show, but more than anything I'm relieved she didn't overhear people ride me about the scary videos.

"Did you hear what happened to Lacey?"

"No, tell me." I already know, but can't tell Bailey that.

"She was walking home from school, and texting someone, and her cell exploded in her hand! Freaky, or what?"

My heart is beating triple time. "Wow, yeah! You always hear about how if you overcharge a cell, it'll explode, but I always thought that was a tall tale. Was she hurt?"

"No. She dropped it really quickly. But it wigged her out." Bailey offers me a piece of Swiss chocolate. "So, what do you need to talk about that can't wait?" She stares at my hands when I take the candy. "Holy wow, how did your hands heal so fast?"

"My aunt has . . . a great Chinese balm," I lie. "So, um, I want to brainstorm with you about my next party, since you're so incredibly creative."

"I won't deny it." Bailey arranges her flowy handmade skirt over her shapely legs.

"I'd like *not* to do a video for the fan page."

"Why not? The videos were incredibly successful. People practically broke my door down trying to get in during Burlesque."

No way I can tell her the real reason. "It's just that, well, I want to switch it up big-time for the next event." I explain the details of Blind Date Confessional—the myriad of dressing rooms, aka confessionals, how blindfolded people will be led into them, how a video might reveal too much about the secret setting.

When Bailey's face gets that half mischievous, half lightbulb-blinking look, I know she's come up with something good. "Got it!" she crows, jiggling a foot.

"What? Spill."

"This righteous animator dude lives in my building. He's in art school so he does jobs on the cheap. He could do a Blind Date cartoon. I could trade that for making him, like, a hat."

"Out-of-the-box awesome. Oh, Bailey, I'll pay the guy." Between the stolen cash and the extra funds my mother sent me, I've stashed a treasure trove for the next event.

"Okay, sure. An animated short could have things you couldn't do in a video so easily. You could give people cartoon bodies and funny voices and put cartoon bats fluttering around. Make it funny and sexy, yet scary."

"Love it!" I exclaim. "Wilson won't have to be involved. I took photos of the place, so I can upload them, plus ones of people that the animator can use to jump off from."

Bailey gives me a look of motherly concern. "I'm glad Wilson won't be involved. I can't help it, Dorianna, he creeps me out." I only nod, so she goes on. "I'll call my animator friend tonight and scope it out. I'll text you if it's a go."

I lean over and hug her. "Thanks, I knew you'd come through."

"Can I ask how you scored the warehouse? Who owns it?"

"Oh, a guy out in Coney Island."

"Which guy? Not Wilson?" I shake my head. Bailey gets up in my face. "Who, then?"

"Um, his uncle."

Bailey frowns. "*Hmm*. How many schools will you invite this time?"

I fiddle with a new bracelet. "I thought I'd . . . open it way up." I shrug. "To anyone."

"That's a horrible idea, Dorianna!" Bailey drops the last piece of chocolate back on its wrapper. "You'll get weirdoes. Even stalkers. I'm worried for your safety."

"It's touching you care about—"

"Think hard about it, girl. What would you get out of a complete mob scene?" Bailey checks the time on her cell. "OMG, you better go. Mom's probably on her way back."

As I scramble down the fire exit, I feel deep pricks of

sadness, followed by relief. I won't have to explain why going viral is so essential. Do I even know why anymore? At least I've gotten what I came for. If Bailey handles getting the items to the animator, and if the animator has no access to my unstable magic, it follows that the cartoon will be free of dreadful changes.

Back at home, I log onto my fan page. Ander's already posted the Blind Date blurb. I'm up to 200,500 followers now, and already have 587 yes RSVPs for Blind Date Confessional. Hot dang, I'm thoroughly stoked. New followers are from Manhattan and the boroughs, Connecticut, and Boston. Even a handful from the Midwest—and California.

Party planning sure is an effective distraction from angsting over Ander and Lacey. I chuckle over how I zapped their cells. No texting to help the illicit lovebirds mate.

Ander will be impressed by my hipster animation for Blind Date Confessional. No one beats me in the fascination department. In comparison, Lacey's a snooze. Before long, Ander will be bored with her and come running to me. Then, Lacey will drag herself to my party just to see how I did it.

This party will be the spectacle of the year. Even timid Cat and Lisbeth will shuck off their misgivings and show.

Taking a break from my laptop, I slip on my newest dress: a silver metallic number that clings to my curves. I pose in the mirror while I experiment with hairstyles. Day by day, my skin is more dewy, my figure slimmer and hotter, my lips fuller. Yesterday, one of the girls even asked if I'd gotten lip enhancements, they look so Hollywood starlet. Last week, a dazzlingly handsome older man handed me a business card from a modeling agency and suggested I come in for an open call. "You're *now*—edgy, sexy, arrogance in the eyes, but still fresh. You're what all of the magazines are looking for," he declared.

I'm considering it. Now, making love to the mirror, I stroke my arms, my hands. No burn scars, no blemishes whatsoever. I glance at a photo of myself on my desk, taken before I moved here. In this new picture, I have no more wonky teeth and I look a fresh-faced fifteen, not my real age, a couple weeks shy of seventeen.

My love affair with myself is cut short when I think to recheck the YouTube beach fiasco. Back at my laptop, heart thumping, I see that the giant eyesore has tons of comments I can't bear to read. Instead, I press play. The beginning's unchanged, except it's proof beyond a doubt that I'm younger and prettier now—as if I'm aging backwards.

But as it plays on, at the part where the flowers used to spring magically from my hands, the items now pouring out are knives and decaying fish. My likeness stares out at the viewer and screams new threats: *You're my victim in the warehouse of pain. Confess your sins, guilty one. Confess or be trapped in my purgatorial elevator of death.*

"Freaking W-T-F!" I bleat, and press stop. I cover my face for a long, jarring time. Then, with horrified fascination, I press replay—same bad magic. My fingers tremble as I fumble for Wilson's number. Texting won't cut it for this conversation.

"Hello, Dor." He picks up after just one ring. *Expecting me?* he doesn't even have to say it out loud.

"Try harder to take those goddamn videos off of YouTube," I splutter. "I'm begging you."

"The videos won't let me."

"That's crazy. They're not people! Did you write YouTube a help message? Double-check their tutorial on how to delete?"

He sighs. "It's *you*. I told you before. The unpredictable

magic in you wants them there."

"Bull! I've had enough consequences. I've burned people, stolen . . . How many more will I get?"

"Dor, worry about that later. These trailers will attract a thrilling, danger-loving crowd. The kind that hangs out at late-night clubs, reads witchcraft stories and watches cult horror films."

"Holy freaking shit, Wilson." I sink in my chair, click my phone shut, and begin to cry. Inside, my beast hoots with glee.

That night, I have a nightmare. My father and I are in his defunct church. He's showing a film, to which people are shaking their heads. It's my YouTube video, but even worse. I'm screaming lewd things to my fathers' followers: *You stupid pigs. How can you follow a manipulating con? You deserve to wallow in your own manure. I have no respect for you, and my father is a waste of life. His church is based on lies. Follow me instead, fools! Follow me into the warehouse of death.* In the dream, utter disgust is etched on my father's face, as if *I'm* the con.

I wake, wracked with chills, gripping my pillow for dear life. The moon outside my window is shrouded behind clouds. I have a strong urge to creep to the shelf and pull out my dad's old devotional book.

Trembling, I throw off my covers and creep across the room, one cautious foot in front of the other because I don't dare turn on the light. This act seems so dangerous, that bright illumination will expose me.

Making it to the window, I open the curtains another inch. A dim beam from the streetlight makes it possible to distinguish one book from another. I reach for the slim volume and hold it at arm's length, as if the book will contaminate me if I clasp it closer. Propping my cell on my pillow for more light, I crack open the devotional.

Two photos fall onto the bed, but the folded list is still tucked in tightly. My hand is poised above it. With one movement—a spreading open of the paper—I'll know his whole private mess. Understand completely why they put my father in jail. My heart beats so violently that my nightgown top bumps up, down, up.

Not now. Not yet. *Not ever.*

I slap it closed. Picking up the photos, I study them instead. In one, I'm about six, and standing in front of the church, with my dad on one side, my mom on the other. I was the turkey between their white-bread sandwiches.

My father was skinny then, with a pinched-in look. He was hungry, too, I realize. His sparse blond hair was mousy, and his spectacles gave him a schoolmarm air. Although later, my mother grew frail from stress, in this early picture she was husky, with a bulldog-stubborn look. I do remember her laying into Dad, criticizing his wrinkled pants and shirt stains.

And there I am. I resemble my father more than my mother. Even then, I'd learned how to disappear—behind the folds of my mother's dress, behind my blank stare. I put that photo down, and pick up the other.

Dorianna on her sixth birthday, my father wrote, under the photo of me, clutching a stuffed teddy bear. I remember that bear, its button eyes reassuring me that the night witches wouldn't steal me, that the dawn would bring the promise of safety.

My eyes blur with tears. The feelings I had as a tiny girl, a daughter who loved her father, now well up unexpectedly. I never dared feel a thing, after years of my parents' fights, after he went on trial and those church ladies gave me hateful looks, as if the sins of the father . . .

I open up the drawer to my bedside table and shove the photos to the back.

Bailey comes over for the big animation reveal. That way, we don't have to worry about her mom kicking me out of their loft. Armed with pastries from a gourmet bakery and a pot of Sumatran coffee, we settle at my desk.

Bailey slides a thumb drive into her laptop. We watch the animation, chortling at the best parts.

"These characters are amazing!" I gasp.

"Yeah, Tim Burton meets a new kind of *South Park*."

I screech when my cartoony character waltzes onscreen in the metallic minidress.

"Wait 'til you see how he did Cole and Ander," Bailey giggles.

A cartoon version of me invites my guests to traverse a creaky moat and enter a haunted warehouse by the sea. Inside, wall-to-wall guests dance to metal music as bats and flying winged monsters swoop down to terrorize. My henchmen, who look like Ander and Cole, but with zombie cracks in their flesh, blindfold my guests.

By the light of cartoon candles, the Cole and Ander zombies escort blindfolded couples to rooms. Voucher winners go up first. There are funny confessions, like one guy admitting to his date that he sucked his thumb until he was fifteen, and a girl admitting a fetish for popcorn-and-mayo sandwiches.

The animation grows into a pulsing abstract design that blooms faster and faster to the musical crescendo of passionate whoops. The voiceover asks, "Who's *your* blind date?"

"Consider me officially wowed," I gush. "Tell your

neighbor he's a genius." I look uncertainly at Bailey. "W—would you mind uploading it to the sites for me, please?"

"Why not you?"

"It's just that . . . Your touch will be a good luck charm." She arches her brows doubtfully. "I'm hopeless with this stuff," I say. "You don't want Wilson uploading it, do you?"

The mention of Wilson does the trick. She mounts the animation on YouTube and to my other sites. I'm hugely relieved. I haven't touched it with my toxic hands. It's not even my computer. If my theory is correct, these cartoons will never go through any horrid changes.

We finish our cupcakes, licking every morsel off our fingers, and wash it down with steamy coffee refills.

"How come you never invited me over here before this?" Bailey asks, as she clicks into a music video of a band singing while they snowboard.

I watch her sway to the beat. "Umm . . . Those elfin critters in your mom's paintings kept luring me to your place? Your room's the best workshop ever?"

Bailey laughs and clicks into another site. Before I know what's happening, the next video is of *me*, swearing and cackling on that cursed first YouTube surf mess. "Hey! Don't play that!" I lurch forward and press stop.

"Why not?" She stares at me like I've lost my marbles. Bailey's not one to be told what to do. She presses *play*.

"No!" I push her hand away and again press stop.

In a furious gesture, Bailey takes hold of her laptop and moves it close to her, guarding it with her arms. "What's your problem, Dorianna? It's *my* effing laptop!"

"I told you, don't watch that thing. It sucks."

My beast is aroused and infuriated. *Let her see,* it scolds. *Frighten the mortal.*

I press on my ears. "Quiet!" Problem is, it's not yelling *into* my ears, but *from inside out.*

"What's wrong with you?" Bailey's moved her chair away from me, and she's peering at me with the pity and horror that one saves for loonies who rip off their clothes and careen through supermarkets, spilling jars of tomato sauce over the waxed linoleum.

"My ears, they're killing me." I bite down on my bottom lip to stop an imminent howl. The skin on my tongue rips and I taste a warm burst of blood. Why does the beast explode with bile at the very worst times? Does it have it out for me? I can never really tell if the beast is me, or an alien thing that's invaded me. Either way, it has a mind of its own.

Bailey squares her shoulders. She marches the laptop safely over to the windowsill, flips it open and presses *play*. "Don't come near me," she warns.

Let her see it, I tell myself. She'll see it eventually, I know that. I'm sick of worrying about it. Bailey, of all people, might get it. She's used to her mother's painted monsters.

My beast sniggers: *Terrorize her.*

I'm able to control myself by chewing more jagged holes in my mouth. That is, until the part in the video where I say I want to trap people in my elevator of death. At that, I leap over my desk with superhuman speed to shut down Bailey's laptop for good.

"Lay off!" she yells as I slam down the lid.

"It's done, you saw it all. Happy now?" I hiss between gritted teeth. My eyes narrow at her in reptilian hate.

Bailey is icy, too. "What happened to the video? Is this Wilson's doing? Is he trying to attract stalkers and murderers to your next party? Tell me, Dorianna!"

She's giving me an out, I realize—Wilson as my out. Bailey can't stand thinking that I'm to blame, because that would mean her best friend is plotting some serious nastiness.

I'm sick of this magic, the secrets and lies. I might've

wanted this when I started school, but all I want now is to be a normal kid, have a friend or two, even if it means I'm no longer beautiful.

Confess. She won't believe you anyway, mocks the beast.

"Bailey, It's all me!" I explode, tears raining down. "I made those nasty changes."

Her skin looks green. "Why? Why would you do that?"

"I can't control it. I made a vow, Bailey, and now I can't take the stuff off. You have to believe me." It's such a huge relief to blurt out the truth. I'm suddenly desperate for Bailey to believe me. Inside, my beast jabbers like a monkey gone mad.

"Vow?" Bailey shrills. "What craziness is that? You sound like Wilson." She slides her laptop in its bag and backs toward the door. "I know it was him. He dragged you down. Did he feed you bad drugs or something?"

"Why won't you believe me?" I rasp, "I'm not on drugs or crazy. I'm telling the truth! It's not Wilson. . . it's me. I have some weird power, Bailey. But it's scary, because even my powers can't delete the videos. They want them there. It's the price I have to pay."

"You *are* hallucinating! *Wilson's* messed up your videos," Bailey yells. "He's out to destroy you and make you psycho. Can't you see? Oh, Dorianna, you're so lost."

"It's me, it's me," I wail, and then choke down the beast's fresh round of curses.

"If you keep protecting Wilson and refuse to tell me the truth, then I'm out of here." Bailey steps backwards into the hall, as if she doesn't dare to turn her back.

Told you so, told you so, sings my beast.

"I need you to believe me. Why won't you believe me?" I sob as Bailey races downstairs and out the front door.

25

Your audience controls you, you cannot control them.
—Simon Cowell

B efore I decide to cut school indefinitely—to protect people from my unstable magic—I go one more time. On the way to history class, I catch a blur of Bailey's red hair bobbing down the hall, as she cuts class to avoid me. Tory, too, stops talking to her minions when she spots me, and the whole group takes off in the direction they've just come from. Lacey and Ander stroll side by side past my old locker and toward me. About twenty paces away, they see me, mouths agape. They shift gears and scurry down another hall.

I'm so hurt. Despite the angry objections of my beast, I don't want to hurt them back. I'm tired of the magic, of the lies. I meant what I said to Bailey.

But the magic's not done with me. To Lacey, without intending to, I send a spike of molten energy. A second later, I hear her distant, high-pitched yelp of pain. On some level, it satisfies me. On another, it makes me absolutely nauseated. It's like the delight of eating something sweet that I've become allergic to, and will soon make me violently sick. An unworldly illness creeping up on me, that no one can diagnose.

By noon, I want to bolt, though there's still vital business to take care of. If this is my last day here, I *do* still need my magic. I need to charm as many people into going to Blind Date Confessional as possible. It's my desperate swan song. Before I figure out how to stop this thing, or let it eat me alive.

Now that Tory has pretty much bailed, I've taken on all the publicity. I've posed as my fans on social media, listed the event on sites, and printed out cards. This morning I left stacks of cards everywhere—in the senior lounge, the front hall, even the ladies' room. Huge job. I feel a twinge of begrudging admiration for Tory. But it soon curdles into bitterness.

And now, I stand at the entrance to the final frontier, the lunchroom.

Ava pauses as she breezes by, to glance at a card. She appraises me with sloe-eyed condescension. "Word is, you had a nervous breakdown or a disastrous acid trip."

"Absolutely not. Who said that?"

"Oh, you know, the grapevine." She tosses her big hair, today laced with silk flowers.

So, Bailey squawked. *Some friend.* "I'm in perfect form," I insist. "Come to Blind Date Confessional and see how perfect."

Lacey waltzes up to Ava and makes a show of air-kissing her. "What's up, girl?" she chirps, as if Lacey wasn't heart-broken last week that Charlie dumped her for Ava.

These girls switch allegiances so fast it takes my breath

away. I shake my head in disgust. Charlie must've already dumped Ava and found yet another juicy flavor of eye candy. How I ever entertained being friends with Lacey is a mystery to me now.

She glances at the invite. "Now that you set Bailey's place on fire, the only followers you'll have from now on are strangers, people who don't know your con. I may consider going, though, if I'm up for a train wreck."

I stare at Lacey's blistered hand holding a new cell phone and stifle a laugh. *Bailey's place isn't the only thing I set on fire.* If only she knew who exploded her cell. . .

My awakened beast is itching to catapult these two bitches into the air with all the force of its magic, and smash them down on their backs. Imagining the satisfying crack of their bones gives my inner creature a spasm of toxic pleasure. But business is business. I need this flea-ridden rat pack at my next party—simple as that. Mustering up mayhem, I coo, "Yes, do come. We'll see whose train crashes first." I send them a dose of persuasive energy to speed their decision. *You'll come, yes, you will, to the biggest event this whole stinking school will ever witness. You will, you will.*

Then I mince away. "What's the date on that party?" Ava drones from behind me.

In a silky, intoxicating, soundless voice I imprint the date in her brain.

I'm not hungry. Haven't been since that frightful video incident with Bailey, but I might as well grab a free bite of rice and beans on my last day here.

Part of why I want to drop out is that my mystique will be greater if people are wondering about me. But I'm also deeply weary of the façade, and bruised by Bailey's rejection. Magic hasn't made people love me. It's cheating. I wanted them to accept me without magic, but now I can't even get respect *with* it. I long to get rid of this toxic power, but I've no idea how.

Next, I run into Cat and Lisbeth. Or more accurately, seeing them make a wide arc around me, I send a beam of persuasive energy their way—just one more time. *You'll come to greet your queen. You'll come to greet your queen. Do as I say, right now.*

Cat and Lisbeth, wearing baffled frowns, swerve back toward me. "Uh, hi?" Lisbeth says. "Haven't seen you around for a while."

"Great to run into you!" I give them each a friendly pat on the back. "Looking forward to seeing you girls at my Blind Date Confessional Party. Have you logged onto my anonymous Web site and created your secret avatar name, so we can pair you up?" I wink.

Cat's eyes dart over to me and back to her friend. Lisbeth's mouth opens and closes fishlike before she blurts, "Sure we will. Won't we, Cat? Right after band practice."

Cat nods mechanically, as her irises swell.

"So, it's settled," I sing. "You'll have a blast."

"We'll have a blast," replies Lisbeth, in a robotic echo.

Even a conjurer has some morals. I'm so done.

On my way to the lunch line, I spot Ander again, and my breath catches in my throat. He still lives in a huge, raw part of my heart, and I hate how badly that wounds me. It would be so easy to glamour him again. Have him run over and take me in his arms, right here, in front of everyone. So horribly tempting.

Instead, I take cover behind a group of sophomores, as he stands near the start of the lunch line, talking to the bookheads. Concentrating hard, I sense they're talking about the sociopath Mersault from our latest assigned novel, Camus' *The Stranger*. In it, Mersault murders a pure stranger. When questioned why, he simply says, "Because the sun was in my eye."

Ha. Sun glare, sunburn, Sungirl, I think in automatic progression. Eyeing the notebook in Ander's back pocket, I grow ravenous to finally see what he's writing. Someone bumps into me. Hard. It's no accident. I wheel around. "Charlie!"

"It's rude to stare," he scolds. My mouth flaps open, speechless. "Look," Charlie starts, balancing the weight of his loaded tray between his big hands. "You and I, we don't need to even pretend we're friends."

Makes sense. I gaze at him, ready to hear what he'll say next. "So?"

"So, what I want to tell you is out of no allegiance to you, or Ander, or my effed-up brother, Wilson." Charlie blinks his dull brown eyes at me, and I wonder for the millionth time how this beefy-taco prepster in pinstripes and cords could ever be related to his elegantly devious goth brother. "It's for your own edification," he promises.

I'm tempted to say, Edification, good vocab word. Did Wilson teach you that? But, I keep my cool. "M'kay. Shoot."

Charlie nods toward Ander. "I saw you staring all lovesick at old Ander there."

"And?" My beast is suddenly jockeying for me to bite this fool's nose off.

"Get over it," says Charlie. "Ander's head over heels for Lacey. Always has been." Charlie lets out a snort of air. "Well, there was that short interval when you entered the picture. You must've pulled some magic on him, but the spell's over."

"Think so, huh?"

"Yeah. You got beautiful overnight, I'll give you that. But the days of Ander fawning over you are past. Best move on." Charlie stares hard at me. How far in can he see? "I always thought you were witchy," he says. "Figured you took lessons from Wilson. So, honey, if you want to cast a spell to make Ander wish he hadn't cheated on you, be my guest."

"He cheated on me?" My pulse jumps. "How do you know? You don't even talk to him."

Charlie snickers. "I talk to Ava and all the other beauties. Word's out: Ander spent the night with Lacey, and not just sleeping." He grins.

So, Ander has gone all the way with Lacey. This hits like a punch to my sternum. Does Charlie know of my powers? How could he? I watch him waddle away. The guy really is one beer-bloated jock. My beast snarls in agreement.

Glancing over at Ander, some huge tectonic plate in me scrapes open and invites in a black, oily alchemical mix. I hiss, "You're no longer safe from me, Ander."

Inside my beast somersaults, delighted.

I snake closer. Ander still hasn't seen me and I aim to keep it that way. Two tables away, I huddle by the condiment stand, pretending to grab napkins and pepper containers. His notebook is folded in his pocket. I focus on it, until it looms large in my mind's eye. Then, I beam over rays of compressed energy. My head heats from the effort. Again, I aim another blast its way. *Up and out, up and out.*

His back pocket bulges. I send another energetic nudge. Inch by inch, as if an invisible hand is pulling it up, the notebook rises weightlessly.

Next, I focus on Ander, persuading him softly but firmly. *Walk away. Do it now. Don't feel your notebook as it slips from your pocket and slaps on the floor. Don't question, don't worry, don't turn around and see me. Do it, do it. Do it!*

Ander says one last thing to his friend, as the notebook falls. Oblivious, he advances toward the lunch line. No one sees the journal as it slides over to where I half-face the wall.

I throw the pepper packets and napkins I've been clutching back on the condiment stand, snatch the notebook and thrust it in my pack. As I hurry toward the door, a flock of enthusiastic ninth graders surround me, all babbling at once:

"Sungirl, where've you been??"

"What should I wear to Blind Date? I know you said sexy party stuff, but . . ."

"My friends in Queens all want to go. Thanks for opening it up to anyone."

"Did you pair me with someone hot? I want Keanu Baker from Debate Team."

"Ooh, yeah."

Reflexively, my arms reach out to shove them away. I need to see that notebook. But I remember, through a dizzying fog, why I came here in the first place. I pull out a stack of cards. I should be grateful that these little ninth graders need no persuasion to fawn over me.

My fans eagerly take the cards. "Put these in coffee shops, theaters, wherever," I demand. Then before they can detain me further, I burst from the room.

I lock myself in a bathroom stall and pull out Ander's journal. Feeling the weight of his opus in my greedy, trembling hands, I revel in my take.

Around me, girls complain about tests, teachers, streaky makeup, and clueless dates. I hear the flush of toilets and the clip of heels as I crack open the creased notebook.

Many of Ander's early entries are three-liners that he's scribbled out. And then there's a short piece about the made-up Padro and Angie.

Lacey was right—there is no long novel. No *Extortion Portraits*. Not even a micro-novella. So, Ander has told a tall tale about how prolific he is.

I sink down into the seat, disappointed.

But as I continue to flip through the pages, the soft hairs on the back of my neck stiffen. There are pieces about me—poetic, lyrical paragraphs. One about our first day on the beach, and about the time we kissed at Havana's. Ander didn't exactly use the word love, but close.

Falling for D. It surprises me. She's so plain. And I only took her out to Coney that first day to get back at L.

My heart thumps hard against my ribs. The world beyond the notebook diffuses into white noise as I search for more clues to Ander's feelings.

D is stunning now. How can a girl change so fast? I never thought anyone could make me almost forget about L.

That word "almost" sticks in my craw. Breathlessly, I read on.

W is a thief, yet imagines himself a stud. He steals D from me with his charm. Charm is cheap, manipulative. Why does everyone want to steal something from someone else? C stole my agility when he mangled my leg. Or was W the real thief, when he grinned maliciously down at me during that accident, and I felt my bone crack wider? Something's wrong with W. I knew it when he tortured that capybara.

A few passages later, what's left of my well-being drains away.

D is a thief too. She steals my attention and my love from L. D steals friends from other people. Insatiable. She wants to steal my old girlfriend, who no longer even belongs to me so I can't try to get her back.

It's strange. When I was with D my cell phone broke. And L's exploded across town at the same moment. That scares me. D scares me.

Who is this D? What does she want?

She doesn't feel human. She's pure obsession, pure hunger.

Why do I feel like one of her followers? Loving L, yet following D .

. .

I throw the book down on my pack and clutch my head between my hands. Try to slow my frenzied, shallow breathing. Glancing at the open journal, I see one last line.

D is my subject!

"Your subject?" I mutter. What does that even mean, that I'm Ander's servant? That he plans to use my life as material? Takes a nerve. I'm glad I broke my pledge not to glamour him. Flushing the toilet, I picture Lacey, Ander, Ava . . . well, not Charlie—at least he told me the truth—whirling down with my used toilet paper.

The last class before I walk out is Lit. Ander will be there, along with Lacey. My first thought is to march into class and dump the notebook on his desk, and then observe, gleefully, the horror of discovery spread across his face—that I now know he's not a real writer. That I know who he's decided upon, even if he never intended to tell me.

What about the Blind Date Confessional Party, though? It's more important to lure Ander out there than confront him now. I want to lock him up with me in one of those claustrophobic changing rooms. Force his guilty confession. I want him to witness the reach of my following beyond our dinky school.

What will assure his attendance? I remember how desperate he was to get his cell back, knowing that he'd left incriminating texts on it. I could keep this notebook, and text him the morning of the party, say that I found it, am safe-keeping it and will give it to him that night, if he attends. *Yesss.* My gut burns with the corrosive delight of revenge. Revenge is so much easier to feel than betrayal.

Later that afternoon, back in my room, I log onto my fan page. Unfortunately, Lacey was right. Tons of classmates have unfollowed me after writing scathing comments.

practicing witchcraft now? You look the part

not stickng around to see what happns in yr elevator of death!

UR 2 sick 2 follow

UNFOLLOW THE BEAST

Growing hair on your chest?? Creepshow!

But there are new fans as well, mostly strangers. In fact, I have 498,546 followers and 938 RSVPS to Blind Date. *Staggering*. Gives me the giddy willies.

No matter how famished I am for followers, there can never be enough. I revel in each new number for five, six minutes, when the inevitable jitters hollow me out. The only thing that fills me back up is to log on an hour later, and see a huge new headcount.

As Wilson predicted, there are some serious hardcore freaks among this new bunch. And, man, their spelling sucks.

whup me sun-boar… torture me in ur elevator

yummy she devul b in my snuff film

Paint us bloody, bringun my bike gang from the Bronx wit me

I recheck the old videos. The beach one still has me screaming about the elevator of death, but even louder. The capybara video now has me flogging the poor beast.

I feel like I'm choking from lack of oxygen.

With an unsteady finger I press play on the new animation. This one will be okay. . . I've had no contact with it whatsoever. Same greeting to my fans, same cartoon zombies leading kids to the rooms, but right near the end, when it pans to the elevator, something new appears: a curling cartoon cord of smoke, escaping through the elevator door.

I rub my eyes and play the accursed thing again.

Same mean coil of dark smoke. "What?" I challenge the empty room. "It doesn't mean a goddamn thing!"

26

The ratings come in, you're happy for five minutes, then the insecure madness comes in.
—Simon Cowell

During the last two weeks before the party, whenever I think I'll go crazy if one more classmate unfollows me, —or if I get one more creepy post from a perv who wants to cast me in his demonology flick—inevitably, Wilson shows up.

He'll appear on the same subway, in my neighborhood cafe to buy me a smoothie, or dressed to kill with a black rose and an offer of dinner. With his dizzying charm, he chips away at my resolve to turn away from my lies and manipulations, my desire to reject the magic that more and more I see as repellent. And each time he tells me more about the work he's done on the warehouse.

"I installed candle sconces," he tells me over one dinner, "and lots of mirrors. Put in a sound system, too."

"That's awesome, Wilson, but I can't pay you back. I have to save for the party drinks."

"Don't worry, Dor. My uncle has cases of stuff out there."

"What kind of stuff? The vodka?"

"That and more."

I'm not keen on underage kids chugging, though his fervor recharges my flagged enthusiasm.

I miss seeing Bailey. Every day I dress as if I'm headed to school, and then wander around the neighborhood until my aunt is safely gone. I sneak back home, get online, and obsessively check my stats until my feet fall asleep. By the time I venture into the kitchen, I'm past the point of wanting to eat. Sometimes I make tea and a burnt piece of toast.

My beast is always chiding me: *Shape up. Get more excited. Rejoice in your evil.* I can't help it, though. I truly don't care about the upcoming party. In fact, I almost can't wait until it's over, so I can sleep more days away.

Since I'm alone with no one to overhear me, I often shout at this thing eating me up inside. "Quit lecturing me, or I'll cut you right out," I say, to which I double over in pain as it gives me a swift boot from the inside out.

Ander texts me twice. He asks if I've seen his notebook and, as an afterthought, asks how I am. I send one cryptic text back, saying I look forward to seeing him at the party.

"One more week," I mutter in a curiously flat voice as I cross off days on the calendar. "One more week until Blind Date Confessional rocks New York."

"Dorianna?" My aunt won't stop knocking. "I know you're in there." She jiggles the handle.

I hoist myself up on the bed and stare at the door. My

head aches, my eye sockets throb, yet my ears are fully attuned. I hear my aunt's frustrated sigh, and a gentle thud as she rests her head on the other side of the wooden doorframe.

"I'm wondering if you'd like to get a sandwich. We haven't talked in a while."

I stand slowly, legs and chest aching. It takes too much energy to walk. Wrapping my sweater closer, I tighten its belt. I haven't been eating. Glancing in the mirror, I still look beautiful, even glowing. I don't know how that's possible, as wasted as I feel. Padding to the door, I crack it open.

My aunt tries to smile, but she's obviously shocked to see me so gaunt. As if she hasn't seen me whittle down, day after day. "Want to walk over to Molly's Cafe for dinner?"

"I'm not hungry."

"You could get soup. Or tea," she suggests before I can protest soup as too filling.

"Okay," I sigh, "give me a minute."

"Sure, sure."

She sounds so relieved that a weak flutter of sadness passes through me. It passes quickly, returning me back to that familiar hollowness. More and more, I suspect that Blind Date Confessional will not satisfy, as my millions of followers haven't. Nothing's made a grain of difference in my world, which has become as flat as the pre-Pythagorean earth I learned about in history of science.

I rake my hands through my disheveled hair, and clip it back. Another glance in the mirror proves that as numb as I feel, my eyes still blaze, and my skin positively vibrates with translucent life. Why?

That last day at school, a friend of Jake's made note of this irony. "Have you been sick?" he asked me. I asked why he assumed this. "Because you look so beautiful," he replied.

My flush of delight was followed by distaste. Some girl back in Indiana had suffered from anorexia, and the boys had fawned over her waiflike figure—gross, equating sickness with beauty.

I suit up in leather pants, a pair of heavy gold earrings, my black boots and leather bomber jacket. These accessories will, like armor, hopefully lend me strength.

My aunt and I walk to the diner in weighted silence, as if neither one of us wants to cut open the air with something as piercing as actual suspicion. I suspect she'll grill me on why I haven't been at school. I'm already strategizing for the counterattack.

We settle into a comfy booth halfway to the back, where we have privacy. The waitress approaches, smacking her gum, and asks for our order. I hear her mind percolating. *Gorgeous girl, but the motorcycle getup? Pretentious. This poor mom has her hands full of diva.*

"I'll have black tea." I glower at the waitress and hiss under my breath. "And she's not my mother." The waitress startles visibly.

Aunt Carol raises her brows at me. "That's all you want?"

I hear the waitress's silent crack: *That, and give her a punch in the nose.*

Catching her eyes, I say, "Dry toast . . . and a punch in *your* nose."

Now, the waitress's mind is near screaming. *Weird bitch.*

After the girl takes Aunt Carol's order and minces away, Aunt Carol turns to me. "You snapped at that waitress for no reason."

"We have some bad history is all," I improvise. "So, how've you been?"

My aunt wrings her hands. "Well, the radio station is always busy."

"Yeah? What specifically are you working on now?"

"Getting more interviews, and subscriptions."

Subscriptions, funny—I never realized that she's also engaged in the business of gathering more followers. Maybe we aren't so different after all.

"I know I've been working late, but . . ." She smiles. "I hope I'm never too busy to spend time with my niece."

The waitress shoots me a dirty look as she delivers our drinks.

Aunt Carol's eyes fill with care and worry. "How are you, Dorianna?"

Uh oh, here it comes. I gulp down tea and flinch as it scalds my mouth. "The planning for my next event takes all my time. And school, you know, homework."

Her forehead creases. I sense that she's suppressing a barrage of concerns or allegations.

The waitress plunks our food down before scurrying away again.

Aunt Carol salts her eggs. I cut my toast. The food gives us both an excuse to table any heavy discussion. Aunt Carol digs into her omelet, while I take stingy nibbles of the dry toast.

It's strange how until recently, I always felt famished, always ate big portions of food, yet I was still hungry. But of late, my hunger's curled inwards and shriveled, and though my belly still feels hollow, it's no longer from hunger. I can hardly stand to eat. The magic isn't helping—not at all. In fact, I feel it biting at me. How the hell does one get rid of something invisible and untouchable? How can I fight it? I've tried to counteract it with good acts. I've tried to stay away from people. Is this shriveling up what happens when you get ready to die?

As my aunt swallows her last bite of omelet, I sense the

loud rush of questions press against her vocal chords, and I brace myself for the onslaught.

"Dorianna." She places her silverware on her plate. "I'm worried about you. You've been spending all your time out in Coney Island."

"There's so much to do to get ready for the event out there."

"It's not the best neighborhood."

"Look, I turned seventeen a few days ago. I'm old enough to—"

"Dorianna!" Aunt Carol's mouth falls slack. "You should've reminded me. I missed your birthday. I feel terrible."

"S'okay. I hate birthdays." My mother sent me a card. But I wasn't in the mood to let anyone else know. "What did you want to tell me?"

Her tone sharpens. "I got a call from your school."

"And?"

"They say you've been cutting classes. Is this true?"

"No!" Nosy jerks. They should be glad. I'm saving my classmates from getting injured by my unpredictable beast. If they only knew. . .

"They say you've been doing more than cutting a class here and there. They say you've been cutting school for days." Aunt Carol's jaw hardens in a way I've never seen. It scares me. She's suddenly the spitting image of my father.

Blood explodes upwards, into my skull. My beast awakens and roars. Leaping up, I get ready to run out of the diner, but dizziness overtakes me. From the corner of my eye, I see Aunt Carol reach out, and I feel the firm yet cool touch of her hand on my forearm. A cool wet compress on a third-degree burn.

"Sit, please. I'm not here to yell at you," she declares.

"Then what are we here for?" I'm still wavering.

"Sit, Dorianna. You look ill."

I sink into the cool leatherette of the booth. My blanked-out eyes stare off past the glass door, and into passing traffic. *Whoosh.* Cars. Red, blue, silver. Yes, this must be what it feels like to be on the edge of death. Still, I'm dangling on a thin strand of hope—so easily breakable.

"Tell me, sweetie, what's the matter?" My aunt's warmth permeates right through my leather armor. I soak it in, secretly, greedily.

"I'm tired. I'm . . ." You'll never understand what it's like to fight your own evil, I want to confess as my eyes blot with tears.

The beast is mocking me now. Inside, it's bleating, *Traitor! Quiet. Stay on your own side.*

I whisper. "Tell me one thing."

"Of course. . . what's that?"

No, my beast yells soundlessly. *Spill the food. Break the dishes. Run!*

"What was my father like? When he was my age?"

Fool. The beast claws my insides, as if it's an entirely separate being, and not just my demonic side trying to claim me. Grabbing my middle, I double over, still not sure how to fight this part of me, except by pure effort of will.

"Are you okay?" asks my aunt, her eyes widening.

"Bad indigestion. I just wanted to ask . . ."

Aunt Carol gazes into her coffee cup, as if its creamy swirls will trigger a memory. "Well, your father at seventeen was very quiet. Plain, not ugly, but people overlooked him. Didn't pick him for neighborhood baseball games, or for drives to the custard stand at night." Her face lurches into a sad smile. "I always felt guilty, because although I wasn't the homecoming queen, I always had a group of friends." She looks up at me. "Why do you ask?"

I shrug. The beast is quiet for the moment, probably

crouching, ready to sink its fangs into my sinews and do more serious damage. I'll take that risk. "I know my dad's not exactly the trendy subject of the day, what with him being in jail." My aunt coughs nervously. I go on. "I was wondering if he was always . . . so messed up."

Her cheeks flush. She looks back down at her coffee. "Not my favorite subject."

"I need to hear it."

"He was ignored—by our parents and his classmates. I guess he got tired of it."

My arms erupt in gooseflesh. I think of Wilson telling me he was the black sheep, and of how kids in Indiana used to call me 'It' and then nothing at all. I think of how deathly tired I'd become of it. "Is that why he changed? Why he got in trouble?"

"I don't know, Dorianna. I'm not sure he got in that much trouble."

I clunk down my cup. "Not much trouble? Then why's he in jail?" I still haven't read his entire list, but something's rotten as hell. "Don't you think he did what they said he did?"

My aunt flushes again, this time all the way to her ears. "Absolutely not! I know my brother. He's weak, but no criminal."

The waitress approaches with the check. A smirk's on her face, as if she's overheard the conversation. The second she walks away, I launch back in.

"I could understand one person ganging up on my father for a personal vendetta, but how can so many people be wrong? Four women came forward and pressed char—"

"He wouldn't do anything to a woman that she—"

"But he was persuasive. I remember him talking me into going to his church all the time. Promising me ice-cream

cones, new dresses. He conned me into singing that stupid
Sun hymn, into playing with the kids of his stupid girlfr—"

"Enough!" Aunt Carol snaps her purse open, angrily
extracts some bills and slaps them on the table. "I won't
listen to you denigrate his name."

"Why am I here, then? Why did you agree to have me
sent here?" My voice rises higher. "Wasn't it to get away from
my father?"

"No! It was so your mother could snap out of it. Your
mother was always a wreck."

"Hey! Talk about denigrating people."

"Sorry, Dorianna. We shouldn't have brought this up. It's
too loaded. He's my brother. I'm sorry." She edges out of the
booth.

I know, then, that there are limits to what people can
stand to see about themselves and their loved ones. I don't
want to be like that. On some level, it's even more chilling
than Wilson's wickedness. I resolve to figure out how to see
beyond my own warped mirror. To do that, I'll need to find
the courage to smash it to shards.

My aunt and I slink back to the brownstone as silently as we
came. Inside, I trudge upstairs, get online, and mechanically
check my fan page, my texts.

One, from Bailey. A bolt of grateful hope strikes me. My
ex-friend still cares . . .

*Hope you're okay. Worried about you. Felt bad to avoid you in
school. Things got too weird & still are. But was wondering if we could
meet up & go to the Blind Date party together? for old times. - Bailey*

I text her back. *Of course! D*

Springing off my chair, I pad to the bookshelf, and inch

out the devotional. I crack it open to where my dad's list is wedged. With trembling hands, I extract it. "This shit has gone unread too long," I whisper, "too damn long." I place it in the studded, silver pocketbook I bought to match my silver party dress. "I'm going to read it. Really, really soon."

27

There is no blue without yellow and without orange.
—Vincent van Gogh

ailey and I lean over the boardwalk railing. Lampposts on either side cast just enough dim light to see only a narrow band of Coney beach ahead, though I clearly hear the black seawater crash in. Drinking in the mysterious peace of the moment, I'm not ready to make my grand entrance. "It's hard to believe we've never gone out to the beach before this."

"*Hmm.*" Bailey takes a long side-glance at me. "You've gotten so thin."

"I haven't been hungry." I adjust the loose silver dress around my bony hips.

"I'm worried about you."

"Thanks, Bailey. I don't want to process, though. Can't we just have fun?"

"Sure, I'm a fun girl." Bailey tries out a grin, though her

eyes leak concern. "Hey, it's a full moon." She points skyward.

"It is. I love its spooky yellowish green."

"To get that in oils you'd mix cadmium yellow with viridian green," she says as if she's trying to tell me something else without actually saying it. "Cadmiums and cobalts —radioactive colors are always the brightest."

I draw my coat tight. The boardwalk is treacherous with these wild wind currents whipping around the closed stands, launching soda cans in the air like grenades. "Shall we walk over?" I don't want to go, even though we're late. I'd rather stay here with my old friend.

"Question is, are you ready? It's bound to be a mob scene."

"You can be my bodyguard."

"Don't think so." She makes a worried face. "You may have to be mine."

We walk down the ramp, taking care not to let our spiky heels stick in the wooden slats, and head toward the old Nivomonsky Bathhouse.

Bailey looks amazing in her sea-green handmade gown, which perfectly compliments her red hair. But watching her lift her long skirt over a section of pavement littered with shards of glass and half-eaten pizza crusts, I'm glad I have on the short silver dress, even if it's cold. We laugh as we peer into the bumper car arcade to watch the local freaks smack it up. Further on, Bailey marvels at the spotlighted sideshow murals that I point out.

I admire Bailey. And I'm grateful for her loyalty. She stuck by me through the fire damage I caused, through Tory and Ander's defections. Bailey was the only person to finally get in touch after I dropped out of school during these last lonely days. She was the only person who at least tried to believe that I knew what I was doing when I invited every metalhead and party hound in the country to this meetup.

Too bad she doesn't believe me about the vow. Who would? Still, it's incredibly painful that neither my aunt nor Bailey can handle my various truths: my father's degradation. My dangerous, dark magic. I can barely handle them. But somehow, telling the truth is linked to finding my way back to health. If I could figure out how to get my soul back, I would never give it away again. Will there be more dangerous consequences tonight?

"Wow, these people are loud," Bailey notes. The clamor thunders out from three whole blocks away. "Not our normal school crowd, huh?"

I flinch. "Don't rub it in."

"It's hard, Dorianna. I feel as if I'm walking on—"

"We missed each other. Concentrate on that?"

"True. Okay."

As we walk closer, a cavalcade of drunken catcalls rings out. The front of the warehouse is lined with Harleys and brawny wrestler types. One shirtless dude with a leather vest has Viking-style braids. Another, bearded guy is smoking a fat, stinky cigar. They're definitely older than high school. In fact, I don't see one person from class.

"Hey, baby," calls a guy with sleeves of tattoos on each arm. "You don't look as spooky as you do online."

"Yo, Sungirl!" The phalanx closes in on us—for a kiss, for autographs, for free feels.

"Don't!" I slap the braided guy's hand off my rear as I lurch backward. My calves scratch against the splintery warehouse wall. I clutch my silver bag to my ribs. No one's getting Ander's notebook, or my father's list. *No one.*

"Don't get uptight, Sungirl, just want to warm my hands on your orbs," he growls.

"Lay off her," Bailey warns. Rough laughter follows us inside.

Wilson has mounted the candle sconces all along the interior hall and the flames create dancing ghouls on the rough-hewn wood panels. Bailey and I exchange uneasy glances. The place reeks of sweat and cheap cologne. Still, it feels good to feel something, even zigzagging nerves, after my listless days alone.

But I don't trust my own excitement anymore. It's too linked to my beast.

I offer Bailey a faint smile. She squeezes my hand in return. "Your moment," she says in my ear.

Yes, my viral extravaganza. I toggle between exaltation and a mounting dread that I cannot name. When the next wave of kids sees me, they chant, "Sungirl, Sungirl, Sungirl!" as they enfold me. Marching forward, I take claustrophobic breaths. My palms up, the corrupted queen bestows dubious acceptance on her subjects.

Bailey takes up the rear, using me as a barricade. A third wave of followers presses in on the second. I shove my way farther inside. It's like a freaking ocean of undulating bodies.

"Sungirl, my priestess!" A tall guy in monkish robes bows.

"I can't believe it's you!" shouts another stranger, as if we're long-lost friends.

A husky guy tries to fold me in a drunken bear hug, but I manage to shrug him off.

"Where are all the women?" I ask Bailey without turning. I can't hear her answer over the brash music and roaring crowd. Scanning the room, I do spot ladies dancing. Though a few, like us, seem to be fending off unwanted advances.

Walking in farther, I resort to physically shoving people away, only to find them pressing against me more persistently. Lots of people are smoking cigarettes and it's making me cough. I smell liquor too, fruity, rotten.

"Pick me for your blind date, Sungirl!"

"Autograph my balls."

Hands reach out and grab me. I always wanted this kind of admiration, but now, it's threatening. My senses tell me these new followers would tear me apart and swallow me if they could. I reel around for Bailey. She's gone. Must've slipped out a side door. Can't blame her. Where's Wilson? At least he could play chivalric guard. I don't dare open my silver bag to text him. Someone might rip my cell or the bag from my hands as a Sungirl souvenir to sell on eBay.

My breathing quickens as I near the stage. Someone barges into me from the rear and I stumble. Is this what happens before you get trampled? I've heard stories about bargain hunters who camp out all night in front of Walmart to be there when those doors open. They want to be the first to buy a trendy laptop on sale, only to be trampled to death and have their photos appear on every sensationalist news show.

A primitive, defensive panic roils up in me and jettisons out through my eyes. Its sheer force propels a kid into the air. In turn, the beer-sopped horde continues to heave the guy up and up, mosh-pit style.

Someone grabs at my dress. I hear the rip of fabric. Spinning around, I send out another blast of fearful, atomized energy. This time an entire knot of kids lose their balance and fall on the people behind them, and those behind them, in a crazy game of torso dominoes.

As I send bodies careening, the mob finally edges back to give me space. It's not as if I'm trying to do it, but my shattered nerves serve as detonating bombs. My fingers, my chest crackle with painful charges.

In a burst of mad adrenaline, I rush onstage. Now that

I'm finally above the mob looking down, I can try to relax as the crowd, crazy batter in an overflowing bowl, folds back into itself.

Safe. From here, I see that Charlie's here with Ava, and even Lisbeth is here with Cat. I wave to them, take deep breaths and launch into my speech. At least Wilson has set up a mic or my voice would never carry in this chaos.

"Blind Date Confessional is the third Sungirl party. Thanks for traveling from all over to be here in historic Coney Island. I'm amazed that it's truly gone viral." I pause while the room erupts in cheers. "We have guests from Boston, Connecticut, the Midwest, even a few from California!" Again, I wait out a deafening roar of approval. Curious, Wilson still hasn't appeared. So unlike him not to want any part of the spotlight.

I go on. "Each of you will be escorted to a private room, with your secret date that we paired you up with on my anonymous site. Our escorts, Cole and Jake, are waiting by the stairs to guide you up." I point to them, in their zombie costumes. "Voucher winners had their pick of dates and rooms, so they'll go up first." I reel off names. Heads turn as the winners snake over.

"Share your darkest secrets with your date. You'll be blindfolded, so identities remain confidential—unless of course, you want to peek. Okay, go!"

With that, the multitude, yelling and fist pumping, makes a frantic beeline for the escorts.

There's a chill, and then a stutter in the flickering candle sconces. A familiar musk cologne and the acidic scent of preternatural intensity swirl around me. Wilson's nearby. He's a vibrating cloud of disquiet, but I can't exactly place him.

Let him lurk in a dark corner. I'm not here for him. I rigged the ticket numbers in order to have a blind date with

Ander. This will be our very last date, where I will come clean with him, and force him to come clean with me, before I return his notebook.

Thankfully, this horrid event is almost over. After this, I'll make it my business to find out who I could be that's better than this, this . . . cheater girl. I picture *Marie Claire* girl, tacked to my locker weeks ago. I don't want to be her, either. Beauty matters, but not like that, not superficially. What matters is to be someone who does the right thing even when no one is looking.

Such a liar. . .You've learned nothing. The beast twists my gut into bloody pretzels. Doubling over, I leave the stage.

Greedy arms reach for me again. They clutch at my dress, ripping it further, and exposing my ribs. In an automatic torrent, my beast sends the guy flying, and I hear my attacker groan.

I defend you, my beast whines, *yet you still resist me.*

I ignore him. He will only spout more deceit if I engage.

"Have a good date," Jake says as he blindfolds me. He knows nothing of how I suffer my hateful beast, nor will I tell. "Room 335," he says. "Shall I escort you up, Sungirl?"

"No, thanks. Just watch out for Bailey. Have you seen her?"

"She's up with Cole."

"Oh, Jake, you don't know how happy that makes me to hear."

Oh, Jake, you ignorant mortal, mocks my beast. Thankfully, Jake hears nothing.

"Seen Wilson?" I ask him as an afterthought.

"Earlier. He went up and—"

"Forget it, doesn't matter." I cock back my blindfold, so I can advance, step by step, to the second floor. Halfway there, I examine the rip in my dress. "Geez," I mutter, "I can see my bra and ribs." Sighing, I continue on. With every step, the rip flaps open. At the second-floor landing, a guy headed down-stairs, thrusts his hand through the open seam and gropes me, hard.

My enhanced reflexes knock him soundly to the floor.

"Ugly wench!" he snarls. *Some fan.*

Among the people zigging my way is a heavyset female with a nose ring. The woman recognizes me and dives for one of my expensive black pearl earrings. My soft ear flesh tears, and I feel a searing pain. Brushing a hand over my earlobe, it comes away bloodied. The woman, already escaping to the main floor, literally has a piece of me in her fist. My animal sight hones in on her as she disappears into the human fold. Against my better side, my inner beast unleashes a maelstrom.

Its force throws the woman, who's made it as far as the back railing, into the air and smacks her down on its hard wooden balustrade. Upon impact, the pearl earring flies out of her thieving grip. I hear a gurgle low in her throat. I feel absolutely awful about her injury, but I can't backtrack. The woman will survive. There's more important business than retrieving that earring. I take the stairs at a frantic clip toward the third floor.

Loud bellows and explosive pops well up from below. A man yells, "Put those back!" followed by more protests. "Don't blast them inside, you fool!"

Oh. Hell. No. I remember Wilson describing an entire office full of fireworks. Someone must've busted the lock.

"Don't be a wuss," a guy bellows over the heavy metal. "There's a whole room of this stuff."

"Look! There's vodka, too—cartons and cartons."

"Par-teee!" booms a third guy.

In my mind's eye, I see the partygoers rip open boxes and distribute vodka, whiskey, and— oh, lord—more fireworks. I

shoot a furious blast of energy downstairs, in order to stop
them. I have to. The warehouse is all wood.

My supernatural action causes a deafening melee of
"What the fuck?" and "You're crushing me."

Is Wilson playing a disappearing act on purpose? He has
to know that maniacs are raiding the offices. *Consequences for
all,* I imagine him saying, *you won't escape them tonight.* Fury
and fear rise in me as I sweat up the last steep flight of stairs.
An overwhelming pain streaks up my left calf, and reduces
my progress to a hobble.

At the third-floor landing, I twist around to see what the
problem is. The splintery wall has scraped my leg so badly
that the skin is raised in bloody, woody ridges.

It's my fault that magic found me, and wrapped itself
around me in a stranglehold. If I hadn't been so greedy to look
good and have this damn following, I could've had a normal,
sucky time at school. I could've tried to make things better on
my own, like most people do. I've cultivated this lousy magic
from shame, and kept it going with my shameless actions. "I
hate these powers," I mutter. "I'll figure out how to kill them."

You'll never figure me out!, screams my beast. *I'm unstoppable!*

Clutching the railing, I'm reduced to panting. Need to
rest until I get a decent lungful. It doesn't help that I haven't
eaten protein for weeks. Surviving on tea, candy, and burnt
toast has made my heart feel as if it's scraping an escape
hatch through my chest cavity with toothpicks.

I need to get inside a changing room, alone, to wrestle
with my demons. I jiggle a doorknob. Locked. Someone yells,
"Taken." I try another. Same thing. The third door opens to
my touch. I collapse on the bench and fish for the list in my
silver bag.

"Time to smash the warped mirror," I chant.

Groping for the LED on my keychain, I click it on, place it

on the bench, and angle it up. Each time I unfold another crease in my father's list my chest seizes up. This must be what it's like to have a heart attack. Flattening out the last fold, I force myself to read the last eight entries out loud. My beast tries to stop me. It pokes a crooked finger up my throat. Choking, I read it anyway.

2. Sherry: *Needed a father figure for her terror of a son. Came over, gave him a what-to. Shelled out movie $ for him, in order to cozy with his mom. Took her for a joyride. Snagged my second member. Who says I'm not all things to all people?*

3. Lori: *No backbone. Loser secretary. Told her she was exciting/su-perstar material, could be in films. That wishy-washy type will believe anything. Next member snagged.*

4. Sandy: *This one I actually liked, but too smart to control. Joked about how I played con games. She needed a "digital manipulation." That got me another member.*

5. Alison: *Had to get her girls out of the way. (Two eldest onto me.) Convinced her they were out to get her $. She joined church and donated big $. *** Keep a close eye on the situation. May need further persuasion.*

6. Alix: *Had to jump this divorcée's bones in church supply closet to nab her before she could move out of state. She joined church next week. My mighty scepter does the trick.*

. . .

7. Tina: *EZ as a fly on sh*t. Promised her a ring and a job. Gave her a cubic zirconia and a clerical church job. Boom, snap—next day, a new member.*

8 & 9. Mia and Mara: *Promised them jobs at my church. Mara got another job offer. I lost it. She called me controlling. Both ready to defect. Couldn't have that. Had to promise use of my car. The wife raised a stink about that. *** keep an eye on these blackmailing fiends.*

10. Lynn: *Never should've touched her. Nympho daughter kept flirting with me. Both joined church, but the underage nympho flapped her jaw afterward to the cops in jealous rage.*

After what? Jen's mother was named Lynn . . .

Oh. My. God. It was Jen who blew his cover: that last brave, underage girl—he must've tried to rape her. But, Jen flirting with him? No way. My father must've had a totally warped view of her to rationalize his perverted behavior. Why didn't Jen tell me? I could've tried to help. No wonder she couldn't be my friend anymore. She was traumatized, terrified.

I'm sick. I lower my head and gag, but there's nothing in my stomach. Gripping my bony skull, I drop it between my legs to flow a few tainted drops of lifeblood back to my brain.

No wonder he's in jail. No *wonder*. . . My own father's a debauched criminal, who preyed on women to do his bidding, have sex with and line his pockets with cash.

My beast bellows bilious shit at me. *What's wrong with a little fun with the opposite sex? Don't go puritan on me, devil-woman. As if you're any different. Having fun with these hot male followers of yours? Hmm?* Its laughter erupts from my mouth in great, belching cackles.

"Shut your dirty mouth!" I yell back. "I'm through with you. You hear?"

In response, my beast hurls me off the bench onto my bloody calf.

I struggle to my feet, and thrust the list in my bra. The way people have grabbed at me, I don't trust my pocketbook to keep it safe. Staggering out the door, I take testy steps. I feel cleaner. Braver. I'll try to find Ander. Confess my betrayal.

Ander, the tortured dream lover with an old man's limp on that first sweet day on the beach—the only person who half paid any attention to me before the magic. Ander, mountain man of ripped jeans, sea-blue T-shirts, and old-school plaid button-downs.

Ander, mysterious author with a mysterious notebook I was always reaching for but could only catch with black magic. Ander, disappointing turncoat. He's virtually fed on me in a parasitic attempt to enliven his stories. I'll present him with the evidence.

Ander will be sitting behind door number 335. I made a manual switch of the tickets at the last minute—a small act of mischief compared to when I snatched that notebook right out of his pocket and read its contents.

Wilson doesn't need to know about the ticket switch. He doesn't need to know about anything anymore, except that people are looting his uncle's office. Maybe he orchestrated that, too—the blameless maestro of disaster who steps back and pins the crime on his minions.

"Ander!" My voice is a rasp as I stagger to door 335. "Ander, I need to talk." My hand rests on the knob as I try to get a read on him. Why can't I get a clear one? He's often hard to read, but I always get sense of his body, his

weight on the floor. Why does the vibe feel so
wrong? Why?

I fling the door open, and almost fall over my feet when I
see Wilson sitting on the narrow changing bench. Removing
kid gloves, he tucks them fastidiously in his jacket pocket,
and looks up at me with a sly grin.

"What are you doing here?" I gasp.

"That's a bit of a rude hello." Wilson stands, and moves
his lusty gaze across me to pause on my breasts and then on
my ripped dress. "What happened?" He sounds genuinely
alarmed.

I step back. "Where's Ander?"

"No idea."

"You switched him out of here, didn't you?"

"Now why would I do that?" Eyes still steady on mine,
Wilson advances toward me, his heavy brow creasing. "Your
leg is cut."

"It's nothing. Where's Ander?"

"I told you, I don't know." With his grasshopper fingers,
Wilson grasps strands of my disheveled hair and lifts them as
he studies my ear. "You've lost an earring. Sweet Dor, how?"
With the cuff of his purple sleeve, he wipes blood from
my ear.

I reach out to stop him, but my movement slows.
Wilson's face takes on an eerie animal intensity, as if he's
holding himself back from leaning over and licking my
wound. I wonder if he licks it whether his own magic might
heal it or burn it?

I slowly extricate myself. "You must know that I switched
the ticket pairings. I put Ander in this room. You were
assigned to room 348."

Wilson snaps his jacket sleeve back over his cuff. "Yes,
and I switched my ticket to this room. Room 348 bored me."

"Then what room did you switch Ander's ticket to?"

"None. I told him to get out. When he found out you'd rigged him up in here, he went willingly."

Pain stabs me, this time not from my wounds. "I don't believe you."

Wilson affects a pout. "That lame-brain girl you paired me with in room 348 was an insult to my sensibilities."

"*Lame*-brain? Lucy Lane is only the best math student in the school."

"She can't enchant me like you," he murmurs as he moves closer.

I'm level with his tri-circled necklace, and overcome with its glint. His charismatic energy draws me in. Bleary-eyed, I stumble back. "I don't want to enchant anyone anymore. I'm done with magic. I need to find Ander." I move toward the door. Wilson blocks me.

"Done with magic? It's not done with you. There are fatal penalties for trying to weasel out of a spell." He bursts out laughing, and then abruptly returns to seriousness. "Ander doesn't want to talk to you. He has no interest in your lovelorn pleas."

It only stings a little this time. I no longer believe anything Wilson says. He's layered in lies. That must be the definition of a demon—a nonhuman entity consisting of lies. If I'm part demon, then to purify myself I'll have to tell only brave truths from now on. Like Jen did when she told the authorities about my father. I may not know how to stop the magic, but I can tell a truth. I can do that. "Ander needs to talk to me," I insist. "And it's none of your business, Wilson. I'm sick and tired of you, you . . . telling me every move to make."

"Dor, you wanted my help with this event." Wilson's fury gives his voice a tremulous quality. "You told me you loved this warehouse."

"Not anymore." Again I try to wriggle past him. Not happening. I'll need to catch him off guard.

"Everything I do is for you," he declares. "That night that I climbed in though your window, and you were so upset, I spent hours with you, trying to comfort you."

"What does that have to do with this party?"

"I built this whole warehouse to your specifications."

"I appreciate the stage and all. What other specifications are you talking about?"

"Dor, I followed your instructions to a T."

Every second I stay in here feels more wrong. Dangerous. I get up in Wilson's face. "Followed what instructions?"

He swivels around toward the framed beach poster to the left of the door, and removes it from its hook. "All for you."

My stomach churns. I can't tell this time if it's the clamoring of my beast or my nausea rising again. Where the poster hung I now see a grid of embedded video monitors, labels under each. "What is this?"

"You wanted spy cams in each room. You wanted secret videos made of all of the people you hate, remember?" His sunken eyes bore into mine.

"I was *joking*," I say, incredulous. "I was really, really mad, at the time."

"Joking, eh?" Wilson barks out a brassy laugh and grabs my arm. "You were dead serious. You went on about it for hours. I didn't spend hard-earned money from my media creations to waste it." He guides me to one of the monitors. "You want to know where Ander is?"

"Not from you!" But the beast in me already knows. I brace for the dreadful assault to my eyes.

"Find him on this." Wilson flicks on all of the monitors but one. They illuminate in a full-scale digital nightmare of shadowy moving figures.

On one screen, there's just enough dim light to see

Lisbeth with her hands all over Cat. They're going at it, still wearing their blindfolds, as if that will absolve them of any misplaced guilt for their passion. Sad, that they can't just be proud. In another, Ava's new friend, the freckled Fiona, is lap dancing for Charlie Cheater, her skirt hiked above her hips. A third monitor shows Ava being mauled by the braided party crasher with Viking shoulders.

Bailey's there on the next screen. I inhale sharply, praying that my one real friend is safe. She's talking, with her blindfold—and clothes—in place. Who's the blindfolded guy next to her, stroking her cheek? Relief floods into me when I realize that it's Cole. I allow myself a grateful sigh. Until I see the next monitor and cringe in debilitating pain.

In it, two bodies intertwine in the dark space, moving, up and down. A shirtless girl with light hair is making soft, guttural noises as she straddles the other figure, a tall guy with long arms and a familiar body—a body that I've lain with in my very own bed.

"Turn it off!" I scream and lunge for the button.

Wilson blocks me. "There's one more," he says in a flat, dead tone that raises hard goose bumps on me.

"You sick freak! Be done with it so I can get out of here."

He flicks on the monitor that's still dark.

Scrunching up my eyes, I desperately focus in on the murky, shapeless space. As I do, the back walls become clearer. The room's the size of the changing rooms, but more square. "What? I don't see squat."

"Remember our final plan?"

Final. That word is terrifying. My beast giggles soundlessly.

"Oracle? Ring any bells?" Wilson's grin is pure malevolence.

"Can't say it does."

"Well, then, sit back and get comfortable. Maybe it'll come to you."

"No. Let me out of here." I push past him, but he shoves me back on the bench.

"Not until I get what I came for." He moves his long, simian face so close to mine that I feel his fiery breath on me, his prodding, insect fingers on my ribs. His mind works its toxic persuasion into my gray matter. It drugs me, caressing and lulling me to that place before sleep.

Fight it, whispers a female voice so small I barely hear it.

I'm already woolly-headed, syrupy. Happy to space out this whole meetup and the meaning of this tiny room. My body relaxes into Wilson's square shoulders. He moves his lips over mine and parts them with his adder tongue. Expertly guides my body to press in on his.

"I've loved you for so long," he whispers into my bloody, raw ear. I feel the flesh bubble and knit itself together, as if he's applied herbs directly to it. His hand cups my breast—a perfect fit, as if his hand has always belonged there. He moans low and throaty as he draws me closer.

As he presses a long, firm leg between my legs, I moan with him.

"My love, my devil girl, my Dorianna. I've spent every night dreaming of this moment. I've been so lonely, so lonely."

I've been lonely, too—lonely no matter how many new followers and so-called friends I made. Back in Wabash, I always thought that if I only had a few admirers, I'd be satisfied. Nurtured the way a hearty, healthy meal does. But, no . .
.

Lately, I've been famished for people. Soul deficient. Always. No matter how many heads turn my way in school, or how many hip new followers I gain when I log on each night, I never ever have enough. The hole in me is always gaping, threatening to engulf me in its deep, anaerobic emptiness.

Wilson understands this, that's what his energy tells me. He's saying that we can fill each other up. Devour each other.

As he presses his lips harder on mine, something nags at me: the word *devour,* and then the word *follower.* A half-hour ago, crazed followers almost crushed me. Ten minutes ago, my father's list taught me he would break any moral code for followers. Another follower has shredded my ear. What will Wilson do to me? What has he done to other girls? What have *I* done to others? What might I still do?

The recesses of my mind boil with a garbled horror. In the wells where my memories languish, the conversation Wilson and I had that night in my room about the oracle wafts up. "The oracle . . . the cables," I mumble, with a growing, dreadful awareness.

Again, that desperate voice in my head: *Fight it. Fight it with all of your strength.* Whose voice? *Lacey's.* Just like that day when we sat across from each other at my kitchen table.

Wilson begins to stroke my inner thighs with his leg. I pull back sharply. So drunk am I on his glamour, this pulling away is as difficult as flying.

I shove him. This gives me strength. His eyes flicker open. He loops his arms around me in a proprietary motion. "Get out!" I slough off his ever-rushing persuasion as if it's a hard shower of radioactive waste.

"Not until I get what I came here for." He glares at me, head to head. I see through all of his layers, beyond his little-boy persona, the misunderstood black sheep. He's made a choice, at some point before he met me—a gleeful choice to do wrong.

I made a choice, too. I thought I was so clever that I could easily bargain with my power. Or ignore the oath's malevo-lent side and hope it would dissolve on its own. That didn't

work, and when it flared up stronger, more rebellious, I tried
to rationalize it. I said to myself, "I'm only out of control
once in a blue moon," or "I'll never do it again." But I
committed more horrific acts, while my inner beast raged on,
unvanquished, growing stronger.

After that, I began to bargain with my powers—do good
deeds to balance out the bad—make dinner for my aunt, and
buy Bailey chocolate shakes. But for all the wrong reasons—
only because I expected something in return, even demanded
it.

I ended up stealing from my aunt and my mother, no
better than a common thief. I tried to be creative with my
powers instead of destructive. But that only caused a fire in
Bailey's loft that freaked Bailey's mom right out. In pure
frustration, I blamed others—Wilson, Lacey, the bullies from
Wabash, my father.

Looking now at Wilson's blood-red eyes and demon face,
I see an absolute mirror of what I've become: a demon that
Wilson wants to devour and destroy.

He forces me against the bench and yanks up my dress.
Begins to slide down my panties.

Jerking up with my sudden and considerable strength, I
push him. His face peels back into a raw thing, and then
down another layer, to a red skull with burning, bleeding
eyes.

"How dare you?" he snarls. I swear I see a forked tongue
working inside his mouth. "Ungrateful bitch!" When he
plants his mouth on mine I bite, feel the firm meat of his lip
crunch under my teeth. Black, rotten blood oozes out. Before
my eyes, it sizzles and knits together.

He pins me down harder, undressing me with one hand.
I'm no match for his beastly strength. Desperate, I look over
his shoulder at the monitors. Now Lacey and Ander are
hastily dressing, then leaving the room.

They're headed for the elevator. The building begins to shake, not from the nearby roller coaster, but from my hatred and jealousy and outrage. The same supernatural force that caused the doors to Wilson's uncle's office to pop open, and those elevator cables to unravel.

See? my beast claims, *You're only making things worse.*

Or did Wilson loosen those cables? I remember us joking about the elevator of death. Oh, no, dear mother earth.

It doesn't matter who's to blame. The only thing that matters now is saving them.

As much as I ever hated Lacey, I don't want her to die.

"Oracle of death!" blare the monitors. It's my voice—on every monitor now, my demon blood betraying me.

I scream the scream of a she-devil and release every last shred of power. Shove Wilson off. His body flies up and crashes into the wall. Grunting, he charges from overhead, soaring from venomous powers. He hits down so hard that I hear the crack of my own broken rib. The building sways from the clash of our magic.

From the hallway, panicked shrieks rise up, and an odor of smoke. Did I cause another fire? Summoning a last drop of adrenaline, I body slam Wilson to the floor, and smash my studded metallic pocketbook in his face.

Before he can recover, I hurl myself at the door and break its hinges. I streak down the hallway toward the elevator as my damaged rib clicks.

Too late, laughs my beast.

In my mind's eye, I see Lacey and Ander already halfway down the shaft, screaming for mercy as one of the cables completely snaps.

"What the heck?" Someone stumbles out of a room half-dressed.

A breaker of people crashes my way, rolling for the stairs. "Fire!" they yell. "Get out!"

I race past them. The only thing to do is to try to pad Lacey and Ander's inevitable fall. Downstairs, there's further chaos. Boxes of vodka and fireworks have been torn open. Smashed bottles crunch underfoot. Overhead, splintered wood planks dangle from firework blasts.

One of the motorcycle riders is swilling from an open bottle. But most kids are beating a fast path out, as flames sprout on a section of office floor and spread from the spilled alcohol. I pray Bailey and Cole are long gone.

"Dial 911!" I yell at Jake, who has miraculously appeared. "And, people—either run to safety or help me with boxes. Please!" Dashing into an office, I haul out cartons of old towels and keep on shoving them into the bottom of the elevator shaft. "Help! Jake! Anyone! We need to pad Ander and Lacey's fall." Jake and his friend help without question.

From the elevator, Lacey screams, "Ander! Do something! We're hanging sideways."

"What do you want me to do?" Terror rings out in his voice.

"Grab something! Brace yourself," I shout into the open shaft to where the contraption dangles crookedly. "I'm padding the floor in case . . . the last cable goes."

"Dorianna?" Ander's voice. "Is that you?"

"Don't listen to her!" Lacey shrieks hysterically. "She wants to kill us. She's trying to kill us!" She shouts this over and over.

"I'm opening the door," Ander says. "Lacey, I'll climb out and catch you."

"Ander, don't!" I caution. "Hold still. Don't stress that last cable."

The building shakes from another monumental force— Wilson's or the roller coaster or mine? The fire crackles louder. Thick smoke clouds my vision. The few people helping are coughing.

"I lost my footing!" Ander yells.

The energy has shifted into something more precarious. I see it all in my fevered mind—his body flailing, arms reaching out to grasp something solid, his back coming first, Lacey bending over the open door, trying to grab his hands.

Ander crashes down, landing hard on the boxes.

Racing toward the elevator, I see something worse than I sensed—the last cable shredding, one fiber at a time. Ander is partly under the damn thing. "Roll out, Ander! Now!" I warn.

I lunge for him as he starts to roll out. The cable squeals like a runaway train. In a torrent of unforgiving air, the elevator smashes down onto Ander's right hand. His curdling shrills ring out. Horrified, people scream with him as they leap back to safety.

"Oh, my god, oh, my god, oh my—" I moan as Ander yanks his arm away with his crushed hand dangling from his wrist. Jagged white bone peeks through his flesh as blood spurts to the beat of his heart and splashes thick and red across the wooden floor.

"Someone call for help, now!" I yell. Busting open another carton of towels, I wrap as many as I can around his wrist. Press hard on them as he groans.

"Witch, what are you doing to him?" Lacey has started to crawl out of the elevator.

People stand in frozen revulsion. As Ander bleeds through the towels, Jake hands me more. Flames spread to the walls, licking and crackling. The sooty, oily smoke fills the room.

Lacey clambers to Ander's side, screaming hysterically. "You're going to kill him—get away! You're going to kill my love, you insane witch!" She grabs a hunk of my hair and yanks hard. "Get off him, you sicko!"

If I loosen my grip on the soaked red towels, Ander will bleed to death. Lacey cradles him and sobs, all the while cursing at me. His eyes are pressed shut as he writhes in pain.

Thankfully, the ambulance arrives quickly. Most people have retreated outside, continuing to hack from the smoke. The EMT transfers Ander outside too, and does triage, hooking him up to a myriad of tubes and carefully transferring him to a narrow stretcher. Then, they swiftly remove the sopping towels and bandage his raw wrist. During all of this, Ander is barely conscious. At last, after receiving an injection, he stops twisting in agony.

The driver eases me away. "We've got him covered. You all need to step far away from the building and wait for the police and firemen."

The EMT guy eyes my ripped, bloody dress and legs. "You're bad off, too. Shall we take you along for observation?"

"You don't get it," Lacey shouts at the driver, "that girl tried to kill him!"

"No way!" Jake yells at Lacey. "If it wasn't for her, your boyfriend would've died."

"Shut up, all of you," Jake's friend scolds.

"I'm okay," I insist. "Just get him to the emergency room. Fast."

Lacey scuttles into the ambulance, shooting me one last despising glare.

As the blare of the ambulance fades and the fire engines grow louder, I slip away and stumble to the Stillwell subway.

Enduring shocked stares and sloppy with blood, I stagger home. I only go there to pack, to scrub off the blood, and to send an e-mail to Ander, telling him how very, very sorry I am. My aunt is out with friends. I'm grateful for that. I couldn't deal with anything more, except the necessary actions.

I log onto my fan sites one last time, to witness that every

single video on those warehouse monitors is already magically posted—the one of Cat and Lisbeth, the one of Lacey
and Ander going at it, and Ava being mauled by the Viking
creep. All of the videos have strange scratches, as though my
demonic claws have scratched right through to the digital
cells. Every last one has my voice on it, shrilling about the
elevator of death, and a disembodied hand, opening and closing, stamps every video with gore. I've lost all of my school
followers, and there are already threats from parents who
want to press charges.

My beast cackles with mirth.

"You'll get yours," I growl at it as I throw a change of
clothes and a toothbrush in a bag.

I scrawl a note for my aunt, saying I'll get in touch with
her soon. That I'm going somewhere safe, that I love her. I've
never told her that. But I mean it. Then I ride that godforsaken subway back to Coney for one last piece of business.

The list burns in my pocket. How could I have ever read
that first entry and not seen the parallel?

I stagger into the gray cinderblock building I saw on those
walks with Wilson—the detention center for teens. My beast
is cursing me out, making every step forward as hard as
keeping my feet on pavement in the cone of a tornado.

I sense Wilson's aura, dense and heavy like black tar on
my back. He who so neatly disappeared when the shit hit the
fan. Wilson, the lying coward, is peppering my mind with
criticisms and vicious put-downs. His voice mingles with that
of my own beast. *You'll never be anything but a demon. Don't even
try. Ugly girl. Plain girl. You were the weakest of all of my clients. Not
even proud of your evil. Not even worth remembering.*

As I enter the building, a medicinal odor hits my nostrils.

And the starkness of the building's military green fills my eyes. Approaching the front intake area, I gather the strength for one last round of magic.

"Can I help you?" a heavyset black woman asks, pen poised.

"I need to be admitted."

"Well, now, hold on." The woman gives me a suspicious once-over. I've scoured off most of the blood, but surely look a fright with all of my bruises and cuts. "What've you done?" she asks me. "The intake process takes a while. We don't have folks just waltzing in, asking to be committed. Usually a parole officer, or a policeman hauls—"

"I need to be locked up. Now!" I well up my last energy reserve and beam it to the woman, who puts down the pen and reaches for her phone as if she's about to call for backup. "I'm not safe. Please!" My beast kicks and thrashes me. It's all I can do to stay upright.

She starts to punch in a number. "I've never heard anything like—"

I shoot out another barrage of desperate energy. It arcs from my eyes, my fingertips, my chest: Lock me up, please, for a long, long time, no questions asked. I'm dangerous. Hurry, lock me in solitary.

The lady drops the phone and stands up, eyes emotionless as plastic saucers. Fumbling for her keychain, she robotically escorts me down the hall. "Well, now, we don't need that paperwork after all," she slurs.

"No, we don't. Solitary. Hurry!"

Once inside the cell, I heave an exhausted, grateful sigh, and crash onto the inch-thick mattress. Despite the tyrannical tantrums of my beast, I fall into a deep, dreamless stupor.

28

Never give up, for that is just the place and time that
the tide will turn.
—Harriet Beecher Stowe

I'm shocked to see Bailey standing in the visitors' lounge a week later. I never told her I was coming here. They must have called her from the number in my confiscated cell phone. I shuffle toward her. "You shouldn't have come here."

"I know. My mother told me not to."

"I don't deserve a visitor."

"Probably not." She steps closer. It's clear by her bloodshot eyes that she's been crying. In contrast to her normal flair, she has on a tatty sweater and clear-framed glasses. Her fiery hair is pinned into a hasty heap. She's clutching a wrapped package.

Something for me? I don't deserve a present. "Want to sit?" I lead us to a round table with metal chairs bolted to the floor. My regulation blue shirt and pants look funky, but the only truly mortifying thing on my mind is the dangerous turn of events at Blind Date Confessional.

"Thought you should see this." She unfolds a newspaper clipping, all the while keeping her eyes glued on me. It reads:

Party Turns Disastrous at Old Nivomonsky Bathhouse

Coney Island, NY—A party organized online by high-school junior Dorianna Gilliam of Park Slope, Brooklyn, took a dangerous turn when it went viral. The out-of-control mob from all boroughs, as well as hundreds of unsupervised teens from across the country, rampaged through the building, drinking stores of black-market vodka and setting off cartons of illegal fireworks. The resultant fire spread, burning the historic Nivomonsky Warehouse nearly to the ground. High-school student Ander James was badly injured, when an unstable elevator shaft crushed his hand. James is in stable condition at New York Methodist Hospital, where doctors were forced to amputate the crushed hand at the wrist.

I stop reading. Tears cascade down my face. "Oh, my God, I tried to keep pressure on his hand until the ambulance came. I tried, I tried, I tried." I shake, as more sobs wrack me. The beast, enraged by my remorse, scratches at my insides with pointed claws.

More than how badly its scratches hurt, I'm deeply ashamed of its lingering presence. I want to cut the evil critter out with a knife. But I know the beast is my own shadowy side, and if I actually used a knife, I'd die. "It's my fault," I manage as I endure a hard shove from the inside out and double over. Now that I'm determined to pay penance, it's out to destroy me.

"Are you sick?" Bailey watches me clutch my belly.

"Don't... . . . worry about me. I'll survive. How are you?"

"Holding up. Thanks for warning everyone you could to get out of that warehouse."

"Not everyone," I whisper. "Not Ander."

"You tried. I'm sure you saved his life when you applied pressure on his arm." Bailey doesn't sound convinced. Why would she?

"Where's Wilson? They put him in jail, right?"

The pink drains out of her face. "Read the rest of the article."

The owner of the warehouse, Grigori Minoff, could not be reached. Neighbors say he is out of the country for an extended period. His nephew, Wilson Warren, who was house-sitting Minoff's Surf Avenue condo, was last seen at the party, but has since disappeared. His estranged father arranged a search warrant, warning that his son could be dangerous. The police found Minoff's condominium cleaned out, except for a bare stage set in a back room.

"Oh, no!" I exclaim. "They need to get him into custody. Charge him with reckless . . ." My words trail off. If I'm being totally honest with myself, the right person is already in custody.

"It's bizarre. He's gone. *Poof.*" Bailey's eyes look as spooked as I feel.

Of course, Wilson would get away with just about anything. Swoop off, a diseased, guiltless spirit in the night. Ready for another victim, in another place and time. Wilson is beyond repair. I'm probably beyond repair, too. But if I have to serve ten, even twenty years to try to starve the beast, I will. Through good deeds, and not for the camera this time. Only do things for others, asking nothing in return. I'm so, so ready to serve. If only the beast would stop clawing me raw. I read the last paragraph.

Provocative video footage from the meetup has appeared on YouTube, and angry parents are threatening to sue Dorianna Gilliam or the building's owner, Minoff. Yet they lack evidence. In an inquiry to YouTube, the online company could not find the actual identity of the person posting the videos. Investigators are conducting further inquiries into the matter. Gilliam's aunt says her niece vanished, leaving only a note that did not explain her whereabouts.

"I'm going to call my aunt. I'll need to make restitution."

"I figured you would. You can turn this around." Bailey curls her hand over mine. The sensation is so startling it gives me shivers. "I'm sorry I didn't believe you," she whispers.

"Huh?"

"The things you said about making a weird vow. How you couldn't control it."

I gaze into her friendly eyes. "Why believe me now?"

"I don't know." She tugs on a stray lock of hair. "I only know you were dead serious when you said it, and desperate for me to believe you. And I let you down by not believing you."

"But you said that I was playing a game, or that I must be hallucinating."

She runs her finger over a dent in the table, nodding faintly. "I know. I can only understand it when I think about Mom's paintings—those elves and trolls." She lets out a rush of breath. "Maybe there are more layers to reality than we want to believe."

"Or maybe I'm nuts, like you said."

"I don't think so. Here." She hands me the bulky package. "Open it."

I carefully peel off the tape at one end of the wrapping and a quilted blue jacket falls in my lap. "Oh, Bailey!"

"I made it." She shivers. "I'm glad I did. It's cold in this place."

I hug her, and put on the jacket. It softens the hollows of my sunken ribs. "Wow, it's so beautiful. I don't know how to thank you."

"Thank me by getting better, by eating, by taking care of yourself, Dorianna."

"And by not putting anyone—like Wilson—on a pedestal anymore?" I crack my first tentative smile.

"Especially Wilson!" She glances at her watch. "Got to go. I'll try to visit again soon."

"You take care of yourself, too." I hug my friend again. "Will you please tell Ander that I'm so, so very sorry?" Bailey nods, but by her troubled expression, it's clear that I'm no longer welcome in Ander's world.

If I really want to apologize to him, I'll need to do it anonymously, through a good act. I need to figure out how. As I wave good-bye to Bailey, the beast gives me a boot so brutal, that it knocks me to the floor. This will not be an easy fight.

I know my powers are gone in a singular, clear moment. But the steps toward it come gradually, through three years of difficult acts, while I'm incarcerated.

The first act was calling my aunt, and trying again to tell

her the unvarnished truth. I admitted to taking her money. She was angry, but insisted that I couldn't possibly be accountable for all of the damage out at the warehouse. Over the violent assaults of my beast, I persisted. That one landed me in the infirmary, with two broken ribs.

Another was when I wrote to my mother in Wabash, confessing all.

Months later, when I recovered enough to move around, I called my father, who was still in jail, serving extra time for fighting with an inmate.

"Hello, Dad?" I was staring at his list, which I taped to the foot of my bed.

"Dorianna? Is it really you? It's been so long. I was expecting you to call long ago." He sounded sorry for himself.

"I was, um . . . busy with the new school."

"How's Aunt Carol's? Heard you were on the East Coast. Having fun?"

So he didn't hear about the warehouse fire or me stealing his sister's money. "New York is . . . I like the big city." I paused, gathering my words, steeling my nerve. "Look, I need to ask you something, Dad."

"What is it?" His tone shifted to sudden irritation.

"Regarding your sentence and all—"

"Let's talk about something more cheery, shall we?" he scolded. "Why dwell on the past?"

"It's not exactly the past. You're still in there. And I really need to ask you."

"If you must." In his voice was a sharp warning not to cross him.

I ignored it. "I wonder, do you ever regret the lengths you went to get those women to . . . join your church?"

He coughs. "*Excuse* me?"

"You heard me."

"First of all, that's no business of yours. Second of all, it's not as if I tied and gagged them. I did nothing wrong, they came to me of their own accord."

A rape victim came seeking molestation of their own accord? Really? Does a lack of accountability run in our family genome? I choked down bitter disappointment. "You absolutely stand by that? You never hurt anyone?"

"No, and I fully resent you accusing me of it. How could you, Dorianna? Whose side are you on? My sister believes me."

"You only needed followers."

"Yes! That's right." His tone was eager now, relieved. "So, you do understand."

"Oh, I understand. More than you can imagine."

In my mind's eye, I pictured the photo of me and the stuffed teddy bear, and the photo of me sandwiched in between my parents. No tears welled up, only a firm resolve. "Thanks, Dad, I got what I called for."

"Wait, Dorianna? I've been so lonely. How's school and—"

"Got to go now, Dad. Take care." I hung up. The beast in me belched and snarled. But I felt it die a little, and that was great, great satisfaction.

I'm more at peace, eating and sleeping better, and my uncanny sense of hearing and smell has dulled. I notice it now and then at the lunch table, when I try to fathom what someone is thinking. Less and less can I glean any real information. . . less and less can I detect the turnipy, black-tar odor of guilt on a new resident.

One day, I decide to test it in a group workshop.

Six residents are sitting around in a circle, talking about

staying sober after release, and how they'll maintain the narrow path of squeaky-clean honesty.

My friend, Aisha is talking. "Problem is, I have no one to put me up."

That's a lie. Aisha has spoken to me about an older brother in Jersey she might go to, though he's unemployed and is therefore not the best prospect. I concentrate hard to suss out *why* Aisha is lying. I send out that directed radar that used to ping back the thoughts of almost anyone. Nothing. I can't even read Aisha's poker face.

Next, I try to smell the dread and tension in a new inmate's body. I've always been able to smell fear—like stew left out in the heat for a week, mixed with the burn of rubber. Nothing. Not even when I lean forward, bloodhound style, and Aisha laughs at how silly I look "as a dog."

I try to feel my inner beast, even a nudge, but he's been fading for a while, like a terminal patient whose muscle mass has morphed into feeble gristle. The final test is to focus on the empty chair and try my best to burn it, like I did to the door at Aunt Carol's. Nothing happens except sweat rolling down my forehead onto the bridge of my nose. I swipe it off with pure, unfettered joy. It's over. I can go back into the world, start again from the ground up.

The beast in me is dead.

29

There is no exquisite beauty . . . without some strangeness in the proportion.
—Edgar Allan Poe

E ighteen years later
I walk into the bookstore and my breath catches in my throat. Facing me is a pyramidal book display built with at least forty identical novels. Each novel proclaims *DORIANNA* in bold red type over a hot-yellow background, with a hazy, steamy snippet of beach in the distance.

The stunning girl on the cover has her head thrown back, worshipping the sun. Her tresses seem to switch in the sea air like an auburn flag. Arrogance and hunger lurk in her gaze. Although I'm not exactly this Dorianna, it's a perfect effigy to my old self.

I give myself permission to laugh. "Years ago, I would've killed for this exposure," I mumble under my breath. Now, it just feels strange, removed. Like someone else's life.

Before coming here, I tamed my thick hair into a ponytail, and applied a minimum of makeup. I'm still as beautiful as I was in high school, but it's no longer my manner to stress over fashion. Squaring my shoulders, I adjust my ribbed gray jersey, hoist my shoulder bag farther up, and march forward with a smile, grateful to have made it this far.

Over the loud buzz of conversation, I feel another wash of anticipation. The place is packed. Quickly, I grab one of the last seats in the back row. Craning my neck, I try to make Ander out from the rest of the men. Can't say for sure which guy he is. Most of the people here are urban, intellectual types.

A store rep walks to the podium and she makes introductions. "We are proud to present the acclaimed debut author, Ander James. He's making a splash in the New York book world, and the entire country, with his searing portrait of a troubled, power-hungry girl. Part horror story and part cautionary tale about power run amok, *DORIANNA* will leave you breathless."

My cheeks heat up, but I steady myself, taking comfort in my anonymity. I can hardly remember the girl I was eighteen years ago. Why would anyone in his or her right mind hunger for fame? The gaunt starlets falling in and out of rehab and relationships always seem so lost. I was lost, too. I ache, remembering how I felt during those horrible times.

My gaze fixes on Ander as he mounts the podium. He's about thirty-five now. His face has grown square, his body more solid, and his sideburns have an early frost of gray. He wears glasses and a collegiate tweedy jacket. These changes at first make me sad, then jealous. Aging is a part of life I'll never experience. Eternal youth is my only scar of power.

I think of the tree outside my window in that detention facility. How I watched its seasonal changes. The wonder of how its tree buds formed, and swelled into leaves, green for a season before folding into brittle, red corpses, only to make room for the next set of tender buds. It seems so wondrous a circle. Like its own natural magic.

I have to accept who I am this time. Forever.

I have no powers to mesmerize anymore. I've purged myself of them through my hard work in the detention center, including work with other troubled kids. As soon as I got out, I settled into an apartment in Bushwick, one of the few parts of Brooklyn I could afford. It was far from Wilson, as I could not chance him finding me.

My first job was waitressing. After that, I found an office job at an agency that helped place troubled teens in homes. With the modest amount of money I saved, I eventually paid back my mother and aunt what I owed them and began sending anonymous cash to Ander through Bailey, for his medical bills.

In the winter, I helped dig out people's cars stuck in the snow. In the summer, I sprayed their stale sidewalks down. I always offered to sign for neighbors' packages if they were stuck at work. I earned my GED from an online course. Mostly, I healed from my fledgling connections with people— my doorman, the teens at the center, and from Bailey's occasional visits.

Her first visit was when she gave me the handmade jacket. She visited a lot after that, and told me again and again how sorry she was for not believing me. I helped her through troubles with her family, and when her marriage broke up with Cole. But when she started filling out and soft worry lines emerged on her forehead, for a time, she retreated. It's one thing to believe in the abstract that someone can't age. But witnessing my smooth face and lithe body, well, Bailey clearly couldn't face even the subtle changes.

She moved up to Vermont, where she remarried, had

three boys in fast succession, and started a children's clothing company that made it into all of the trendy department stores—because her fashions rock, and she's always been a talent to be reckoned with. Eventually, Bailey found her way back to Manhattan and enrolled her handsome, redheaded boys in the best alternative charter school.

She also found her way back to me. I'm still wearing Bailey's blue jacket, frayed at the cuffs and hem.

"I'm your old-fogey friend," Bailey often laughs, holding me at shoulder's length to wonder again that I still look seventeen.

"My best old fogey friend ever," I always reply, giving her a reassuring hug.

Healed by connections without expectations—free of the itch of the con.

My one remaining blemish—eternal youth—is there to remind me there are consequences, even after healing. If this is the last price, I will happily pay. And pay. So, when my sadness that I can't grow older alongside my friends crops up, I count my blessings. No more hunger for followers or famished, sickening longing. The voice in me speaks with one heart.

Ander begins to read, and I freefall into the dream of his powerful prose. He's rendered me so well on the page that he's managed to capture me more convincingly than Wilson ever did in those phosphorescent videos.

I haven't forgotten that. A chill passes over me, and a dark presence shrouds the room. Could Wilson be in this very audience?

A month after the warehouse fire, he chased me down, and found me in the detention center. He charmed the guards into letting him in to speak with me. It was only my preternatural senses, still with me in that first year, that smelled his lust to dictate my every move. Only my enhanced hearing that heard the frantic beat of his rancid heart and my inner sight that saw the sick gleam in his eyes through steel doors. This warned me early enough to alert the guards. As long as I still had those powers, I was able to shake the guards from the stupor of Wilson's spell. Convince them to keep me safely locked in, and him out.

But my uncanny senses have long since been smoothed back to normal. No longer can I rely on them to alert me of Wilson's, or anyone's, presence. I glance around nervously. No tall, menacing man with coal-black hair and a slick camera. I remind myself I am stronger than evil. Wilson's powers lack oxygen, they are fueled by pure anaerobic toxins. Surely he has less power over those who live and breathe among the healthy. With a sigh, I turn back to Ander.

After the reading, I hurry to take my place in line for an autographed copy. The line winds around four entire book-shelves.

Glancing over to the row of mostly empty seats, I spot a familiar woman sitting near Ander's author table, fixing her adorable daughter's barrette. Her hair is a dull blonde. Her face has a roughness, as if she'd been through stress, but at one time was the queen of something.

Lacey. It's Lacey for sure. I feel the ancient stab of pain, followed by a letting go. Lacey and Ander are right for each other after all. Charlie was right, too: I was only a blip.

A blip that inspired a book.

I inch forward in line. Finally, one person away, Ander looks up. His eyes are underscored by sallow half circles, no doubt from long hours hunched over his laptop. As he studies me, his expression changes from a vague confusion to a startled aware-ness. Then the person in front of me plunks his book down and Ander is drawn back into the business he came here to do.

Silently, I rehearse lines. "Pleased to meet you, how did

you come up with the idea for this book?" Too fake. I know precisely how he came to write it. He lived it.

The customer in front of me is done, and walking away. My turn. Ander smiles up at me, showing the stains of too much coffee, too much time gone by.

Time is a thief, too, in its way.

I plunk down my copy of *DORIANNA*. Ander opens it to the title page. I gasp when his metal claw grips the pen. I caused that. He's a writer, and I made it so he can't even write with his flesh-and-blood fingers. Tears spring to my eyes.

"Who should I sign it to?" he asks. Before I can answer, he apparently sees my tears, and something else I can't conceal. "You, um, you look so much like someone I used to know," he whispers.

"Oh!" I brush tears away. "Are you sure?" Maybe I shouldn't have come here. Revealing myself to him was not my goal, and now . . .

"Yes, you look like the girl who I wrote about, who inspired this story."

"But I couldn't be. I'm only—"

"—What, about seventeen?"

I nod. Seventeen going on thirty-five.

"The Dorianna in my novel would be about thirty-five. But it's uncanny, the resemblance." He puts down his pen and shakes his head. "Sometimes I wish I could talk to her again."

"Oh?" My chest seizes up with hope.

"I would tell her I felt horrible for betraying her." An embarrassed chuckle escapes him. "When you read this, you'll see I was in love with two women at the same time— Dorianna and my wife. And I never had the nerve to tell Dorianna the truth, that I cheated on her."

I swirl with such a storm of emotions I have to lean on the table.

"Gee, I'm really spouting off." He grins apologetically. His eyes are still milky blue, smart, and soulful. But I can no longer read his thoughts. I can only understand him through his words, which are sweet medicine.

The man behind me taps my shoulder. "Lady, almost done? There's a line here."

"Give us another minute," Ander insists. His metallic claw is again poised above the book. "You haven't told me who to sign it to."

"Oh . . ." I stumble. Then it comes. "To the sun."

"How eerie." Ander jots my words down. "That's exactly what Dorianna would've said."

"Well, ha! Synchronicity rules." Tell him the truth. No more lies, my heart stutters.

"Hey, Lacey." Ander's calling to the woman with the pretty daughter. "There's someone here who's the spitting image of Dorianna. You won't believe this."

When she glances over at me, her eyes fill with animal fear.

"Listen, the man behind me needs a turn," I blurt. "But I just want to say . . ."

"Yes?" Ander's full attention is back on me.

"She betrayed you, too."

"Who?"

"Dorianna. She looked at your journal, the one in your back pocket, and read it."

"How do you know?" Now he's caught Lacey's look of fear.

"The important thing, is that you both betrayed each other, and . . ." I place my hand gently on Ander's one warm hand. "She's sorry. She forgives you, too."

Picking up my book, I turn and swiftly walk away. I hear

the man in line making a snide comment about hogging the author's attention. I hear Ander, Lacey, even their little girl calling after me.

But the past is the past, and the future is bright as a perpetual sun.

If you liked *Pictures of Dorianna*, see Catherine's other novels at catherinestine.com and subscribe to her newsletter there for book news, events and sales. *Pictures of Dorianna* Book Club and Class Discussion Questions follow!

ACKNOWLEDGMENTS

I'd like to give special thanks to Holly Kowitt, Maggie Powers, Sarah Cloots and Nancy Rawlinson. You all played important roles in helping *Pictures of Dorianna* blossom.

And of course, thanks to the original inspirations: the German Faust myths, Christopher Marlowe for his *Doctor Faustus*, Oscar Wilde for *A Picture of Dorian Gray* and all the other iterations of this supernatural trope.

I figured it was high time for a female Faust lead! Thus, the inimitable and outrageous Dorianna.

ABOUT THE AUTHOR

Catherine Stine is a *USA Today* bestselling author of historical fantasy, sci-fi thrillers, paranormal romance and YA fiction. Her novels have earned Indie Notable awards, a RWA Sheila award and New York Public Library Best Books for Teens. She's from Philly, lives in Manhattan and the Catskills and loves spending time with her beagle, writing about fantastical creatures, gardening, and meeting readers at bookfests. Find out more at catherinestine.com

Join her mailing list for launch news, events and sales.

BOOK CLUB AND CLASS DISCUSSION QUESTIONS

What are Dorianna's strengths in the beginning? After the Burlesque Party? During and after the Blind Date Confessional Party?

What are her weaknesses? In the beginning? The middle of the novel? Toward the end?

How do the changes in Dorianna's videos parallel her own transformation to the dark side?

How do the themes of hunger and consumption play out? What's eating at her? What and who is she consuming?

Talk about the themes of truth telling and lying. How do they play off each other?

What about the theme of power? Have you ever felt that you were in a situation where your own power grew beyond your control? What did you do about it?

Is power a good or bad thing? What makes the difference?

What does Ander really think of his friend, Wilson? Why is he sometimes uncomfortable around Wilson?

What human aspects does Wilson stand for? Literally? Symbolically?

Who is conning who (Ander and Dorianna), (Dorianna and Wilson)? What is the author saying about the nature of betrayals and lies?

What is the author saying about the good aspects of social media? The bad aspects?

Does change usually happen from the inside out, or the outside in? Discuss.

Who is your favorite character in Dorianna? Why?

What are the parallels between Dorianna and her father? The differences?

Does Dorianna reach a point where she tells the truth? Is it too late? Why or why not?

Do you believe people can make reparation for their evil or bad behavior? If so, how?

In what ways is eternal youth a harsh consequence?

Visit catherinestine.com to see her other novels, subscribe to her newsletter or read about her events.

www.ingramcontent.com/pod-product-compliance
Lightning Source LLC
Chambersburg PA
CBHW062019170626
46813CB00001B/219